Big Girls Do Cry

CARL WEBER

Dafina
BOOKS

KENSINGTON PUBLISHING CORP.

DAFINA BOOKS are published by

Kensington Publishing Corp.
119 West 40th Street
New York, NY 10018

ISBN-13: 978-0-7582-3181-9
ISBN-10: 0-7582-3181-4

Printed in the United States of America

DEDICATION

*This book is dedicated to my good friend,
the late Reverend Joseph Simmons Sr.
May you rest in peace, my friend.
I hope to see you again one day.*

Prologue

The taxi pulled into the circular driveway, rolling to a stop in front of the expensive double oak doors of the large brick colonial. Roscoe, the driver, a fortysomething dark-skinned man, placed the car in park and turned toward the woman in the back seat.

He smiled to himself. He liked the way she looked. She was just his type of woman, thick and pretty, with skin like a chocolate bar. Oh, and even more enticing were her large, melon-sized breasts. Yes, sir, Roscoe sure loved a woman with big titties and some meat on her bones. And this one was as fine as she could be. He had thought about asking for her number or perhaps offering to show her around Richmond when she first entered his cab at the airport. Over the years, Roscoe had bedded many a lonely female passenger after picking them up at Richmond's bus station or airport. All it usually took was some small talk and an invitation to one of the city's many bars or eateries for a drink. But this sister had spent most of the ride on her cell phone, probably comforting some insecure boyfriend or husband afraid her fine ass would wind up with a Southern charmer like him. Now that they had reached her final destination, he would have to make his move quick if he was going to bed this plus-sized beauty.

"That'll be forty dollars, ma'am." He smiled, revealing a mouth full of gold teeth.

Tammy, a woman in her late thirties, didn't notice his unattractive smile or his country accent, things that would have surely caught her attention and gotten under her skin if she weren't already preoccupied with looking at the house they'd just pulled in front of. She would never admit it to anyone back home, but a twinge of jealousy swept through her body as she stared at the house. The large colonial was at least twice the size of her Jamaica Estates home back in New York, and compared to her yard, this house's land appeared to be big enough to hold a football field or two.

This has to be the wrong address, she told herself. *They can't afford this.*

"Are you sure we're at the right house?" she asked without moving her head, her mind still trying to process what she saw before her.

"Yes, ma'am. You said Four James River Lane, didn't you?"

Tammy glanced at the paper in her hand, then looked at the large number 4 on the house. "Yes, that's what I said."

But this can't be her house. It just can't be. Tammy's thoughts were consumed by jealousy.

"Then this is where you want to be. Do you want some help with your bags?"

She reached in her purse for her wallet. "How much do I owe you?"

"Forty dollars. I usually charge fifty when I come out here to Chesterfield County, but havin' a pretty woman such as yourself in my cab, I feel like I owe you. Maybe I could show you around town. They're having an all-you-can-eat rib festival down at Shockoe Bottom tonight. My name's Roscoe." He offered her his hand.

Tammy rolled her eyes and shook her head, flashing the two-carat diamond ring on her finger.

"My name is *Married,*" she snapped, "and my husband's name is Foot in Your Ass."

She was about to go on putting this homely, gold-tooth fool in his place, but before she could continue, she saw someone come out of the house. A light-skinned woman, big, but not quite as large as Tammy, came running toward the taxi. That's when Tammy knew there was definitely no mistake; she was at the right address. But how the hell did her best friend get a Mc-Mansion like this? And who the hell were they robbing to pay for it?

Tammy handed the driver two twenty-dollar bills, then stepped out of the car. She was usually a pretty good tipper, but with that country-ass come-on the driver just tried, she figured he'd forfeited his tip.

Egypt threw her arms around Tammy's neck and pulled her in closely. "Tammy, girl, I missed you something awful." She placed a huge red-lipstick kiss on Tammy's cheek.

Tammy smiled at Egypt when she let her go. She'd missed her friend too. They had a lot of catching up to do, and even more importantly, she wanted to know how Egypt and her new husband, Rashad, could afford such a nice house when they earned far less than she and her husband did. Or did they?

"Girl, you moving on up, aren't you?"

"You think? Come on in and let me show you around." Egypt was grinning from ear to ear. She knew Tammy had to be envious, and she loved every minute of it. "You can leave her bags by the front door," Egypt instructed Roscoe.

Tammy followed her friend. Yes, she wanted to see her house. She wanted to see if the inside looked anything like the outside.

Tammy and Egypt had known each other for almost thirty years and had been best friends since they'd met. But even best friends could have rivalries. As close as they were, the two of them had played a one-upsmanship game when it came to material things since they were teenagers. Tammy, however, had been winning this competition handily the past ten years because of her marriage to her successful husband, Tim. She had thought the title would be hers for a lifetime, but as she walked into the flawlessly decorated foyer of Egypt's house for the first time, she was afraid that the tides had changed.

As a matter of fact, she was so amazed as she followed her friend from room to room that she barely noticed the people sitting in the large family room until Egypt shouted out, "BGBC in the house!" and the people in the room all stood in unison and echoed, "BGBC in the house!"

Tammy couldn't help but blush. She smiled at Egypt, who gave her a thumbs-up. It was one of those moments in a woman's life when she feels a sense of accomplishment. One of Tammy's dreams was actually becoming a reality, and she couldn't have been prouder. She'd come to Richmond for two reasons. One of them was to catch up with her friend, who she hadn't seen since her wedding the year before. The other was to be in attendance at the first meeting of the Richmond chapter of the Big Girls Book Club. She'd started the club five years ago in New York with only one rule: you had to be at least a size 16 to become a member. With the success of that first book club, which had swelled from five members to almost thirty, Tammy had the dream that someday there would be BGBC groups in cities all over the country. Her best friend was helping her realize that dream.

Tammy glanced around the room. There were more than a dozen people there, but she felt as if she knew four of them personally because of her conversations with Egypt. Of course, there was Isis, Egypt's older sister and former member of the New York chapter of the BGBC. She'd moved down to Richmond a few months ago to get away from the hustle and bustle of New York, or so she said. Only time would tell if that was her true motivation. Tammy had a suspicion that there were more personal reasons involving her sister.

Then there was Loraine Farrow, Egypt's boss and one of Richmond's leading businesswomen. Loraine was a tall, well-dressed woman in her early forties. Despite her 275-pound figure, she was very attractive. She owned a large public-relations firm in town. Tammy liked her right off the bat, not just because Egypt had said she was a take-charge woman who didn't take smack from anyone, but also because of the way Loraine carried herself. It was obvious from one glance that she was a woman of class who deserved respect.

While Loraine exuded everything good about being a black woman in her forties, the woman standing next to her represented everything bad. She had a very attractive face, with two huge dimples on both cheeks, but Tammy's first impression of LaQueta Brown was that she was a hot mess. Her clothes were too loud; her blouse was way too tight for a woman her size; her skirt was too short; and from what Egypt had told her, she was so damn boisterous it could make you sick. She put the *g* in *ghetto* and really didn't care.

But as much as Tammy was appalled by having LaQueta in

the BGBC, there was only one member she disapproved of on principle. That member was Jerome. Oh, yes, Jerome was a man, a very handsome man at that. Perhaps even a little too handsome. Tammy argued with Egypt about him for almost two weeks on the phone, but her friend wouldn't budge on including him in her BGBC chapter.

"Our club has only one rule, Tammy," Egypt had argued, "and that's that members have to be at least a size sixteen. Well, we put him in a dress, and he meets the size requirements."

"But he's a man, Egypt!"

"So? It's not against the rules. And he reads everything from romance novels to Mary Monroe to L. A. Banks."

Tammy was so puzzled by Egypt's insistence on Jerome joining that she accused her of sleeping with him. "Sounds to me like someone's trying to keep their boyfriend close and not raise any eyebrows."

Of course, she got a denial and some very choice words back.

"You know what? Fuck you, Tammy. I've never cheated on my husband. Not once! Can you say the same?"

There was silence; then Tammy said, "That was cold, girl."

Egypt didn't mean to be so spiteful and throw Tammy's business in her face, but sometimes it was the only way to keep her friend in line. "I'm sorry, but you need to stop. You know I would never mess around on Rashad."

"I also never thought you'd invite a man into our book club. So, as the president, I must say no."

"You may be the president, but this is my chapter, and if I can't run it the way I see fit, then there isn't going to be a Richmond chapter."

Egypt knew how much Tammy wanted the club to go national. She took a gamble, but the gamble paid off. Tammy finally gave in, and the core for the Richmond chapter was formed.

Now, Tammy settled in to a plush armchair in Egypt's living room and watched as her friend got the meeting under way.

Egypt

1

"So, what's this thing Rashad's doing to make all this money? And how can me and Tim get down?" Tammy asked as we walked into the Tobacco Company, one of Richmond's most well-known eateries and watering holes. We'd left my house after our book club meeting, because Tammy was leaving in a few days, and I really wanted some time alone with my best friend. "Girl, you been holding out. I'm supposed to be your best friend. Why I gotta come all the way down here and find out that your man's making all these country-ass Negroes a small fortune? All you had to do was pick up the phone."

I ignored Tammy, letting her continue to ramble as the blond hostess asked us, "How many in your party?" I put up two fingers and watched the young woman pick up two menus and then motion for us to follow her to our table. Tammy, who hadn't stopped speaking since we'd arrived, walked alongside me. At our table, the hostess placed the menus next to our plates and we sat down.

"Juan will be your waiter, and he will be right with you," the hostess told us before she walked away. I picked up my menu and began to peruse the selections, while Tammy was still talking.

"Egypt, you didn't hear a word I said, did you?" Tammy asked.

When I didn't answer, she tapped her spoon on her water glass to get my attention. "Earth to Egypt. Earth to Egypt. Are you there?"

I'd heard most of what she'd said, but my mind just wasn't in the conversation. It was elsewhere. Don't get me wrong; it wasn't as if the subject wasn't interesting. I was very proud of my husband and his work. And let's face it, who better to show off to than Tammy, the woman who had been throwing her and her husband Tim's money in my face for the past ten years? But for me, this wasn't a time to be petty. I had more serious things on my mind that I wanted to discuss, only I didn't know how or where to start. I had a favor I needed to ask Tammy, and it wasn't a small favor by any stretch of the imagination. It was the kind of favor you ask only of your best friend, because it was the kind of favor only a best friend would grant you.

"I'm here, Tammy. I'm sorry. I just have a lot on my mind." I looked up from the menu.

"Well, girl, you need to get your mind right, because we need to talk." She sat back in her chair. "I'm hurt."

Hurt? What the hell did she have to be hurt about? I mean, I knew she was jealous of my house, but damn. I'd watched her eyes flash like a camera as she took in and memorized my décor and the color scheme that ran throughout the rooms. Hell, half the members of the book club were whispering in my ear about how her nose hooked around every nook and cranny of my house during and after the book discussion. Knowing her, she was pissed off about some color scheme I'd picked out that was too similar to one of the rooms in her house. I could see her now: When she got home, she'd be telling everyone in New York that my whole house was biting her style.

Well, she needed to get over it. Imitation is a form of flattery.

On the ride over, I noticed she was furtively checking out my designer pantsuit and my Louis Vuitton purse when she saw the Bloomingdale's bags in my trunk. Shit, I had always had nice things and wore nice clothes when I was in New York, but I'd always gotten them from Marshalls, T.J. Maxx, and Filene's Basement, not Bloomingdale's and Saks like her. She was used to me shopping on a budget, and it was obvious she just couldn't get over how I'd come up in the world. I loved her to death, but we'd always been "frenemies." I knew Tammy had a competitive nature, but I still couldn't understand how she could take my success personally. What the hell did she have to be hurt about? It was just my time to shine.

"Ummm, what exactly are you hurt about?" My eyes were locked on her as I waited for an answer.

"Well, I was talking to that sweetheart of a woman, Loraine, after the meeting, and she told me that she just gave Rashad a six-figure check to invest—and that half the book club has their money invested with him."

Was I missing something? She genuinely looked upset about people being invested in my husband's company. Maybe she wasn't the woman I should ask to do me this favor. "I had no idea you'd be interested. I thought you and Tim were through with the stock market after all the money you lost last year."

She raised her voice. "You didn't tell me he was investing in solar and wind energy. Everybody knows that's where half of Obama's stimulus package money went. Oh, and you damn sure didn't tell me he was doubling everybody's money. Loraine told me he's one of the top money managers in Richmond."

I smiled proudly. I loved it when people said good things about Rashad. He worked so hard to provide for me, and I loved him so much. I honestly don't know what my life would be like without him.

"I told you he was running a hedge fund, didn't I? You do remember that, don't you?"

"Yeah, but you should have told me how much money y'all was making."

Oh, my God. Can you believe the audacity of this woman? Tammy had always been materialistic, but she was acting like I was taking food out of her children's mouths. "Look, Tammy, that's Rashad's thing, not mine, okay? Me and him have a deal. He makes the money; I spend it. Besides, I told you to have Tim call Rashad last year, didn't I?" This was what I hated about her. She never could take responsibility for anything. It was always someone else's fault when things didn't go her way.

There was silence for a while. It looked like I'd put her in her place, but looks can be deceiving. "Okay, well, now we want to invest." She reached in her bag and pulled out her checkbook. I put my hand up to stop her. I had to draw the line somewhere.

"Look, if you want to get into the fund, then talk to Rashad when we get home. I'm sure you and him can work something out. I ain't got time for that. I've got enough problems of my own."

I guess my eyes must have taken on a downcast look, or Tammy realized I wasn't the one to help with her investment needs, because all of a sudden she asked, "Hey, girl, are you feeling okay?"

I forced a bright smile, thinking about all the things I had to be grateful for—all except for that one thing. The one thing I wanted most in the world and would give up all our newfound wealth for.

"Yeah, I'm fine." I tried to sound cheery, but water was welling up in my eyes. Truth is, I was a wreck inside. "Oh, Tammy," I confessed, "I don't know what I'm gonna do. I feel like my world's falling apart." I took my napkin and wiped my eyes as tears fell.

"What? What's the matter?" I didn't answer right away. "It's your sister, isn't it," she said with certainty. "You know, I never thought having her stay at your house was a good idea."

Tammy had always hated the idea of Isis moving down to Richmond and living with me. She'd given me quite a few valid reasons why I shouldn't allow it, but I always thought Tammy's real reason was that she was afraid Isis and I would become closer, and that would somehow affect my friendship with her. What she didn't understand was that, although I was close with my sister, I was much closer to her.

"Nah, Isis has been good. Other than her running up my phone bill calling that no-good fool Tony in New York, me and her are good. Matter of fact, I've seen some of those black and yellow real estate books lying around, so I think she's looking for an apartment."

"Thank God for small favors." She reached across the table and took my hand. "It's not Rashad, is it?"

"What! No," I said quickly in his defense, taking back my hand. "He's done nothing but love me and take care of me. I couldn't ask for a better man."

"So, what is it? What am I missing?" Tammy looked into my

eyes. "You've got everything a woman could want: a beautiful house, a nice car, and a handsome husband with a good job who loves you and you love him." She stopped, and whatever scenario she dreamed up in her head in that moment caused a worried look to appear on her face. "Don't you? You do still love him, don't you?"

"Oh, my God, of course I do, Tammy. More than anything in this world." I gave her a genuine smile, and she seemed to relax a bit.

She let out an exaggerated sigh. "I knew that. I just wanted to hear you say it. You two make a beautiful couple, Egypt. When I see you together, it really makes me happy."

For the first time, Tammy really sounded sincere. I didn't hear a hint of jealousy in her tone, and the truth is, she had no reason to be jealous of my marriage or our achievements. I guess you could say we were equally matched as friends for the first time— that is, except for the one thing.

"Egypt, what's going on? What's bothering you?"

Finally, I decided to broach the subject that had been on my mind all night.

"Tammy, we're friends, aren't we?"

She leaned in closer to the table. "Of course we are. You know you're my girl. I'd do anything for you." I was glad to hear that. The only question was, did she mean it?

"Well, I'm glad you said that, because, Tee, I need a favor— no, I don't even know if you'd call this a favor. I need your help with something. And you know I would never ask you for a favor if it wasn't really important to me."

Tammy sat back in her chair with a look of disgust that caught me off guard. "No, Egypt. The answer is no!" she said adamantly.

"What do you mean, no? I haven't even asked you the favor yet."

"You don't have to, because I'm not having a threesome with you and Rashad. Having one with you and Tim was enough to last me a lifetime," she said loud enough for half the restaurant to hear. I felt my high-yellow face become hot, and I'm sure it was bright red. Part of me wanted to walk out of there right then and there. I could feel the other patrons' eyes all over me. I swear I'd never been so embarrassed in my life.

Three years ago, before I was even seeing Rashad, I did have a threesome with Tammy and her husband. The whole thing was crazy. Looking back at it, I can't even believe I agreed to it. I still can't believe Tammy even asked me to agree to it. But she did, and I did. All because she wanted to give her husband the ultimate birthday present, and she didn't trust anyone else with her man. Well, when it came down to it, she didn't trust me either. She swore Tim and I started having an affair after that one crazy night. It couldn't have been further from the truth, but Tammy's jealousy really sent her over the edge for a while. Don't ask me how we still remained friends after that, because it almost ruined our friendship, not to mention her marriage.

"Tammy, you got me all wrong, girl. I wasn't going to ask you to have a threesome. I swear to God." I put my right hand up in the air. "Ugh. Just the thought of Rashad being with another woman turns my stomach."

"You weren't going to ask me that?" I could hear relief in her voice, but she studied my face as if she doubted I was telling the truth.

"No!" I said assuredly. "I don't even know where that came from. I'll never do anything like that again in my life. You know that mess was painful for all of us. Why would I even think about getting into a situation like that again?"

"Damn, I'm sorry. I don't know why I let my mind play tricks on me. But with Rashad's birthday coming up, I just knew that's what you were going to ask me. I—" Suddenly she stopped speaking, and her head went from side to side.

I looked around to see people staring at us like we had on clown costumes. One woman at the table next to us was glaring so hard I had to say something to her. "What are you looking at?"

"Egypt, don't worry about her."

"People need to mind their own damn business." I wasn't normally so rude to strangers. I guess the tension of my situation and the fact that I just had to defend myself from Tammy was really getting to me. Either way, it made the woman finally look the other way.

"Look, stop beating around the bush. You said you need a favor. What is it?"

"Okay, I'm sorry." I turned to her, hesitating for a second before I spoke. I really couldn't believe I was about to tell her my secret, but part of me was happy to share it with her and get it off my chest. "Rashad and I didn't tell anybody, but I had a miscarriage a few months ago."

"Oh, Egypt, I'm so sorry."

"We didn't want to tell anybody I was pregnant until I was three months," I explained. "Then when I lost the baby, I couldn't talk to anyone about it other than Rashad. Until now."

"Oh, Egypt, honey, you should have told me. I would have come down sooner." Her eyes looked like they were tearing, which caused mine to tear again. It was good to know that she really cared. "I would have been here for you."

"I know, but it gets a little worse."

I hesitated again, and Tammy said, "Girl, if you don't tell me what's going on . . ."

"I'm sorry. It's just a little hard to talk about." I took a deep breath. "I just got the report back from my doctor—"

"Are you all right?" She reached out and held my hand for support. "Seriously, you okay?"

"I'm fine, Tammy, far as I know—except for one problem. I had an endometrial biopsy. . . ."

"Oh, no, girl, don't tell me nothing bad. Please don't tell me they think you got cancer or something." She closed her eyes as if she was afraid to hear what I was about to say. She was being awfully dramatic about everything, and I hadn't even gotten to the favor yet. But that was Tammy; she never did anything in an understated way. I just hoped all this concern she was showing for me translated to her wanting to grant my wish.

"No, really, I'm fine. I just had it to see if my uterus could support a pregnancy."

"And? What'd they say?"

"It can't. I can't." I felt the tears rising, but I bit my lip and held them back. I was an emotional wreck, but I didn't want to show it in the restaurant again now that the other patrons had finally stopped staring. "Rashad's sperm count is excellent. It's me who can't get pregnant. My womb won't hold a baby."

Tammy leaned back in her chair and folded her arms. "Girl, just relax and it'll happen. These doctors are always saying stuff like that. The next thing you know, you got crumb snatchers running around everywhere."

Damn, so much for my sympathetic friend. I guess she was so relieved that it wasn't cancer that she just brushed my feelings aside. She didn't realize how badly I wanted to have a baby— Rashad's baby.

"No, my doctor says the chances of me sustaining a pregnancy are slim to none. I'm barren, Tammy. I can't have a baby." I buried my face in my hands. "What kind of wife can't give her husband the baby he wants so badly?"

"Girl, you need a second opinion. I know plenty of women whose doctors said they couldn't have babies, and they're pushing strollers right now."

"You don't understand. This is the fourth doctor we've talked to."

That made her pause. All of a sudden, she didn't look so confident. I guess she realized that her words of encouragement were falling on deaf ears. "Damn, what're you going to do?"

It was now or never. I mounted the courage to ask my best friend the ultimate favor. "Actually, the question is, what do we want *you* to do, Tammy?"

One of her eyebrows went up, and her mouth kind of hung open. I could see by her expression that she had just figured out what my favor was.

"I know this is a lot to ask, Tammy, but will you be the surrogate for our baby?"

Tammy's hand flew to her heart, and she looked even more shocked now that she'd heard the words. "You need to stop playing, 'cause I know you ain't serious."

"I am serious, Tammy. Serious as a heart attack. Will you be our surrogate and have our baby for us?"

"I told you, you need to stop, Egypt. This shit ain't funny. You nearly gave me a heart attack for real." She waved her hand at me, then laughed. "Me having another baby. That shit is funny."

The fact that she could laugh at this situation was starting to piss me off. I folded my arms, locking my eyes on hers like laser beams. "Do I look like I think something is funny? I'm asking you for a favor. I want a baby." She just didn't understand how important this was to me.

Tammy's face softened. "Oh, my God. You're really serious about this, aren't you?"

I nodded, waving a strand of hair out of my eyes. "Yes. Never been more serious about anything in my life. Please, Tammy. You don't know how much this would mean to me and Rashad."

She paused, rubbing her temples as if she suddenly had a throbbing headache. If there was ever a time I wished that I was a mind reader, this was it. I couldn't even imagine what was going through her head or what decision she would make. All I knew was that I wanted—no, needed—her to do this for me, no matter what the cost. What I wanted was a yes, though with the way this conversation was going, I would have settled for a "let me think about it."

She sighed, lowering her head, then lifting it to look me in the eyes. "This isn't any small favor you're asking."

"I know that, but I'm desperate. You don't know how much I want to have a baby of my own."

"Well, why don't you adopt? There are plenty of black babies who need a good home. My friend Tina from Hollis just adopted a beautiful baby girl." She made everything sound so simple.

"Rashad doesn't want to adopt. He wants his own baby. His own flesh and blood. He's the last male in his family. He wants his family bloodline to go on. You can understand that, can't you? And without your help, he's not going to get it." I couldn't help it. The tears just started flowing. "I feel like leaving Rashad so he can find a woman who's not broken."

She handed me her napkin. "Look, don't talk like that. You are not your sister. Everything's going to be okay."

I lifted my head and wiped my tears. "So, you'll do it?"

"I don't know what I'm going to do. This is not a decision

you make in five minutes. I've gotta go home and think about it. Plus, I have to talk to Tim."

A glimmer of hope. "I understand. I love you for this, Tammy." I got out of my chair and gave her a huge hug, praying that she would make my dreams come true.

Loraine

2

Have you ever heard the cliché "get a life"? Well, that's how I felt, like I needed to get a life as I watched Jerome work the room on his way up to the karaoke machine at the Soul Cafe in the west end of Richmond. Of course, Jerome and his charismatic behind knew everybody and had to shake every man's hand and kiss every woman's cheek on his way to the stage. I swear I could sit there for hours watching people watching him. It was comical the way folks just seemed to be drawn to him, including me.

I let out a laugh as he walked by a table occupied by a man and woman in their late thirties. The woman was leaning against the man, who had his arms wrapped around her waist. Her head was facing forward, but her eyes were following Jerome like a hungry lioness about to pounce on a zebra. What really made it funny was that her man was doing the same damn thing behind her back. Oh yeah, the down-low brothers were in full effect here in Richmond. I actually felt bad for the sister. Part of me wanted to walk over there to pull her coattails and tell her exactly what her man was doing, but I'd learned the hard way that you can't tell a sister shit about her man that deep down she doesn't already know.

I'd let Jerome talk me into coming over to the Soul Cafe for a drink following our book club meeting. Well, at least that's what I was there for. Jerome, on the other hand, was there to get all the women's panties wet with his damn-near-professional singing voice.

"Good evening," Jerome's deep voice boomed as he took the

microphone from the DJ. You could hear the sighs from the women in the audience already. He really knew how to work the crowd.

One woman shouted out, "Good evening to you, Tall-Dark-and-Handsome. What you doing later tonight?"

The crowd busted out laughing, then settled down as the background music for Luther Vandross's "Always and Forever" got started.

As he prepared to sing, Jerome strutted in front of the crowd in his navy blue Brooks Brothers suit and pale pink shirt with matching handkerchief. Now, Jerome was a very good-looking guy who was always dressed as sharp as a tack. But when he opened his mouth to sing, that good-looking guy transformed into the finest guy in the room. His voice just seemed to reach out and touch you. And when you heard him sing for the first time, it was like having your first orgasm, and all of a sudden, you understood what all the fuss was about.

When Jerome finished his song, everybody in the room was on their feet. As usual, he'd done his damn thing. I can't tell you how proud of him I was as I stood there clapping my hands, watching him shake one hand after another as he made his way back to our table.

"Excuse me, miss." I looked up. A very attractive, tall, curvy but thin woman, probably in her late twenties, was standing next to me. She was wearing a microskirt and a blouse that left nothing to the imagination. She was just the kinda twiglike bitch a sister my size couldn't stand.

"Yes, can I help you?" I put on a fake smile, because I was in the public-relations business, and you never know who could be a potential client—although I doubted it very much in this case.

"Umm, do you know him?" She pointed at Jerome, who was still shaking hands and kissing cheeks about halfway from the stage.

I nodded. "Yes, I know him."

"Well, is he single?" Little Miss Size 8 looked so excited. I don't think she even considered that Jerome could possibly be my man. I wanted to bust her bubble and say, "Hell no, he's not single. He's my damn man!" But she didn't care if he was single or not. None of these heifers who chased him down ever did. But the truth of the matter was that he wasn't my man. He hadn't been my man in years. He was just my friend now. I was okay with that, because Jerome would do anything for me. He was the best friend I had in this world.

"Uh-huh, he's single." I nodded. "But—"

She cut me off, pulling up a chair like we were old friends. "Do you think you can introduce me? I think he is so fine."

I smirked at her presumptuous behavior. She was smiling so hard I could see every tooth in her mouth.

"Yes, he's a very handsome man," I replied.

"No, girl, he's not handsome; he's lollipop-licking fine, and I got me one hell of a sweet tooth."

I sat back in my chair to enjoy the show, because this was going to be fun. I absolutely loved watching women pursue Jerome. They always made fools out of themselves. I was sure from her confident attitude that this one had already planned out exactly how she was going to seduce Jerome. The only question now was, would he allow her to do it?

"Well, who do we have here?" Jerome smiled as he sat down at the table a few minutes later. His forehead was sweating profusely from all that moving around onstage, so I handed him a napkin to wipe his brow.

"Thank you," he said.

He had a handkerchief in his breast pocket, but Jerome never used it to wipe his sweaty face or blow his nose. It was a fashion statement, and Jerome never messed with a fashion statement.

"Umm, Jerome, this is . . ." I gestured toward the woman but had to stop in midsentence when I realized the little hussy hadn't even told me her name. Before I could say anything else, she stuck her hand in Jerome's face to introduce herself.

"Hi, I'm Tiffany. I was just telling your . . . your . . ." She waved her finger in my direction cluelessly, and it pissed me off. I told you she didn't give a damn if he was with me or not.

"She's my best friend." Jerome smiled at me.

"Oh, is she? Well, that's nice. I thought she was your sister. Y'all do favor." The woman fake-smiled at me, then turned back toward Jerome. It was obvious to me that she felt I was blocking and wished I would leave, but that wasn't happening. What she didn't know was that like the handkerchief in Jerome's breast pocket, I was a fashion statement, and I never went out of style. I wasn't going anywhere.

Jerome turned back toward me again. "Yes, I guess we do favor."

Obviously that wasn't the direction she wanted the conversation to go, because she stuck her hand in Jerome's face again. "Yes, well, like I was saying, my name is Tiffany, and I absolutely love the way you sing."

Jerome beamed with pride. "Wow, thank you very much, Tiffany. It's a pleasure to meet you. My name's Jerome." He took her hand, but instead of shaking it, he lowered his head and kissed it. Within seconds, old girl's cheeks were flush with color and she was looking at me as if she had won some great battle. Why she was looking at me at all, I don't know.

"So, can I buy you a drink?" Jerome asked.

She nodded, and Jerome motioned for the cocktail waitress. He ordered us all drinks, and for the next hour, I watched a respectful conversation become one of assumption and innuendos. It was amazing to me how these young women would just tell all their personal business to a perfect stranger with the expectation that they'd get him into bed. Well, after a while, I decided to break up their little Dr. Phil session so I could go home and get some sleep.

"Jerome, you said we were only going to be here a half hour. Well, it's been almost two hours. Whatever happened to one drink and we're out? I have to go to work in the morning."

Jerome glanced at his watch. "Jeez, I'm sorry, Loraine. I just lost track of time talking to this beautiful young lady. Let me just finish my drink and I'll drive you home."

Tiffany cut her eyes in my direction and I smirked. I'd just pissed her off. Oops, too bad. Besides, she may not know it now, but I was doing her a favor.

"You really leaving?" She put on this sad face that I'm sure worked on most guys really well—but Jerome wasn't most guys.

"Afraid so, Tiffany. It was a pleasure meeting you." He finished off his drink, then stood up.

"So, what are you doing when you leave here?" I could hear the desperation in her voice. She didn't want him to leave; she wanted to continue the conversation. Jerome had that effect on people. Not only was he handsome and could sing, but he also had a deep side that made him even more attractive. God, there is nothing like a man who can stimulate both your mind and your body.

"Well, I have to drop Loraine off; then I'm going to head back to my place and curl up with a good book."

I could see her eyes sparkle when he said he was dropping me off. *Girl, you do not want to go there,* I said to myself.

"So, why don't I meet you back at your place?" Damn, slut! She went there. Why did they always have to go there? She could have just asked for his phone number. Why did they always want to go to his house or have him come to theirs on the day they met him? Did any of these women have any respect for themselves? Oh well, I guess she deserved what she got from this point on.

"You wanna come over my house tonight?" Jerome asked.

She nodded. "Yeah, I wanna come over your house."

He raised an eyebrow. "So, what exactly do you think we're going to do at my house at this time of night?"

She stood up, moving close enough for her breasts to rub up against his chest. If he'd lowered his head a few inches, their lips would be locked in a kiss. If she hadn't already done so, she was making her move. "I don't know. I'm sure we'll think of something better than curling up with a book."

Jerome stepped back, folding his arms to regain some of his personal space. "That's what I'm afraid of."

"You don't have to be afraid of anything. I'm not looking for a commitment. I'm just looking to have a good time." She licked her top lip shamelessly. At this point, I was invisible to her.

"Look, Tiffany, I think there's something you should know about me."

"Please don't tell me you're married."

"No, never been married," Jerome said calmly. "But—"

She cut him off with a little attitude. "But what? Here I am damn near throwing myself at you, and you acting like you sleep with men or something."

"There is no *something* about it. I do sleep with men."

This was always my favorite part. I loved watching as women processed what he had just told them. Why did they always assume he was straight? None of them ever asked the right question.

"Excuse me? What did you just say?" Her head was rolling around her shoulders like a bobblehead doll.

Jerome added a little bass to his voice. "I said I sleep with men."

"Stop playin'." She laughed. Their first reaction was always denial.

He gave her a stern look. "How many men would lie about something like that?"

Her jaw dropped and her bottom lip began to quiver like Mushmouth from *Fat Albert*. "Oh, my God. You mean to tell me . . ." She couldn't even look at him anymore. All of a sudden, he was the invisible one, and she turned her attention toward me. "He's bisexual?" The truth had finally settled in, and she was now looking to me for answers.

"Ain't nothing bisexual about him. He likes dick more than both of us."

Tiffany glared at me for a full three seconds before turning back to Jerome. "Ain't this some shit?" she said as she walked off.

Jerome shrugged. "I guess she don't want to come over anymore."

I laughed and gave my friend a hug.

If you haven't figured it out yet, Jerome is gay—very gay—and there is nothing he likes better than proving to me that he can pull people from both sides of the fence. It used to bother me, years ago, when he first came out, especially since we used to date. That can be a blow to any woman's ego when the man she's having sex with decides to announce that he doesn't even like women. But now I was past that, and I couldn't imagine him any other way.

"C'mon, friend, take me home." I hooked my arm in his, and we strolled out of the club, right past Tiffany's evil glare.

Isis

3

I sat down on the living room sofa, poured myself a glass of wine, and then eased back to read Keith Lee Johnson's *Little Black Girl Lost 5,* our next book club selection. I'd read the other books in the series when I was in the New York chapter of the BGBC, and I really enjoyed them, so I was looking forward to reading part five.

I hadn't gotten through five pages when Rashad walked past the sliding glass doors, blocking out the sun and casting a large shadow in the area where I was sitting. I watched him inconspicuously for a moment. He was gazing at the pool as if trying to decide whether to get into the water. He looked cute pacing back and forth in the red-and-white Nike sweat suit I'd gotten him last Christmas. Had to give credit where credit was due; he really was a fine-ass man. He was one of those men who got even better looking as he got older. Maybe it was his newly shaved head, but he looked more distinguished, if you know what I mean.

A satisfied grin crept up on my face when he unzipped his jacket. Apparently he'd made a decision to take a dip in the pool. Rashad always seemed to be working, and I was glad he was about to tear himself away from his computer and Black-Berry to finally enjoy the pool his money built. He'd worked hard to afford this house, and he deserved to enjoy it. Heck, maybe after I finished a chapter or two, I would just join him. It had been a long time since the two of us had enjoyed a swim together.

My grin became a full-fledged smile as I remembered a night many years ago, when the two of us sneaked into his neighbor's aboveground swimming pool to skinny-dip. Thank God the owners of the house were on vacation; otherwise they might have gotten quite a shock. I still can't believe I let him talk me into it. Not that I have any regrets. I swear I'll never forget that night as long as I live. The moon, the stars, the warm water . . . Oh, and let's not forget the best part—the off-the-charts sex! My smile was now a devilish grin that I covered with my hand. That was one of the most memorable sexual experiences of my life, and for the moment, all I could think of was the best way to re-create the past.

I fanned myself, then picked up my wine, draining half the glass with one gulp. I glanced back over toward him, thinking naughty thoughts I had no business having at midnight, let alone at twelve o'clock in the afternoon. Besides, he was my sister's husband now. Fucked up as it was, he was off-limits. So, I tried my best to ignore all the fantasies swirling through my mind and get back to my book. Keith Lee Johnson, here I come!

That idea went totally out the window when Rashad's shadow began to sway around the room in a very sensual way. When I looked up, Rashad was slowly gyrating his hips as if he, too, were lost in the memory of our past escapades in a pool. From that moment on, my eyes never left him as I put the book down next to me on the sofa.

I finished that glass of wine and poured myself another as I watched the show. And I do mean show, because the way he was shaking his ass as he eased off his jacket put him in a class of his own. Now, I'd seen my share of male strippers, but they didn't have anything on Rashad. He was moving so smoothly as he eased off his shirt.

He had to know I was watching. There was no other reason for him to be dancing like that. He might be married to my sister, but I knew that deep down, he still felt something for me.

By the time his shirt was off, my chest was heaving, and when he untied his sweatpants and they slid to the ground, showing off a Speedo, I broke out into a cold sweat. I was sitting on the edge of the sofa, waiting to see what he had planned next.

Then, out of nowhere, he spun around like he was a member

of New Edition, showing me his package from the front just long enough to get my imagination working overdrive before he turned back toward the pool. I watched as he dove into the water, and when he moved out of my range of vision, I decided it was time to read my book out by the poolside.

Finishing off my wine, I picked up my book, the glass, and the bottle. I opened the sliding glass door and stepped onto the patio, taking in the afternoon heat. It felt good as I walked over to a lounge chair, swaying everything I knew he liked. I'd lost a lot of weight due to a recent hospital stay, but I was still a thick girl with an ass and a half. I tried my best to give the impression that I didn't even realize he was in the water and that I had not paid any attention to his little striptease—that is, until he splashed some water and shouted, "You coming in or what?"

I dropped my book, clutching my chest as I turned around toward him, pretending to be in a panic. "Oh, my God, Rashad, don't do that. You nearly scared me to death."

"Ahhhh, sorry." He froze, staring at me as I walked toward the edge of the pool. "Didn't know you were there."

Sure you didn't.

"How's the water?"

"Great." He swam toward my end of the pool, his eyes moving their way up from my ankles to my thighs. I'm sure he was trying to look up my dress. I stepped a little closer so that from where he was situated in the pool, he could get a glimpse of my purple panties. He swam a little closer.

Oh, you naughty boy. This isn't for you anymore. Not unless you can keep a secret.

"You taking a swim?" It sounded more like an invitation than a question.

"Why you ask me something like that? You looking for some company?" I teased coyly.

He tried to wear a blank expression as he treaded water silently a few feet from the edge of the pool, but I knew what he really wanted. I'd always known what Rashad wanted, and right now, he wanted me in the water, sliding up and down on that hard dick of his. It was a good thing I loved my sister.

"I asked you a question, Rashad. Do you want some company?" My voice was as calm and as nonchalant as it could be, but it had purpose.

"Actually, I did want some company, but—"

I cut him off with a confident smirk. "All you had to do was ask. You didn't have to put on a striptease to get my attention. What if my sister was back from dropping Tammy off at the airport?"

He replied matter-of-factly as he pointed toward the second floor of the house. "She is."

Shit! I held my breath as I turned toward the house. The absolute last thing I needed was for my sister to see him flirting with me—or, even worse, me flirting with him—after everything she'd done for me lately. She would be devastated, and our parents would never forgive me. She had done what only a sister would do for me: She saved my life. Against the protests of all my family, she opened up her house to me during my truest time of need, inviting me to live with her and Rashad after my latest suicide attempt.

And, yes, I did say *latest*. I know, crazy, right? Unfortunately, it was crazy but true, and I had the scars on my wrists to prove it. I'd tried to end my life three times in the past few years. My last attempt would have succeeded if my ex-boyfriend hadn't broken down the bathroom door and rushed me to the hospital. Why would an apparently strong-willed black woman do such a thing? Why else? Because of a goddamn man. A man named Tony, who for three years of my life was my entire world. A man who led me to give Rashad up to my sister. A man whom I couldn't let go of, even after I found out he was married and I confronted his wife. A man I wasn't willing to live without, even though I knew I could do better. A man I tried to kill myself over.

When I got out of the hospital, Egypt asked me to move to Virginia and live with her until I was back on my feet. Most of our family was against it, as I said before, but I did have to get out of New York and away from Tony. If I didn't, I would be right back where I was—or worse, in a cemetery. So I accepted her invitation and awkwardly moved down to Virginia with my sister and her husband—my ex-boyfriend. Things had been going pretty smooth so far, and hopefully they would continue to, as long as I figured a way out of the mess I might have just stepped into.

My eyes traveled to the second-floor balcony, where the sliding glass door was still open. Dear Lord, what had I just started? If the ground could have opened up and swallowed me whole, it wouldn't have been deep enough. There was no doubt in my mind that Rashad was telling the truth, and my sister had seen his striptease and quite possibly heard my flirting. How the hell could I have been so stupid? So blind? Shit, if I knew Egypt, she was probably on her way downstairs with Rashad's gun right now. My sister was known for her temper. She could fly off the handle faster than anyone else I knew.

I whipped my head back toward him. "Oh, my God, she's going to kill us. You know that, don't you?"

"I doubt that," he replied rather arrogantly. "'Cause I didn't do anything wrong."

"You didn't what? Are you—" My jaw dropped. So that's how he was going to play? Act like he didn't do anything. Wasn't that just like a damn man? Always willing to take the pleasure but never the pain. At that moment, I would have bet a hundred dollars he was going to leave me hanging out there to dry like this was all my fault and that somehow I made him do a striptease.

"Rashad, you—"

He blurted out, "Honey, I think we've been busted," but he wasn't looking at me when he said it.

I glanced back over my shoulder, and there was Egypt, walking out the sliding glass doors with a purpose. She didn't have anything in her hands, so that was a blessing, but her facial expression was not a happy one. I bit my lip as she approached, bracing myself for a smack. Thank goodness it never came.

Instead, she apologized to me. Apparently she hadn't heard what I'd said to him. "Isis, I am so sorry. Rashad was just having a little fun. We didn't even know you were there. Did we, honey?" She sounded sincere. And, more importantly, I was off the hook.

I turned to Rashad, who grinned that boyish grin of his that used to melt my heart. He apparently had been putting on his little show for my sister, not for me. Or at least that was the story he was sticking to.

"Nah, babe, I didn't have a clue she was there." He was such a bad actor; I'm surprised Egypt didn't catch on right then and there.

"Don't worry, Egypt." I shrugged it off. "I wasn't really paying him any attention." I flagged my hand in dismissal, then began to walk toward the house. I have to admit, my ego was a little hurt at the thought that he had been doing his little strip-tease for my sister and not me, but I still wasn't convinced that was the case. There was something about the way Rashad said he didn't have a clue that told me differently, especially when I looked up and realized that the sofa I'd been sitting on was clearly visible from outside. Now that I had time to think about it, I decided he was probably putting on a show for both of us.

Jerome

4

I read the last page of M.T. Pope's drama-filled novel *Both Sides of the Fence,* snapping it closed before placing it on the bed next to me. "Damn, now that was a good read," I said to myself, picking up my phone and dialing my best friend Loraine's number. I'd started the book around five-thirty when I got home from work, and here it was a little after twelve and I was finished. I had to give Isis, my fellow book club member, a pat on the back. She'd made the recommendation of M. T. Pope's book a few weeks ago, but I'd only picked it up today, because I'd already finished this month's selection for our next meeting, and I didn't have anything else to read. I didn't usually read gay fiction, because most of the time, it just seemed like fantasy with everyone living happily ever after. But this book wasn't just real; it was thought-provoking. I almost felt like I was reading about myself with the way the main character kept having relationships with married men.

Yes, I had a thing for married men. I loved me a man with a ring on his finger, especially, if by chance, he was in denial and considered himself straight. Breaking in a supposedly straight man was always a challenge. When I finally turned them out, they would shower me with money and gifts for "showing them the light." I smirked happily as I admired my well-decorated bedroom. Everything in it was given to me by some unsuspecting woman's husband.

"Hello." Loraine's voice on the other end of the phone snapped me out of my thoughts.

"Hey, girl," I said.

"What you doin'?" she asked. "I thought you were with some man when I didn't hear from you."

"I wish," I replied. "All I been doing is reading. These lips ain't seen a dick in three days. I think I'm going through withdrawal." I fell back on my bed dramatically for effect, even though I knew she couldn't see it.

"You are a hot mess. You know that?" Loraine laughed. "If you're so damn horny, why don't you call Big Poppa?"

The corners of my mouth curled up into a grin. *Big Poppa!* Just the sound of his name got me all worked up. Big Poppa was the nickname for my sugar daddy, and he sure was sweet. Loraine and I made up the name years ago, because he was, for lack of a better word, big. Really big. He was also the only man who could truly steal my heart if he wanted to. He was kind and sweet and treated me like gold when we were together. Ain't no reason to lie; despite the fact that I saw other men, I was in love with him. There was no question in my mind that I would drop everything if he'd leave his wife and settle down with me. The only problem was, he wasn't having any part of that. Shit, I could fix his favorite meal, then suck his dick until he was unconscious, but when he woke up, he would put his shit on and go home to his wife. Deep down, I think he loved me. It was our lifestyle he was afraid of. I'd gotten used to it by now, but I still hoped that one day he would realize we were meant to be together.

"No can do, Loraine. I ain't calling Big Poppa. He already told me not to call until the weekend. Last time I broke one of his golden rules, he cut me off for two months. So, I guess I'm just going to bed frustrated."

"Well, honey, I'm available if things get too backed up down there. A fake mustache and a strap-on and you'll never know the difference from the back," Loraine joked. We both laughed, but part of me always felt that she was only half joking when she made little comments like that.

I'd known Loraine a long, long time, since we were in college at Virginia State, to be exact. Believe it or not, we even dated during our freshman year. To this day, she still swears I was her first; I know she was mine, male or female. Of course, that was before I came out of the closet, admitting to myself and the world that I was gay. The good person and friend that she was, Loraine took it pretty well when I came out to be with this married professor who picked up on my vibe and finally turned me out.

Loraine told me a few years later that the reason she didn't get upset was because deep down she always knew I was gay. I kind of find that hard to believe, because I always considered myself a man's man. I wasn't one for acting feminine, and I was not attracted one bit to feminine-looking or -acting men. I had nothing against them, mind you. I just wanted people to look at me for who I was: a masculine man who just happened to sleep with men.

"Raine, I love you to death. I would do anything for you, and I know you would do anything for me. But fucking me in the ass is not something I want you to do, so get that shit out your mind." We both laughed so hard behind that.

"Well, then, I suggest you make a call to one of your many sponsors."

"Hmmm, I might just do that." I smiled at the thought. "Look, I'ma bring you that M. T. Pope book tomorrow. It's the bomb. I put it up there with E. Lynn Harris."

"Really? Then don't forget it," she replied. "Look, I gotta go. I took a Tylenol PM and it's starting to work."

"Okay, get you some rest. Night, Raine."

"Good night, Jerome." I hung up the phone thinking about her last statement. Maybe I should just call one of my "sponsors." I had a real craving for some lovin' and a taste for some dick.

Despite what I said to Loraine, I had thought about calling Big Poppa, though I was sure he couldn't get away from his wife and probably wouldn't answer his phone. He stuck to our schedule religiously and refused to see me any other time. I guess I was just going to have to wait until our weekly rendezvous on Sunday. But I wasn't going to let that stop me from enjoying myself. I reached over on my night table and picked up a small piece of paper with a name and number on it. I dialed the number.

"Hello." The man who answered sounded groggy.

"Hello . . . ah . . ." I had to look at the paper. I had forgotten his name that quick. "Is this Peter?"

"Yes, this is Peter. Who is this?"

"Hey, Peter, this is Jerome. We met at the gas station the other day. You know, the big black guy? You said I looked like a football player?"

"Hold on a moment," he whispered, and the phone became muffled, then silent. He was probably trying to get out of bed and as far away from his wife as possible to speak with me.

Finally, I heard, "Hi, Jerome. How you doing?" in this overly excited white-boy voice.

Yes, he was a white man. I didn't discriminate when it came to the bedroom or whose money I took—especially when he was as fine as Peter, with his George Clooney looks. Mmm, mmm, mmm, I could just eat his fine ass up. I know plenty of people, male and female, who would be jealous if I showed up to a function with him on my arm.

"I'm doing all right. Been thinking a lot about you."

"I've been thinking about you too." I could hear the smile in his voice.

"Really? Penny for your thoughts."

"Good thoughts. No, more than good thoughts."

"How good?" Damn, I was starting to want this white boy bad. He knew the right things to say.

"Really good." He wanted me too. I could tell.

"Were they good enough to get you out tonight?"

"I wish I could, but what about my wife?" Always the wife. But I wasn't giving up that easy. I never did.

"What I've got for you is only going to take fifteen, twenty minutes tops."

"I don't know, Jerome. I don't think she's going to go for that."

The hell with her! It's not what she wants. It's what I want. He just didn't understand how good this was going to be. It was time to make him understand what he'd be missing.

"Bet she wouldn't go for giving you a blow job tonight either, but I will. Best you ever had, and that's a promise."

There was silence on the line, which meant he was mulling

over my offer, fighting with himself on whether he should stay home or go get his dick sucked. He wasn't like most of the guys I went after—he told me at the gas station that he'd been with men before—but he was still in denial. I knew I could win him over, though, because the other thing he'd admitted to me was that he'd never been with a black man. From the way he had been looking at me, I gathered he was having a real bad case of jungle fever.

"Okay, where you want to meet?" His desire finally won over his conscience.

"You remember the gas station we met at?"

"Uh-huh, the BP on Jefferson Davis Highway."

"Well, there's a short-stay hotel across the street. Meet me in the parking lot. No need to wear any underwear. They'll just get in the way."

"I'll be there in ten minutes."

"I'll be there in fifteen. Get us a room." I hung up the phone, wondering if he was going to make it back home before his wife woke up, because we were going to be there a hell of a lot longer than the twenty minutes I'd promised him.

Egypt

5

"Oh, yeah, baby. That's it. Take that shit. It's all yours, boo," I cooed into my husband's ear.

For lack of a better word, he was fucking the shit outta me, and every stroke was bringing me closer to an orgasm. All I needed was for him to hit the right spot one more time, and I swear I was going to explode. I locked my ankles around his and held on to his waist, grinding my hips against his every time he entered me. Rashad could be very long-winded when he wanted to be, so I always tried to hold out and reach my orgasm with him, but sometimes it just got too good to me, and I had to let it go. I couldn't help myself. I let out a long moan, and when I finally did explode, my entire body tightened and then contorted underneath him. I can't even imagine the faces I made as I climaxed, but I felt so good I didn't give a damn. My God, did he know how to bring out the beast in me.

By the time I had regained control of my body, I was ready to make him come. And, believe me, I did know how to make my man come when I wanted him to. I lowered my hands, taking hold of his butt cheeks to pull him in deeper. Then, lifting my head, I nibbled his earlobe with my lips, whispering as I dug my fingernails deep into the round flesh of his buttocks.

"Come on, Daddy. Give Momma that love juice. I wanna feel your come deep inside me." It's amazing what a few words and a little pleasure/pain can do to take a man over the edge, because within seconds, Rashad was moaning and groaning loud enough for the entire neighborhood to hear.

"Baby, I'm coming!"

I placed my hand over his mouth. "Shhhh, baby. You're being a little too loud. You're gonna wake up my sister."

"Huh?" He stopped moving and glared down at me like I had robbed him of something. Considering he'd been in the middle of his orgasm when I quieted him, I guess he sort of had a point. But he knew how I felt about getting all loud with my sister in the house. We'd had this conversation before, so I really didn't see why he was acting all indignant now.

"What is wrong with you?" I asked.

"If you have to ask, then it really doesn't matter." He rolled off of me, staring at the ceiling. I heard him mutter, "This is bull-shit."

"Rashad," I whined, trying to snuggle up against him, but I knew he wouldn't forgive me that quickly. He'd explained to me plenty of times that he didn't care who heard us having sex. As far as he was concerned, we were a married couple, and anyone who had a problem with the fact that we had a healthy sex life would just have to deal with it.

That was fine with me, too, except when it came to my sister. I didn't know how to explain it to him—hell, I barely under-stood it myself—but something just felt weird to me knowing she could be listening to us. It had something to do with the fact that Rashad used to be her man. She could imagine full well what he was doing to make me scream, which was why I never allowed myself to go there when she was in the house. When we had the house to ourselves, I would scream and moan like a porn star. I guess that made it even more frustrating for him when I held back.

He'd been dealing with it pretty well up until now. Tonight the look on his face told me he'd reached his breaking point. Damn. Why the hell did I have to bring up my sister? I tried once more to explain my side.

"I just didn't want Isis to hear us having sex. It's embarrass-ing."

"Embarrassing! No, you didn't just go there. Look, this is my damn house. If I want to scream while I make love to my wife, I should be able to holler from the top of the damn roof. So should you."

I felt bad that he was frustrated, but his angry tone put me on the defensive. I couldn't believe he was so upset.

"C'mon, Rashad. You know what I mean."

"I sure do."

The next thing I knew, he'd rolled over and turned his back to me, threatening for the first time since we'd been married not to kiss me good night.

"Aw, baby, don't be like that." I reached out and tried to turn him back toward me, but he yanked his shoulder away. His back formed a wall between us. "Rashad, don't do this. Talk to me."

"I would, but I'm afraid your sister might hear us. Wouldn't want to disturb her freeloading ass while she's getting her beauty rest—if you know what I mean."

I sighed. Our conversation felt like a CD stuck on repeat. He was forever putting down my sister, but the way I saw it, she just needed some help getting back on her feet. "She's not freeloading. She's just staying here until things turn around for her. We talked about this. You agreed she should stay with us until she got better."

"I agreed to three months." He turned over to face me. "She's been here almost a year, Egypt. You swore it would be only three months. Shit, she ain't even got a job yet. Eating us out of house and home."

"I know, baby." She was my sister and I loved her, but Rashad was right about everything he'd said. You could look at the situation and see that Isis was taking advantage of us to a certain extent. Shoot, I was just thankful that he hadn't mentioned that she hadn't so much as picked up a broom since she arrived.

"Rashad, you're the best husband in the world, and you have been so understanding. You know Isis ain't wrapped too tight. I promise I'll talk to her about getting a job tomorrow, okay? I just can't see her out in the cold."

"I know, but, you know, this is awkward for me."

"Awkward how?"

"Uh, are you kidding? I used to sleep with her, remember?" he asked with a bite to his tone.

"How could I forget? I mean, I know you used to be together, but I thought that didn't matter to you anymore." Yeah, I know I was being a hypocrite. The fact that they used to be a couple was always in the back of my mind too. It's just that he'd promised me he never thought about their relationship anymore, so it irked me that he still felt awkward. Or so I thought. His explanation was actually a little deeper than that.

"I don't know. I always feel like I'm walking on eggshells when she's around. I can't explain it except to say sometimes I think she feels she's the wife."

I jackknifed straight up in the bed. "She what?"

Rashad hesitated for a second. I folded my arms and raised my eyebrows, waiting for an answer. I loved my sister, but I knew she had done some devious shit in the past. I wouldn't have expected her to do something shady with my man, but now Rashad had me wondering.

"Well?"

"I'm not going to lie to you. She looks at me kind of funny."

He knew Isis well enough to interpret her face, so if he said she was looking at him funny, it was about to be on between me and my sister. I reached for my robe.

"Did she say anything to you? Did she come on to you?" I asked, digging for more details.

"No, not in so many words. It's just little things."

"Like what? Don't start getting evasive now."

"I don't know. It's just—"

"Wait a minute." It was time to cut to the chase. "Has she ever tried to kiss you? Offer you the goodies or anything like that?"

He shook his head. "No, I can't say that she has, but I know when a woman wants me, Egypt."

"Hmmph." I wasn't sure how I felt about what he'd just said. I might have been mistaken, but I thought I saw a flash of pride cross his face. He was a man, after all, so I'm sure his ego was loving it that my sister was sending him vibes that she still wanted him. But then I started getting worried. Was he feeling awkward because he was having trouble controlling himself around her? Maybe it wasn't my sister. Maybe he was the one who needed a warning.

"Let me make one thing clear: That's my sister. If anything ever happens between you and her, I will kill you both." My voice was trembling, and my chest was heaving. "Now, are you telling me that my sister shouldn't stay here because she wants to fuck you? Because I'll get up and kick her ass out right now."

I was out of the bed now, about to head to the door.

"Egypt . . ." he called out, and I stopped, turning to face him.

"Like I don't have enough stressing me out, waiting to hear from Tammy about this whole surrogacy thing. Now you throw this shit at my feet."

For a moment, we both fell silent, and tension filled the room.

"Well?" I asked.

"Maybe you're right. Maybe we're both stressed out about this whole baby thing, and I'm just a little too sensitive."

"You didn't answer my question. Do you think she wants to fuck you?"

He shook his head. "No, your sister doesn't want me. She wants that married dude in New York. I'm probably just reading too much into things."

"You sure?" I asked, eager to accept his explanation and avoid a fight with him or my sister.

"Yeah." He extended his hand, pulling me back onto the bed.

He kissed me, and I tried to relax. I tried putting the conversation out of my mind, but the best I could manage was to push it to the back. I definitely wouldn't forget it. I wasn't sure if Rashad really believed he had misread her or if he was just trying to stop me from kicking her ass. Either way, it was something I was going to keep my eye on. It was time for me and my sister to have a long-overdue conversation about her living arrangement.

I kissed my husband back, this time initiating our lovemaking. From now on, if he wanted to scream, he could scream all he wanted. I know I was going to add plenty of theatrics from now on.

Isis

6

I bit my lip as I squirmed around on the bed. Rashad's moaning was like music to my ears as my fingers gently stroked my clit, bringing me to one hell of an orgasm. He was such an attentive lover, always putting my pleasure in front of his, so I was sure he was doing the same for my sister as I jealously listened to them make love.

I know you must think I'm one sick bitch getting my shit off while listening to my sister and her husband having sex, but what the hell was I supposed to do? As large as this house was, the walls were paper thin. I mean, damn, I'm only human. Here I was in bed trying to get some sleep, and the next thing I knew I was awakened by the two of them trying to break their bed. Rashad's sexy ass was moaning and groaning like he was about to bust a supernut, and my sister's screaming was letting the world know she was getting the best dick in three states. The way I saw it, there were only three plans of action: bang on the walls and tell them to keep down the racket, keep listening and let my fingers do the walking, or walk down the hall and join them. In truth, joining them was out, if only because I'm selfish and don't like to share, unlike my sister, who has been in threesomes before. Banging on the walls was also out because it was only going to get me eye rolls from both of them at the breakfast table tomorrow morning. So, by letting my fingers do the walking, it was a win-win for everyone. They got theirs, and I damn sure got mine.

Hell, it wasn't the first time I got off listening to them, and it damn sure wouldn't be the last. Only problem was, I was getting sick of using my hand. Rashad, although flirtatious as hell, still hadn't made a move on me yet. Oh, it was coming. I'd taken him down memory lane enough times in the past few weeks to assure myself of that. In fact, my sister probably owed her little love-making session tonight to the seeds I'd planted in her husband's head. Sooner or later, he was going to want the real thing, not the younger imitation, but that wasn't doing me any good right now. I hadn't had any real dick in almost two months, and I was about due.

I picked up the portable house phone and dialed the one person other than Rashad whom I would love to fuck. It was time to get something in motion so I could get my groove on real soon.

"Hello?" a woman answered on the third ring. I was so taken aback by the sound of her voice that I couldn't say anything. "Hello?" she repeated. What the hell was she doing answering his cell phone? "I know it's you."

You don't know shit, bitch, I thought. *It's a fucking blocked number.*

"I can hear your crazy-ass breathing, Isis."

Stay calm, girl. Don't let this bitch get to you.

"What, did you escape from that nuthouse again?"

I'll show you crazy, heifer. Just say one more thing. One more fucking thing.

"Let me guess. You're going to attempt suicide again, and you wanted us to know. Well, stop trying to kill yourself, for Christ's sake, and do it. You won't get any tears out of me. I'm sick of you calling my husband. Can't you see he don't want you? Why don't you get your own man?"

"He is my man, bitch!" I couldn't help myself. I knew he was going to be mad later, but I just couldn't help myself. "The only person I'm going to kill is you. And if you keep pissing me off, I'll do it in front of your kids."

"Oh my God, you are one sick woman. Stop calling my husband!"

Her name was Monica. She was a school secretary in some hick town in upstate New York, and I couldn't stand the bitch—mainly because she was living my life, or at least the life I would have had if her husband, Tony, my ex-fiancé, wasn't such a lying son of bitch. Too bad for me that I loved him more than life itself.

"Let me talk to Tony," I demanded.

"Are you out your mind?"

Click. The phone went dead. That wench actually hung up on me. I couldn't stand when people did that. I dialed the number again. She answered on the first ring.

"Nobody hangs up on me, whore."

"I'm calling the police. This is harassment."

"Call 'em, bitch. Think I care? By the time they get to your house, you'll be a corpse. Now put Tony on the phone!"

Click. She hung up again. This wench was really pissing me off. I dialed the phone again. This time it went straight to voice mail. She must have turned off his cell phone. I lay back in my bed, frustrated. I tried to calm down, but I really wanted to kill that bitch. Hell, upstate New York was only an eight-hour drive. I could be there in the morning, waiting for her to come out the door on her way to work. A smile crept up on my face as I imagined choking the life out of her.

My cell phone rang. I reached over to the night table and looked at the caller ID. I was going to kill Tony. He was supposed to put my number under someone else's name, but this bitch was calling me back. I hit the green button, connecting the call without saying a word.

"Isis?" It wasn't her; it was him. I was like a deer caught in headlights. I didn't know what to say or do. All I knew was that I didn't want him mad at me.

I'd been in love with only two people in my life. One was Rashad, who, as you know, was now married to my sister, and the other was Tony. I lost Rashad to my sister because of my love for Tony. A few years ago, Rashad and Tony had actually battled it out for my affection. Tony had won not just the fight, but also my heart, with a huge diamond engagement ring and a wedding proposal right in front of a bruised and battered Rashad. I'd finally found my prince charming in the form of Tony—only my prince turned out to be a frog when I discovered he was already married with two children. I can't begin to tell you how humiliated I was. I'd already begun planning my wedding and had even bought a wedding dress.

Crushed, I decided to seek refuge with the one man who'd always loved me unconditionally, a man I was sure wasn't married and would marry me without hesitation—Rashad. Sadly, he was absolutely devastated by my decision to be with Tony and had turned to my sister for a shoulder to lean on. To this day, I still do not understand why Egypt would do it, but instead of a shoulder to lean on, she offered him what was between her legs.

If you think discovering out Tony was married was an arrow through my heart, it felt like I'd been hit by a bazooka when I found out about my sister and Rashad. Between what was going on with me and Tony and the craziness of finding out about Egypt and Rashad, I had a mental breakdown.

Believe it or not, it was Tony who got me through it, with a wife and all. By the time I got out of the hospital that first time, I just needed to be loved, and Tony was there for me, despite what everyone else thought. So, I put aside my holier-than-thou attitude about seeing a married man and went for mine.

For two years, I competed with his wife for his affection. I honestly felt like I was winning for a while, especially since I saw Tony almost every day and made sure that when he did go home to Monica, he was tired and sexually drained. But I had to give it to her; that bitch just wouldn't give up.

She actually resorted to what I considered to be some really dirty shit when she started using the kids as weapons against me. She knew Tony loved his kids. They were his one weakness. So, she moved them to upstate New York and made Tony transfer his job so he couldn't see me. She had him on such a tight leash that I barely saw him once a month.

I felt like I was going to die inside. One weekend, right before he was to leave, I took an entire bottle of pills. I wasn't trying to kill myself, just get his attention. I wanted him to prove that he loved me by staying with me and nursing me back to health like he'd done in the past. My plan actually worked that time but failed miserably the next time, which was how my sister ended up taking me in.

"Isis. You there, baby?" I loved it when he called me baby.

"Yeah, I'm here." I knew I sounded like a child. He brought that out in me.

"Everything okay?" He was always concerned about my well-being.

"Yeah, everything's okay. Except for that crazy bitch you're married to."

"What did you say to Monica?" He didn't sound mad, but there was no doubt he wanted an answer right then and there. "She's on the warpath."

"Nothin'. I just asked for you. I wasn't expecting Monica to answer the phone. She caught me off guard."

"Yeah, I can imagine. Sorry about that. I went out for a while and left my phone behind."

I sighed thankfully. He could never stay at me for long.

"Let me ask you a question."

"Anything, Tony."

"You didn't threaten my kids, did you?"

"Hell no, I didn't threaten your kids. I love your kids, Tony. They're a part of you." I'd hated the little brats ever since their mom used them to take Tony away from me, but he didn't know that and never would.

"I didn't think so, but Monica's talking about getting a restraining order."

"Tony, I don't know why you don't just leave her. You could move down here, and we could get a place. That woman is crazy, baby. You've said it yourself."

"You know I can't leave my kids, Isis."

I never won this argument, so it wasn't worth going down this road. Best I kept to the subject at hand—getting some dick. "I know you can't leave your kids. But how about for a weekend?" I crossed my fingers. "Can you leave them for the weekend to come see me? I miss you, baby, and so does Miss Kitty. You wouldn't want me to have to give her to someone else."

"I know you ain't planning on giving away my pussy." Tony was one jealous motherfucker. Despite having a wife at home and not hitting this in almost two months, he still considered this his pussy. He couldn't stand the idea of anyone else getting some of this.

"Well, then you need to handle your business before the job is given to someone who can."

"Don't play with me, Isis. I'll be down there this weekend."

"Now that's what I'm talking about. I heard my sister say they were going to New York for the weekend. We'll have the house to ourselves."

"Sounds good. I'll see you on Friday."

"Friday it is." I could hear Monica in the background. "You gotta go, don't you?"

"Yeah," he said sadly. "Don't wanna piss her off too much. Last thing I want is for her to block me from coming down this weekend."

"I know that's right, baby. Just call me tomorrow."

"Aw-ight. Love you."

"Love you too." I hung up, wondering if he was going to keep his promise or not show up because of his wife like he'd done the last two times we were supposed to meet. Well, if he didn't show up this Friday, I damn sure was going to show up at his house on Saturday.

Loraine

7

"He's home," Jerome blurted out in disbelief, as if he were reading my thoughts as we pulled into the driveway of my Southside Richmond home. The "he" Jerome was speaking about was my husband, Leon, whose tricked-out black Mercedes was impossible to miss. Leon had been missing in action for the better part of a week. He'd walked out of the house after we had yet another argument over money.

Leon was a very prideful man, and he was having a hard time adjusting to me being the breadwinner in our house. I just couldn't seem to make him understand that we needed to save. He'd lost plenty of money trying to get in on so-called ventures that never went anywhere. I didn't know where the hell he spent the rest of it, but he was never able to keep money in his pocket. Considering I was making the majority of that cash, it was pissing me off how careless he was. On top of that, he was asking me to give him his interest in the public-relations firm so he could invest it in Rashad's hedge fund. Because I wanted more details about the investment before I said yes, he got pissed off, said I needed to stop trying to control him.

In the heat of the argument, he'd smacked the shit out of me on his way out the door. Of course, I was pissed at first, but once I calmed down and thought about it, I realized I had pushed him too far. I had said some pretty belittling things to him, and I guess he had just reached his breaking point.

You see, it takes two to argue, and I'm a sister who is used to making her point, so I say whatever is on my mind and let the chips fall where they may. It seems that with my husband, I had made one point too many, and he decided to end the argument by picking up his keys and heading for the front door. You just don't walk out on me, so I snatched his keys from his hand and blocked the door. That's when he called me a bitch.

I've heard that saying: "Sticks and stones can break your bones, but words will never hurt you." That's crap. Don't nobody call me a bitch to my face and get away with it. I slapped the shit out of him, and trust me, I'm a big, heavy-handed black woman, so I know that shit hurt. What I totally forgot was that even though I'm big and heavy-handed, I'm still a woman. When his hand came across my face, I slid down the door and the pain reminded me that he was a man. I didn't try to stop him from leaving after that.

"You should have changed the locks," Jerome said.

After Leon left that night, I'd called Jerome for some comfort. I tried to convince him that the whole incident was my fault, but he wasn't having it. He'd been trying for the longest time to get me to leave Leon. To him, there should have been no question about kicking Leon out after he put his hands on me.

"You want me to put his ass out, Loraine? 'Cause I will," he said as I unfastened my seat belt. "All you gotta do is say the word, girl, and his ass is gone. Ain't nothin' but a thang." Jerome tried his best to stay calm, but I could hear the anger in his voice.

I understood how he felt, but that didn't change the fact that I loved my husband and still wanted my marriage to work. In truth, as I looked at his car in the driveway, all I could think about was whether he was home to stay or just picking up some clothes to leave again.

"No, Jerome. I can handle it." I forced my voice to sound confident, but deep down, I was hopeful at best.

Jerome shook his head. "You gonna take his ass back, aren't you? That man put his hands on you, and you're taking him back."

I stared blankly at my friend before speaking. Maybe it was because he seemed to have no problem jumping from one lover to the next, but Jerome just didn't get it: I loved Leon too much to give up on our marriage. "I'm going inside to talk to my husband, Jerome. It's not his fault he hit me. I hit him first."

"If that's your story." Jerome locked his eyes on mine. "He still shouldn't have put his hands on you. He don't got the right. Not after all you've done for him. That man wouldn't have a roof over his head if it wasn't for you." Jerome looked disgusted. "That man doesn't deserve you, Loraine. You're too good for his no-good jealous ass. Sooner or later, you've got to let go, or he's going to drag you down with him."

"Will you stop it? He's not jealous, and he's not going to drag me down. He's just going through a hard time with the construction industry in such a slump. Now's the time I've got to support him, not knock him down."

"Well, next time he blackens your eye, don't call me—unless you want me to go to jail for knocking his ass down a flight of stairs."

"There won't be a next time."

The way he looked at me said, *Sure there won't.*

Ignoring his eyes, I leaned over, wrapping my arms around his two-hundred-plus–pound frame and giving him a kiss on his cheek before reaching for the door handle. "I love him, Jerome. Just remember that I love him."

"I know you love him, sis. That's the only reason he's not wearing these size fourteen gators in the crack of his ass." Jerome blew me a kiss. "I swear that must be some really good dick."

"Don't you wish you knew?" I smirked as I stepped out of the car.

"We're friends, Loraine. That's not something you want me to pursue. Or have you forgotten my track record with married men?"

We both burst out laughing. "Don't even try it, Jerome. If I catch you near my husband, we gonna have a problem."

"Hey, don't get your panties in a bunch. I'm just teasing, girl. You know he ain't even my type."

"Please. Your type is anyone with a big dick swinging between his legs."

"Hmm, you're right about that. But anyway, listen, are you sure you don't want me to come inside? Just to make sure everything's aw-ight? I mean, he has gotten out of hand before."

"No, no, I got it, okay? I'll see you at work in the morning."

"Are you sure?" He leaned across the passenger seat and looked in my eyes. I knew what he was doing. Jerome was very good at reading people's faces. But I wasn't lying; I wanted him to leave so there wouldn't be any confrontation.

"Yes, absolutely."

"Aw-ight, girl, I'll see you in the morning." He sat back up in his seat. "Keep your head up. Remember, tomorrow's the big meeting."

"How could I forget? Good night, Jerome."

I walked to the door, preparing myself mentally before placing my key in the lock and turning the knob. I had no idea what to expect from Leon. Truth is, I was glad he was home but was afraid of where things might go.

As I entered the foyer, I noticed him in the living room situated off to my right. He was sitting in the love seat by the window with a drink in his hand and a bottle of Hennessy resting on the end table next to him.

Is this his first drink, or one of many?

Suddenly, I wished I had taken Jerome up on his offer to escort me inside. Leon had never been too much of a drinker, until a few years ago when his construction company fell upon hard times after he lost a government contract. I couldn't tell how many drinks he'd consumed, but a drunken Leon was not the person I wanted to deal with tonight. I was hoping he'd be sober so we could talk. I missed talking to him; lately all we did was argue.

"Where you been?" he asked without emotion as I entered the room.

He had some nerve asking me that after being gone all week, but I answered him nonetheless. "Jerome and I went to—"

"So, you been hanging out with that sissy again?" Leon let out a disdainful laugh. "What the hell is it about that faggot you like so much anyway?"

Oh, boy, here we go. I hated Leon's homophobia.

"I like him because he's my friend, Leon," I stated flatly. "And if you think he's so much of a sissy, why don't you tell him that to his face?"

"You know me, baby. I'm a lover, not a fighter," he said with this stupid smile on his face.

That black eye I had last week says different. "You're not funny, Leon."

Leon frowned at me. "You act as if you like him more than you do me."

"Damn right, sometimes I do. Jerome's like a brother to me. When your ass isn't around, he's always there for me. I love you, Leon, but sometimes I don't like you."

"Look, I apologize. I didn't come home to fight. I came home to be with my wife."

That made me feel a little better, but I was still not convinced he was being sincere.

"So, why did you come home, Leon? I thought you were leaving for good."

"This is my house, and you're my wife. I just needed a few days to cool off." He smiled and sipped on his drink. He even had the nerve to look sexy. "Plus, I got a call from Rashad. He congratulated me on being fully vested in his hedge fund. No need to fight if I got what I wanted."

"True," I replied. To be honest, that's the way I saw it too. That's why I gave Rashad the money. I loved my husband enough to let him win this one.

"He said you dropped off a cashier's check."

"Yeah, I did."

"I'm a little confused. You said you couldn't afford to give me my interest in your company."

It's our company. Why can't he see that? We're supposed to be a team.

"What I couldn't afford was losing my husband. I went to the bank and got a loan." I could tell he was shocked. I just hoped he was grateful, because I'd put our financial future on the line to keep our marriage intact.

"Thank you, baby. This is gonna be big. You'll see."

"I hope so, Leon. That's a lot of money to give to one person. Every financial person I know warned me against it." If I hadn't already made money with Rashad—with a much smaller initial investment, mind you—I probably wouldn't have done it.

"It will be. So, where have you and your *friend* been?" Interesting, now that he felt he'd won our fight, Leon refrained from taking jabs at my gay friend.

"We were just out for a few drinks."

He finished off his drink with a laugh. "Oh, and here I am thinking you was out with the fat girls book club."

"No, the Big Girls Book Club," I replied, hating that lately he had to put down everything and everyone I was associated with.

"And you are a big girl, aren't you? My big girl!" He smiled sincerely, standing up. Everything he had said up to now had sounded derogatory, but now his voice had a seductive tone to it. So did the way he approached me. "You are still my big girl, aren't you?"

I didn't answer, but I did remember why I missed him and wanted him home so bad. I loved Leon. I loved him to death. He was smart, funny, and a great husband—when he wasn't consumed with self-pity and doubt.

I took in his handsome six-foot-five frame. Leon was as fine a forty-five-year-old man as you're going to find. He was tall, chocolate, and slim. There was a little gray around the temples, but when he entered a room, women paid attention.

In the beginning, I found it hard to believe that a man as successful and as handsome as he was could be so attracted to a big-boned sister like me, but he was. I learned shortly after we started dating that Leon had always been a chubby chaser. I didn't have anything to worry about when it came to the Tyra Banks and Beyoncé types, but if Mo'Nique or that woman who plays the mother on Tyler Perry's *House of Payne* ever came around, I was taking my husband and heading for the hills.

He winked at me as he came closer, undressing me with his eyes while taking in my full-figured curves. He had a way of making me feel like I was absolutely the most beautiful woman he'd ever seen.

"I missed you, baby." He stepped closer, sliding his arms around my waist. "I'm sorry. I didn't mean to call you out your name. I was just frustrated. I didn't mean to lose—"

I placed my hand over his lips. "It's okay. You're just going through a hard time."

He lowered his head until his lips covered mine.

I almost submitted to his advances, but I caught myself in time. "Stop, baby. We need to talk."

I gently pushed him away. I didn't want to fight about money anymore, but we still had some unfinished business to discuss. I wanted to talk to Leon about his leaving. Would he promise to never hit me again? Was he back to stay? Most of all, where had he been for the past few days?

Suddenly Leon reached down and cupped my breasts in his hands. It was a soft, feathery motion, which slowly built momentum, but there was an expert manipulation of my nipples. He knew my spot. Although I still wore my suit, I could feel the heat starting to rise inside me from his touch. He began kissing my neck, and my knees gave way.

Every woman has her own special erogenous spot, the one that can take her from an ice princess to a sultry tigress in a nanosecond. Well, Leon knew mine after five years of marriage. All resolve melted when his hand found its way under my blouse and made direct contact with my breast. I felt myself ready to spread my wings. Besides, it had been a while since we'd made love.

"Stop," I moaned, but I felt my back arch, my arms roping around his neck as he kneaded my nipples. His lips worked their way up my neck to my lips. I opened my mouth and took in his tongue. "No, Leon. Not now," I murmured. My mouth said no, but my body screamed yes.

"You know you want it," he whispered. I didn't answer with words but guided his head back to my neck. He worked his way up and down my neck, opening another button of my blouse with each succulent kiss. Next thing I knew, he'd gently pushed me down on the sofa. My blouse was fully open now, with both his hands kneading my exposed breasts. He wasted no time bringing his lips to my nipples, sucking them like a newborn babe. I'd never felt such heat, such animal passion with Leon. It was like he was a totally different man. If it were possible, I would say this was the best our sex had ever been.

His skin against mine felt like fire. His fingertips were touching hidden crevices he'd never touched before. I have no idea how or when our clothes came off, but somehow they did. When Leon mounted me, my body was ready and begging to be satisfied. I don't think I'd ever been that horny in my entire life.

With all that being said, I was afraid things were not going to end up as planned. You see, Leon, who was a very well-endowed man, had run into some major stamina problems the last few years. It was a secret I'd kept even from Jerome, because the last thing I wanted was for anyone to think my husband was less than a man in the bedroom. The frustrating part was that Leon was such an egomaniac in the bedroom that he didn't have a clue. Things were so bad in my sex life that I hadn't had an orgasm in almost six months, and I'd given myself that one; however, I was determined to get mine tonight.

"Slow, Leon. Take it slow," I pleaded.

"Girl, I know what I'm doing. You know you like that shit hard and fast," he said as he entered me like a bull. I tried to hold his hips to slow him down. I was so sexually charged that I would need only a few minutes to reach my climax. All I had to do was get him to hold off a little while longer and we'd both be happy. Hell, I'd be elated.

He was doing great for the first minute or so. I honestly thought this was going to be it. He was actually going to make me come. I was so pleased that I whispered encouragement in his ear. "That's it, Leon. You're gonna make me—" Just when I was about to reach my climax, he stiffened his back and collapsed on top of me.

No, no! I screamed inside. *You're almost there. Just move your hips a few more times.*

But it never happened, which was not good at all, because when Leon was finished, he was done, end of conversation. I hated it, but he'd been that way since we first started dating.

I bit down on the inside of my lip. It took me a few seconds to get over my disappointment. One side of me was glad that he came so fast, because it made me certain he hadn't been with another woman after our fight, but the other side felt cheated. I wanted to come too. He'd gotten me all hot and bothered, but for what? Nothing!

We were lying on the living room floor, clothes strewn all over the place. I could hear Leon's ragged breathing piercing my ear. Another few minutes and he'd be asleep.

Finally I made a move. "Leon." I shook him, hoping he could recharge and we could go for round two. Instead, Leon lifted his shoulders and looked down at me. "Whew! Girl, girl, girl. That *was* good, wasn't it? I told you that you liked it hard and fast."

Good? Was he crazy? Hell no, it wasn't good. I was just getting started. I wanted to jump all over Leon's selfish ass, but I didn't want to risk our tenuous reunion and send him back out into the streets.

So I did something I was getting good at. I pretended I'd had an orgasm.

"Yeah, babe. That was great." I tried to look satisfied. "Why don't we do it again?" Couldn't hurt to ask. Maybe I'd get lucky. The second round always seemed to last longer than the first. At least, that's what I remembered.

"Nah, if I give you too much, you'll get spoiled." Leon gave me this silly grin as he eased off my body and picked up his clothes. He slapped my thick buttocks as he headed toward the stairs. "I'll see you upstairs. I'm going to take a shower."

As I lay there, listening to the shower running upstairs, I thought about what it would be like to be with someone other than Leon. Then I snapped out of my fantasy and thought, *When the hell would I have time to meet another man when I'm always busy working?*

Egypt

8

It had been more than a month since Tammy and I went out to dinner. She still hadn't given me a definite answer as to whether she would be a surrogate for me and Rashad. Every time we talked, she'd give me the runaround, telling me not to worry and that she and Tim were still mulling over the idea. I wouldn't admit it to Rashad, but I was starting to think the answer was going to be no—that is, until two days ago, when she and Tim asked us to come to New York for the weekend. My guess was that they were planning on telling us that we were going to be parents. At least, that was my hope. I couldn't think of any other reason Tammy would ask me to visit. I knew my best friend pretty well, and she was a coward for the most part. If she had bad news, she would tell us over the phone, not face-to-face.

So, there we were on a plane to New York. I was so excited I could hardly sit still through the hour-long flight. Rashad, on the other hand, was stone-faced and quiet. He barely moved during the entire trip. Ever since I'd told him of Tammy and Tim's request for us to come to New York, he'd taken a wait-and-see approach. Rashad was always the levelheaded one between us, but I knew my husband, and he was excited inside.

"You okay?" I asked when we landed. Rashad was usually the first person out of his seat belt, grabbing our bags so we could get off the plane. But this time he just sat there waiting patiently with his seat belt fastened as other passengers disembarked. "You haven't said more than a few words since we took off."

He patted my knee and gave me a little smile. "I'm fine. Just thinking, that's all."

"Thinking about the baby?"

He nodded. "That and what to say to Tim."

I gave him a puzzled look. "I don't understand."

Rashad put his hand over mine. "Maybe it's a guy thing, but what do you say to a man who lets his wife have your baby?" His voice cracked, like he was trying to hold back powerful emotions. "I don't know how I'm going to repay him."

"Neither do I, sweetheart. Neither do I." I leaned my head against his shoulder.

We didn't say much as we walked hand in hand from the gate to the luggage claim area and then to the rental car kiosk. From the airport, it took us only fifteen minutes to drive over to Tammy and Tim's Jamaica Estates home.

Surprisingly, things weren't as tense as I expected when we arrived at Tammy's house. We were greeted with warm hugs and kisses. I was almost beside myself with anticipation. It took all my strength and self-control not to cut to the purpose of our visit and ask them for their decision right then and there, in the middle of the foyer.

As I walked through the house, I noticed that Tammy had redecorated quite a bit. She, with her sneaky self, had stolen my color scheme and even decorated her foyer like mine, using a grandfather clock and a chandelier. Nevertheless, I was so wound up about getting our baby that I decided to forgive Tammy and her pettiness. I was going to have to deal with a lot worse from her during a pregnancy, so I might as well get used to it now.

Finally, we were seated around the living room of their five-bedroom home. Once everyone was settled down with a drink, that tension I'd been expecting took over the room. It seemed like nobody wanted to speak. We were all staring at each other like a bunch of fools, each waiting for the other couple to speak.

Finally, I just blurted out, "So, Tim, Tammy, what did you guys decide? Am I going to be a mommy or what?" I crossed my fingers, rocking back and forth in my seat. I didn't think they were going to say no, but I was nervous as hell. Rashad took my hand in his to calm me down.

Tim coughed against his fist, then cleared his throat. "Egypt, I know you and Tammy are good friends. . . ."

"Yeah, and?" I didn't mean to interrupt Tim, but I couldn't help myself. He was taking too long.

"Calm down, baby," Rashad said under his breath. "Let the man speak."

"Thank you, Rashad." He cleared his throat again. "As you know, this wasn't a small request. We had to give it a lot of thought and consideration. We've even prayed about it."

Tim was beginning to get on my nerves. We didn't need all this buildup—just get to the damn point. "Come on, cut to the chase. Are you going to let Tammy be our surrogate or what?"

Tim heaved a deep sigh. His words came out in a rush. "No, Egypt. I'm sorry, but we can't do it."

"Huh?" I turned to Tammy. She wouldn't look at me. This had to be some kind of damn joke. "This isn't funny, Tammy."

"We're not laughing, Egypt," Tim answered for her. "We know how bad you want a baby. We just can't help you."

"Why not?" My eyes filled with tears, but I bit my lip and held back my pain.

"Well, Tammy is thirty-eight, and carrying a full-term pregnancy at her age could be a health risk. Plus, she's overweight." Tim was enumerating his points with his fingers, as if he had practiced this little spiel. "If she carries a baby, it could push her into diabetes. We've got Michael and Lisa to think about as well. My children deserve to have a mother while they're growing up. People still die in childbirth in this country, you know."

"Tammy won't die," I assured Tim. "And she's been overweight since you met her. And we're willing to pay for her to have the best doctors." I knew I was babbling, but I couldn't help myself. I had been so sure they were going to say yes, and now that Tim was refusing, I felt like someone had let me unwrap a beautiful gift and then taken it back. "She could go on bed rest the entire pregnancy."

Tim's voice was firm. "No, we've thought about it. Tammy—I mean, we—can't afford to lose a year of our lives. I'm sorry, but we have to put our own family first."

I turned back to Tammy, appealing to her. "I know this is a lot to ask, and I wouldn't ask you for this if I wasn't desperate, but I just want a baby of my own."

"I know, Egypt, but I haven't lost my weight from my last baby." Tammy, wringing her hands, had tears in her eyes.

I felt if I could just get through to her, she could convince Tim to go along with our plan. "You know I would do anything for you, and I have." I gave her a pointed look, since Rashad didn't know about the threesome I had had with Tim for Tammy.

Tammy continued, "Tim's right, Egypt. Having a baby would be like losing a year out of our lives. I'm sorry, but I just can't do it."

Rashad stood up, his back ramrod straight. "Come on, honey. Let's go. Tim, Tammy, we thank you for your time." He was polite but obviously pissed. I rarely saw this side of his personality.

"Why can't you guys stay for dinner?" Tim asked. "Tammy made those beef ribs you like so much, Rashad."

"No, thank you." Rashad kept his eyes straight ahead.

I turned to Tammy one last time. "Tammy, please. I'd do it for you."

She didn't answer. She just looked down at the floor with her eyes full of tears. I now had my final answer. I wanted to throw myself at Tammy's feet and beg her to have our baby, but instead, I got up and followed my husband to the front door, sobbing softly.

"Stop crying, baby," Rashad said, putting his arm around me as I got into the car. "If it costs every cent I have, we'll find someone to have our baby."

Tammy followed us outside, crying too. "Don't be like that, Egypt. We're still friends. Don't take it personally. I would do it if I could."

"What are you trying to say, that this is Tim's decision, not yours?" I turned to Rashad, who was now sitting in the driver's seat. He just shook his head as if he could read my mind. "Tammy, I've known you long enough to know that if you wanted to do this, Tim couldn't stop you. No, this was totally you. Tim's just backing you up."

"Egypt, I can't."

I put my hand up. "Don't, okay? Just leave it alone."

"Listen, why don't you ask Isis to do it? She's your sister, and the baby would be more than half yours. It would have your bloodline too."

"Don't try to push this off on my sister. You're the one who's supposed to be my best friend. But I guess it's pretty obvious how lopsided our friendship really is." I tapped my husband's leg so he could get me as far away from her as possible. I dreaded the flight home. Unlike the trip to New York, where I was full of anticipation, I was returning home with my hopes shattered.

Loraine

9

"Are they here?" I tried to keep my excitement down as Jerome walked into my office. I'd been expecting some very important people for a two o'clock meeting, and it was ten after when he walked in.

Jerome didn't answer me at first. He just closed the door behind him with his head hanging low. I didn't like the way he was acting at all, because his body language had *bad news* written all over it. I just hoped and prayed it didn't have anything to do with my two o'clock meeting.

"Okay, spill it. What's wrong?"

"I just got a call from Ms. Jericho's office. The meeting's been canceled. They've decided to back someone else. I'm sorry, Loraine."

I ran my hand through my hair as I tried to comprehend why they would cancel a meeting that they'd asked for. Had I done something wrong? Was this whole thing some sick joke to play with my emotions? Dammit! I slammed my hand down on my desk.

"You've got to be kidding me. I been kissing these women's asses for over two years." If anyone else had been in the room, I would not have shown this much emotion, but Jerome was my rock, my best friend, my confidant, and my right-hand man all rolled into one. "How the fuck can they do this to me?"

"They didn't." Jerome laughed. "I was just playing with you. They're in reception."

"Ooooh, Jerome, I'm going to kill you." I pointed my finger at him, looking evil but feeling relieved. "That wasn't funny. You almost made me cry."

"Sorry, I just couldn't help it. You've had a stick up your ass all week, waiting for these people to give you what you deserve. I had to have some fun with it."

"That's not fun. What you did was cruel. This is important to me."

"I can see that. Don't worry. You're gonna knock 'em dead." He winked at me.

"How do I look?" I chewed nervously on my bottom lip.

"Seriously? You need to put on a little blush." Jerome gave me a pointed look, lifting his eyebrows. "Stop chewing your lip. You know how dry they get. Oh, and put on some lipstick too."

I straightened the lapels of my pink suit, reached into my purse, and pulled out my compact. I patted makeup over my face and used a little beige concealer to cover the circles under my eyes. I lined my lips, then put on a neutral-colored lipstick. I slid on my Sarah Palin eyeglasses, then turned to Jerome for his inspection. He nodded his head in approval.

"Now that's what I'm talking about. Go get 'em, girl," Jerome whispered, making a circle with his right thumb and index finger.

"Well, then, let's get this show on the road." I spun my desk chair toward the door. "You can show them in now."

While I was waiting, I contemplated how I got to this point, something I did before any serious meeting or decision. I thought about my life. I'd started my own public relations firm at the age of twenty-nine, with the help of Jerome. We'd gone through good times and bad together, and our company was still running strong. Jerome had been there for me in lots of ways, including accompanying me to events that my own husband—who only wanted to watch TV, play golf, or look for the next get-rich-quick scheme—was never interested in attending. Sometimes it felt like if it weren't for Jerome, I would not have any social life at all. Jerome had it going on. Sometimes it was as if I were living my life through his life, since my personal life was so boring.

But all that was about to change. I straightened up my face and put on my professional façade as Linda Brooks, Leigh Seabrooks, Nancy Jericho, and Kim Garner walked into my office. They were all high-powered members of my sorority. My *sorors,* as I liked to call them.

After a round of pleasantries, I said, "Have a seat, ladies. To what do I owe the pleasure of your visit?" Of course, I knew what the meeting was about, but it wasn't the type of thing you admit to until it was formally put on the table.

Nancy Jericho spoke up first. She and Kim Garner were the state presidents for the sorority in Virginia and Maryland, respectfully. "You've been on the national board in the past and held state office twice. You really made an impact during your tenure."

"Thank you. We all must do our part." Suddenly my intercom buzzed. I hit the button, and Jerome's voice came through the speaker.

"You have Mariah Carey on line one."

I pressed another button and said, "Tell Mariah I'll call her back later."

"You also have Usher's PR people on line two—must be damage control about that divorce."

"Tell his people I'll get back with them. And hold all my calls until my two o'clock is finished."

I spun back around in the chair to face my visitors. I could see they were impressed; I was too. I wish I had Mariah Carey and Usher as clients. That Jerome was always playing games; although, from the looks on my visitors' faces, it may have actually helped.

"I've been following your career for some time," Kim spoke up. "You've been voted businesswoman of the year for the past two years."

"You're just the type of leader we need," Leigh added.

"For what?"

"Well, let's just say quite a few members of the sorority have their eye on you. You're on a short list of people we want to run for national president." Linda sounded excited.

"We need new blood in there, Loraine, young blood," Nancy stated.

"Now, I'm not one to talk about my sorors, but the average age of the board is seventy," Kim added.

"I—we—know you can do the job, Loraine," Leigh said.

"Well, I'm honored." I was all smiles. "Tell me more. Wait, let me order coffee. Coffee, anyone?"

All three women nodded.

I turned and buzzed Jerome on the intercom. "Jerome, please have your secretary bring in coffee and some refreshments for my guests."

"I'm on it," Jerome replied. I cut off the intercom. In business with Jerome, I gave orders, he didn't question them, and I didn't often say thanks. He was on a job—a six-figure job at that—so when it came to work, he was my girl Friday.

"I'm flattered, but you've got to tell me more."

All three looked at me approvingly. I could feel their sincere respect for me as a woman who was capable of getting the job done. But as they talked about the pros and cons of running for office, my mind wandered to my marriage. If these people only knew what my home life was like.

I cleared my throat. "Well, I've got to discuss this with my husband."

"That's right," Leigh commented. "We wouldn't want something like this to come between you and your husband."

"I'm sure he's a secure man to be able to live with such a dynamo like you," Nancy commented, trying to feel me out.

I've never liked how women are always trying to check out your relationship with your husband. But they were barking up the wrong tree if they thought I was going to tell them anything different about my marriage. I was so good at doing PR, I knew just how to paint a pretty picture of a marriage. "Leon is the greatest. He always wants what's best for me, and he loves to see me shine."

"Well, then I'm sure he won't have any problem with you running for our national president."

I smiled, hoping they were right and that Leon wouldn't have a problem with it. All I needed was one more thing for us to fight about.

Isis

10

I climbed up the stairs, a breakfast tray in hand. Plenty of times I wished I was the lady of the house, and today I was enjoying the next best thing—I was playing lady of the house while my sister was gone. Since I couldn't lay up in the house with Rashad, I had the next best thing—Tony, who was visiting for the weekend. He'd managed to sneak away from his wife, feeding her some cock-and-bull story about having a conference to attend. Too bad he had to lie to her, but he'd been lying to me for years. I was elated.

"Hey, baby," I cooed as I put the breakfast tray over Tony's sheet-clad nakedness. "I made you breakfast—your favorite."

Tony surveyed the tray, grinning. "Eggs, bacon, sausage, pancakes, fresh-squeezed orange juice, and coffee. I could get used to this."

"So could I! That was some good lovin' you gave me last night, baby."

Goodness gracious, if my sister had any inkling I had Tony laid up in her bed, screwing him like there was no tomorrow on her expensive silk sheets, she'd kill me. But to be perfectly honest, that just made the whole thing that much sexier.

"You like the way I put it on you last night, huh? Well, there's more where that came from," he teased, slapping my ass under my sheer negligee. I got moist right away. It reminded me of when I lived in New York, and Tony and I would role-play that he was a burglar who had broken into my apartment. He would tie me up and spank me until I told him where my valuables were. I'd always end up confessing that they were inside my panties, and he'd have to take them off to get them.

"Promises, promises. What I got last night was a ten on the Richter scale. I don't think anyone could perform that good two nights in a row."

"Oh, you doubt me?" His face said what his mouth didn't: He was up for the challenge.

"Eat your food and let's find out."

He picked up his fork with a smirk, "You do realize that when I finish this, it's about to be on?"

"So, hurry up and eat. I'm about to start without you." I lay on the bed next to him, hiking up my nightie. I closed my eyes and moved my right hand to my eagerly awaiting pussy. Sliding my fingertips over my wet lips to moisten them, I began to rub my clit gently. It felt so good I let out a moan. I could hear Tony trying his best to wolf down his food. Even though he was eating, I was sure he was watching my every move. He loved it when I masturbated in front of him.

I decided to mess with him. "Oh, damn. I'm so wet, I'm gushing. I just need something to fill me up." I slid a finger inside myself, and the next thing I knew, I heard a loud crash that scared the crap out of me.

I opened my eyes to see the tray of food all over the floor. Tony had the sheets pulled back, totally exposing his nakedness. His erection was pointing at me like a Viking sword. Before I knew it, we were making love for the umpteenth time since he'd gotten there. He was thrusting his penis inside, sending me over the top again and again.

"That's it, Tony. Give it to me," I hollered as he exploded inside of me. "Oooh, baby, make me a momma! I wanna have your child!"

"Huh, have my child?" Tony pulled out of me faster than if I'd just told him I had gonorrhea. "What are you talking about?" He looked down in my face.

"I wanna have your baby." There. I'd said it.

"Where the hell is this coming from?" He rolled off of me.

"It's always been there. I just figured we'd get married first— oops, that's right, you're already married. So I guess I'll have to have my baby out of wedlock." Yes, I said it, and I did have an attitude.

"What if I don't want a baby?" He had the nerve to have an attitude too.

"Oh, so you don't want me to have your baby? Why not?" I sat up. "Hmmph. So, I'm good enough to fuck but not good enough to have your child. Is that right?"

Tony reached down to his dripping penis as if he wanted to pull his sperm back up in it. "This ain't cool, Isis. It's not cool at all. You know I'm married."

"I didn't hear you hollering about being married just now when you was all up in me, raw dog, busting a nut. I thought you said you love me."

"I do, but—"

I cut him off. "But what? You want your cake and eat it too? It's not that easy."

"No, but my wife will take me for everything I've got if you come up pregnant."

"She ain't got to know. I've accepted that I'm the other woman, Tony. You just have to keep treating me like I'm not."

"I ain't trying to have no more kids, Isis. My kids are older—finally. I'm glad to be through with diapers and bottles." He groaned in disgust. "No way will I go back down that road."

"But you love kids. You're always talking about your kids. Besides, if I have a baby, then me and you can be together like we planned. I'm glad I stopped taking those pills."

"Wait a minute. Don't tell me you stopped taking the Pill."

I couldn't lie. I didn't answer, though. I guess the look on my face said it all.

"Aw, shit! I knew I shoulda stopped fucking with this crazy bitch." Tony started talking to himself as if I wasn't even in the room.

I didn't pay his crazy comment any mind. I just looked at him and said, "Time to man up, Tony. Either you love me or you don't. Either way, if I'm pregnant, I'm having your baby."

Tony hit the palm of his hand with his fist. "This is some bull-shit, Isis. Some real underhanded bullshit."

"Like the shit you've done to me over the years isn't some bull? You fucked me up so bad I'm living with my sister and my ex. I lost a good damn job because I lost my mind over you and your lies. So if you want to talk about underhanded, look in the fucking mirror."

I watched him get up and slip the sheet around himself. He ran to the shower, and the next thing I knew, he was dressed and down the stairs.

"Tony, I love you." I followed him to the front door. "We can do this. We can raise this baby."

Just as the words fell out of my mouth, I looked up the walkway and saw an irate-looking Egypt and Rashad stalking toward me. They'd come home early. Tony flew by them without a word, his overnight bag clutched in his hand.

"Isis, what is going on?" Egypt called out. I saw Rashad looking mad, but I didn't care what they said.

I ran upstairs, locked my bedroom door, and put my legs up against the wall to make sure that none of Tony's sperm escaped out of me.

Jerome

11

"You did what?" I almost dropped the phone. I was so surprised at what I'd just heard. "Can you repeat that, please?"

"I told my wife I was gay and that I was leaving her for a black man," Peter, my little George Clooney look-alike, said to me.

"You shouldn't have done that, Peter."

"Why not?" he asked adamantly. "I can't lie about who I am anymore or how I feel. For the first time in my life, I feel alive."

"Yeah, but leaving your wife? She'll take you to the cleaners."

"I don't care. She can have it. I just want to be with you. I think we can have a life together."

Oh, boy, here we go again. You know, if I could bottle these lips and sell them, I'd make a million dollars. No, I'd make ten million dollars, 'cause these dudes be losing their minds when I suck their dick. Whatever happened to never let 'em see you sweat?

"Look, I've been having a good time with you. And I really appreciate the diamond bracelet you bought me last week, but I never said anything about us being exclusive."

"But I'm falling in love with you. I never felt like this about anybody before. Just give me a chance. I know I can make you happy."

Now, this is why I never had people other than Big Poppa come by the crib. Never knew when one of them would get too attached and cross over the line to stalker status.

"Look, Peter, no offense, but the feeling's not mutual. I like you, but I'm nowhere near in love with you. I'm not even sure I know what love is."

"You can learn to love me. For now, I have enough love for both of us."

Damn, this guy just didn't understand the meaning of "it ain't gonna happen."

I tried to reason with him. "You need to take a deep breath. I think you're confusing good sex with love."

"I don't think you're taking me serious, Jerome. I didn't come out of the closet because I was confused. I came out because I'm in love, and I won't take no for an answer."

"Listen, I can't have this conversation now. I'm with some people. Let's talk about this some other time." I closed the phone without even waiting for him to respond. This dude was gonna be a problem; I could feel it.

"What was that all about?" Loraine asked, sipping on her drink. We were at T.G.I. Friday's having a drink after work. It was kind of a ritual every Friday.

"Remember that fine-ass white guy I told you I was seeing? The one who looks like George Clooney?"

She nodded. "Yeah, the one who sent the roses to the job?"

"Mmm-hmm, that's him." I shook my head. "He just told me he's in love with me, and he's divorcing his wife."

"Damn, Jerome, you're a pimp," Loraine said with a smirk. "What do you do to these guys?"

I shrugged my shoulders rather shamelessly. "I don't know. Just spreading around what God gave me, treating others the same way I want to be treated."

"In other words, you suck the hell out of their dicks."

"Among other things."

Once Loraine stopped laughing, she said, "All jokes aside, don't you feel sorry for his wife? The poor woman probably had no clue. Probably got kids too."

"Poor woman my ass. Poor me. She's getting rid of him. If she had a clue, I wouldn't have to deal with his crazy ass."

"Oh, please. You know you love it when they leave their wives for you. I can see your ego getting bigger by the second." She leaned back in her chair and glanced around the restaurant to check out the other patrons. "And speaking of ego boosts, you might wanna check out the bar. I think somebody is looking at you."

"Really?" I tried to play it cool by not turning my head toward the bar. "Male or female?"

"Male," Loraine replied. She wouldn't look me in the face—probably because she would have busted out laughing.

"Hmm, what's he look like?"

"Tall, cute, very chocolate." She tilted her head to get a better view. "To be honest, Jerome, he's fine."

"Now, that's what I'm talking about." I turned my head slightly to sneak a peek, then changed my mind. I needed a bit more information. "Can you see his left hand? He got on a ring?"

"Not sure. Hold on." She reached into her purse and pulled out her glasses. "Yep, he's got on a ring."

"He still looking?" I picked up my drink, finishing it with one final gulp.

"Yep, but he turns his head every time I glance over there. He really is cute, Jerome."

I couldn't help myself anymore. I had to see this tall glass of water she was talking about. I turned my head toward the bar and had to do a double take. He wasn't fine; he was *fiiiiinne*!

"What do you think?"

"I think he's just your type," she said.

"Isn't he, though." I was grinning like a Cheshire cat as I picked up both of our glasses. "You mind?"

She shook her head. "Go for it."

"I will."

I got up and walked with a purpose across the room, weaving in and out of the crowd until I was standing at the bar next to Mr. Good-Looking. He was even finer close up than he was from our table.

"What can I get you?" the bartender asked.

I didn't waste any time. "Can I get a watermelon martini and a goblet of your best cognac? And give my friend here a refill on whatever he's drinking."

He held up his glass, which was nearly full. "No, I'm cool."

"You sure?" I gave him a smile. I could usually charm them pretty quickly with my pearly whites.

He didn't bat an eye. "Yeah, but thanks."

I have to admit, my ego took a hit. "Not a problem. My name's Jerome. Yours?" I offered my hand; he took it. His hand was firm yet soft. Definitely not a blue-collar guy, but he didn't ride a desk either.

"I'm Michael. Michael Richards. Nice to meet you, Jerome."

"Pleasure's all mine," I said as I let my eyes travel down his tight body. Mmm, mmm, mmm, I couldn't wait to get him undressed.

"So, that was you sitting over at that table in the corner, right?"

Now that's what I'm talking about, I thought. This brother didn't waste time and play games. He just got down to business.

"Yeah, that was me. I saw you looking." I decided to make the next move. "I think you look good too. I'm going to a dinner party later tonight. Maybe you'd like to join me. Think I could get your number?"

"Whoa! Whoa, hold on there, fella!" He threw up his hands, palms facing me, with an uncomfortable look on his face. "It's not that type of party. You got me all wrong." Michael shook his head and started laughing. Wasn't a damn thing funny, as far as I was concerned. "You know, I've got nothing against gay men, but that's not my thing. Besides, I was looking at the woman."

I guess we're going to play this the hard way. Another brother in denial. This was going to be fun.

"Oh, excuse me. My bad. No harm meant." I put my hands up, mimicking his earlier gesture so that he would calm down. "So, you're interested in the woman I was with?"

"You could say I've been interested in her all my life." Michael probed, "I take it she's not your girlfriend."

All his life? This guy wasn't just in denial; he was weird.

"No, she's my good friend, though. I look out for her—if you know what I mean."

"I've got an idea." He turned and looked toward our table. "I haven't seen Loraine in almost twenty years."

"You really do know her?"

"Know her? I was in love with her."

I was beyond confused. Raine had told me about some of the guys she dated in the past, but she ain't never told me about anyone this fine, and I was sure she would have remembered. I screwed up my face, and I guess I must have given him a pretty suspicious look, because he protested right away.

"Hey, I'm not crazy. She was my older sister's best friend. I had a crush on her since I was in eighth grade." He kept looking over at her.

"Wow, so you're from Norfolk?"

"Born and bred. Lived two doors down from Loraine."

"Why didn't you come over to the table? I'm sure she'd love to see you."

"Little nervous. I was afraid you were her husband or boyfriend. You know how people are. I didn't want to cause any drama for Loraine."

"That was nice of you." The bartender brought me my drinks. "So, you still like her, don't you?"

He nodded. "What's not to like? She's gorgeous."

"Why don't you come over to the table with me and join us?" Usually I'd get a little jealous when a man I found attractive didn't show me any interest, but if by some stroke of luck this guy could get Loraine away from Leon, I think I'd do cartwheels. "You and Loraine can catch up."

He slid off his bar stool. "Thought you'd never ask."

I led him across the room. "Michael, this is Loraine. Loraine, this is Michael. But then again, you two know each other." I couldn't stop smirking at my friend. She was going to have to explain later how she let this guy get away.

Loraine peered up, looking rather confused. "We know each other?"

Michael eased into the empty chair. "You don't remember me, do you?"

"Probably because I don't know you."

Did I make a mistake bringing this guy over here? I still didn't know what was going on, but it was starting to look like I might not be the only one with a stalker. Things got even creepier when the dude started talking.

"If I don't know you, how come I know you have a small, starlike birthmark right under your left butt cheek? Your favorite ice cream is mint chocolate chip. Your favorite color is red, or at least it used to be." If he didn't know her, he sure knew a lot about her. "Oh, and you love foot massages."

"Jerome, your friend is not funny. Now that you had your fun, the joke's over."

"What do you mean, my friend? I thought he was your friend." I was about to get real indignant with this kook. I placed my hand on his shoulder. "I think it's time you leave."

"Wait a minute! I admit I was having a little fun, but you do know me, Loraine Farrow. I'm Michael. Michael Richards, Lisa Richards's little brother . . . your high school best friend. Don't you remember you gave me my first kiss when we were playing spin the bottle?"

Loraine's hand flew to her mouth. "Oh my God! Mike." She stared at him like she was still trying to process everything. "Mike Richards?"

"That's me." He had this weird proud smile on his face. I swear his chest puffed up a little as she checked him out. "But they call me Michael now."

"I barely even recognize you. You're so, so . . . ."

"Thin," he said with a laugh. "I lost a little weight. I had gastric bypass surgery about five years ago. Plus I work out."

"I'll say," I chimed in.

"My God, how much did you lose?" Loraine asked.

"Three hundred and fifty, give or take."

Loraine stated the obvious: "You look good, Michael."

"Good enough for a date?" He actually sounded nervous. I had never seen a brother who looked this good acting like he was afraid he'd be turned down. This whole scene was just getting weirder by the minute.

"You know I been waiting to ask you out for twenty years."

"Yeah, right. You are so crazy," Loraine told him. "This isn't high school. Besides, I saw that ring on your finger." She winked at me.

"What, this?" He took off a gold band with a colorful stone. "It's not a wedding ring. It's my college ring. I used to wear it as a pinky ring, but since I lost all the weight, my ring finger's the only one it will fit on."

Game, set, and match. I didn't know about Loraine, but I was convinced. The only question I had was, did he have a gay friend or one hiding in the closet who needed a push out?

"Hey, Loraine," Michael said with a charming smile, "seriously, I'd love to take you out to dinner."

Egypt
12

When we pulled up the driveway and I saw the black Cadillac Escalade with New York plates, I knew exactly who was in my house. To come home after hearing Tammy's bad news and see his car just pushed my anger to a new level. Why the fuck my sister would have that sorry-ass excuse for man in my house was beyond me. His lying ass was the root of all her problems, not to mention the fact that he'd beat Rashad's ass back in the day. He was nothing but bad news, but she refused to give him up and move on with her life. Isis had gone too damn far, and we were about to have words.

From the way Rashad was reaching toward his glove compartment, I was pretty sure words were the last thing on his mind.

"Baby, what are you doing?" I asked, lifting my knee so that the glove compartment wouldn't open for him.

"I'm getting my shit so I can get that nigga out my house. Now move your leg."

"No!" I shouted defiantly. I raised my knee to block him even further. "You told me that you should never handle a gun when you're emotional or angry. Baby, right now you're both." I placed my hand over his, my eyes pleading with him to calm down. "I know my sister is wrong, and I'll deal with her—I promise—but let's not do something stupid just because we're mad at Tammy and Tim. Please. I'm trying to avoid visiting you in jail."

"I want that motherfucker out my house, Egypt."

"I know you do, baby. His ass is leaving as soon as we get in the house. And my sister's ass is going to be right behind him. Come on."

We both stepped out of the car and headed up the walkway. They must have heard us pulling up, because Tony headed out the door toward his truck with a purpose. That son of a bitch passed us and didn't even speak, which was probably for the best, since Rashad couldn't stand his ass. It wouldn't have taken much to get him to head back to the car and get his gun.

My sister, on the other hand, acknowledged our presence, but only by slamming the front door when she saw us coming.

The first thing I did when I entered the house was head for the stairs. Rashad was right behind me, talking about dragging Isis out of the house by her hair. With him being so angry, I took his threat seriously. I had to stop him halfway up the stairs. I was pissed at Isis, but I didn't want things to turn violent. "Baby, go back out to the car and bring our bags in. Let me handle this, please." He didn't say a word, but his body language spoke volumes. He was disgusted and looked like he wanted to hurt somebody. "Please, baby," I repeated. He wanted to take his anger about what happened in New York out on someone, and my sister was the most logical choice. Only, even though she was an ass for having that man in our house, she didn't deserve what was rightfully meant for Tammy and Tim. I pleaded one last time, "Please, Rashad. For me."

He turned around and walked down the stairs. "I want her out of my house by Friday. You hear me?"

"Yes, baby. I hear you," I replied, then headed up the stairs, stopping in front of Isis's door.

They say if you love someone, let them go. Well, that was what I was about to do with my sister: Let her ass go. I reached for the doorknob, surprised to find it was locked. How could she lock doors in my house? She was really pissing me off. "Isis, open this door."

I could hear movement, but she didn't reply. I slammed my fist on the door three times. "Open this door! This is my goddamn house!"

I waited for a few seconds, then said, "You think I don't have a key to this door?" I stomped down the hall to my bedroom to retrieve the key. When I entered my room, all I could do was gasp, hand over my chest, as I took in the disaster area I called my bedroom. "Oh my God. No, she didn't have him in my room!"

Orange stains, probably from juice, were splattered on our carpet, along with what looked like pancakes and—oh no, syrup. The lamps were turned over like these two fools had been having one wild whoopee-making session. Strawberries and rose petals were smeared all over my comforter. Crumbs and a break-fast tray were sitting on one side of our bed. Let's not forget the bottle of whipped cream that sat on the nightstand. Over in the corner, balled up like it had just been thrown to the side, was my husband's favorite robe. What had she been thinking? Had she been thinking at all? Dear Lord, could it get any worse?

That's when I noticed the bed was made with my brand-new three-hundred-dollar silk sheets. I hadn't even taken them out of the package yet, and this broad had the nerve to use them. When I pulled back the top sheet, I saw what looked like dried up semen in three places. *Oh, hell no, this heffa didn't have sex on my new sheets without a condom!* Just the idea that she came into our room made me see red. I was furious!

"Isis!" I screamed, running back to her bedroom door.

I didn't even care about the key anymore. If she didn't open that door, I was going to break it down. Like most siblings close in age, Isis and I had had our share of physical fights over the years. I happened to be the winner of most of them. "Open this fucking door! I'm not playin' with you no more, Isis! I want you the fuck out my house!" I started to pound on the door again and heard her fumbling with the lock. When she finally did get the door opened, she looked like a hot mess, hair all over the place. And if it wasn't bad enough that she had that man wear-ing my husband's robe, she had the nerve to be wearing mine.

"Take my goddamn robe off!" If my expression didn't tell her how serious I was, my two clenched fists must have, because within seconds, she was standing there half naked, handing me my robe.

"I can explain." I could hear the sincerity in her voice, but then again, she always sounded sincere when her back was up against a wall. It wasn't going to work this time, though. I was done.

"Explain what? What the fuck you going to explain? How you disrespected me? How you took my kindness for weakness? What the hell was you thinking about, bringing that mother-fucker in my house, desecrating my bed?" I was so mad that I was nauseated.

"I'm sorry," Isis muttered, looking down. "Things got a little out of hand, but I was gonna clean up before you got back. You told me you were coming home Sunday."

"Oh, so you guys were gonna play house all weekend at our expense? I can't believe you did this shit. The least you could do was have a decent man in my house. Isn't he still married?"

"He don't love her."

"And he loves you?" I almost laughed.

She nodded pathetically. "Mmm-hmm, he sure does."

"Then why doesn't he leave his wife for you?" She didn't have shit to say about that. "We trusted you, Isis."

"I said I was sorry. What else do you want me to say?" She turned away from me. I spun her back around so that she was facing me.

"Sorry ain't good enough this time. I can't keep babysitting you. I want you out of my house by Friday."

"Huh?" She looked at me like I was betraying her by finally putting my foot down. I'd let her get away with too much for too long. Clearly she wasn't ready to act like a responsible adult. "You can't do this. Where am I gonna go?"

"Call Tony. If he's so in love with you, I'm sure he'll get you a spot, 'cause he just fucked you out of a place to stay." I didn't re-alize it, but I was so upset I had tears in my eyes. I hated what I was doing to my sister, but it was for her own good and mine. I knew she didn't have any place to go, unless by some miracle that idiot Tony came through for her, which I seriously doubted. From her reply, I don't think she had much faith in him either.

"Give me another chance, Egypt," Isis pleaded. "I won't mess up again. I swear. The only place I got to go is Mommy and Daddy's."

"You should have thought of that before you disrespected my

house. I want you out by Friday. And I'm not going to change my mind."

With that, I turned and left, almost blinded by my own tears. In a rage, I went to my room and changed the sheets. I picked up the room and blotted the carpet, hoping Rashad didn't see the mess. He was already acting weird. In fact, he had been so quiet since we left Tammy and Tim's house that he was scaring me. Lord, could things get any worse?

Loraine

13

I was sitting in front of Michael Richards, quite possibly one of the most handsome men I'd ever met. Only this wasn't the first time we'd met, and he sure didn't look like the same kid I'd known since he was four years old and his family moved down the street from us.

I knew Michael had had a crush on me when we were younger, but he was my best friend's little brother. When I was a senior, he was only a freshman, so he was just a silly little kid to me. Oh, I was nice to him, and I got on the older boys when they teased him or called him Fat Mike, but I never once thought of him in a romantic way. Besides, I had my pick of guys in high school, and Mike wasn't the kind of guy who would have gotten a second look from me, even if he was my age. Not to sound conceited, but back then, who didn't have a crush on me? I was a big girl, but I had a nice shape, and guys used to fall all over me, because I had big titties and a fat ass.

Now I was almost a hundred pounds heavier, and plenty of men just considered me fat. The tables had surely turned. Michael had lost all that weight, and he was stunning. I felt like I needed to catch my breath just looking at him. The surprising thing was that even though he was certifiably gorgeous, he still seemed to be infatuated with me. I was beyond flattered. I mean, I knew I was still attractive, but we 250-plus-pound women don't get men who look like Michael asking us out every day. Unfortunately, I was faithfully married, and dating was prohibited.

"So, Loraine." Michael's voice cut into my thoughts. "You

wanna go out to dinner with me sometime? I know this great Italian place down in Chester."

How in the world was I supposed to keep my composure when this gorgeous man was inviting me to dinner? I mean, I loved my husband, but there was that small part of me that was dying to say yes.

I turned to Jerome for a helping hand with my dilemma but quickly realized that was useless. He was sitting on the edge of his seat, leaning forward with both arms on the table like he was watching the season finale to one of his favorite sitcoms. It crossed my mind that somehow he had something to do with Michael asking me out on a date. My good friend had been trying to get me to step out on Leon for quite some time now.

"So, Raine, what you gonna do? Can't you see the man is waiting for an answer?" Jerome chimed in.

"Mind your own business, Jerome," I snapped. I was still trying to figure this all out. Did this man really want to go out with me? And was it wrong for me to even be fantasizing about saying yes?

Michael was shifting around in his seat, obviously still waiting for an answer. I knew I couldn't say yes, but I couldn't imagine saying no to such a fine man, so I avoided both by changing the subject. "So, how's your sister?"

"She's good. Divorced with three hardheaded boys. She's talking about going back to school to get her master's."

"Good for her. Tell her I said hello when you talk to her."

He kept staring at me. I tried to avoid looking too deeply into his jet-black bedroom eyes, and that's when I noticed his full lips. I loved full lips. They made me think naughty thoughts.

I bet he could make me come with those lips. I bet he could make me come over and over again. . . .

"So, what do you do for a living?" I asked to get my mind out of the dangerous place it was going.

He smirked. Was it that obvious I was trying to avoid answering his question? "I used to be a CPA; I guess technically I still am, but I gave all that up when I lost the weight. I'm a nutritionist, physical trainer, and sometimes a motivational speaker now."

"That's great. Let me know if you need any PR work done. Ever thought about doing a DVD or an infomercial?" I handed him a card.

He smiled warmly. "That'd be great . . . but I don't usually mix business with pleasure, so maybe you should answer my question before we take this any further."

"Umm, what question?" Yes, it was a lame attempt at avoiding the subject again, but I was running out of ideas. And apparently, Michael was not giving up without an answer.

"I asked you if you'd like to go out to dinner with me."

I was usually a decisive woman, but in this case, I truly didn't know what to say. He'd already asked me out twice—or was it three times? I really wasn't sure. The point is I still hadn't mentioned I was married. What the hell was wrong with me? This was so unlike me. Was I actually contemplating a date with this man? Or was it a roll in the hay I was looking for? Jesus, was either of those a road I really wanted to go down?

"Can I ask you a question?"

"Sure. Ask me anything, as long as you answer my question after I answer yours."

"Why me? Why ask me out? Are you just into fat girls or something?"

"Oh, shit!" Jerome damn near spit out half his drink. I'd almost forgotten he was there.

Michael sat up straight in his chair. Unlike Jerome, he wasn't laughing. He was as serious as a heart attack. "I wouldn't care if you weighed eighty-six pounds, Loraine. It's not your size I'm after; it's the woman inside you."

Good answer. Jerome looked like he wanted to applaud.

"I wanna date the woman who made it her business to call me just plain Mike, not Fat Mike, when I was in high school. The girl who didn't run into the bathroom to wash her lips after she had to kiss me during a game of spin the bottle. I could go on, but I think you get what I'm trying to say. So, no, I'm not into fat women. Not unless the fat woman is you."

This time, Jerome did applaud. "Damn, that was some deep shit. You mind if I use that? Switching the gender, of course."

I'm sure my face was bright red from all the blood rushing to it. I took a sip of my drink, hoping it would cool me down, but it didn't. It had the opposite effect. If we weren't in T.G.I. Friday's, I think I would have made love to him right then and there. No one had said anything that nice to me in my entire life.

"Jerome, can you excuse us for a second?"

"You want me to leave?" Jerome was staring at me like I'd just turned off his TV right in the middle of a really good show.

"Yes, I'd like to speak with Michael alone, if you don't mind."

"Fine. I'm going, but you damn right I mind. As much stuff as I let you listen to." He got out of his seat in a huff, pouting as he walked away.

"Sorry about that. Jerome doesn't understand the meaning of *personal* or *private*."

"I understand. So, does this mean we're on for a date?"

I wanted to reach out and hold his hand. Oh, how I wished I didn't have to turn him down. "Michael, I want to thank you for asking, but I can't go on a date with you."

"Why not?"

I couldn't look him in the eyes. "Because I'm married."

He looked down at my hands. "I don't see a ring on your finger."

"That's because I've gained so much weight in the last few years, my hands have swollen." I saw his lips turn down.

"Oh, I'm sorry. I didn't know. I didn't mean to be disrespectful." He stood up from his chair, looking a little embarrassed. "Loraine, it was good seeing you again. Tell your husband he's a very lucky man."

The mention of Leon sent a little stab of pain through my heart. The way things had been going between us lately, I doubted he'd agree that he was lucky to be with me.

He took a step toward the bar, then turned back. "If you weren't married, would you have said yes?"

He had no idea just how close I'd come to saying yes even though I was married. But it wouldn't do me any good to admit that to him, so instead I nodded and said, "Yes, if I was single, I'd go out with you." In another place and another time, Michael Richards most definitely would have been mine.

He smiled boyishly, like he'd won even though he came in second. I watched him walk toward the entrance, and then, through the window, I saw him get into his car. I didn't take my eyes off him until he drove away. I suppose it was for the best, but we never even exchanged numbers or e-mail addresses or anything. I wondered if it would be another twenty-something years before I'd see him again.

Egypt

14

I felt like my entire life was falling apart when Jerome came to my desk solemnly and told me Loraine wanted to see me in her office. I figured it was a foregone conclusion that I was about to be fired, and there really wasn't anything I could do about it, because stupidly, I'd brought the whole damn thing on myself. Sure, Loraine and I were friends, but she was a businesswoman first, and there was no way she was going to let me get away with skipping work the past week without so much as a phone call. Not to mention the fact that I missed three key meetings with clients.

Yep, I was getting fired.

I followed Jerome to his desk, which was situated in front of Loraine's office. I'd always found their little seating arrangement strange, because although Loraine was the face of the company, Jerome helped her build it from day one. On paper he was the company's vice president, but most people, including the majority of the company's employees, thought he was just a glorified assistant. It appeared that was just the way the two of them wanted it.

"Any idea why she wants to see me?" I asked Jerome.

"I think you have an idea, sis." There was a tad bit of attitude in his voice that I probably deserved. Especially since he'd called my house, cell phone, and texted me to see if I was all right, and I never responded.

"Yeah, I guess I do."

"Just be straight up with her, and you'll be okay. Don't play games like you did with me."

I nodded and he opened the door so I could walk in. Loraine was sitting behind her large cherrywood desk glancing at some files. I sat down in one of the chairs in front of her desk as Jerome stepped out of the office, shutting the door behind him. It took her a full two minutes before she looked up over her reading glasses to acknowledge that I was even there. Those were two very long and uncomfortable minutes. I sat there nervously and thought about how I was going to break the news to Rashad that I'd lost my job. My life was stressful enough already without having to add searching for a job in this economy to my list of worries.

Finally, our eyes met. Loraine and I saw each other socially at our monthly book club meetings, and she was perfectly nice then, but now she looked nothing short of menacing. I'd never been in trouble at work before, but I'd heard from other employees that Loraine was no joke when she was mad at you. I was experiencing firsthand how true that was.

I decided to fall on my sword and weaken the blow before she had a chance to speak. At least that way I'd be able to get in a word edgewise. "Loraine, I know I cost the firm a lot of money. I know I should have called and I didn't. But I was having some personal issues that I just couldn't deal with. So if you're going to fire me, I understand."

Loraine stood up from her desk, and the way her large frame was looming over me, I suddenly felt tiny and fragile. I was actually scared for a minute when she threw down the file she'd been holding. "Fire you! Girl, I should kill your ass."

Kill me? Well, damn, I know I'd messed up, but did she have to take it that far? I was about to protest, until she explained herself and I realized I had read her all wrong.

"You had us worried to death. I'm surprised poor Jerome is even speaking to you. Don't you ever do that shit again."

I was actually left speechless for a minute while I tried to process this whole scene. I'd been imagining myself jobless and depressed, and now it seemed that wasn't Loraine's intention at all.

"You mean I'm not fired?"

"Not if I get an explanation about what the hell is going on. Egypt, you're my friend, and my friends are like family. I don't socialize with many people I work with, other than Jerome. But somehow, you and I clicked. We've broken bread in each other's homes. To me, that's special."

Wow, I didn't know she felt that way. I guess we were closer than I thought. Now I felt bad that I hadn't at least called the office while I was out.

"I'm sorry, Loraine."

She waved her hand as if to say there was no apology necessary. "So, what's going on, girl? Your marriage falling apart?"

"If it hasn't already, it will be."

"He cheating." She spoke as if it was already a certainty, not a question. Why was that the first thing everyone asked when a relationship was having problems? Not every man cheats. Sometimes it's the woman who causes the problem—by not being able to have a baby. Yes, I was back at work, but I still hadn't stopped beating myself up over the fact that I couldn't give Rashad a child.

"No, he'd never cheat." At least I hoped he wouldn't. I didn't even wanna imagine anything like that, but the way my life was going lately, I suppose anything was possible. Lord, I hoped things never got that bad between us. If I caught Rashad cheating, I think I would die.

"Are *you* cheating?" She leaned back against her desk and assured me, "If you are, I'm not judging—just looking for answers."

"Hell no," I answered adamantly. "I love my husband. I don't need anyone but him."

"Then what? You didn't just skip work the past week for nothing. Where the heck were you? What were you doing?"

"It's a long story, Loraine. You really don't want to hear it." She considered me a friend, but I wasn't quite ready to go there with her yet. I was barely able to admit to myself that my body was unable to bear children; it wasn't something I wanted to discuss with my boss.

"Yes, I do want to hear it." She glanced at the clock on her office wall. "And it's ten-fifteen. You don't get off until five. I think we have enough time."

"Loraine, I don't know what I'm going to do. My life is falling apart at the seams." I hoped this vague answer would be enough to stop her from asking more questions. Unfortunately, as soon as I admitted it out loud to her, the pain that I'd been trying to control burst forth, and I was in tears.

In an instant, Loraine was by my side, patting me on the back to soothe me. But I couldn't stop the tears.

She waited until my sobs had subsided a bit, and then asked, "What's wrong? Is there anything I can do?" She handed me a tissue.

"I don't even know where to start. My sister's lost her mind, and I think my husband hates me." It felt good to finally get some of this off my chest. I used to be able to vent to Tammy whenever I was feeling down, but for obvious reasons, I didn't feel like she'd be much help to me these days. And since Rashad was hurting just as much as I was, I had been trying my best not to burden him.

"Rashad? The man who sang to you in front of the entire office at our Christmas party last year? No, that man loves you."

"That was before he found out I couldn't have his child." I shocked myself by how easily I'd said those words. Boss or not, I realized how much I needed a friend right now, and Loraine was offering.

Suddenly, an idea came to me. "Loraine, you know a lot of people. Do you know anyone who would be willing to have a baby for us?"

"So, that's what this is all about?" Loraine shook her head. "You guys having trouble getting pregnant? I know a great fertility doctor. Dr. Anderson is the best in Virginia."

"I know. We've already seen him."

"Did he help?"

"He tried, but it didn't work. That's why I'm looking for a surrogate."

She thought about it for a second, then said, "No, I don't know anyone. Maybe that's not a good idea to have a complete stranger anyway. You know that could open you up to black-mail."

"You think someone would do that to us?"

"Heck, yeah. Either the birth mother turns out to be shady, or she changes her mind and doesn't want to give up the child. You hear it on the news all the time where the court rules for the surrogate to keep the baby. From what I understand, most states allow the birth mother to change her mind for a whole year after the baby's born."

"I actually knew all of that. Rashad and I researched pretty well before we decided to go ahead with surrogacy. That's why we asked my best friend, Tammy. You remember her from our book club meeting, right?"

"Yeah, the one from New York."

"Uh-huh. She and her husband already have a boy and a girl, so we weren't worried about them wanting to keep our child. We were even willing to pay them any amount of money."

"I take it she said no?"

I nodded sadly and wiped away a tear that was trickling down my cheek. "They said Tammy was too old to carry another child, plus they were concerned that her weight would be an issue."

"Well, I can't say I don't understand how they feel," Loraine admitted. "I never wanted to have children when I was younger, but I used to think that maybe I'd get pregnant once my career was established. Now I know for a fact I don't want any babies. I can't imagine how hard a pregnancy would be on my body."

"But women are having babies in their forties all the time these days."

"True, doctors can make it happen, but it doesn't mean it's the right thing for everyone."

All of a sudden, Loraine's advice wasn't helping very much. Her sympathy for my situation seemed to have turned into sympathy for Tammy. I was starting to feel stupid sitting there bawling in front of Loraine, especially since her motto was "Big girls don't cry; they get the job done." Only, not all of us were as strong as her and could put up with everything.

"Well, I'm only thirty-seven, and I want to have a baby now."

I guess my snippy tone made her realize she wasn't being very supportive, because she apologized. "I'm sorry. I know this must be terribly hard on you and Rashad."

"We've got everything in life that we want—except for a baby."

My tears had started flowing freely again. She sat quietly and waited while I got myself under control.

"Why don't you ask your sister?"

I shook my head. "Not an option."

"Why not? I thought you two were close. She lives in your house."

I had also learned recently that she was jealous of me and my husband, but I couldn't tell that to Loraine. "It's complicated."

"If she's your sister and she really loves you like she says she does, she should be willing to do it. You hear about that all the time on the news, grandmothers giving birth to their own grandchildren and things like that."

"I don't know. . . ."

Loraine approached the situation logically, like the businesswoman I knew her to be. "I don't see why not. She's living up in your house for free. This could be her way of repaying you. I'm not one to talk about family, but it would be her way of getting a job, since she doesn't seem to be trying to find one."

I felt a slight twinge of guilt for letting her talk about my family that way, especially since I hardly even let Rashad say anything about Isis, yet I couldn't help but agree with her assessment of the situation. It dawned on me that maybe that was my problem: I was being so emotional about the whole darn thing. If I looked at it like Loraine was, like a problem to be solved, and took my feelings out of the equation, it kinda did make sense to ask my sister. After all, Isis was laying up on us for free, and after the stunt she had pulled with Tony, she owed me—especially since I hadn't yet forced her to move out.

I wondered if she would be willing to have our baby. Loraine was the second person who had suggested her. I hadn't consid-

ered it when Tammy said it, because I was so upset, but now . . .
I didn't know.

Maybe it would work.

"Loraine, do you think I can go home a little early today?" I
asked, my mood more hopeful than I'd been in a long time. "I
need to talk to my sister about a few things."

Isis

15

"Shit!" I was so damn angry. Why is it always when you don't want to get pregnant that it happens so damn easy?

I looked down in the toilet and saw evidence that my period had just started, ending any hope that I might be carrying Tony's baby. Ever since he came down from New York last weekend, things just seemed to be going from bad to worse. It was starting to look like I went through all that aggravation of pissing off my sister and getting kicked out of her house for absolutely nothing.

I grabbed a tampon. It wasn't like I couldn't get pregnant. Two years ago, Tony got me pregnant, but I wasn't trying to have a baby by a married man back then. I was still trying to get over the fact that he had a wife, so I did what I had to do and took the abortion route. Hindsight being twenty-twenty, now I wished I'd had the baby; then I'd have Tony's ass right where I wanted him—with me.

I heard a rap on the bathroom door. "Isis, you in there? I need to talk to you."

It was Egypt. My heart started thundering in my chest, because I knew things were about to get even worse. Today was supposed to be my moving day. Actually, it was supposed to be last Friday, but Mr. and Mrs. Sunshine seemed to be going through their own patch of stormy days since they'd returned from New York, so they hadn't pushed the issue. I didn't know what was up, but neither one of them went to work at all last week. Rashad, who wasn't much of a drinker, was putting away shots of Jack Daniel's like an Irish sailor. Hell, he was getting so drunk I almost jumped his bones a couple of times, figuring he'd never even remember it in the morning. Of course that didn't happen, though, because my sister was in the house twenty-four/seven.

I knew she was depressed, because all she did was clean and cry. The more she cleaned, the more depressed she was. After the first day, the house was spic-and-span, but she just started cleaning all over again. Whatever it was between those two, there was definitely trouble in paradise.

Still, I was in no better shape today than I was a week ago, when Egypt gave me the boot. I'd been trying to get her to sit down and talk to me all week. I was hoping to talk her out of giving me the boot, but I wasn't even sure she realized I was in the house until this morning, when she passed me on her way to work and told me she wanted me out by the time she got home.

Now here she was, home hours before I was expecting her. Egypt was the only thing standing between me being homeless or going back to live with Momma and Daddy, and this was my last chance to get her to change her mind. I opened the door and hung my head low, trying to look pitiful.

"I'm still packing." I just hoped Egypt would have mercy on me.

"Come down to your room. We need to talk." She wasn't being mean, but she wasn't being nice either, so I couldn't read her.

When we got to my room, I sat in the chair across from my suitcase, which was lying on the bed. I was praying she wouldn't look in it, because I hadn't packed a thing. "What's up?" I asked.

She had the weirdest look on her face. She didn't look angry, like I would have expected her to. In fact, she looked like she was about to cry. Oh my God, was she going to tell me I could stay before I even started begging?

"Isis, do you love me?"

Where the hell was this coming from? Was she feeling guilty about kicking me out? 'Cause if she was, I might as well play along.

"What kind of question is that? Of course I love you. You're my sister. I may not act like it all the time, but you, Momma,

Daddy, and Rashad are all I got." I knew I was laying it on a little thick, but her smile told me I was headed in the right direction. I think she wanted to forgive me. Suddenly, I felt a glimmer of hope.

"Look, I'm sorry about what happened last weekend. I showed bad judgment, and I disrespected you and your house. That was unacceptable, and I'm sorry." Talk about kissing ass.

"I need to know something, Isis. And please don't lie to me."

"Okay . . ." I had no idea where she was going with any of this. All I knew was that I was feeling more and more confident that I wasn't going to be packing my bags after all.

"Are you still mad at me for marrying Rashad?"

Oh yeah, she was feeling guilty all right. A little more ass-kissing and I'd be home free. "Little sister, I got over Rashad a long time ago. I consider him my brother, not my ex-boyfriend, so don't you worry about that." I did my best to plaster an innocent look on my face. "I hope I haven't given you any reason to think otherwise."

Egypt smiled at me, but she still looked sad. "I can't tell you how glad I am to hear that, because I need to ask you a favor. A big favor."

This whole thing was getting weirder by the second. Somehow, the tables had turned, and she sounded like she was the one in trouble, not me. But, whatever. As long as it meant she wasn't kicking me out, I would agree to whatever favor she needed. I mean, how bad could it be?

"Anything. Just name it."

She took a deep breath and sighed, like whatever she was about to say wasn't going to be easy for her. Once I heard what she had to say, I understood why. "All right, this is the deal: Me and Rashad have been trying to have a baby since I had the miscarriage, and we haven't been able to conceive."

"Wow, I'm sorry to hear that." I remembered how heartbroken she'd been when she miscarried. Rashad too. He'd wanted a baby when we were together, but back then, he wasn't getting the milk without buying this cow. It's amazing how life can throw you a curveball, though, because if I could do it all over again, I would have been the one sleeping in that master bed-

room, and me and Rashad would have a few little rugrats running around by now.

"Well, I have a proposal for you," Egypt continued.

I sat quietly. I had no idea where she was going with this, but
I was intrigued. Maybe they needed me to vouch for them with
an adoption agency or something.

"We want you to be our surrogate."

I almost fell off my bed. "You want me to be what?"

"A surrogate."

"A surrogate? You want me to have a baby for you?" I had to
be sure we both shared the same definition of that word.

"Yes, Isis, we want you to have a baby for us."

That's when it hit me like a ton of bricks, and I just blurted
out, "Oh, my goodness. You're barren? You can't have a baby?"

I regretted it as soon as I said it, because her eyes started tearing up, and her lip was trembling like she was about to cry. She
was a backstabbing dirty bitch, but I still loved my baby sister.

"You want me to have a baby for you and Rashad?" I asked,
trying to sound a little more sensitive this time. I really wasn't
trying to hurt my sister's feelings, and even more importantly, I
was trying to keep a roof over my head.

"Please, Isis. You don't know how much this would mean to
Rashad and me," she said in a shaky voice.

"So, if I say yes, who's going to be the biological father to this
baby? Am I supposed to go out and find some dude off the
street?"

"No, of course not. Rashad's going to be the father."

"Really?" Oh, this was getting freakier by the second. My
head was so full of questions it felt like it was going to explode,
but it didn't take me long to start scheming.

Was she actually going to let Rashad and me make a baby the
old-fashioned way? After all the months of trying to get him
back in my arms, it looked like now Egypt was going to practically hand him over on a silver platter. Well, damn. If she wanted
to, I sure was willing. I'd give them a baby, too, but I was going
to make sure it took a lot longer than they expected before I conceived. Shit, the second Egypt walked out the door, I was going
to start taking my birth control pills. Just the thought of being

able to get my swerve on with Rashad whenever I wanted—with her permission—was making my day.

But then, as if she were reading my mind, Egypt said, "We'll have to go to my doctor and get everything set up. It takes a lot of planning to do artificial insemination. You do understand you'd have to give up the baby and all rights to it, don't you? Rashad's lawyers would draw up the papers."

I'd be lying if I didn't admit I was disappointed that I wouldn't be able to knock boots with Rashad, but then again, I wasn't that naïve. I knew it was only wishful thinking. I didn't actually think she'd be that stupid.

I could, however, see the desperation in her eyes. She thought this baby was the answer to all her prayers, when in all actuality, it was quite possibly the answer to all mine. If I had Rashad's baby, he'd be indebted to me for the rest of his life. He'd probably even leave Egypt for me if I offered to have another baby for him.

I know she's my sister, but all's fair in love and war. Rashad was my man first. I might have made a mistake by choosing Tony over him, but maybe fate was about to turn in my favor after all. Maybe I was being given a second chance.

"So, what do you think?" Egypt had fingers on both hands crossed. "Will you be our surrogate?"

"If it's a girl, will you name her after me?" I smiled, but she didn't. I don't think she understood what I was saying. "Just kidding. I'll do it. I can see how much you want this baby."

"You'll do it?" Egypt sounded surprised and thrilled, like someone who'd just hit the lottery and still couldn't believe it. She grabbed me, hugging and kissing me, getting me all wet with her tears. She was crying, and so was I. Don't ask me why.

"Girl, you my sister." I hugged her back warmly. "I got your back." *As long as you don't turn it on me.*

She released me, wiping tears from her eyes. "Oh my God, Isis, I love you so much. I can't thank you enough. You're not going to have to do anything. I can't wait to tell Rashad."

She looked like she could float on air at any moment, but I brought her back down to earth real quick. Yeah, I needed a place to live, but I was not about to go through nine months of pregnancy and not get compensated. "So, don't we have to talk money?"

"Money?"

"Yeah, don't surrogates usually get paid for their services? You know, so they can't make a claim on the baby?" Time to get paid.

Loraine

16

It was Sunday, and I'd slept in late, something I tried to do on the weekends, since I generally got up at six in the morning during the week. I was lying in bed, curling my toes, feeling lazy. I gazed over at the clock on the nightstand to see if I still had time to get my butt out of bed and off to church for the eleven o'clock service. The red 11:42 staring back at me said, *Nope, not a chance.* Only way I was going to make church was if Reverend Simmons just happened to get a little long-winded.

I'd planned on getting up and going to church when I first heard Leon getting ready to leave around eight, but as soon as he heard me stirring, he started kissing on my ears and neck. As usual, he got my engine going but just couldn't get the car started. That was all right, though, because when he left to go golfing, I finished what he'd started with a fantasy of that sexy Michael Richards. I'd satisfied myself so good that I put myself back to sleep until a few moments ago. I don't know why God made orgasms, but I'm sure glad he did. I stretched, arching my back as I purred like a satisfied Siamese cat. My body hadn't felt this good in a long time.

Since I wasn't going to church, I figured I'd pass the time reading a book. I picked up *The Cartel 2,* by Ashley and JaQuavis, off my nightstand. People other than Jerome and Leon didn't know it, but I loved me some street lit. I could read about pimps and hoes and gangsters all day long, and Ashley and JaQuavis were two of the best at writing that gangster shit. Their stories reminded me of when I was a child in the seventies, living in Norfolk. I used to sneak off and read Donald Goines and Iceberg Slim books behind my parents' backs.

As I moved over to Leon's side of the bed to make myself more comfortable, my toes got entangled in something tucked under the sheets. I laughed, figuring they were Leon's boxers. Like everything he did in the bedroom lately, he must have been trying to get them off quick. I reached down, pulling them up, and did a double take when I saw a pair of cheap red cotton panties instead of my husband's usual plaid boxer shorts.

"What the . . . ?"

The thing that bothered me was that they were my size, but they sure as hell weren't mine. They looked like they were purchased at Kmart. I did my undergarment shopping in a much pricier place than where these came from, and I wore only thongs. I looked closer at the underwear, then dropped them when my mind comprehended what I had in my hands. Holding some woman's used panties was nothing compared to the fact that I'd slept with them rubbing up against me. Just the thought made my skin crawl. That was just so disgusting; I didn't even want to think about it. What kind of woman leaves her panties behind anyway? She had to know they were missing with an ass that size.

I got out of bed and headed to the shower, wringing my hands. I felt a real need to get clean. When I finally got past the whole underwear thing, the most troubling thought was that this could only mean Leon had some woman in my bed. Was that fool crazy? Had he lost his mind? Didn't he know that if I found out, I would kill him? I was so upset I couldn't even cry.

I needed to talk to someone, to sort out my feelings and weigh my options. I stepped out of the shower and headed for the phone.

I called Jerome. The truth was, I hated to tell him something like this, since he already didn't like Leon, but I had to tell someone who wouldn't tell my business. Jerome was like my personal safe; he kept all my secrets.

He answered on the second ring. "Raine, this isn't a good time."

"I'm sorry, but I need to talk to you," I whispered into the phone, as if Leon were standing right next to me or might walk into the room at any second. I think it was my own thoughts and fears I was afraid of—as if putting these thoughts into words would destroy me and our marriage.

"Where are you? And why are you whispering?" he asked.

My voice went back up to its normal tone. "Oh, sorry. I'm home by myself."

"Well, I'm not. I've got company," Jerome hissed back, making it clear he wanted me to get off the phone. "Big Poppa's here, and we're naked, if you get my meaning. You know he don't like to be disturbed when we're getting busy. Call me back in an hour."

I know how he cherished every moment with Big Poppa, but he should have known I was in a crisis and I needed him.

"But, Jerome—"

He cut me off. "Are you in any physical danger?"

"No."

"Then it can wait. I'll call you back. Love you. Gotta go." With that, he hung up. I'm telling you, gay men can be more flighty than women when they're getting some dick.

I sat there, dumbfounded. Who else could I confide in? The truth was, there was no one else. Over the years, I had given up quite a bit for the sake of my marriage. I had lost touch with so many friends, because Leon claimed he didn't like them for one reason or another. In most cases, they didn't like him either, and they weren't shy about telling me why. Most of them said they thought I deserved better, but I always ended up siding with my husband. Apparently, that decision was a bad one, because now that I had found evidence of him cheating, I had no one to talk to.

You know what? Fuck confiding. It was time for confrontation. I was not letting Leon get away with this. It was time for me to be the same woman who everyone in the business world knew me as. I never let anybody in my office get away with shit. I was all up in their face, demanding answers for whatever they'd done wrong. I was a powerful woman. So why should I let Leon get over just because he was my husband?

I walked over to my closet, grabbed my Sunday best, and got dressed. Twenty minutes later, I climbed in my car and drove straight over to Chesterfield Country Club.

"Could you tell me what hole Leon Farrow is golfing on?" I

asked at the clubhouse desk. I didn't know if they could actually give me that information, but if not, I was prepared to walk all eighteen holes of that course until I found his cheating ass. What I was not prepared for was the clerk's response.

He looked down at his computer. "Leon's not golfing here today, ma'am. Next tee time I have for him is Thursday."

I tilted my head. "You sure?"

"Yes, ma'am." He nodded.

But I didn't trust him. He was a man, and as far as I was concerned right then, every last one of them was suspect.

I walked out of the clubhouse and looked around the parking lot for Leon's car, which, it turned out, really wasn't there. I couldn't believe this shit. Where was he? Obviously he wasn't playing golf. By now, I was convinced that he was over at that hussy's house, screwing her. The problem was, I had no idea who she was or where to even start looking for them.

Fuming, I drove home to search for more clues, but instead I found Leon's car parked in the driveway. I jumped out of mine and strode to the door with a purpose. I wanted to stay calm, I was trying to stay calm, but I was anything but calm. My husband was about to meet the new me.

The second I hit the door, I was screaming his name. "Leon! Where you at?"

He walked out of the kitchen, carrying a sandwich. "What are you screaming for? I'm right here."

I placed a hand on my hip and went straight to the point. "Where the hell have you been?"

"I told you I was going golfing." He took a bite of his sandwich. It was so obvious he was trying to appear nonchalant. He couldn't even look me in the eye.

"Oh, really, you went golfing?" I was about to teach him that he wasn't a very good liar.

"Yes, I went golfing."

"Where? Because I just came from Chesterfield Country Club, and you sure weren't there."

He stared at me for about five seconds, probably in disbelief that I had finally woken up to his crap. He was so busted. But that didn't mean he wouldn't try to squirm his way out of this.

"I don't know why you didn't call me. I could have told you I was at Brandermill Country Club. What the hell you looking for me for anyway? I figured you'd be reading one of your ghetto books this afternoon."

Oh, no, he was not going to turn this around on me, trying to make me look wrong for checking behind him. Those red cotton panties I'd found gave me all the reason I needed to go looking for his ass. "Stop lying, Leon. I know you was with some big-ass woman. Admit it. For once in your life, be honest about something."

"For once in my life? What the hell are you talking about? I'm not admitting to shit, because I ain't did shit! Now, what the hell is this all about?" His temper was escalating pretty quickly, probably because he was pissed that he was caught in his lies. I guess he thought he could intimidate me into backing down, but he was wrong.

"You want to know what this is about?" I reached into my bag and pulled out his bitch's bloomers. "It's about these!" I held them out for him to see.

He shrugged his shoulders. "Why exactly are you showing me these? I've seen your underwear before. Personally, I like your red thong with lace better." He laughed, and I wanted to smack him into next week.

"I don't see a damn thing funny. These cheap-ass things are not mine—but I did find them in our bed." I threw them in his face. "So, would you like to tell me whose they are?"

Leon stuck with his confused routine. "Our bed?"

If I wasn't so pissed off, I'd have to give him credit for his acting ability, because the confusion on his face looked almost genuine. Maybe the damn fool had been practicing in front of a mirror.

"Yes, our bed. Now, who the hell do they belong to? And why did she leave them in my bed? Y'all trying to send me some kind of message? 'Cause I got it loud and clear."

"What message? I still don't know what you're talking about. And you best watch your tone of voice with me."

I was not about to watch my goddamn tone of voice or back down. "Oh, so you're going to lie right to my face?"

"I ain't got to lie. And I ain't got time for this nonsense either." He waved his hand in dismissal, then turned like he was about to walk away.

"Don't you walk away from me!" Before I knew it, I hauled off and smacked him as hard as I could. His sandwich went flying.

"What the —?"

Uh-oh. My hand had barely made it back to my side when I realized I'd made a big mistake. What the hell did I hit him for?

Leon stood there for a second before his hand touched his face. It probably took that long before his brain registered the pain of my slap. He looked shocked. I'd seen the look before; it told me I should run.

"Leon, baby, I'm sorry," I pleaded, backing away from him as I spoke. "I didn't mean it. I just got mad because you was lying to me. I'm really sorry, baby. I didn't mean to—"

"Woman, didn't I tell you about putting your hands on me?" Before I could move, he smashed his fist into my chest so hard that he knocked the wind out of me. When I didn't go down, his other fist landed two punches into my stomach. This time, my knees gave out, and I hit the ground hard.

"Didn't I tell you about laying your hands on me?" He touched his face again, looking crazy, like he wanted to hit me some more. "If you left a mark on my face, I'm gonna kill your ass."

I was sobbing and shaken, but I found the resolve to demand, "I want you out of my house." This time, I'd had enough.

"I ain't goin' nowhere. This is my goddamn house!" Leon hollered.

"Get out! I mean it. Get the fuck out my house!" My words were strong, but when he took a step closer, I cowered in fear.

"If you really want me out, then you're gonna have to sell this house. Then you can give me half that business of yours and anything else you own. I ain't going away cheap. Oh, and you might as well give up that fantasy about running for sorority president, 'cause the day I walk out the door, I'm going straight to the Internet and posting those naked pictures of you. So think about it. You really want me out?"

"I hate you." I couldn't believe how fast he rattled off his list of demands and threats. It was almost as if he'd been expecting this day to come, and he'd planned his speech in advance.

"Oh, please," he said with a smirk. "You hate me right now, but you won't hate me in a couple of days when you need an arm ornament or you get lonely. Besides, Loraine, don't nobody want you but me." He no longer looked like he wanted to hit me, but his words hurt just as much as the punches.

"You act as if you're the only man who would ever want me." Michael Richards's face flashed in my mind for a moment, lessening the pain of Leon's words. But, of course, he didn't know what Michael had said to me, so he scoffed at the idea that I could be considered attractive.

"Had any offers lately? You couldn't even keep that faggot from turning gay when he was your boyfriend. When I met you, you hadn't had any dick for two years, so I think you know the real story. Ain't nobody want you but me."

I tried to get up. When he saw me struggling, he reached out his hand to help.

"Don't touch me." I swatted his hand away.

"Look, I'm not gonna hit you—as long as you don't hit me. We just need to keep our hands off each other. And don't be getting all upset and try calling the police, because I gave you a love tap. You did hit me first, remember. You lucky I didn't hit you in the face."

He offered me his hand again, and I refused again. I would never admit it to him, but I knew I was wrong for slapping him first. But then again, what was I supposed to do with the rage I felt after learning that his ass was cheating on me? It was humiliating.

I was tempted to pick up something and knock his ass out. My eyes searched the room for something to hit him with, but he must have figured out my intentions.

"Look, everybody's gonna keep their hands to themselves, right?" He clenched his fists as a warning. "I know you're mad, but you did hit me first. Don't get your ass beat twice."

Twice! I never thought I'd get my ass beat down like this in my own house once, even if I did start it. Before it had been just a slap, but this time, Leon had hit me in the chest and stomach like a man. He was right about one thing, though: I was grateful he'd hit me below the neck so I'd be able to hide the bruises.

Part of me still wanted to call the police to get his ass back. The other part of me didn't want to turn another black man over to the criminal justice system. Besides, with my luck, I'd be the one who ended up in jail for hitting him first.

He bent over and picked up what was left of his sandwich. "I'm sorry this had to happen. Why don't you go upstairs and get cleaned up. I'll take you over to the River Tavern for dinner."

"I don't want your fucking food." I glared at him evilly as I walked toward the stairs. After all this, I still hadn't gotten a truthful answer on where he had been or whose underwear had been in my bed. He might have won this round, but the war was far from over. Turnabout was fair play.

Egypt
17

I glanced at the clock radio on Rashad's side of the bed. It was 10:05, and he still wasn't home from work. He was usually home by seven, eight at the latest. I wish I could say I was just starting to get worried, but that would be a lie. I'd been worried since five o'clock when I called his cell, and it went straight to voice mail. I'd been blowing up his phone ever since, with the same result. My mind quickly ran through a million different scenarios, each one with an unhappy ending. He'd been drinking so much lately, ever since Tammy said no to surrogacy, and I had a bad feeling about him not answering my calls. I prayed he hadn't gotten into an accident and hurt himself.

I wanted him to come home so I would know he was safe, and I wanted to tell him the good news. I wanted to put all his concerns to rest so we could be happy again.

It was sad but true; neither of us had been truly happy since my miscarriage. I wanted a baby of my own so bad, but more than that, I wanted my husband to be happy. And right now, the only thing in the world that would make him happy was a child of his own, conceived from his seed. I was sure he was starting to resent that his wife couldn't bear his child. Not that I could blame him. I'd been beating myself up over the same issue ever since I found out I couldn't have his baby.

For the first time in our marriage, I felt like I was losing my husband because I was less than a woman. Oh, he'd never admit it, and knowing him he'd try to stand by me. But the way he watched every child who passed us at the mall told me a different story. His lack of patience and recent short temper were showing me he was starting to fall out of love with me. If this past week was any indication of our future, our marriage wasn't going to make it.

He was really messed up over this baby thing, but I refused to give up on us. So, I'd orchestrated the impossible. A few hours ago, I'd asked my sister to be our surrogate and she agreed. I hadn't had a chance to tell Rashad, because he was missing in action. Now all I had to do was find him so that I could tell him the good news, and both of us could start living our lives again.

Finally I heard his car pull into the driveway. I wanted to run to the door and curse him out for scaring me and not answering his phone, but this was not the time to be the annoying wife. I waited for him to come upstairs to our room.

"Hey." I waved casually, as if his lateness didn't bother me at all. He nodded as he entered our bedroom.

When I got up to kiss him, I was pleasantly surprised to find he didn't reek of alcohol as I expected. Still, he didn't look great. He was wearing a suit, but he wasn't his usual well-groomed self. His eyes were bloodshot. His always-shaved head and face had a week's worth of growth that accentuated his receding hairline and his bald spot.

I wanted to ask him where he'd been, but that wasn't important now, because he was home safe.

"I've got good news." My voice was full of excitement. I couldn't wait to put a smile on his face.

"Is your sister gone?"

I shook my head. He wouldn't be thinking about her in such a negative way once I gave him my news. "No, but she—"

"What did I tell you this morning?"

"I know, but hear me out first."

He waved his hand at me, looking disappointed. "Not now, okay? I just want to take a shower and go to bed."

"But—"

"I said not now, Egypt, damn!" He stormed into the bathroom and shut the door so I wouldn't follow him.

This was not turning out at all like I had planned. It looked like I had to deliver my news in a different way. "I found someone who agreed to be our surrogate!" I yelled, hoping he would hear me through the closed door.

I heard him shut off the faucet, and then Rashad stepped out of the bathroom. In spite of being bloodshot, his eyes revealed his excitement. "You did?"

I was so relieved to see a glimmer of happiness in his eyes that I had to hold back tears of joy. "Yes, I did."

"Who?"

"My sister."

The room fell silent for a few seconds. Just like that, the sparkle was gone from his face, replaced by a dumbfounded look. "Do you have a sister I don't know about?"

"No, just Isis."

"This isn't funny, Egypt. You know damn well your sister isn't going to have a baby for us." He stepped back into the bathroom again, but I ran behind him so he couldn't shut me out this time.

"I wasn't trying to be funny. She really said she'd do it."

He leaned over to turn on the shower. As he undressed, he said, "Yeah, just to fuck with us. Picture your sister having a baby for us. She's just stalling so we won't kick her ass out."

Could he be right? Had I let my sister dupe me? She knew I was desperate to have a child, and maybe she saw that as her opportunity to stay put, because Lord knows she didn't have too many other options. He was definitely putting some doubt in my mind.

Still, for the past few hours, I'd been over the top with excitement, thinking our problems were solved. I couldn't let go of hope that easily. "Rashad, she sounded pretty sincere."

He stepped in the shower and closed the curtain. "Since when does your sister do anything if there's not something in it for her? Can't you see that she's playin' you for a place to stay?"

"Maybe you're right, but she did seem pretty interested in when she was going to get that money."

The shower stopped, and he poked his head out from behind the curtain. "What money?"

"She asked me for thirty grand as a surrogate fee."

He considered what I'd said for a moment. I was expecting

him to tell me there was no way we were paying Isis to have our baby, but instead he said, "Did you tell her she'd have to sign papers giving up all her parental rights?"

"Of course I did. I'm not stupid."

"And she agreed to it?"

"Yeah. I told you she sounded sincere."

I tried to suppress my smile. Rashad looked like he was warming up to the idea, but I still felt like I had to proceed with caution. Clearly there were "special issues" with my sister that we had to consider, number one being her past history with Rashad—and his belief that she might still want him. "We even talked about you and her."

"What'd she say?"

"She told me she was in love with Tony and that you were like her brother. Always looking out for her best interests. She even said she was happy for us."

"And you believe her?"

"Yeah, I do." I wanted so badly for things to work out. Every cell in my body wanted to scream out to Rashad, "Just say yes!" But I had to understand where he was coming from too.

"Babe, I know this isn't going to be easy, but what other option do we have? I'm so scared that if we can't have a baby, we're not gonna make it," I admitted with a shaky voice. "I know Isis has her problems, but I believe she'll have the baby for us if we give her the money."

He pulled me close to him, and I held on tight, releasing my pent-up tears. When my crying subsided, he took a step back and said, "We might want to get her a place as far away as we can once the baby is born. She's always talking about L.A."

"She is, isn't she?" We were both grinning now.

"It could work," Rashad said, and I felt the tension leave my body. "But I have a question for you," he said. "Can you handle your sister being pregnant by me?"

I had already thought about this during the hours I waited for him to come home. "As long as she signs those papers saying she's having *my* baby, and I know you love me, I'll do what I have to do."

He reached out and pulled me close again. "I love you. And I know the sacrifice you're making for me."

"I love you too. And I'd make any sacrifice for you." He pulled me into the shower, kissing me. We might not be able to make a baby together, but that night, we did what we did best and made sweet, passionate love.

Jerome

18

I sat at the bar of the NCO Club at Fort Lee Military Base down in Hopewell, nursing a goblet of cognac. Soldiers had always been a hard bunch to figure out, so I mainly watched as Loraine danced the night away with not one or two, but three brothers at the same time. Don't ask me what had gotten into Ms. Conservative, but there she was, strutting her stuff on the dance floor, where she'd been since the moment we set foot in the place. I couldn't put my finger on it, and she wouldn't admit it, but there was no doubt in my mind that something had changed her in the last month or so.

Of course, it was possible that the pressure of running for president of her sorority was getting to her, and she was just trying to unwind. Whatever it was, she sure was letting them brothers get all up close and personal. One brother was feeling all over her ass and titties like he planned on taking her home. If I didn't know better, I would have thought he had a good chance, too, but unlike me, Loraine knew where to draw the line.

When the song ended, Loraine headed toward me, followed by two of her three dance partners. One in particular, the one who was all over her, looked like he was more my type than hers, not because he was gay, but because he reeked of being married. The guy had a shadow on his left ring finger, a telltale sign of a wedding band that had been recently removed. He was wearing a suit that most men would wear to work. Oh, he dressed it up with a bright yellow shirt, and he looked decent, but a clothes whore like me could spot that he really wasn't prepared for the club scene. What really gave it away was the wing-tipped shoes. No single man would ever show up at a club with those on his feet.

My guess was that he'd left the little lady home with the kids to go out with his buddies, probably for the first time in months. He wasn't necessarily looking to get laid, but if it happened, he wouldn't turn it down, as long as he could get his ass home at a reasonable hour. I was going to pull Loraine's coat on him, but why spoil her fun? The chances of her and this guy hooking up were slim to none, especially since she'd driven us to the club and I needed a ride home.

"Hey, Jerome." Loraine reached over to the bar to retrieve her drink, still moving her head to the rhythm of the music. "Phew! Now, that was fun. I think I could dance all night."

I tapped her on the shoulder. "Excuse me, miss. Where is Loraine, and why have you stolen her body?" We both laughed.

"What, a girl can't have a little fun?" She fanned herself with her hand as she sipped her drink.

I leaned in and whispered, "From the looks of things, you trying to have twice as much fun as everyone else." I motioned in the direction of her two handsome dance partners.

"Now, Jerome, as long as you've known me, have I ever been selfish?" She gestured to the men. "Fellas, come here."

"Jerome, this is Terrance." She slid her arm around the waist of the man I suspected was married. "Terrance, this is my best friend, Jerome."

He offered me his hand. "Nice to meet you."

"Likewise." He had a handsome ruggedness to him. If Loraine didn't know what to do with him, she could send him over my way any time she liked.

"And this handsome young man right here is Thomas."

I took his hand, and he gave me a nice firm handshake. Thomas was kinda young, early thirties at best. He was a big guy, with well-maintained dreads, which were not something I usually found attractive, but there was something about him I liked.

"Um, Jerome, Thomas was admiring your suit and tie."

"Yeah, I like your style. It's hard to find suits for guys our size," Thomas complimented.

I was just about to tell him where I get my suits when Loraine cut in. "Maybe you two should sit down and talk so you can tell him where you got them. I'm sure you guys have a lot in common." Loraine winked at me twice, our signal for *I think he's in denial.*

"Ohhh, okay, that's a good idea. Grab a seat, Thomas. Let me buy you a drink."

"Come on, Terrance. They're playing my song." Loraine headed for the dance floor with Terrance in tow.

Thomas sat down in Loraine's seat.

"So, you like the suit, huh?"

"Yeah, it's tight. I've been trying to find something like that for a while. I just can't find them in my size. Where'd you get it from?"

"Believe it or not, a little hole-in-the-wall called Al's Men's Shop on Broad Street in Richmond."

"Man, I been by there. That place is a hole-in-the-wall." For a man so big, he had a sweet innocence to him. After being around him for a few minutes, I could tell Loraine was right: He was in denial.

"No question. But have you ever been inside?"

"Nah, can't say I have. Just didn't look like someplace I'd want to go inside of."

I leaned in a little closer to him. "Never knock something until you've tried it. There's a whole new world out there for you. All you have to do is be brave enough to open the door."

He nodded his head, and I couldn't help but wonder if he understood my meaning and was giving me the go-ahead. Only time would tell, and I could be a patient man when I needed to be.

Thomas and I chitchatted for almost an hour and went through several rounds of drinks. He was an interesting guy, a former minor league baseball player who had a cup of coffee with the Atlanta Braves in 2002 before blowing out his knee. He said he really missed the camaraderie of being out there with the team. The more we talked, the more I was starting to think that what he really missed were the *boys* on the team.

More than once our eyes locked, only for him to turn his head or look away abruptly. Now I had no doubt that Loraine was right about him. Even though he told me he had a fiancée, he also mentioned on several occasions that there was something missing from his life. That he always felt different. To a man like me, those were all buzz words for *I'd like to be with you, but I'm afraid to make the first move.*

Good thing I wasn't afraid at all.

About twenty minutes before the club closed down, I made my move. "I'm going to go out on a limb here, but would you like to get out of here and take a drive somewhere?"

I didn't have to wait long for his answer. "Yeah, I think I'd like that."

He had no idea how much he was going to like it.

"Good. I'll be right back." I walked over to the dance floor, where Loraine and Terrance were slow dancing. I tapped her on the shoulder. "I'm gonna take off. You gonna be okay?"

She lifted her head off his shoulder, giving me a warm smile. "Do I look like I'm in bad hands?"

"No, you look just fine. Call me when you get home." I kissed her cheek, then turned my head toward Terrance. "Take care of my girl and make sure she gets home safe."

He saluted me. "Yes, sir. She's in very capable hands."

"I'm sure."

"Don't do anything I wouldn't do, Jerome!"

"I'm sure I will." I started to walk away.

"I'm not."

I looked back toward them. Her head was back on his shoulder, and she waved good-bye with her fingers.

She wouldn't do anything with him, would she?

I wouldn't know the answer to that question until I spoke to her later, so I put Loraine out of my mind and followed Thomas out of the club and to his car, a 2009 Lincoln Navigator.

"Nice ride," I said as I got in and buckled my seat belt.

"Thanks. With everything going on in the car industry, I got a good deal. Where we headed?"

"Just get on Jefferson Davis and drive north. We'll know when we get there."

There wasn't much said on our drive, but my hand inched

closer and closer to Thomas's thigh. It took me somewhere around ten minutes, but eventually my arm was resting on his thigh while my hand massaged the inside of his leg. I didn't meet with any resistance. At a stoplight, I leaned over and began to kiss his neck and nibble at his ear. I could tell he liked it from the way he rolled his neck around and purred when I kissed a certain spot.

"I think maybe we should pull over. There's a short-stay motel right across from that gas station up there." It was time to get a room and seal the deal. He'd started driving erratically when my right hand began massaging his penis through the thin material of his pants. If I went any further, he'd probably end up driving off the road and killing us both.

Thomas followed my instructions to the letter, parking his truck in the motel lot so that I could get us a room. I guess sex is a universal language, because the entire time we drove, he hadn't spoken a word, yet I knew exactly what was on his mind.

Two hours later, we walked out of room 24. There was a couple standing by the night window, waiting for a key.

"When can I see you again?" Thomas was speaking under his breath as we walked to his truck. He was trying to look inconspicuous, as though he was not with me, but I could tell he was already sprung. He had that overeager glimmer in his eye that my men get when they first admit they like to have sex with men.

For me, it was like breaking in virgins when I got these downlow men. They were the ones I liked the best. They were generally the biggest freaks once I shattered their facades, and the sad thing was, their wives had no clue. I'd had rappers who tried to act like gangsters, and I'd had celebrities. I'd had them all—and almost every last one of them was a married man. Maybe Thomas's fiancée would figure it out before they walked down the aisle . . . but I doubted it.

"I'll call you." I tried to sound vague. It was, of course, the weekend. I didn't want to mess up my precious time with Big Poppa. Until I was sure that he wouldn't be coming over any time during the weekend, I couldn't make any promises.

"You got my number, right?"

"I got it."

"Lock it in your phone, man."

"I said I got it, Thomas."

"Look, man, I really had a good time. We should do this again soon."

Damn! On the way there, I couldn't get him to say a word. Now I couldn't get him to shut up.

"Jerome!"

I heard a voice behind me. I pivoted around to see who was calling me.

"Peter?" What the hell was he doing at the motel? And why did he look so bad? He was a far cry from George Clooney now. Something was definitely wrong with this guy. I was starting to think he'd lost his mind for real.

"Jerome, how could you do this to me?" He held his hands out in a pleading gesture. He was actually crying like a little bitch.

"What the fuck, Peter? Are you following me?"

"Not this time. I was just sitting here reminiscing. This was the first place we made love, so it's special to me, and like some type of omen, you showed up. God sent you to me, Jerome."

"Man, you are fucking nuts." I didn't mean to sound so cold, but I can't stand a weak-ass man, especially one who's trying to make me feel guilty. Shit, I had been nothing but honest with the guy. I never told him we were going to be together. Was it my fault if he fell in love?

He looked over at Thomas, who had stopped pretending he wasn't with me and was now standing by my side. "You don't need this guy. Just give me a chance. I'll do anything for you. I love you." Peter began bawling like a little girl, which further turned me off.

"Yo, who is this guy?" Thomas asked.

"Nobody important."

"Nobody important! I left my wife and my kids for you. I have lost all my friends so that I could be with you. Now you're gonna tell this man that I'm nobody important?"

"Didn't nobody tell you to leave your family." I turned away from Peter.

Thomas offered to defend me. "Just say the word, Jerome, and I can whip this white boy's ass with one hand tied behind my back."

"No." I sighed. "This is just someone who doesn't know that no means no. Just get in the truck so we can get out of here. Can't you tell he's crazy?"

Peter turned to Thomas. "Mister, I don't know who you are, but run while you can; get out of this mess. He'll ruin your life. I swear he's Satan. He'll make you fall in love with him and then break your heart."

I loved me some married men, but it was times like these that reminded me I was playing a very dangerous game.

Isis

19

I'd been texting Tony all day, but he hadn't answered me back once, which was pissing me off. I had his number, though. I couldn't wait until that jealous motherfucker found out I was pregnant by Rashad. He was going to flip his wig. He hated Rashad just as much, if not more, than Rashad hated him. I know this probably sounds absurd, but my period couldn't be over fast enough so they could shoot me up with Rashad's sperm. I decided not to go on the birth control pills, since we were not going to be getting pregnant the natural way. No, I wanted to get pregnant as soon as possible. Once I was pregnant, I was going to make quite a few people grovel and pay.

I heard a knock on the door. It had to be Egypt. She had been in and out of my room all afternoon. Ever since I had agreed to have Rashad's baby, she'd been asking me a million questions. I wanted to scream, *What the hell do you want?* But there was still the remote possibility that she could change her mind and kick my ass out on the street, so instead, I said sweetly, "Come in."

"Hey, Isis." To my surprise, it was Rashad who walked in, wearing his bathrobe. I had to admit he looked better in it than Tony did. We were going to have some really good-looking kids.

"Hey, Rashad," I replied happily as he shut the door.

I sat up in the bed, and one of my breasts almost fell out of the opening to my nightgown. I didn't even attempt to cover myself up. He'd seen everything I had to offer plenty of times. I'm sure he knew that all he had to do was ask, and it could be his again. If he didn't, I'd let him know soon enough.

"What's up?"

"I just wanted to say thanks. Egypt told me what you're doing for us."

To my surprise, he was all choked up, and his eyes were glistening with tears. I'd dated that man for ten years, and I'd only seen him cry twice—once at his father's funeral. The second time was the day I chose Tony over him, probably the stupidest thing I'd ever done.

"Hey, it's okay." I cleared a space on the side of the bed and patted it, signaling for him to join me. He sat down, and I said, "You don't have to thank me."

You could kiss me, maybe even fuck me, but you don't have to thank me.

He looked me straight in the eye. "Yeah, I do. I'm not stupid. I know this wasn't an easy decision for you to make. I just want you to know I will never forget it."

"Mmm-hmm." I rubbed his back, thinking that he had no idea how easy it really was for me. I mean, have Rashad's baby and have him forever indebted to me? It was a no-brainer.

"Egypt told you I'm going to take care of all the doctor's bills and medical expenses, right?"

"Yeah, she told me." His concern was so cute. I couldn't wait until I had cravings so I could send him out in the middle of the night to get me ice cream and pickles. I think I was going to love being pregnant.

"You don't have to worry about anything. I swear I'm going to take care of everything."

Be careful what you ask for, big boy, because when I get off my period, I'm going to have one hell of an itch. You think you'll be able to take care of that?

"I know you will, Rashad. I'm just a little scared, that's all." I wrapped my other arm around his neck, and we hugged. I wasn't really scared, but I would do or say anything if I thought it would bring me physically closer to him. What I really wanted to do was pull him back on the bed, open his robe, and make that baby right then and there. Lord have mercy, just being close to him was making my juices flow.

"It's okay. I'm here. I'm always going to be here." He hugged me tighter, and I almost melted.

I slid my hand down his back. It would have been so simple to slide my hand inside his robe and claim what had been mine for so many years before my sister stole it. But she had just been at the right place at the right time, 'cause she sure didn't win him by being able to fuck him better than I could. We were together for a long time, and if there was anything I knew, it was how to satisfy him. All he needed was a reminder of the paradise between my legs, and that would be it; he'd be sneaking in my room every night. Only thing stopping me was my period. Then again, I also gave a pretty mean blow job, so maybe we could start there.

Just as I was working up the nerve to suggest it, there was another knock at the door. Damn!

I moved away from Rashad just as Egypt walked into the room. Another few minutes and we'd all be headed for divorce court. I wondered if she'd be as shocked to find Rashad's dick in my mouth as I was when I found her half naked at his place the first time. I know, I know . . . I was engaged to Tony at the time and had already broken poor Rashad's heart. Well, what about my heart? Of all the millions of men in this world, my sister had to choose my ex-fiancé—not ex-boyfriend, but ex-fiancé—to screw. I sound bitter, right? Well, that's because I am.

"Baby, you forgot this in the room." She handed him an envelope, which he in turn handed to me.

"What's this?" I asked.

"You said you wanted thirty grand plus expenses to be our surrogate," Egypt answered.

Can't she tell I was talking to him? I was looking at him when I asked my question. How can she not know I was talking to him?

"That's five thousand. You'll get another five when you sign and notarize the papers Rashad's lawyers are going to draw up. Ten thousand more when we have confirmation you've made it through the first trimester, and another ten when you deliver and hand over the baby."

The way she was talking, it sounded like I was selling something on QVC, and she was explaining the easy payment program. It just seemed so impersonal, nothing like the way Rashad

had spoken to me before she entered the room. Then again, she wasn't going to have the connection to the baby that Rashad and I were going to have. She was only going to be the baby's mother in name, while Rashad and I would be the baby's biological parents.

I opened the envelope and glanced at the cash. I could feel my sister's eyes on me. I'm sure she was judging me in some capacity. What she should have been doing was kissing my feet for agreeing to all this.

"It's all there," Rashad said. "You can count it. We wouldn't short you."

I tossed the envelope on my night table. I guess it was time to get this show on the road. "I know you wouldn't, Rashad. It was never really a concern. All I want to know is when do we go to the doctor?"

Once again, Egypt took over the conversation. "I made an appointment for next Monday. Don't worry, I'll drive you." She was so damn pushy. How could he stand her?

I barely acknowledged that I heard her words as I turned to Rashad. "You gonna be there?"

He nodded happily as he got up from my bed. "I wouldn't miss it for the world."

"Neither would I," I replied. "Neither would I."

Loraine

20

I was mad when the lights came on and the music stopped playing, signifying that the club was officially about to close. I was having such a good time. I just closed my eyes, holding on to Terrance like the music was still playing. Lord, forgive me, but I didn't want this moment to end. I would have traded my soul to the devil if we could just keep dancing for a few more hours. I couldn't remember the last time I had this much fun. Not only was the dancing great, but also the attention that Terrance and the other men gave me made me feel alive again. To hell with Leon's cheating ass and his bullshit put-downs. Tonight confirmed that men still desired me and that sexy wasn't a dress size; it was an attitude.

"Um, Loraine," Terrance whispered in my ear, "I think we're the only ones left on the dance floor."

I took one last sniff of his coconut-oil cologne, then reluctantly lifted my head off his shoulder, my arms still wrapped around his upper back. I glanced over at the bar. He was right. It was completely empty, along with the dance floor. I couldn't even remember hearing them announce the last call. Damn shame too. I could have used another drink. I was already a little buzzed, but one more watermelon martini and I would have been feeling just right.

"I think it's time to go."

I rested my head back on his shoulder. "Do we have to leave?"

"Yeah, but that doesn't mean the night has to end. I know this place where we can dance until the sun comes up." He gave me a squeeze, then let me go, taking hold of my hand.

I hesitated for a moment, but he tugged at my hand gently and told me, "Trust me."

A few minutes later, I followed his car off the military base and onto I-295 toward Emporia. After a fifteen-minute ride, we got off the interstate and traveled down a long, winding road. Ten miles later, we pulled over near the side of what looked like an old barn, and he got out of his car. There were cars parked all around, and I could hear people laughing and music playing inside, so I opened my car door to get out. I'd barely gotten my foot out the door when Terrance came running over, shaking his head.

"No, no, I just stopped here to get a bottle. The place we're going is BYOB, but it's much better than this."

"Are you sure? We're kind of far out in the country, aren't we?" I asked.

"Trust me." He flashed me the sweetest smile, and that was all I needed to put my mind at ease.

"Okay, but don't leave me out here alone too long." I got back in my car to wait.

He disappeared into the front door of the shack and then quickly returned with a bag. He opened my passenger side door, sliding into the seat next to me.

"Go 'head down this road." He pointed and I just drove. I didn't even ask about why he was leaving his car.

Up until this point, I'd been on autopilot. I never asked where we were going. I just assumed it was some after-hours place out here in the country. But at about the same time my martini buzz started subsiding, my sensible side woke up. Why the hell was I going to some juke joint way out in the country with a man I barely knew? For a moment, I was nervous, wondering if I was driving myself into some sort of trap. If I needed to be rescued, would my cell phone even get reception way the hell out here? I looked over at Terrance to see if his face would reveal any sinister thoughts in his head, but all I saw was a man who couldn't take his eyes off me.

"I'm so glad I met you tonight," he told me.

And just like that, I relaxed. This man was just looking to have a good time with me, and he was sure showing me a good time—something my husband hadn't done in a long time. So that's why I was here, traveling down a dark country road with someone I'd just met, behaving in a way I never dreamed I would. I wanted to pay Leon back for everything he'd done to me. Oh, I still loved my husband; I couldn't help it. But those panties were like a dark shroud hanging over me, and the only way to cleanse myself of it was to get even. I wanted him to feel the same way I did.

Terrance told me to turn down a dirt road that didn't look like it was traveled by many people. I couldn't imagine any kind of party spot being down here, and my heart rate picked up a bit. Maybe he sensed my nervousness, because he slipped one of my CDs into the player, and Alicia Keys's soothing voice came on. It helped a little, but still, that road was getting kind of spooky. It reminded me of something out of a *Friday the Thirteenth* movie.

"Hey, turn off your lights," he said.

I looked at him like he was crazy. It was pitch-black outside— I mean, damn, even the moon was hiding—and he wanted me to turn the lights out while I was driving. He seemed nice enough, but now I was really starting to worry that I'd allowed myself to leave the club with some nutcase. I casually reached down with my left hand and took my mace from its hiding spot on the driver's side door.

"Why in the world would I turn off my lights?" I asked.

"Because I asked you to. And you trust me."

I stopped the car.

"You're taking this trust thing a little far, aren't you? And where the hell are we going? I haven't seen a car or house since we turned down this road."

"We're almost there. Come on. All you got to do is drive with your lights out for about fifteen seconds and we'll be there. Come on, trust me."

I was going against my better judgment and everything I'd ever been taught when I turned out my lights and started to drive down that road in the pitch black. I was still holding on to my mace tight, though. One false move on his part and I was going to set his eyes on fire.

"One, two, three, four, five . . ."

Terrance turned up the music as I counted.

". . . thirteen, fourteen, fifteen."

"Stop the car!" he yelled.

I jammed my foot on the brake, switched the lights on, and then dropped my mace back into its hiding place.

"Oh my God." In front of us was the most beautiful man-made waterfall I'd ever seen. I stepped out of my car, standing there in awe, until I felt his arms come around my waist from behind.

"Pretty, huh?"

"Gorgeous." We stood there for a few minutes and just took in its beauty. "What is it—a dam?"

"Yep, there's a larger one a couple miles up the road. Most people don't know about this one, mostly just fishermen."

"How'd you find this place anyway? You're a fisherman?"

"I'd like to think so. A friend of mine took me fishing down here about three years ago. I caught a ten-pound bass down by those rocks."

"Nobody has ever taken me somewhere like this."

"Tonight might be a first for a lot of things."

He reached into the car and changed the music. Bobby Womack's song "If You Think You're Lonely Now" was playing.

"Can I have this dance?" He put out his hand. I took it, and we began to slow dance, my head on his shoulders, my arms around his neck, his hands on my ass, our bodies so close an ant couldn't walk between us. We picked up right where we left off.

I guess we were dancing that way for a half hour before he whispered, "I think you're beautiful." I lifted my head off his shoulder and turned it so that we were face-to-face. I knew what was coming next but made no attempt to stop him.

He kissed me and I kissed him back. Leon had never been much of a kisser, other than the occasional peck he'd give me before he left for work. Even when we were intimate, we never really kissed. I was pleasantly surprised when Terrance slid his tongue in my mouth. I offered no resistance.

"I want you," he whispered when we broke the kiss.

As much as I wanted him too, I still wasn't sure if I could go all the way. I'd always prided myself on being faithful, and I looked down on women who tipped around on their husbands—double dipping, as Jerome called it. I thought it was disgusting, but now, with Terrance nibbling on my ears, I just didn't know anymore. Maybe those women had a reason for stepping out. I mean, after what Leon had done, who could blame me for getting even?

Still, it wasn't a simple decision for me to make. I had the proverbial angel and devil on my shoulders, as I battled with my conscience.

Okay, you've gone far enough. The kissing was one thing, but if you take this any further, there will be consequences to pay. Don't cross that line. Do the right thing. Get back in your car and take your butt home.

Then Terrance would hit the right spot on my neck, and I'd think, *Girl, forget that good-girl shit. What's it ever got you? It got your ass beat, a black eye, and a cheating-ass husband. Go on and get yours. Leon's cheating on you, isn't he? Where do you think those panties came from? Then he had the nerve to hit you, and he's the one cheating on you? Naw, go on and handle your business.*

Could I do it? I wondered as conflicting thoughts waged war in my head. One thing was for sure: If I did do it, I'd have to keep it to myself. I couldn't let this sort of thing get out, not even to Jerome, particularly now that I was being considered for a national position as president of my sorority. He was my best friend, and I wasn't in the habit of keeping secrets from him, but I didn't think it would be hard to keep my mouth shut about this one. I'd already had practice when I made the decision not to tell him about the panties and the last beating. I loved my friend, but if I did this, I was taking this secret to my grave.

"I want you," he whispered again.

"I want you too," I whispered back. "Did you bring any condoms?"

Egypt

21

"Now, just try to relax. You're going to feel a small amount of pressure as I enter your vagina. Possibly a little discomfort when I enter your cervix and uterus, but it won't last for long," Dr. Collins told Isis.

She was on her back, naked from the waist down, with both legs in the stirrups covered only by a paper sheet. She glanced at me. I wasn't sure if she was scared, but I reached out and held her hand. Anytime I'd ever heard a doctor talk about discomfort, it usually meant pain, so I was trying to comfort her the best I could.

"You okay?" I asked.

She nodded and then grimaced when Dr. Collins ducked under the sheet to insert this long tube thing up inside her vagina. She squeezed my hand tightly. I leaned down and kissed her on the cheek. Yes, she was in pain, but she had no idea how much I envied her. I would have taken a hell of a lot more pain than that to have Rashad's baby.

"Ow!" Isis shouted. She was squeezing my hand in a vise grip. "Oh my God, Egypt! This man is trying to rip my shit apart."

"Dr. Collins, you're hurting her. Can you be a little gentler?"

He ignored me and pushed that thing in farther.

Isis and I had been pretty tight before I started dating Rashad, but I'd never felt as close as I did now with my sister. She'd been poked, prodded, and tested for almost a month without a complaint. I had to give it to her; she was showing herself to be a real trooper, a true sister, and a good friend in every sense of the word. It was almost as if she wanted this baby as much as Rashad and I did. I didn't know if I'd ever be able to repay her. Up until recently, I thought she might still have a problem with me being with Rashad. Now I couldn't believe I'd ever doubted her sincerity.

Many people would have said it was my own fault if my sister did hate me. I was the one who had broken what some would call the cardinal rule of dating: Thou shall not date, fool around with, or marry your girlfriend's or sister's ex. Plenty of women would say I should never have messed with Rashad. On the other hand, those who saw it my way would say that Rashad was fair game once Isis became engaged to Tony. I didn't know which one was right, but I wouldn't second guess myself, because there was no doubt in my mind that Rashad was my soul mate.

I honestly didn't know if I could have been as forgiving as my sister. Oh, she was mad in the beginning, but she could have tried to make my life a living hell, and she never did. That's a big part of why I always kept my eye on her. She'd given me a pass, so I was obligated to stand by her side during her times of trouble.

I was truly blessed to have the relationship I had with my sister. We'd gotten past any differences, and now she was making the ultimate sacrifice for me. I mean, to give up nine months of her life to conceive a precious little baby, then give it up to Rashad and me so that we could be parents . . . It was truly a humbling experience.

On the bright side, the way things were going, I really felt like I was participating in the whole process. And believe me, the process was not simple, for my sister or for Rashad. For the past two days, he and I had been coming to the doctor's office so that he could masturbate and give them a sperm sample. When he finished, they washed his sperm through a special process, and only the strongest swimmers were used for the insemination process.

Rashad had been taking the whole thing very seriously. He was so concerned about his sperm count that we hadn't had sex in more than a week. Now, that might have been good for the process, but it sure as hell wasn't doing me any good. I was used to getting some at least two or three times a week. A sister was about due, if you know what I mean.

I knew I would be all right, though. Now that Isis was being inseminated, Rashad promised me tonight would be our night to celebrate. As I stood there and let my sister squeeze the hell out of my hand, I distracted myself from the pain by daydreaming about the great sex I had to look forward to.

"Ow!" Isis shouted.

I glanced over at the doctor. He could ignore me if he wanted to, but I was going to snatch that thing out of his hand and show him how it worked if he kept hurting my sister.

He must have sensed my thoughts, because he announced, "Don't worry. I'm done."

Just like that, it was over. Isis was inseminated. The doctor and Rashad had done their parts; now it was up to Isis and God to do the rest.

"You okay?"

"Yeah, I'm all right," she grunted. "We did it."

"No, Isis, you did it, and I love you for it."

"I love you too."

To say this was an intense moment was an understatement. A little more than a month ago, Isis was a beacon of controversy in my household, and now she was an angel of hope. She didn't know it, but she'd single-handedly saved my marriage. Soon, Rashad and I would be parents, and our family would be complete. For the first time, it truly sank in: I was going to be a mommy.

"So, Doctor, when will we know?" I was so anxious that I could barely sit still. "What are the chances she'll get pregnant?" He'd answered this ten times already, but I wanted to hear him explain it again. I'm sure I wasn't the first mother-to-be to ask a million questions.

"Good. The chances are very good that Isis will get pregnant. She has a strong uterus, which can support a pregnancy. She was ovulating during our insemination."

"That's great." I couldn't wait to go outside to the waiting room and see Rashad. "Do you think it will take a long time for Isis to get pregnant?"

"Now, that I can't say. You're just getting started. Most couples don't get pregnant until the third or fourth try. We'll just have to wait and see. If it doesn't work this month, we'll try next month when she ovulates. But like I said, her body temperature indicates she's ovulating, and our tests show that she has healthy eggs. It's just a matter of fertilization. Each month, we will keep track of her cycle and do the insemination, until we get the results we're looking for."

"I hope I don't have to go through this no more," Isis said. "It hurts."

"Well, go home and keep your feet up. If you have any discomfort, you can take Tylenol."

Dr. Collins left the room, and I helped Isis dress. She was acting so helpless that you'd think she'd already had the baby, but I was enjoying every minute of it. Taking care of her was the least I could do to show my gratitude.

We walked out to the waiting room, smiling and holding hands. Even sharing a bedroom growing up, we had never been this close.

Rashad still looked a little disappointed that he had been forced to stay in the waiting area. He wanted to come in during the insemination, but I told him no. I mean, he did used to sleep with my sister, and no matter how close I was feeling to her right now, there was still that part of me that was determined to make sure my husband never again saw her naked.

"Well, how did it go?" he asked.

"We have to wait before we find out if this round worked, but the doctor says he's sure it's only a matter of time before you're a daddy," I told him with a smile.

He stepped closer and wrapped his arms around both of us. Here I was with the man I loved and the sister who was giving us the most beautiful gift. I felt so loved. This was a moment I would never forget.

Isis

22

On our way home from the doctor's office, we stopped at Chesterfield Town Center Mall at my suggestion. I loved to shop and so did my sister, so I was hoping to pick up a few things and have Rashad pick up the tab. He was so giddy about me walking around with his sperm up inside me, I could probably get him to buy me just about anything if my sister weren't around. If I had known he was going to be rich and that having a baby was this important to him, I would have let him knock me up years ago.

I was in a really good mood as we strolled through the different shops, spending Rashad's money like he had an endless supply. It was almost as if we were both married to him until Egypt took his hand, leaning against him playfully. I watched them kiss, and my blood began to boil. I'm not sure why, but lately that kind of shit angered me. Probably because Egypt just loved to rub it in my face that she was with Rashad and I wasn't. She'd been doing a lot of that lately, and it was pissing me off. *Well, let's see her rub it in my face when I'm carrying his damn baby.*

Speaking of pissing me off, Egpyt really did it this afternoon at the doctor's office when she wouldn't allow Rashad to be in the room while they inseminated me. Hell, he and I were the biological parents of this baby, not her. Who the fuck was she to say he could or couldn't be there when our baby was being conceived? If I had my druthers, we'd be making the baby the old-fashioned way, and she'd be the one waiting outside the room for the results.

It was time to see how much this baby thing was really going to get me. When I saw the sharpest maternity outfits in a store display window, I called out, "Ooh-wee, let's stop here."

Egypt, who had been in a good mood lately, said, "We haven't even done the pregnancy test and you're already acting like you're pregnant. You need to slow down."

She didn't see, but I gave her the nastiest look.

"Look, I've been turkey basted to death, and I should be pregnant. I got a good feeling," I said. "Let's get an early start."

The truth was, I already felt a little different, like the first time I was pregnant. I don't know, just a little warmer than usual, like my temperature was elevated. They had this early pregnancy test we could do at home, so we might know in about ten days.

"Aw, let her go in and look and see what she likes," Rashad said.

Egypt let out a good-natured sigh. "Okay. Girl, you are getting spoiled already. These clothes look rather expensive."

"Well, I'll just get a few nice pieces; then the rest I'll buy secondhand."

"No, you won't wear thrift-shop clothes," Rashad said. "We want you to be in a good frame of mind while you're pregnant. That way the baby will have a good disposition. I read that in the baby books."

Those two had all these baby books from before, and they had pulled them out and reread them now that I was trying to get pregnant for them. If I didn't wish they were broken up, I'd think they were a cute couple.

I picked out the cutest and most high-end clothes I could find. When Egypt protested, Rashad said, "Let her get them."

After I had tried on many outfits, I said, "Ooh, Egypt, I'm so thirsty. Could you go buy me a lemonade at the lemonade shop next door?"

While she was gone, I got a whiff of some fresh pastries. "Rashad, you think you could go get me a Krispy Kreme donut over across the way? I'm already getting cravings. I'm almost sure this is it."

Rashad grinned and nodded, then left to get my food.

I almost laughed out loud. I had both of them at my beck and call, and I wasn't even pregnant for sure yet. I started daydreaming about what it would be like when I did conceive. And if we found out it was a boy, then that would be even better. Rashad was already acting a fool, so I knew I'd have him wrapped around my finger once the baby was on the way. After that, I could promise him more kids, and he would definitely want to leave Egypt. Yeah, things were certainly looking up for me.

Loraine

23

It was five in the morning when I tiptoed nervously up the stairs, carrying my heels in hand. I'd just come back from the waterfall with Terrance, where we'd made love on a blanket under the stars. It was the most memorable night I'd spent in a very long time.

The sex was good—not earth-shattering, but good. It could have been much better if I hadn't been so distracted with guilt over cheating on Leon. As much as I wanted to get even with him, a part of me still couldn't get past the fact that I was breaking vows that were meant to be honored for life.

I had to give Terrance an A for effort, though. I think he sensed my hesitation, and he sure as hell tried his best to make me see stars. He came damn close too. Regrettably, every time I was on the verge of climaxing, I'd think of Leon. Talk about a mood killer. What that told me was something I already knew: I loved Leon, and deep down inside, I wished it was him who was making me feel that way. I'll tell you, trying to have revenge sex wasn't all it was cracked up to be.

Now that I was home and the thrill of the moment was gone, I was kind of glad I didn't have an orgasm with Terrance. If he had made me come, I might have been, for lack of a better word, wide open. That would not have been a good thing, because in spite of everything, I really did want my marriage to last. But I was also smart enough to realize I'd been so starved for attention that it would be easy to become attached to a man who could bring me the physical joy Leon hadn't cared enough to give lately. Jerome always liked to say, "It's easy to confuse good sex with love," and at this point, a good orgasm might have had me falling head over heels for someone who was not my husband.

So, I came home feeling like I'd accomplished my mission. I'd set out to get even in order to move on with my life and my marriage. He'd cheated; now I'd cheated, so we were even, although he'd never know it. I wasn't going to step outside my marriage again—not unless Leon gave me a good reason. As much fun as it was, it just wasn't me.

When I walked into our bedroom, Leon appeared to be fast asleep. It was times like these I wished he snored so I could be sure. I glanced across the room to the bathroom door. All I had to do was make it fifteen feet, and I'd be home free. I needed a shower in the worst way. Not that Terrance was a dirty man, but I felt like his scent was all over me. It was a mixture of sweat, sex, and his coconut body oil. I kind of liked it, but I was sure Leon wouldn't find it very appealing, so I headed for the bathroom and a hot shower. Unfortunately, I wasn't able to walk three feet, let alone fifteen, before I heard the ruffling of sheets.

"Loraine?"

I froze in my tracks, turning my head toward the bed. Leon sat up like he'd been awake, waiting for me all night. *Please, don't come over here. Please, don't come over here.* The absolute last thing I wanted was for him to get too close before I had a chance to shower.

"Hey, baby, what you doing up?"

"Waiting for you. A little late, isn't it?" He glanced over at the clock radio. "It's five o'clock in the morning. Did you forget you have a home?"

"No, I was out with Jerome. We went down to the NCO Club at Fort Lee." I tried to answer casually, but if I sounded half as nervous as I felt, he was going to see right through me.

"The NCO Club closes at two. Mind telling me where you been?" The tone of his voice made me feel like he knew exactly where I'd been and what I'd been doing. I racked my brain trying to remember if there was anyone in the club who looked familiar, someone who might have called Leon to tell him about the man I was hugged up with on the dance floor.

"We went to the Waffle House to get something to eat. I guess

I lost track of time." I turned to head for the shower, hoping our conversation was over.

But it wasn't. "The Waffle House, huh?" he said skeptically.

I faced him again and crossed my arms over my chest. I tried to sound exasperated by his questions. "Yes, Leon, me and my gay friend went to the Waffle House. Do you have some sort of problem with that?"

"No, I just—"

"Oh, I see. You afraid some man other than you might see me and want me?" He looked a little taken aback by my change in demeanor, and I suddenly felt empowered as I realized how well this tactic was working. "All right, I was in a secluded park screwing some man under the stars. That make you feel any better? Would you like some details?"

Okay, for the record, I couldn't believe I'd just said that either. But the way things were going, he wasn't about to let up, so I took a page from the playbook used by so many cheating men: Go on the offensive and take the focus off yourself, quick. I'd just taken it one step further by admitting the truth, without him realizing I was admitting the truth. Pretty good reverse psychology, don't you think?

He tried to play it off with a laugh. "No, I'm not afraid of anything." Then he tried to assert his manliness one more time. "But you got a home. Don't come through that door after three in the morning again, or—"

"Or what?" My defiance was no longer part of an act. Husband or not, I hated when people threatened me. "I'm a grown-ass woman, and I stopped having curfews when I was eighteen."

"No wife of mine is going to be running the streets until five o'clock in the morning. Or have you stopped being my wife too?"

Uh-oh, he was taking this in a direction I didn't want to go. This was not the time for a long discussion about the state of our marriage, especially not when I was still covered in the scent of another man.

"Leon, it's late. I'm tired. I wanna take a shower and go to bed. I don't wanna argue with you." I started to walk toward the bathroom, but he pulled the sheets back and stepped out of bed.

"Well, I do."

I was struggling to keep calm, but his voice had taken on a little too much bass, and I was afraid this might escalate into something physical in a hurry. I stepped into the bathroom, but he was right behind me.

"If we have to argue to get this thing straight, then we will."

"What do you want from me, Leon?" I was leaning against the sink, still trying to keep my distance.

"I love you, Loraine. I want my wife back."

I had to pause for a moment, because I was so confused by his sudden change. I fully expected the screaming to start at any moment, but all of a sudden, he was speaking to me almost like he might start crying or something.

Then it dawned on me that he might be faking. Maybe this was some sort of trick. Maybe he knew something, and he thought that he could lull me into confessing if he faked vulnerability. I decided my best plan of action was to stay the course. If I changed my attitude and showed some weakness now, he would know something was up.

"Oh, now you want your wife back. You should have thought about that before your nasty-ass bitch left her panties in my bed."

He raised his hand, still with that sad look in his eyes. "Loraine, I swear on my dead grandmother, I have no idea where those panties came from." Wow, he was really working hard. He never swore on his grandmother—unless he really wanted me to believe him. Too bad I didn't.

"So, what, did I pull those panties out my ass or something? Where did they come from?" Every time I talked about those damn panties, it brought me right back to the moment I found them.

"I don't know." He had the nerve to sound aggravated, and I was about to go off on him for it, but just that quick, he switched gears again. "I really don't know, but what I do know is that I love you, Loraine. I love you, and I don't want to lose you. Please don't throw this marriage away."

I looked in his eyes. If I didn't know better, I would have thought he was telling the truth. I guess that's when my conscience kicked in. What was I getting so upset about? I'd had my night of passion with a hot young man. I'd gotten my revenge. No need to take things too far when I wasn't entirely innocent myself anymore. Besides, this was the first time in more than a year that he'd said he loved me without me having to say it first.

"Loraine, I don't want to fight anymore." He sounded sincere.

"Neither do I."

"I love you. Do you still love me?" He may not have been telling the truth about the panties, but I wanted to believe him. I wanted to believe he loved me, and only me.

"I never stopped loving you. I just want the old Leon back."

He smiled. So did I, and for that moment, we were connected in a way we hadn't been in a long time. He closed the distance between us, reaching out his hand. I took it, and he pulled me in close, holding me tight.

"I love you so much."

"I love you too." He started to kiss my neck and ears, and it felt so damn good.

I was totally lost in the moment; I'd completely forgotten that I still hadn't showered, until he said, "Mmmm, you smell so good. Is that a new perfume?"

Suddenly I felt nauseated. My back stiffened, and my eyes were now wide open. I could feel his tongue licking my neck. What usually turned me on was making me feel sick to my stomach. I didn't know where he was mentally, but I sure as hell wasn't enjoying this anymore.

I tried to push him off me, but he wouldn't let go. "Baby, let me go take a shower, and I'll be right back, okay?"

"You ain't going nowhere. I want you just the way you are." I felt one hand slide under my blouse to fondle my breast as the other unzipped my skirt from behind. His hands were in so many places; he was like an octopus.

"Baby, please let me take a shower. I've been at the club dancing, and everything is sweaty—including down there," I added for emphasis. I took hold of the hand going into my skirt to stop him.

"When we finish, we can take a shower together. Come on, Big Sexy. When we first met, we used to have sex the second we hit the door after a night of dancing." He was determined. The hand that was in my blouse was now pushing down my skirt below my hips.

Dear Lord, I did not want to have sex with Leon after I'd just had sex with another man. That would be too nasty. But the way he'd just professed his love to me, how could I tell him no? Besides, we hadn't had sex in almost three weeks. If I turned him down, he'd get suspicious.

"Leon, please. I just want to take a shower." By now my skirt had hit the floor, and my panties weren't far behind. I tried once again to push him away, to no avail.

"I don't care if you're a little funky down there. When we got married, you said this was my pussy and I could have it anytime I wanted. Well, I want some now."

How the hell was I supposed to respond to that? *Think, Loraine, think*. It was times like these I wished I could phone a friend. I was sure Jerome could help me find a way out of this mess.

And there it was, the answer to my problem. As soon as Jerome entered my mind, I knew exactly what his advice would be. He'd say, *Get on your knees and suck his dick. A good blow job will put his ass right to sleep*. I was going to have to buy Jerome lunch on Monday. He was helpful even when he wasn't around.

I hadn't given Leon a blow job in quite some time, even though I did enjoy giving them. I loved the power it gave me over a man. And I must admit I'd become pretty skilled at giving head after Jerome showed me how to deep-throat a banana about seven, eight years ago. When we first got married, I would have Leon doing the Spider-Man, I would suck his stuff so well. Then, around the time Leon started with his pre-ejaculation nonsense, Jerome suggested I stop giving him blow jobs. He said that sucking on him before we had intercourse may have had a lot to do with his lack of staying power. I was desperate for a solution, so no more blow jobs for Leon. Unfortunately, I don't think he even noticed as long as he got his shit off, and after a while, neither did I.

"Okay, Leon. You want me, you got me. But first you gotta let Momma suck on her chocolate lollipop first."

I guess Jerome was right; men don't turn down blow jobs, because Leon let me go right away, grinning from ear to ear. I reached down to the thin material of his pajama pants and pulled them down. Out sprang Mr. Man, who I very eagerly took hold of as I slid to my knees.

Less than five minutes later, I was in the shower and Leon was in the bed fast asleep.

Isis

24

I'd just come out of the shower, my body wrapped in a large bath towel, when I heard Rashad's car pull into the garage. He'd probably gone down to the 7-Eleven to get the morning newspaper and some coffee. I hurried downstairs to the family room so I could greet him with good news. Minutes before, I'd taken my temperature, and from all indications, I was ovulating, which was important if I was ever going to get pregnant. We'd all been disappointed when my period showed up a few weeks after my first insemination, but this time, I was determined things were going to be different.

For starters, Rashad and I were the ones who were going to deal with the doctors alone, without Ms. Micromanager, who had gone on a business trip to Virginia Beach for the weekend. Now, for the first time in two months, I didn't have to worry about Egypt hovering over me and worrying me to death about how much sleep I was getting or what foods I could eat. Ever since we started this artificial-insemination process, she'd been dictating like she owned my womb or something.

"Rashad!" I yelled as soon as I heard the door open, startling him so much that he almost dropped one of the two coffee cups he was carrying.

"Hey, Isis, I brought you some coffee," he said casually, as if I weren't standing in front of him practically naked. I had to stop myself from smirking, because I knew he was dying to rip the towel off me. I'd always loved teasing him. It made our sex that much more passionate. The only difference this time was that he was trying to be somewhat well behaved because he was married, so it would take a little more work to get him to loosen up. That was no problem, though. I had a plan that was sure to be successful.

"Thanks, but guess what?" I said, holding out a thermometer for him to see.

"Oh, Lord. You're not sick, are you?" The look of concern on his face was sweet.

"No, silly. This is a good thing. I've been tracking my temperature ever since I got my period two weeks ago, and this means I'm ovulating."

"Oh, shit. For real?"

"Look for yourself." I waved the thermometer in his face. Conveniently, my towel dropped from around me. "Oops." I pretended to try to stop it from falling, but when it hit the ground, I waited a few seconds so he could get a good view before I bent over to pick it up. I wrapped myself up again, leaving the towel low enough that my breasts were practically spilling over the top. Then I acted like nothing had happened, bringing his attention back to the thermometer.

"You see what I mean? Ninety-nine point one."

Just as I'd expected, Rashad's eyes were not fixated anywhere near the thermometer. They were glued on my DDD breasts as if he had forgotten just how perfect they were.

"Boy, you better give me one of those cups before you make a mess." I casually took a coffee out of his hands, then glanced at his crotch, where his penis was bulging against the material of his sweatpants. I turned around to set the coffee cup on an end table, bending extra low so he could get a good view between my legs.

My plan was working perfectly. He wanted me as bad as I wanted him, but I still had to play along with this charade. If I jumped on him now and he started feeling guilty later, he would blame the whole thing on me. I was not about to have this explode in my face. No, I would just have to entice him until he made the decision on his own to come back to me.

"Umm, don't you think you should go put some clothes on?" His voice had taken on a lower tone—one I remembered well from the past. He was trying to keep his composure, but it wasn't working, because his hard dick had already given him away.

"Stop trippin', Rashad. Ain't nothing here you ain't seen before," I said flippantly.

"That was then and this is now. Things are different and you know it. Now, go cover yourself up." It was cute the way he was trying to act all faithful and everything. He might do a better job if he kept his eyes off my titties, though.

"Fine, I'll cover up," I said as he sat on the sofa

Instead of leaving the room to get dressed, I sat back on the arm of the sofa next to him. He sighed, but I knew it was just to hide the fact that he was dying to reach out and touch me. Mr. Cover Yourself kept stealing glances at my breasts as I spoke to him.

"So, you still didn't tell me. What should we do about the fact that I'm ovulating?"

"Oh, shit, that's right. We better hurry up and get you to the clinic." He tried to stand up, but I placed a hand on his shoulder to keep him in his seat.

"Yes, we should, but it's Saturday. The clinic is closed."

"Damn." His face fell.

I felt a little bad that he looked so disappointed, but it had to be done this way for my plan to work. This was the one good thing about Egypt being so controlling. Rashad let her handle all the details. She would have known that the clinic always had someone on call in case you were ovulating during hours they were closed. Rashad, on the other hand, didn't know this, which was just how I wanted it.

"I know. Bad timing, to be ovulating on a Saturday. But we have to do something. I just feel like today is the day I'm going to get pregnant."

He paused for a moment to think.

"Damn, maybe I should call Egypt. She'll know what to do."

"No!" I fought against a sudden rising panic. If she got involved, my plan would fall completely apart—not to mention that she might discover what I was up to. "We can figure this out, can't we? We shouldn't have to run to Egypt for everything." I leaned back a little so the towel rode up higher on my thighs. His eyes wandered downward.

"You do know there are ways I can get pregnant other than going down to the clinic, right?"

Okay, big boy, I put it out there. Now, let's see what you do with that.

Rashad lifted his head, his eyes no longer trying to burn a hole through my towel but staring me right in the face. "What are you trying to say, Isis?"

He knew exactly what I was trying to say. He just didn't want to say it out loud, and neither did I.

"What do you think I'm saying?" I leaned forward, staring right back in his face. I came out as the winner of our staring contest when he lowered his head, and his eyes found their way back to my sweet spot. I blatantly opened my legs so the poor guy could finally get a good look at what he'd been wanting to see.

Now, Rashad could have just gotten up, walked away, cursed me out, or even called Egypt, but he just sat there in silent contemplation. I watched as not a muscle moved in his face. It was like he was made of stone—all the way down to my favorite place, where I wanted him to be as hard as a rock.

I studied his face as he wavered between wanting me and wanting to do the right thing. It was either one or the other, and we both knew there would be no going back if we crossed that line.

"Are you saying what I think you're saying?"

"I'm saying we need to get your sperm inside while I'm ovulating."

"You're right, but what about Egypt?"

"What about her? She wants this baby just as much as you do. That's what this is all about, isn't it? The baby."

Again, he was lost in thought, but I took it as a good sign that he hadn't just flat-out said no. "Isis, if she ever found out . . ."

It was obvious we had a trust issue. He wanted to do it, but he was afraid I might throw it in my sister's face one day. What he didn't understand was that when I got finished putting it on him and had his baby, he was going to end up telling Egypt himself about us—right before we walked out the door.

"I'm not going to tell her," I replied with confidence. "Are you?"

He sat back in his chair. "You do know I love your sister, don't you?"

"This isn't about my sister. This is about me getting pregnant so I can have your child." I kept bringing up the baby, because I wanted to hammer home the one thing I knew was important to him. The one thing I could provide for him that my sister could not. "You do want this baby, don't you?"

"Yes, I want the baby." His voice sounded defeated as he patted the empty seat next to him on the sofa. "Come on, let's get this over with."

Finally! It was all I could do not to reach out and kiss him. But I waited. I wanted him to make the first move. Ten years from now, I wanted to be able to tell our children that their father seduced me, not the other way around.

I felt myself getting aroused just sitting so close to him, and I could tell by the way he was breathing that he was feeling it too.

"This is between us, right? We're just doing this to make a baby, right?"

I think he was asking himself the questions as much as he was asking me. If he needed to soothe his conscience by pretending this wasn't lust, I didn't mind.

"Just between us," I assured him.

"Okay, and we'll make sure you get to the clinic on Monday so that if you do turn up pregnant, no one will wonder how it happened."

I smiled and nodded. The fact that he was coming up with his own excuses now told me he was definitely down with the program.

He leaned in close, and that's when I knew he was about to kiss me. A million thoughts raced through my mind in a matter of a few seconds. Just that quick, I had planned the rest of the day. We were going to make love on the sofa; then I was going to make him breakfast. We'd go skinny-dipping in the pool like we'd done when we were young, and, of course, we'd make love in the water. We'd go shopping, and then if we weren't too tired, maybe we'd take in a movie and have dinner somewhere nice down in the West End. When we returned home, we'd leave a trail of clothes from the front door to the master bedroom. We'd make love until he didn't have anything left, and I'd fall asleep in his arms until noon.

I prepared for his soft, full lips to cover mine, but they never did, because, in an example of the world's worst timing, his cell phone began to play "The Beautiful Ones" by Prince. We both stared at each other, listening as the song played.

No! No! No! This can't fucking be happening! I am not going to let her ruin this!

"Don't answer it," I pleaded, but he still reached for the phone.

"I have to. It's Egypt's ring tone." He looked nervous, and the color drained from his cheeks. "You know your sister. She's just going to call back until I answer."

"Rashad, please don't answer it." I'm sure at this point I sounded desperate as hell, but I knew my opportunity to win him back was fading fast. I nearly collapsed when I saw him push the TALK button on his phone. He moved to the other side of the sofa, looking guilty.

"Hey, babe," he answered. "Umm, yeah, everything's fine. Well, except that Isis is ovulating."

What the hell did he tell her that for? Five minutes ago, he was foaming at the mouth at the thought of getting some pussy, and now he was fucking George "I Cannot Tell a Lie" Washington. I had a good mind to snatch the phone from him and tell Egypt exactly what was going on.

"Uh-huh. Oh, really? I didn't know that." Rashad paused, glaring at me. "You're right. I'm sorry. I should have called you."

I wished like hell I knew what she was saying, but from the way Rashad's expression had changed, I was pretty sure it wasn't good for me.

Rashad said, "Babe, you don't have to do that. We can handle this."

Please, please, please don't let her come home. If I could just get another day with him, I could turn this whole situation around again.

"Oh, she's right here." He handed me the phone. "She wants to speak to you."

I watched him walk halfway across the room to get away from me. I was so tempted to hang up the phone, but that would only make her suspicious.

"Hello?" I said, totally unsure of what her mood would be.

"Hey, you sure you're ovulating?" To my surprise, she sounded pretty calm. At least she didn't have a clue what was going on here.

"Mmm-hmm, my temperature was ninety-nine point one."

"Why didn't you call the on-call doctor like I told you?"

I stole a quick glance at Rashad. No wonder he looked so pissed. He knew I was lying. "You know what? I forgot all about that until you just said it. I'll call them right now."

"No," she said in her usual domineering way, "I'll call them. And I'm on my way back now, so I'll see you in about an hour and a half."

"Okay," I said, hoping she couldn't detect that I felt close to tears.

"Let me speak to Rashad."

I handed him the phone. When our eyes met, we both looked away.

Loraine
25

I hadn't heard much about my nomination for sorority president, so I invited about three dozen of the heavy hitters over for Sunday brunch in hopes I could improve my chances. I really did want to be the national president of the sorority, and whenever I decided I wanted something that I deemed obtainable, absolutely nothing could stop me.

Although my sorors came in all shapes and sizes, it was a foregone conclusion that they all loved to eat. So, there was no better way of getting their attention than feeding them some good old-fashioned Southern cuisine.

"Loraine, this chicken and waffles is out of sight," Elizabeth Williams, an elder stateswoman in the sorority, said as she filled her plate at the buffet for the second time.

"Ms. Elizabeth, I wish I could take credit for the food, but, girl, that's my husband's doing. He's the cook in our family. Would you believe he made everything himself?" I glanced over at Leon, who was pouring a Bloody Mary for a guest. When we made eye contact, he winked and gave me an inconspicuous thumbs-up. He really had been a big help in putting this party together.

Leon was an excellent cook, and in spite of our issues lately, he insisted that I should let him prepare the food instead of hiring a caterer. He knew how much this presidency meant to me, and to my surprise and relief, he had been extremely supportive. We'd been getting along better as a couple too. We'd spent many a night the past few months curled up on the sofa together, watching television, laughing, joking, and making love. If I could just get the man to slow down a little so I could get mine once in a while, I think I'd have the perfect marriage. In any case, I planned to give him a special thank-you in bed later that night.

"That handsome man over there cooked all this food?" Ms. Elizabeth dug her elbow into my side gently, grinning from ear to ear. "I'm impressed. Here I am thinking you kept the eye candy around just for the sex. Does he have a single father or older brother?"

We both laughed, but I'm sure it was for different reasons. Her because I'm sure she figured with a fine man like Leon I must be getting it good. And me because she was so far from the truth.

When things calmed down and everyone had their fill of food and drink, I invited all the sorors into my living room for coffee and dessert. There were about twenty women there, all from the mid-Atlantic region. Each one had a lot of clout when it came to influencing the votes of other sorors.

"Sorors!" Nancy Jericho, the Virginia state president said. "First off, I'd like to thank Soror Loraine Farrow and her husband, Leon, for inviting us to their lovely home and this fantastic brunch." There was some clapping, and I nodded my head in thankful acknowledgment. "This was the perfect way for those of you who don't know Loraine to meet her and see what type of woman and soror she is." She walked over and put her arm around my shoulder. "Now, I've known Loraine a lot of years, so I'm asking you what she won't. I'm asking you to help campaign for my soror and friend, Loraine Farrow, to be our next national president!"

There was a whole bunch of clapping, and everyone was on their feet. When they sat back down, Nancy stepped aside so I could be center stage and say a few words.

"I'm not going to pretend I don't want to be president, 'cause I do. But I think I want it for the right reason. I just hope all of you will help support me these next nine months—"

A piercing laugh interrupted me. I turned in the direction of the sound, where a few women on the couch were giggling and whispering. In the center of the group was Soror Alison Bedford, a skinny bitch in her early thirties who I personally couldn't stand. She was one of those women who just sat around and gave orders, because she was always fretting that she might chip a nail or her hair might get messed up.

My personal dislike for her went deeper, though. I had caught her on more than one occasion making eyes at Leon. I'm sure she probably thought she had a chance. What she needed to do was go back in the kitchen and get some more of that fried chicken, because if she wanted to steal my Leon from me, she was a good hundred pounds too light. The only reason I invited her in the first place was because of how powerful her mother, June Bedford, was in the DC metro chapter, which I was going to need to win the election.

When Alison realized that every eye in the room was fixated on her, wanting to know what the hell was so funny, she sat back on the sofa with an arrogant grin on her face. She cleared her throat, looking like she was happy to be the center of attention.

"Loraine, I think you lost something," she said, holding up a large purple thong with both hands. "This is yours, isn't it? It was stuck between the cushions."

All eyes in the room turned to me, and the good will I'd felt toward Leon suddenly evaporated. I flashed back to the underwear I'd found in my bed and realized that he and his bitch were up to their old shenanigans in my house. And to think I actually thought things were the best they'd ever been in our relationship. I could feel the blood rushing to my face, showing everyone in the room just how embarrassed I truly was.

Okay, girl. Keep it together.

Yes, I was embarrassed, but I was not going to let Leon, Alison, or anyone else take away the opportunity that was standing in front of me. I'd worked too hard and wanted it too much to let that happen. I always taught my clients that you can turn any negative into a positive if you have the right attitude. Believe me, I'd deal with Leon later, but first I had to show these women that their future president could deal with anything.

"Yes, it's mine," I said with a slight laugh. "My housekeeper was probably folding clothes on that sofa. Could you look and see if my red one fell between the cushions too? They're the ones my husband really likes." I tried to appear nonchalant as I walked over to Alison to retrieve what I wanted them to believe was mine. "What's wrong, Alison? You look rather surprised. Didn't you know they make thongs in my size?" A few of the larger sorors laughed with me. "Well, they do, and I look good in all of mine." I took the panties out of her hand and smiled. "You see, we big girls can be sexy too. Isn't that right, Ms. Evelyn?" I glanced at Evelyn Mathews, who was one of our sorority's most respected members and a fellow big girl. She pumped her fist in the air.

As I walked back to my original spot to finish my speech, I was sure I'd deflected most of the negative vibes in the room. I'd find out later in the evening that most of the sorors found Leon's and my relationship refreshing and that I'd handled the situation with the panties well. By then, I'd also had a chance to inspect the underwear a little better, and it appeared I wasn't lying when I said they were mine. I did have a pair the same color, same brand, and same size. The only thing that confused me was how my underwear got between the cushions. My housekeeper knew better than to be sitting in my living room when she was folding clothes. I could guarantee you, she and I were going to have words.

Taking that all into consideration, the day turned out pretty well. I'd gotten verbal support from almost every woman who came, including Alison Bedford, although I think she was just going along with her mother. My husband was off the hook, and I for one was very grateful for that. Looked like he was getting that blow job I owed him after all.

"Oh my God!" I let out a scream—not exactly a blood-curdling one, but still a scream.

I was standing in my bathroom about to take a shower and change into a baby-doll nightie. My intent was to get myself all sexy so that I could properly thank Leon for all the help he'd given me with my brunch this afternoon. As I changed, I caught a glimpse of myself in the full-length mirror, with my dress pulled up over my waist. I immediately let go of the dress. What I saw nearly made me break down and cry, which was something I almost never did.

"Everything all right in there?" Leon called from the adjoining bedroom. He sounded alarmed, but it wasn't as if he rushed into the bathroom to see if I was okay.

It took me a minute to regain my composure before I stomped out of the bathroom.

"You all right?" he asked, as if my scream wasn't a sign that something was very wrong.

"I give up!" I threw my hands in the air. "Obviously I'm not woman enough for you, so tell your bitch she can have you, 'cause I'm done. Do you hear me? Done!"

"Now what did I do?" He ran in to inspect the bathroom, then ran out. I had to give him credit; he was doing a good job of playing dumb.

"I should smack the shit out of you. That's what I should do." I raised my hand.

Leon held up his hand to stop me. "Don't go there, Loraine. Remember what happened last time. You put your hands on me, you're going to have to live with the consequences." He closed the fingers of his upturned palm into a fist.

I glared at him for a second. I was so angry that I actually contemplated whether getting one good hit in might just be worth "the consequences," as he'd just threatened.

As tempting as it was, I lowered my hand, remembering the knee-bending pain of my last beat-down. I still had a small tender spot on my chest from where he'd hit me.

"I hate your fucking guts, Leon. Get the fuck out my house."

"Oooooh boy, here we go again. I am getting so tired of this." He shook his head. "So, what did you find now? Wait, don't tell me. I'm hiding a woman in the medicine cabinet, right?"

"You think this shit is funny, don't you?"

"No, I think this is stupid. Especially since you won't tell me what I supposedly did." He looked like he was going to walk away, and I hated that shit.

"You been having some bitch in my house, and you don't even have the decency to make sure she goes home with her damn drawers."

"Loraine, what the hell are you talking about?"

I walked over to the clothes hamper and pulled out the purple thong that Alison Bedford found stuck between the cushions of our sofa. "I'm talking about this." I threw it right in his face.

"You know, maybe you are going a little crazy. You told me—and every woman in the room today—that this was yours." He tossed it to the ground.

"I thought it was," I said adamantly. "But I have only one purple thong."

Leon looked at me strangely. "And so what? What's that supposed to mean?"

I pulled up my dress. "I'm wearing it!" I said angrily.

Leon's face suddenly went blank. He pointed at the other thong on the floor. "Well, whose is that, then?"

"That's what I want you to tell me." I folded my arms and glared at him.

"I don't know. Maybe you have two pair and just didn't realize it? How the hell you put on a thong and don't know what color it is anyway?"

"The only time I notice the color is when I'm wearing something white, which I'm not today."

"Well, if you don't pay attention, then maybe you're mistaken. Maybe you do have more than one purple pair."

It was a good try on his part, but I wasn't going to let him weasel his way out of this. "I'm sure I have only one purple thong, Leon. So now I want to know, how did this get in the living room if I'm wearing my only pair?"

"I don't know." Leon looked befuddled. "I swear on my dead grandmother's grave, I don't know where those panties came from."

I couldn't believe he was swearing on his dead grandmother again. He was stooping to a new low with his lies lately. "You know what, Leon? Get out of my room."

He didn't even bother to protest. He let out a deep sigh, grabbed his blanket, and walked out.

I plopped down on my bed and fumed. I wanted to call Jerome and talk about my latest discovery, but I was too ashamed. Plus, Jerome was always threatening to whip Leon's ass, and I didn't want this thing to escalate into any type of felonious assault. Jerome was my friend, and he would watch my back no matter what, but talking about Leon would only set me up for problems later. Jerome would take my side, which might make me feel better in the moment, but if Leon and I worked things out, Jerome would forever hold a grudge.

Since I couldn't talk to my best friend, I needed another way to soothe my aching heart. I did something I had vowed to myself I wouldn't do: I picked up my cell phone and sent a text message to Terrance, asking him when we could get together again. If Leon wanted to play games, I'd show him how it went. I wasn't going to get mad. I was going to get even.

Jerome

26

It was a little after eight when I reached down from the bed to pick up my pants off the floor. I was searching through my pockets for my BlackBerry to call Loraine, to do a little bragging and let her know I was going to be late for work. There was no way I was going to make it back to Richmond from DC, get dressed for work, and make it to the office by nine o'clock. Hell, I'd be lucky if I made it by twelve. What I really wanted to do was call in sick so I could spend some more time with Ron, the hot new plaything lying next to me. I called him the Energizer Bunny, because he kept going and going and going.

I looked over at him sleeping next to me. *I think I'm in love.*

I know, I know, I was always telling people not to confuse good sex with love, but there is truly a thin line between the two, and Ron took me right there to the edge. My goodness, there was truly something to be said about youthful exuberance, because my forty-five-year-old body felt like it was twenty-five again.

I'd come to Washington, DC, late Saturday, trying to take my mind off Big Poppa, who'd canceled our Sunday get-together to be with his wife. To say I was pissed off was an understatement; I was absolutely furious. I'd waited all week to see that man, purchased the ingredients for his favorite foods, and turned down two dates. For him to cancel at the last minute was just wrong. He did, however, promise that next weekend was mine, and mine alone. I was still pissed off about the whole principle of the thing, but Ron had made me feel much better.

I'd met Ron last night at a reggae club up here in DC. Believe it or not, he was a player on Georgetown's basketball team. Not a starter yet, but now that I'd gotten to know him a little better, he could play on my team any day. I'd seen him and a few of his teammates come in the club about eleven. I wasn't really into young cats; matter of fact, the only reason I even noticed them was because of their height. How often do you see seven or eight men over six foot three together unless you're actually at a game?

Originally I wasn't even paying attention to him. If anything, I had my eyes on his teammate, the seven-foot center with *number one lottery pick* stamped on his forehead. Having a sponsor in the NBA would be a dream come true. He could take my lifestyle to a whole 'nother level. Unfortunately for me and Mr. Lottery Pick, it became apparent early in the night that he was into the ladies. He hadn't given me as much as a glance the entire evening.

Around midnight, I'd just about given up on finding a play-mate for the night, when I got this feeling that someone was watching me. Usually I caught the vibe pretty quickly and could hone in on the watcher, but whoever it was, he was pretty damn smooth, because I couldn't make eye contact to save my life. There was, however, one constant the entire night. Every time I looked around, there was Ron a few feet away, and once I realized that, I knew he was the one. He wasn't obvious at all. In fact, most of the time he was all up in a woman's face, but being gay, even if you are in denial, is like being part of a secret society. We always know how to spot other members of the club. To a casual observer, he was just a regular guy in the club, but in a subtle way, he was sending out a vibe I could pick up. I knew it was only a matter of time before he would confirm he was the person who was watching me.

It happened when I was in the men's room. I didn't even realize he'd come in until I turned around from the urinal to wash my hands, and there he was washing his. Although he was cuter in the light of the bathroom than he was in the darkness of the club, he was nowhere close to being fine. He did have a handsome ruggedness to him, though, that was very appealing, and he had a slammin' body.

"Hey," he said timidly.

"How you doing?" I asked, acknowledging his presence as I turned on the water. Neither of us looked at the other directly, although we were side by side. It was as if we were talking through the restroom mirror.

"I'm aw-ight. How're you?" he replied. His accent told me he wasn't from anywhere north of Richmond.

I wanted to laugh, because it was so obvious he meant for this conversation to continue when he started washing his hands for the second time.

"I'm okay," I said. "A little lonely in this big city. Can't wait to get back to Richmond."

"I know what you mean. Where I come from, Richmond is the big city."

"Oh, yeah? Where you from?"

"You ever heard of South Boston? Not the one in Massachusetts, but the one in Virginia."

"Man, you my homeboy. Of course I heard of South Boston. I'm from Danville. My momma's from South Boston." This was going to be easier than I thought.

"For real? You the first person I met from back home since I been here." He turned, offering me his hand so that we were no longer talking through the mirror. "My name's Ron. Ron Grier."

"Pleasure to meet you, Ron. My name's Jerome." I took his hand, and he gave me a firm shake.

I could feel the chemistry between us, and I really didn't want to let go of his hand, but he gave me no choice when he snatched his back as soon as another patron walked into the restroom.

There was an awkward silence between us as we exited the bathroom and headed back into the darkness of the club. His demeanor changed quickly. I could tell he was scanning the place to see if any of his teammates were watching us. Worried that he was only seconds away from losing his nerve, I made my move.

"Look, Ron, I'm about to get out of here, but if you wanna grab a cup of coffee or catch up on what's going on back home, I'm staying at the J. W. Marriott. Unfortunately, I'm leaving tomorrow morning, so if we're going to get together, it probably should be tonight."

After such a direct invitation, I totally expected him to walk out of that club with me, but instead of saying "Let's go," he just offered me his hand awkwardly. He didn't even look me in the eye. I followed his gaze over my shoulder, turning to see two women about his age approaching us. They stepped up to him and put their arms around his waist. The three of them seemed pretty cozy, so I'm sure they'd been waiting for him the whole time.

"Okay, homeboy. Have a safe trip back," he said.

"Ah, thanks." I shook his hand, feeling like I'd just been dismissed by this young boy as he and the two women walked back into the crowd.

Was he just playing me?

If he was, it was certainly a rare occurrence. My intuition about brothers on the down low was usually pretty damn good. I almost never misread the signals.

I dismissed the thoughts from my head quickly, because it didn't matter anyway. It wasn't like I'd ever see him again. I hadn't even given him my last name, let alone a room number where I was staying.

I took one more look around the club, and not seeing any more interesting prospects, I decided it was time to head out. Looked like it would be one lonely night in my hotel room—until one of the women who'd been with Ron approached me near the coat-check line.

"Ron wanted me to ask you what room that party was in."

Her question caught me off guard. "He asked what?"

"He wanted to know what room that party you invited him to was going to be in."

I gave her the number but wondered if I was doing the right thing. I was happy he had sent her to ask but was still a little unsure if I'd read him correctly. I hadn't told him it was a party, so what did it mean that he was calling it one? Maybe it was just part of his cover, and he was hoping I'd tell these girls it was a private party so he could ditch them with some of his teammates. Or maybe, I thought, I had seriously misread his vibe, and he was just some nice, simple straight kid from the South who really thought I was inviting him to a party. Either way, it was too late now, because I'd already given out my room number, and I had to be prepared that he might show up with the two women—or worse, with a bunch of drunken, homophobic college basketball players.

"So, are you and your friend coming to the party?" I asked.

She rolled her eyes. "No. Ain't no way I'm going to some stinky-ass old people's poker party. I can't stand cigars."

I smiled. My question was answered.

Later that night, about two-thirty, Ron showed up at my room. By three o'clock, we were in the bed buck naked. He had the most incredible, athletic body I'd ever been with and the stamina to go at it all night. Every time I thought we were done, he'd take a brief nap, then climb on top of me, and we'd be off to the races again.

I wasn't sure if he was taking a nap or finally asleep for good, but I figured I'd better call Loraine and let her know I was going to be late.

"Hey, girl," I said when I heard her very meek hello. "Look, I done run into a Greek god up here in DC, and I'm not sure if I'm gonna be back in time to come in."

"That's okay," she said. "I'm not sure if I'm going into work either."

"I hear that. You working from home today? I think I've got everything set with the Sullivan file. I'll e-mail it over to you if you'd like."

"No, don't e-mail me shit. I couldn't care less about the Sullivan project right now. I'm just gonna do me for a change."

Red flags went up in my mind.

"Do you? Loraine, what's wrong? You don't take days off to do you. And if I can paraphrase you, you are the company."

"I know that, Jerome. I just need some time, okay? I've got a lot on my mind."

"What's going on? It's not the sorority stuff, is it? I thought everything went well with your brunch."

"It did. They loved me. And they loved Leon too." The way she said Leon's name told me everything I needed to hear.

"Okay, what did he do now? He didn't put his hands on you again, did he?"

"No, but I wish I could put mine around his fucking neck," she growled.

"What'd he do?" I asked for the second time. "The way you been talking, I thought you was going to put him up for husband of the year."

"I'd like to put a stick up his ass; that's what I'd like to do." Loraine and Leon had their problems, but I wasn't used to hearing her talk about him like this. I sat up in the bed.

"Raine, will you tell me what the hell he's done?" I demanded.

"He's cheating on me, Jerome, okay? That son of a bitch is fucking some whore in my house like I don't even live here."

"Shut up!" I shouted. "You caught him with a woman in the house?"

"No, but I found that nasty bitch's panties a couple of times. If I had caught them in my house, I'd be calling you from my jail cell, 'cause I would have shot both their asses dead."

"Damn, I go out of town for one day and all hell breaks loose."

I glanced at Ron sleeping and thought, *Oh, well, at least one of us had a good night.*

"So, what you gonna do, Raine? You're not gonna stay with him after this, are you?"

She let out a pathetic laugh, but behind it I could hear that she really felt like crying. "First I'm gonna go sit down and finish my eggs Benedict and my mimosa. Then I'm going to take the handsome young man waiting at my table upstairs to the suite I rented so he can fuck my brains out. That's what I'm going to do."

"You go, girl. I'm impressed. Get some for me."

"I already have."

So, she'd finally done it! I had been trying to convince Loraine for the longest time that she needed to get rid of Leon or at least find herself a playmate. I was so happy to hear that she'd gone there.

"What about Leon? You gonna finally kick him to the curb?"

"Nope."

"No?" I shouted.

"Jerome, I don't have to tell you that in everything I do, I have to be better than a man at it. So I guess now I have to be better at being a dog. Besides, it's cheaper to keep him."

"Loraine, this is nothing to play with. You need to divorce his ass."

"I need him right now, Jerome. If I'm going to win the presidency, I need him, so unless things get worse, this is not open to discussion. We clear on that?"

"All right, if that's what you want." I was surprised she shut me down like that.

"Thank you. Now, my food's getting cold, so I'll talk to you later."

"Talk to you later, Raine."

Before she hung up, I heard a beep, so I clicked over. "Hello?"

"What did I do to make you treat me this way?" I recognized the voice right away. It was crazy-ass Peter. He was really starting to get on my nerves.

"Look, man, I'm not doing anything to you, so you need to stop calling me."

"I love you, Jerome. How could you hurt me like this?"

This guy was nuts!

"Man, you don't even know me. How the hell you gonna say you love me?"

"I know you. I know you better than I know myself. And I'm not going to let some young boy ruin it for me."

"What young boy?" How the hell did he know about Ron?

"Oh, so now you're gonna play stupid? Do you know how easy it would be for me to knock on your hotel room door right now?" Jesus Christ, he followed me! This son of a bitch was scary.

The hotel phone rang.

"You can go ahead and answer the phone. It's me."

I reached over to the phone, but then pulled my hand back.

"You're fucking following me?" I was starting to feel more

than a little paranoid, but I didn't want him to know. It would give him the upper hand if he thought I was scared. I had to remain aggressive. "You know what? You're a sick dude. You need to get yourself some help."

He laughed. "You think I'm crazy? Well, you're right. I'm crazy for you, and if I can't have you, nobody will."

Isis

27

I rolled over and woke up on Saturday morning to the sound of Egypt barking orders at the landscapers. The clock next to my bed told me it was almost noon. I probably could have slept until one or two in the afternoon, like I'd been doing the past few days, but I figured I'd probably be the next one on Egypt's shit list if I didn't get my butt up before she came looking for me.

I headed for the bathroom, prepared to do what had become my regular Saturday morning ritual, taking a pregnancy test. So far, we'd made three insemination attempts, and none had worked. I was really becoming concerned. What if I couldn't get pregnant? What if my age had caught up with me and made me barren like my sister? Rashad and Egypt were anxious for me to have a baby, but I wanted it just as bad. I was starting to think that without a baby, there would be no more chances to win back Rashad.

As it was, he had already started paying less attention to me since the stunt I pulled last month. Before that, he was so sweet, practically waiting on me hand and foot so I could relax while I was trying to have his baby. But once I got busted for lying about the clinic, Rashad was definitely keeping his distance. Egypt still waited on me, when she wasn't being a pain in the ass, but it wasn't the same.

The only good news was that he hadn't told Egypt about how I tried to seduce him. If she knew, World War III would have broken out in the house, and I don't think he wanted to take that risk. I think he kept it a secret because he knew that he wasn't entirely innocent. God, would I have loved to find out what would have happened if Egypt hadn't called.

Who am I kidding? I know exactly what would have happened. Egypt just didn't know how lucky she was.

But it didn't happen, because his desire to have a child outweighed everything, and if Egypt kicked me out, that would mean no baby. Yeah, he might have been staying away from me, but he was definitely still excited about the prospect of fatherhood. I could hear him and my sister talking about it all the time, which certainly wasn't helping my mood lately.

In the bathroom, I picked up a small cup and used it to collect my morning pee for the pregnancy test. The package insert said to pee on the stick, but I always used a cup because I didn't like the idea of getting it on my hand. I placed the cup on the counter and dipped the stick in, then left it there while I went about my morning routine.

Looking at myself in the mirror as I brushed my teeth, I wondered if the sadness I saw in my eyes was obvious to Rashad. I tried to ignore the negative chatter going on in my head, but it was hard, because it seemed to be happening more frequently lately.

You ain't pregnant. You know you can't get pregnant with no turkey baster. Now that you want to get pregnant, you won't get pregnant again, so you can just kiss your little dreams about you and Rashad good-bye.

I washed my face and brushed my hair. By then, enough time had passed for me to check the stick, which I was certain would once again be negative. In fact, I was so sure I wasn't pregnant that I barely glanced at it before I tossed it into the trash. Then it hit me. *Wait a minute. That was a positive sign!*

I reached into the trash can, rummaging around until I had the stick in my hand. I looked down, and sure enough, there was a plus sign on the stick. I jumped up in the air and let out an excited yelp. Suddenly, there was hope for me and Rashad.

I ran back into the bedroom and threw on a robe—no more falling-towel tricks for me—then rushed down the stairs, stick in hand. I was moving so fast, it's a miracle I didn't slip and break my neck.

I headed right to the family room, where I knew Rashad would be watching college football. He'd been talking about the big game between Florida and Georgia all week. Originally, I'd planned to watch it with him, as a way of spending some alone time with him. Egypt never watched sports with him, so I figured I could use that opportunity to rebuild his trust and hopefully chisel away at that wall he'd put up between us. Now I didn't need to worry about that. The pregnancy test I held in my hand would be more like a sledgehammer, and in no time at all, the wall would come tumbling down.

I stepped into the room, where Rashad was reclining in his La-Z-Boy chair, eyes glued to the TV.

"Good game?" I asked, trying to contain my excitement.

"Hell, yeah. Georgia's up by three in the first quarter." He barely glanced over at me as he spoke.

"They in Athens or Gainesville?"

"Gainesville, but Georgia's getting seven points on the spread." He finally turned his head in my direction. "You know, I forgot you liked football. You want a beer?" He lifted the top of the small cooler next to him.

I casually placed a hand on my stomach. "No, thanks, but we should definitely celebrate after the game."

"If Georgia wins, I'll buy you and Egypt the biggest steaks in Richmond."

"What about if they lose?"

"If they lose, ain't nothing to celebrate. I got two grand on this game."

"Oh, I don't know about that. I might have something else we could celebrate."

He raised his eyebrows, but I couldn't read his expression. Either he was beginning to understand what I was hinting at, or he was wondering what scheme I was up to now. I spoke up fast before he decided it was another trick and put his guard up again.

"Do you think you might feel like celebrating if I'm pregnant?" I asked.

"If you're—" He stopped speaking abruptly, and I could see the awareness dawning on his face. "Wait a minute. You're pregnant?" He was out of his seat and by my side in a flash.

"Yes, Rashad, I'm pregnant!"

I expected him to joyfully throw his arms around me, but instead they stayed folded across his chest. "Isis, if this is another lie . . . I don't have time for your games today."

Damn, he really didn't trust me at all, and it was starting to annoy me. He could act like I was the one playing games, but it's not like he didn't want to hit it that day too.

"I'm not playing, Rashad. I'm really pregnant."

He turned back to the television like he had already made up his mind that I was full of shit. "Who am I supposed to be, Bo-Bo the Clown? You haven't even been to the doctor yet."

I held up the stick. "I just took a home pregnancy test. This test is ninety-nine percent accurate, and that plus sign means I'm pregnant. Check it for yourself." I tossed it at him. "You convinced now?" I asked as he picked up the stick and examined it.

"You weren't lying?"

"No, Rashad, I wasn't. You're going to be a daddy."

It took a minute for the information to register, but once it did, he was all over the place. He jumped up on the La-Z-Boy and started to do the Running Man. Then he jumped to the floor and wrapped his arms around me and picked me up off my feet. I hugged him back, giggling.

Seeing the joy on his face made this whole process well worth any sacrifice I might have made. I don't think I'd ever done anything in my entire life that had made someone else this happy. There was no doubt in my mind he was going to make a great father—and we were going to make great parents.

"I can't wait to tell Egypt," he said, spinning me around.

"Tell Egypt what?" My sister walked into the room, looking at us like we'd lost our minds.

Rashad put me down and ran over to her, but her eyes were still locked on me. "Excuse me," she said, "but that's my husband you're holding on to." After Rashad's excitement, her stern voice was like a bucket of ice-cold water over my head.

"We were just celebrating, baby," Rashad explained.

"Celebrating what, a football game? You know better, Rashad." She cut her eyes at me again.

"Baby, it's not like that. She's pregnant." He showed her the stick.

In an instant, her face lit up. "Oh my God! We're pregnant! We're pregnant!" Now she was jumping all over the place right along with Rashad, and I was left standing by myself. When they embraced and shared a passionate kiss, I wished I had morning sickness so I could throw up on Egypt's shoes.

"We're pregnant, baby," she said to him with tears in her eyes.

Sorry, I know the moment was supposed to be touching and all, but I wanted to push my way in between them and remind her, *No, bitch, I'm pregnant.*

I bullied my way into their little private party. "I'm so excited, Rashad. It's going to be a boy. I just know it."

I knew I'd made a mistake as soon as I saw the look on Egypt's face. "Don't forget, you're a surrogate. This is our baby, not yours. Don't go getting attached. We're paying you good money to do this."

I couldn't afford to make her an enemy just yet—at least not until I was paid in full—so I waved off her warning as if she'd totally read me wrong. "Girl, I'm just so happy to be a part of this. Of course I know it's going to be your baby, Egypt."

Her shoulders relaxed. "Yeah, you're right. I'm sorry. But you need to lie down. You're going to have to get plenty of rest."

I nodded, gladly heading back upstairs to get some more sleep. I was sure I'd be dreaming of the look on Rashad's face. I'd just made him the happiest man on the planet, and it was only a matter of time before he realized that it was me, not my sister, who did that for him.

Loraine

28

I sat down in a chair on the other side of the waiting room, purposely keeping my distance from Leon, who was reading a magazine with his legs crossed. We'd been living under the same roof for the past two months, but I slept in the master bedroom and he stayed in the guestroom. Not that he liked our arrangement, but what choice did he have? He could either live by my rules or get the hell out, 'cause I was done. As far as I was concerned, all he was good for was as an occasional escort to a party. Once I won the election, I was going to find me someone else. Shit, I didn't really even know why I'd agreed to come here today other than, as he put it, to call his bluff.

"Mr. and Mrs. Farrow, you can come in now," a well-dressed sister in her early fifties said as she stood by the door. I glanced across the room at Leon, who smiled at me confidently. I rolled my eyes. What the heck was he smiling about? He was the one who was about to be put on blast for cheating on me.

You see, this all started about a week ago, when Leon escorted me to my sorority's annual ball. I have to give him credit; when he wanted to, Leon could be a first-class asset. Not only did he place me on a pedestal and make every person in the room think we were the happiest couple they'd ever met, but also every time I pointed out someone who might not vote for me, he'd ease his way over and work her husband, inviting him to play golf or go fishing on his boat. He'd even set up a husbands' poker game. I can't begin to tell you how well this worked, because the next thing I knew, their wives were all up in my face, trying to set up lunches and teas.

Not that his kindness was new. He'd been doing the same thing at home. He'd been so nice to me as of late, you'd think he was running for Pope, the way he was cooking, cleaning, and running my errands. That night, he must have told me a thousand times how beautiful and sexy I looked. I can't lie; we both had a really good time. Under normal circumstances, he would have gone to sleep a very happy man; but when we got home, to his surprise, it was his and hers bedrooms again. You should have heard him begging and pleading for me to give him another chance. I didn't pay him no mind. I just went upstairs and closed my door.

About a half hour later, there was a knock on my bedroom door, which I now kept locked just for this reason.

"Hey, Loraine, can you open the door, please?" he pleaded.

"What do you want? Go to bed." I hated when he did this, always when I was almost asleep. I covered my head with a pillow.

He knocked again, this time lighter, probably with a knuckle. "I just want to talk to you, baby. Please open up." He really sounded pitiful.

"Leon, I'm tired. Whatever it is, it can wait 'til the morning. Now go to bed!"

"I'm not going to bed until I have my say. We can do it face-to-face or through this door. The choice is yours."

I sat up with an aggravated sigh. "Go to bed!" I threw the pillow at the door.

"Baby, I just want you to know I'm not messing with no woman. I swear to God, I don't know where those panties came from. You've got to believe me. I swear on my dead grandmother's grave—"

That's when I had had enough. I didn't feel like listening to him calling on his dead grandmother yet again, so I got out of bed, unlocked the door, and then snatched it open. Leon almost fell in on his face. When he straightened up, I noticed he was wearing a smoking jacket and his silk PJs.

"Who the hell are you supposed to be, Hugh Hefner?"

"Heff ain't got nothin' on me, baby. So, how's my big sexy?" He was talking all smooth, looking at me seductively. He didn't want to talk about our relationship. All he wanted was sex. Leon mistakenly thought sex would bring us back together.

What he didn't understand, and quite frankly most men don't understand, is that when women get mad, all their parts get mad. In other words, Big Sexy's Sex Shop was closed!

"I'm not your big sexy anymore, so go call your bitch."

His so-called seductive smile disappeared. "Loraine, I swear—"

"I know, I know, you swear on your dead grandmother. . . . Oh, please, Leon. Give it a rest, will you? Stop lying and stop calling on your grandmother. That poor woman is probably turning over in her grave right now."

"Loraine, it's been two and a half months. I need you, baby. We need you." Leon looked down at his crotch, then back up to me. Pitiful. That was the look that used to melt me down, but it didn't work this time.

"No. You should've thought about that shit when you was fuckin' some bitch in my bed. But, nooooo, it got so good to you, you even had her in our living room. Where else in my house did you screw her?" Just thinking about some other woman in my house had me livid.

"Nowhere, dammit!" he exploded, grabbing me by the shoulders and shaking me. "I don't know where the fuck that shit came from! All I know is that I want my wife back! Now, tell me, what's it going to take so my life can get back to normal?"

He wasn't hurting me, but it was scary the way he was screaming like a madman as he shook me. I wasn't about to let him know he had rattled me, but the way his veins were popping out of the side of his neck, you would have thought he was about to kill me. I had to be careful that whatever I said didn't escalate this situation, because he looked like he was about to snap, and I did not want to be the victim of a murder/suicide.

"You wanna know what it's gonna take?"

"Yes!" he shouted.

"It's going to take some counseling. You—we—need some help, Leon. We can't do this by ourselves anymore. We both have too many issues. So, if you want us to have a chance, we have to go to some type of counseling."

It was almost unfair. I had just placed him in the ultimate catch-22. The last thing Leon would ever do was go see a shrink. He'd said it a million times when I'd suggested it in the past, when he was clearly going through depression over losing his uncle. He was like most black men; he didn't believe in letting anyone inside his head.

He took a long, deep breath, letting go of my shoulders. It looked like he was calming down, probably trying to think of a way out of this quandary he had now gotten himself into.

"You want us to go to a marriage counselor?"

"Yes, Leon, I do."

"Okay, I can do that," he said.

"Huh?" I was stunned. "What'd you say?"

"I said I'll do it. If that's what it'll take to show you how serious I am, I'll do it. I'll go to counseling. Matter of fact, I'll even make the damn appointment."

I couldn't help it. A short laugh escaped my lips. His actions were getting so ridiculous they were funny. If I didn't know better, I'd think he believed them himself. "Stop lying, Leon. You are not going to make any appointment."

"I'm not lying. You'll see." I was more surprised by this than when I thought he was going over the deep end a few minutes ago.

"Call my bluff."

So, although I didn't let Leon in my bedroom that night, there I was at a marriage counselor with him three days later. As far as I was concerned, it wasn't going to do any good, but Leon seemed as happy as a pig in slop.

The therapist, Dr. Robena Marshall, was a highly respected marriage counselor in the Richmond-Petersburg area. I'd looked her up online, mostly because I didn't trust Leon not to have one of his friends play therapist to trick me. I still couldn't believe he'd actually made the appointment and shown up.

"So, why are we here today?" Dr. Marshall asked a few seconds after we were seated.

Leon and I glanced at each other, but neither of us spoke. We were sitting on a leather sofa across from the doctor, but I made sure he was on one end of the sofa and I was on the other, so that told a story in itself. She looked from one of us to the other, giving our physical space a pointed look. She then wrote something on a notepad.

"Okay, let's not all speak up at the same time." I guess that was supposed to be an icebreaker. Personally, I thought it was rude. "Leon, why don't you start?"

I turned my entire body in his direction when he started to speak. "I love my wife. I love her more than anyone in the world. But my wife doesn't want to be physical anymore. We're just living together like roommates. We're there in name only, and I don't like it one bit. Not at all."

"I see." She glanced at me, her expression neutral, then back to Leon. "When was the last time you two were intimate?"

"It's been two and a half months."

"And how does that make you feel?"

"Like I'm less than a man." As I listened to Leon pour out his heart like he was the victim here, I felt myself getting angry. "Making love to your woman is a natural part of being a man. When she rejects me, I feel worthless. Like she's tearing me apart or ripping at my self-esteem."

"This is bull!" I stood up, pointing a finger at him. "You know why I haven't given you any, and it damn sure ain't got nothing to do with your self-esteem. Why don't you tell her about the panties?"

"Loraine, would you please sit down?"

I ignored the doctor. "Tell her, Leon. Tell her about the panties I found in my bed. Tell her about the panties my sorority sister found stuck between the cushions of my sofa. Tell her."

"I told you I don't know how those panties got there," Leon protested.

"Loraine, I must insist that you take your seat," Dr. Marshall ordered.

I glared at her like I wasn't about to take orders from her, but then I sat down anyway. I felt like knocking both of them out right there in her office, but I didn't want her to take his side any more than she already had.

"Both of you calm down," Dr. Marshall said, still as cool as a cucumber. "Now, Leon, you're saying you don't know anything about these panties, correct?"

"Yep." That lying bastard. I wanted to reach across and slap that lie right out of his mouth.

"So, where do you think they came from?" In all the times we'd fought about this, he'd never offered an explanation for how else they might have gotten there. I was anxious to hear what story he would concoct for the good doctor.

"Dr. Marshall, if I knew the answer to that, I wouldn't be paying you a hundred dollars an hour to help me get back with my wife."

"What makes you think she's going to help you get me back?" I asked. "I don't even like you anymore, Leon. In fact, I'm planning on divorcing you."

Leon's face registered shock, but when I looked toward the doctor, her face was a blank canvas. Either she'd heard it all before and wasn't surprised, or they taught them at whatever school a therapist goes to how to mask their true feelings.

"Loraine, it sounds like you've already made up your mind. Don't you want to try to work things out? Otherwise, why did you come?"

I didn't answer, because I was thinking about this situation. There was a side of me that didn't want to get a divorce, but my proud side couldn't take any more of Leon's shit.

"Okay, Loraine. Besides finding the underwear—which Leon says he didn't put there—what else bothers you about your husband? What other reason do you have to divorce him?"

Leon folded his arms, smirking like he didn't have a care in the world. He had no idea what was coming, but since I was still worked up, I decided to drop a bomb right on his head. "The sex is horrible."

"Huh? Are you serious?" Leon fixed his eyes on me with this incredulous stare, like he couldn't believe his ears. I just rolled my eyes at him, and he turned to the doctor. "And she had the nerve to call me a liar. I thought we were supposed to be honest."

"You are supposed to be honest. What makes you think she's not being honest?"

I sat back and relaxed a bit. For the first time, she sounded like she might be on my side.

Leon stuck his chest out. "You don't understand, Doc. Loraine's body is like a canvas, and when we're in the bedroom,

I'm Leonardo da Vinci. Our lovemaking is like fine art, a master-piece."

"I see." She still wore that blank mask, but I wondered if she was holding back a laugh. Leon might have been trying hard to save our marriage, but his flowery description was taking things a little too far.

As for me, I just folded my arms and studied the titles of the books on her shelves, wishing I had never suggested a visit to a shrink. I had expected Leon to refuse, but I had no idea that I'd end up being the one who didn't feel like talking about what was in my head. But now that I was here, the doctor wasn't about to accept silence from me.

"So, what is it, Loraine? You don't agree with Leon's description of your lovemaking?"

I shook my head. "No. I don't think I was in the room when that picture was painted."

"So, how would you describe it?"

"To use a metaphor like him, I see myself as a high-performance race car, and Leon's the driver. But he only knows how to drive one speed, and that's fast. He has no clue how to maneuver through the curves, so he crashes the car before the race ends—every time." I looked at him, daring him to deny it. I wasn't expecting him to sound so vulnerable when he answered.

"If I was so bad, why didn't you say something?"

"I've tried to tell you, Leon, but you just wouldn't listen. You can't tell me how I'm supposed to feel. I'm supposed to tell you."

"So, what are you trying to say?"

"For the past few years, you've been prematurely ejaculating. I can't remember the last orgasm I had with you."

Leon sat there looking like I just stabbed him in the heart. "You don't have orgasms with me? Well, why didn't you tell me?"

He was almost in tears, and though things were nowhere near resolved, I was starting to feel bad. I softened my tone a little. "It wasn't always that bad. We used to have a lot of fun in the bed-room when we first got married."

"My uncle."

"What about your uncle, Leon?" the doctor asked.

"It started right around the time my uncle died, didn't it?" It took me a second to realize he was talking to me.

"I never thought about it, but, yes, it did start around then." I turned to the doctor. "He was very close with his uncle. Before he died, Leon had been his caregiver."

"I see. Sometimes death can cause mental trauma that's related to our sexual psyche." Dr. Marshall wrote something in her pad before she continued. "How about if you start going out on dates, without any sex? You can touch, you can fondle, but no actual intercourse. Just old-fashioned petting. Couples have told me this method lights up a fire in them like being teenagers."

"Well, I'd like that," Leon said, brightening a little. "How about it, Loraine?"

I shook my head. "That's not the only reason I'm sick of you, Leon. Don't think I will ever forgot that you put your hands on me. I still have a mark on my chest where you hit me." I turned to the doctor. "He's an abusive man."

The doctor glanced at Leon out of the corner of her eye, then wrote something in her notebook.

"Oh my goodness, Loraine. That's not the whole story and you know it. You put your hands on me first," Leon responded. "I was only defending my—"

"Wait a minute," Dr. Marshall interrupted, her eyes on me. "Are you the aggressor? Do you hit your husband first?"

"Well, ah . . ." Damn! This was not going well at all. How did I go from being the victim to looking like the bad guy?

"That's a yes or no question."

"Yes, but you see, I'm a businesswoman, and I'm used to getting on people when they mess up. Sometimes Leon gets disrespectful, and I'm not used to taking crap off of people. I always deal with them head-on, but with Leon, he knows how to push my buttons and he doesn't give. So sometimes he makes me so angry I fly off the handle and smack him."

Dr. Marshall shook her head, revealing a clear opinion for the first time. "That's a no-no. Neither one of you should be physically harming the other."

"You're right. I was wrong," Leon admitted. "Even if she hit me first, I should have walked away. I'm sorry I ever laid hands on her, and I promise I will never hit her again. This is my wife, and I love her. I'm willing to do whatever it takes to win her back. I want my wife, and I want to save my marriage."

"Okay, say that to your wife, not to me."

"Loraine"—Leon turned toward me—"I'm sorry for all the pain I caused you in the past, but I swear I never disrespected you and brought no woman to our bed or in our house. I still don't know how those underwear got there. I swear I'll try to change in the bedroom. You're a good woman, and my life has been better for you having been in it. Please, baby, give us a chance."

I sat there quietly, lacing and unlacing my fingers. I was kind of touched by the way Leon humbled himself in front of another woman, even if she was our therapist. He was laying down all his cards on the table.

"What can I do to make our marriage better?" Leon asked.

I sat there, trying to formulate my answer. "Well, for one, you're going to have to start talking to me more. I'd like to be kissed and held more. I have to build up our trust again, behind these panties. I don't want to have sex again until I'm ready."

Leon nodded in agreement.

Dr. Marshall glanced at her watch, then spoke up. "Well, I think we've made some progress. I'd like to see both of you again next week. How about Thursday?"

"That's fine," I said. I wasn't sure how I felt about everything that had transpired, but I know I felt relieved as hell to be getting out of there. I stood up, and Leon and I headed for the door.

The doctor said, "Leon, I think there are some issues that are a lot deeper than any of us think. I'd like to see you again alone."

Leon said, "If you think it will help with me and Loraine, I'll do whatever it takes."

Wow, did he just agree to go to therapy on his own?

"Loraine, I think you could use a few sessions too. I think you have some anger issues."

I looked at her and concentrated hard to keep my expression as neutral as hers. "No, thank you, Dr. Marshall. My anger issues will be just fine, as long as I don't find any more panties in my house and he don't call me a bitch."

Isis

29

I sat at the table in Momma and Daddy's house in Hollis, Queens, feeling full and satisfied. From the look on Rashad's face, I could tell he was just as happy as I was to be sitting here eating Momma's mouthwatering turkey, instead of that dried-out thing Egypt tried to pass off on us last Thanksgiving. Momma had laid out a spread of turkey, ham, sweet potatoes, carrots, collard greens, stuffing, and candied yams, and I was so glad that my morning sickness had recently stopped. I don't know why they called it morning sickness anyway, since I had been throwing up at all times of the day and night. But now that I could finally hold down some food, nothing was going to stop me from filling my plate three times, not even the disgusted stares I was getting from Egypt. Four months into my pregnancy, she was still as controlling as ever, but I'd be damned if I was gonna let her control what I put in my mouth with all this good food sitting in front of me.

Part of the reason she was in such a bad mood was because she hadn't really wanted to come home for Thanksgiving in the first place. She claimed it was because she didn't think it would be good for me or the baby to make the long trip up from Virginia. Something told me that wasn't her real reason, so I called her on it. I checked with the doctor, who told me that it's safe to travel all the way up until the eighth month. That's when I knew for sure that Egypt's excuse was a lie, because after I got the doctor's permission, she just started coming up with other excuses for why we shouldn't come to New York for the holiday. The only reason she finally agreed that we should all go home was because I told her flat out that if she didn't, I was taking a Grey-hound bus to New York. Even then, it was Rashad who an-nounced that we'd all be going to see Momma and Daddy, because he didn't want me on no bus.

Truth is, I think now that I was starting to show, Egypt didn't want people seeing me, because it would just be a reminder of her own inability to get pregnant. If she had her way, she would have locked me in a windowless room until I gave birth, and then she would pop up with the baby in her arms, like I had nothing to do with it. That wasn't happening, though. I was the one carry-ing Rashad's baby in my womb, and sooner or later, everyone would have to acknowledge that fact.

Rashad, however, was already acknowledging it on a daily basis. Every time he looked at my stomach, he would beam with pride, and he told me at least three or four times a day how grateful he was that I was carrying his child. So, while Egypt was busy trying to control my every waking moment, Rashad was waiting on me hand and foot. Tonight at dinner was no excep-tion.

"Can I get you any more yams, Isis?" He reached for the bowl and passed them to me. I spotted Egypt rolling her eyes, and I couldn't resist the urge to do something I knew would annoy her.

"No, me and my little candy dumpling are saving room for Momma's cobbler." I unbuttoned my stretch jeans and lifted my blouse, patting my growing belly. This always brought a smile to Rashad's face.

Daddy smiled and said, "That's right. Eat up. I want my grandbaby to be nice and fat."

Momma, always the more judgmental one, had a very differ-ent reaction. "Isis, pull your top down," she snapped. "You know better than to do that at the dinner table."

Egypt let out a disgusted sigh. "Welcome to my world, Momma. You should see how spoiled she's getting since she's been pregnant."

My father had seen enough fights between me and my sister to know that this could turn ugly in a hurry, so he changed the subject before I had a chance to jump down Egypt's throat.

"Well, I just hope it's a boy," Daddy said. "I want me a grandson, so stop calling him by sissy names. He ain't nobody's candy dumpling. He's gonna be a man's man."

Momma took the hint and steered away from the touchy subject of my supposedly bad behavior. She asked what she thought would be an innocent question. "So, what do you want?"

"Personally, I want a boy," I answered without thinking. "I've always wanted a little boy."

"Hold on!" Momma shifted her attention to me. "You're just supposed to be the surrogate, and this is *their* baby. Or have you forgotten that?"

Damn, what did I open my mouth for? I suddenly felt like a little girl again. I was always the one getting scolded by Momma, even when we were kids. And Egypt was always right there, watching with a satisfied smirk on her face, just like she was doing now.

"No, I haven't forgotten, but—"

Momma didn't even give me a chance to finish defending myself before she was on top of me again. "This baby is theirs. You may be carrying it, but you are the baby's aunt, not its mother."

"I know, Momma. But—"

"Now, it's a nice thing you're doing for them, but those are your sister's eggs growing into that child. You are just an incubator, so let's not get confused."

Oh, no, she didn't just call me an incubator. I mean, I know she always took Egypt's side over mine, but did she really have to go and disrespect me like that? I felt my face getting hot. I was about ready to explode.

"Karen," my father called out, intervening once again. The room fell silent. My father was a man of few words, but when he spoke, especially with that telltale bass in his voice, everyone listened. "Not at my dinner table, okay?"

Momma sounded humbled as she answered, "Okay, Bobby, but I just want to make sure things are clear. Last thing we need is any more confusion in this family."

I loved my mother, but she sure had a knack for hurting my feelings. Her comment about confusion was an obvious reference to the time I lost control for a while after I found out Tony was married. This time, though, I was in total control, and I was going to make sure she—and everyone else at the table—knew it. "Hmm, confusion, huh? I hate to tell you this, Momma, but if you're confused, it sure ain't my fault."

She raised her eyebrows and opened her mouth, but no words came out. Momma was probably too shocked that I was speaking back to her like this after my father had basically told us all to stop it. I didn't care, though. I was not no incubator, and I'd be damned if I was going to let anyone treat me like I didn't matter.

I gave Egypt an evil smirk, then turned back to Momma. "Or maybe you've been lied to, 'cause these is *my* eggs the baby came from."

My mother's face fell as she looked to Egypt for answers. Nobody spoke, not even my father.

"Is this true?" my mother snapped at Egypt.

The best Egypt could do was nod. She kept her eyes glued to the table, looking like she just wanted to crawl in the corner and die.

Rashad made an attempt to save her the embarrassment of explaining. "Mom, as you know, Egypt's uterus is too weak to support a pregnancy." He paused, but still no one else said a word. "What you don't know, from what I'm gathering, is that her eggs drop very infrequently."

From what he was gathering? So, he had no idea that Egypt was telling lies to my mother and probably to other people, too, about the fact that her eggs were no good. My sister was scandalous! But still, Rashad was sticking by her side, and it was starting to make me a little sick.

"Because of this," he explained patiently as he held her hand, "we weren't able to create any embryos to implant in Isis. So we are very thankful to her for letting us have her egg."

Instead of yelling at Egypt for telling lies, like she would have done to me, my mother wrapped her arm around Egypt's shoulder and kissed her.

"Isis, I'm sorry," Momma said.

Finally, I thought with a smile, she was offering me a little appreciation, but it didn't last long. "It's a wonderful thing you're doing for your sister and Rashad, but what I said before still stands. You can't get attached. This pregnancy is only for you to carry the baby. Don't try to bond with it. This is just going to be your niece or nephew."

I was so sick of Egypt getting all of Momma's affection. Shoot, I was the one saving the day and having the baby, but she still made me sound like some irresponsible fool who wouldn't know which way was up if she wasn't lecturing me about it.

"I know it's going to be my niece or nephew," I said, resisting the urge to roll my eyes and suck my teeth at Momma.

"We are just so appreciative of Isis having the baby for us," Rashad said to break some of the tension in the air.

"Yes, and I'm glad to do it for them." Suddenly, I felt something squirm inside of me. "Ooh!" There was another faint fluttering, and I placed my hand on my stomach when I realized what was happening.

Rashad jumped up. "Are you all right, Isis?"

"I'm fine. The baby just moved for the first time."

"No shit?" Rashad sounded so excited until he looked up at my father. "Excuse my French, Mom and Pop. Can I feel it, Isis?"

I leaned back and placed his hand on my abdomen in the place where I felt the baby. "There it goes again!" I said happily.

He stared at my stomach and waited a few seconds, but nothing else happened. "I guess the baby's still too small," he said. "I didn't feel anything." He moved his hand away, but I knew he was just putting on an act in front of everybody. Maybe he didn't feel it kick, but you can't tell me he didn't feel the same electricity I felt when his hand was covering the baby we'd made together. Oh, yes, I was going to get my man back.

Egypt

30

It was the day after Thanksgiving, the busiest shopping day of the year, and my feet were killing me from walking the mall. Momma, Isis, and I had been over at Green Acres Mall since six o'clock, taking advantage of all the early morning department store sales. It was sort of a family tradition, but to tell you the truth, I wished we had left Isis's spoiled behind at home. I swear she must have thought I was her personal servant the way she ordered me around—in front of my mother, no less.

"I gotta pee," she whined as we walked out of Ashley Stewart. "Where's the bathroom?"

"You always gotta pee. Can't you wait until we get to Red Lobster so I can sit down? My feet are killing me."

"I'm sorry, but this baby—you know, the one you wanted so bad—keeps pushing down on my bladder." She dropped her three shopping bags at my feet. "I would think you'd be a little more understanding. If I hold it too long, I might get a urinary tract infection, and that wouldn't be good for the baby, now, would it?"

I put my hand up to quiet her.

"Just go 'head and pee so we can go sit down and eat. We'll be right here." I pointed at the restroom sign, praying that she wouldn't ask me to come in with her. I was so sick of her acting like she was carrying Baby Jesus. The woman was only four and a half months pregnant, and she'd already started waddling around like she was ready to drop her load.

"Okay, I'll be back."

I watched her walk away as I sat down on a bench. I didn't

know what was worse, the aching in my feet or the headache I was getting from being around my demanding sister. I know we offered her money to have this baby, but she was making us pay in more ways than that. You should have seen the way she could manipulate Rashad to do her bidding. And as if I wasn't waiting on her lazy ass enough, he was downright ridiculous about it. If that woman got my husband out of my bed after midnight one more time to go out and get her a Cherry Coke Slurpee and one of those nasty 7-Eleven hot dogs, I was going to scream. I mean, this baby meant a lot to me and Rashad, but this shit had to stop. She was not about to run me or my husband ragged trying to satisfy her every whim. I was starting to feel like a victim of extortion.

I know I sound ungrateful, perhaps even bitter. Don't get me wrong; I was happy she'd decided to make the sacrifice and have our baby, but this situation was much deeper than that. I didn't know I'd have these feelings of envy and, sometimes, downright animosity. I never thought I'd feel this way, but, yes, I was jealous of my sister—even though I was the one with the husband, the big house, and the fancy cars. I was jealous of her for being the one with the ability to get pregnant.

What really made me angry about the entire situation was that deep down, she knew it. I could see it in her eyes and behind that smirk she tried to hide. She was playing this pregnancy, my emotions, and Rashad's need to be a father to the hilt, and there was nothing I could do about it. But I could sure complain about it, and my mother was the perfect sounding board.

"Momma, this is ridiculous. This is the fifth time she's been to the bathroom since we left home. She is so spoiled." I turned to my mother, who was sitting next to me. Her silence and the look she gave me spoke volumes. She'd been this way ever since last night, when the baby supposedly kicked. All she did for the rest of the night was watch and observe without a word, other than a few whispers to my father. That much silence was totally out of character for her.

"What, Momma?"

"I didn't say anything." She looked away.

"You didn't have to. Now, what's on your mind?" I stepped directly in front of her, and she finally spoke.

"Do you trust your sister?"

I wanted to say, *About as far as I can throw her,* but I didn't want to admit that to my mother, so instead, I said, "Yes. Why?"

"No reason. Just wanted to know."

My mother never asked a question for no reason.

"Don't 'no reason' me. I know that look. What, you think I'm being too hard on Isis because she's pregnant, right?"

She hesitated, and I saw something in her expression that I'd almost never seen in my life. My mother looked like she was contemplating things before she spoke her mind. Finally, she said, "What I want to know is why, of all people, would you ask your sister to have your baby? I thought you took her in to help her start a new life. How did she end up having your baby?"

Oh, boy, here we go. I had avoided talking in detail to my mother about this whole surrogacy thing, because I knew she would have something to say about it. She knew how much I wanted a child, but she also had very strong opinions about me and my sister. In fact, she was the one who warned me about taking Isis into my home in the first place. She just didn't think it was smart with the history Isis and Rashad shared. It wasn't like I disagreed with her, but my sister needed help, and I was not going to stand by and let her suffer. She needed to get out of New York and get away from Tony. Besides, no matter what history they shared, I knew Rashad loved me, and he would never do anything to jeopardize our marriage by crossing the line with Isis.

Now, my sister was a different story. Like I said earlier, I didn't trust her ass as far as I could throw her. Even though I didn't say it out loud, I suppose my mother knew that, which is why she was asking how Isis ended up pregnant with our child. I wanted a child so badly that I was willing to take a chance on Isis, in spite of how complicated the whole situation was. I had to at least try to explain the depth of my pain to my mother.

"The truth?"

"Truth."

"I was desperate. Rashad wanted a baby, and the doctors told me I couldn't have one. The only thing he's ever asked me for, and I couldn't deliver. Without this baby, our marriage might not have lasted another year. So, I did what I had to do. And I'll continue to do what I have to do until this baby is born."

"I understand that, baby, but you couldn't think of anyone other than your sister?" She reached out and patted my hand, giving me a sympathetic look. I was confused. Was she worried about Isis's mental health, or was she saying she was worried about me?

"There was no one else, Ma. We tried to get Tammy to do it, but she couldn't, or wouldn't. And I've heard too much in the news about strangers reneging on the deal. I'd just die if anyone ever did that." I sighed. "So, no, there was no one else." Then, just to cover myself in case it was Isis she was worrying about, I said, "Besides, we're paying her thirty thousand dollars to have this baby."

My mother's eyebrows shot up. "You're paying her?"

"Yeah, it's what we would do for any other surrogate, so why shouldn't we do it for her? Plus, if she gets to be too much of a pain in the ass, I always have that thirty thousand to hold over her head." I let out a small laugh, hoping to lighten the decidedly somber mood, but Ma wasn't having it. She still looked concerned, and it was starting to scare me.

"What is it?"

She glanced in the direction of the bathroom. Isis was still nowhere in sight. "Well, I hate to be the one to say this, but watch Isis. She's my child and I love her, but she's always been determined to get what she wants."

"What are you trying to say?" I think I knew what she was getting at, but I wanted to be sure.

"Your sister's mind is very fragile since her breakdown over Tony, but she's far from stupid. There's a lot missing in her life, and she's looking for something to fill that void. She may be sick, but she's still a woman, and—"

"What do you mean, she's still a woman? You think she'll try to come on to Rashad, don't you?"

"I think your sister's a woman. And women have been known to do some crazy things to get a man, including getting pregnant. So watch your sister and your husband. The two of them are just a little too close for my taste." There was a seriousness to her words that I hadn't heard since she warned me not to let Isis move into my house. I, however, refused to worry like she did.

"Ma! Rashad is so over Isis."

"Now, Egypt, you know I love Rashad. I loved him since the day your sister brought him home fifteen years ago." I felt a tightening in the pit of my stomach. Why'd she have to go mention their relationship? I was much happier just pretending that chapter in our lives never happened.

"But you know the one thing that's never changed about him?" she asked.

"No, what's that?"

"He never stopped being a man. And a man is always going to be a man. Same way a woman is always gonna want a man."

"You don't trust either of them, do you?"

"I don't trust any woman, and I damn sure don't trust no man. That's why I stayed married for forty years and all my girlfriends are alone."

I just stared at my mother, dumbfounded.

"But Rashad would never—"

"Did you hear a word I said?"

I nodded. "Yes, ma'am."

"Good. You know what? I think I have to go to the restroom too."

She left me sitting alone on the bench, speechless and wondering if I should start watching Isis and Rashad a little closer.

Loraine

31

I pulled into my driveway after a really fun day of Christmas shopping with Jerome. My trunk was filled with so many shopping bags that I was embarrassed to even think about what my American Express bill was going to look like. Oh, well. Sometimes you have to go all out for the people you love.

Speaking of the people I loved, Leon and I were starting to put things back together with the help of Dr. Marshall. She'd said that we both had to take responsibility for how our marriage was going, and I was trying to do my part. I wasn't entirely past the panties thing, but I was trying not to let it consume me the way it had been. I'd reached a point where we could have a discussion without me bringing that subject into it, and I hoped that someday it would be a nonissue. To cement my commitment to fixing our marriage, I'd called Terrance and told him I could never see him again.

We'd continued the joint marital counseling sessions, along with Leon going by himself twice a week, and things were definitely improving. I have no idea what they talked about during their private sessions, but it really seemed to be doing Leon some good. Lately, he was beaming with confidence. In a lot of ways, I felt like I was getting the old Leon back.

The upshot of all this was that Leon and I were beginning to communicate. He was one of the smartest men I'd ever met, but he never seemed to think things through during the past few years. Now, not only was his construction business starting to do well again, but he and I also talked every day about every subject imaginable. To me, smart men have always been sexy, so you can just imagine what Leon's looks and his more recent stimulating conversation were doing to me. I was feeling Leon in a physical kinda way for the first time since the thong incident. Funny thing is, we still hadn't had sex yet. There was a lot to be said for all this delaying of sex, because I was getting horny as hell for my husband. Hell, I wanted him so bad lately I'd started masturbating in the shower thinking about him. And from what I'd learned in our last meeting with Dr. Marshall, he was doing the same.

No worries, though, because tonight was the night I planned to make wild love to him. I'd gotten the okay from Dr. Marshall, so while I was shopping, I picked out a nice sheer negligee. I planned to have scented candles burning and soft romantic music playing in the background. I couldn't wait until he got home from visiting his family in Charlottesville, because it was going to be on!

I stopped my car in front of the garage, hitting the trunk-release button so I could retrieve my shopping bags. When I stepped out of the car, I noticed a woman parked on the street in front of our house, getting out of her car. I didn't recognize her, so I figured she was visiting one of my neighbors—that was, until she started walking toward me.

"Excuse me, Loraine?" She placed a hand on her hip, looking more aggressive than friendly. Who the hell was this woman throwing all kinds of attitude my way?

I quickly gave her the once-over. She was a pretty, well-dressed, brown-skinned woman, probably in her early thirties, with shoulder-length flat-ironed hair. She was tall and heavy like me, but much curvier in the hips and chest. Her figure reminded me of mine when I was her age.

"Yes, I'm Loraine. And you are?"

"Oh, I'm sorry. I've heard so much about you that I feel like I know you. Let me introduce myself. My name is LaKeisha Thomas." Just by the way she popped her gum as she spoke, I knew she wasn't the classiest woman I'd ever met. As Jerome would say, her ghettoness was hiding behind some nice clothes and a few proper words. Now that I knew her name, my only questions were how did she know mine, and what did she want?

"Nice to meet you, LaKeisha." I was trying to remain civil with her. For all I knew, she was a soror—one with no class, but a soror no less. I reached in the trunk and pulled out a few of my bags. "What can I do for you?"

She stepped toward the car. "You want me to help you with those?"

"No, I think I can manage." I closed my trunk. "So, LaKeisha, how can I help you?" This woman was starting to concern me. She was a little too forward for someone I didn't know and who wasn't giving up any information.

"I just thought we should meet, since we have so much in common."

I raised an eyebrow. "Oh, really? What exactly do we have in common?"

She took a step back before she spoke, all attitude again. "Leon."

Leon! Right away, this bitch set off bells and whistles in my head. She was right up Leon's alley: a big girl with big titties and a big ass. Dear Lord, this could not be happening to me. Not after all the therapy and counseling we'd been through. I was burning up inside, but I tried to play it cool. No way was I going to lose it right in front of my own house for all my neighbors to see.

"How exactly do you know Leon?" This time, I didn't just give her the once-over; I gave her the complete stare-down, burning her image in my memory in case I needed to describe her to the cops later.

"I think we both know how and why I know Leon. He's my man. We been together almost five years."

I placed my free hand on my car, because my legs almost gave out.

"I beg your pardon? He's your what?" It didn't take long for me to regain my composure. I let my bags go and took two steps toward her, closing the space between us. This bitch was looking for a beat-down.

"Look, I'm not trying to start no trouble." Her attitude disappeared, and her voice was about as humble as they come as she lifted her hands defensively. She was scared, just like she should have been, 'cause I was gonna knock her head off. "I'm not trying to disrespect you either. I just want to talk about this like ladies."

"Well, sister, if you didn't want trouble, why'd you come over here? And if you weren't trying to disrespect me, why did you just tell me you were sleeping with my husband?"

She backed up some more, keeping her mouth shut.

"So, why are you really here?"

"I don't know. I thought maybe if I saw you, I'd get so mad I'd be able to leave him alone."

"And? Did it work?"

She just stared at me silently for a few seconds, and my heart sank. I guess we both knew her answer. She couldn't give him up; she was in love. Part of me understood why, especially after the past few weeks.

"I should go," she said. "This was a bad idea. I'm sorry." She took a few more steps backward, then turned toward her car. I wanted to run after her and beat the shit out of her, but if I did, I was sure I'd end up killing her. Neither she nor Leon was worth it.

"You love him, don't you?" I shouted.

She stopped, turned around, and nodded. "Yeah, I do."

"Hold on a second." I walked toward her without aggression, stopping about ten feet from her so she would know I wasn't going to attack her. "You said he's your man? Prove to me that you're sleeping with him."

"What do you want me to tell you?" she asked with a twinge of confidence.

"Tell me what Leon's ass looks like."

Without hesitation, she said, "He's got long scars across it from where he got beat as a child." That was enough confirmation for me to know she was telling the truth, and it made me nauseated just thinking about it.

"You know what, LaKeisha? You can have him." I took off my rings as I walked toward her, handing them over. Believe it or not, she took them and stuck them in her pocket. This woman had no class.

"I just want to know one thing. Why'd you leave your nasty drawers in my house?"

"I—" She stopped for a minute, looking a little confused. "I don't know. It seemed like a good idea at the time."

I could have smacked her for that. I guess from the look on her face she could tell.

"I should leave."

"Yeah, I think you should." And with that, I walked away from LaKeisha, picked up my packages, and went in my house and slammed my door.

I climbed up the stairs and sat on the edge of my bed to ponder my situation. I was crushed. I don't think I'd ever been that hurt, and I'd had my share of low moments in the past year. My first thought was to call Leon and curse him out. I changed my mind, though, deciding I didn't even want to hear that bastard's voice or his lies. Did he ever really love me?

Instead of calling Leon, I dialed Jerome's number. Thankfully, he was still at home.

"Hello."

"You alone?" I said through the tears that spilled as soon as I heard my friend's voice. I guess when it comes down to it, big girls do cry. "I need to talk."

"Sure. You all right? You wanna come on over?" Everyone should have at least one friend like Jerome.

"No, I'm not all right. I could use a drink. Actually, I could use a couple drinks. You still have that bottle of Grey Goose?"

"Yeah, I still have it."

"I'll see you in fifteen minutes." I hung up the phone and wiped my eyes. That cheating bastard of a husband didn't deserve my tears.

Isis

32

I'd been up in my old room for the past fifteen minutes, listening on the other end of the phone as Egypt's boss, Loraine, boo-hooed about how her husband, Leon, had been cheating on her. To be totally truthful, it was never really my intention to listen to their conversation in the first place. I'd actually picked up the phone, because I needed to make a call. I had no idea I was going to be entering a conversation in the middle of drama central, but the first few words I heard were so good, I couldn't put down the phone. It was like listening to a *Jerry Springer* episode.

Evidently, some woman Loraine's husband had been messing with had been leaving behind her panties in Loraine's house as a calling card, which, I might add, was a stroke of genius if you're trying to piss someone off. That's letting a bitch know that not only was I up in your house, but I was also up in there fucking too. To top that off, the woman strolled right up to Loraine's door and made it very clear that she'd been sleeping with her husband and had no intentions of stopping anytime soon. I didn't know who this woman was, but we needed to sit down and talk, because I was impressed. I'd confronted Tony's wife, Monica, a few years back, but things didn't go nearly as well as they seemed to be going for this mystery woman.

What I didn't understand was what a smart woman like Loraine was thinking. I'd seen her husband before, and as fine as he was, she should have been watching his ass like a hawk. I know if I had a chance, I would jump on his fine ass myself, four and a half months pregnant or not. Men that fine don't come around every day.

Oh, you're probably saying that I should stop thinking about other people's husbands; I should be worried about other people's feelings. Well, if you haven't been able to figure it out yet, I don't give a shit about anybody's feelings but my own. I had my heart stomped on before, and the lesson I learned was that being nice is way overrated. That's what I would have told Loraine if I was the one talking to her: Go kick that other woman's ass, and then kick your husband's ass. But instead, I had to listen to my sister give her the usual sappy "Oh, how sad," without offering a real solution to the problem.

"Loraine, I'm so sorry this is happening to you. What are you going to do?" Egypt asked.

"I'm on my way home to kick his no-good ass out my house; that's what I'm gonna do!" Looked like my girl Loraine was more like me than I'd realized.

"My God! Well, be careful." Egypt could be such a wimp. "Are you taking Jerome with you?"

"I don't need Jerome. I got two friends who agreed to come with me—Smith and Wesson. I'm sure they can handle Leon better than Jerome ever could."

Damn, that Loraine was no joke!

"Okay, well, as long as you're bringing someone with you."

I so wanted to take my hand off the receiver and scream, *She was talking about a gun, stupid!* But I knew it was time for me to hang up the phone, because if my sister said one more inane thing, I was going to curse her out for real, and I didn't want to risk being caught eavesdropping. I placed the receiver back on the phone, wishing I could be a witness when Loraine went to take care of business. In the meantime, that mystery woman of Leon's had inspired me with all kinds of ideas.

The next morning, I got up early and went downstairs, where I found my father sitting in his lounge chair, reading the paper.

"Daddy, can I use your car to go out to Long Island? Coco's in town, and I'm going to meet her at IHOP."

"Sure, baby," Daddy said. "Just be careful. You have precious cargo on board now."

"I will." I gave him a kiss on the cheek and headed out, glad that I was a daddy's girl. He'd handed over the keys without a second thought, whereas Momma would have asked a million questions. And just like she always did, she would have grilled me until I admitted the truth: I wasn't going anywhere near an IHOP, and I hadn't talked to my friend Coco in ages.

I put the Hudson Valley, New York, address into Daddy's GPS and started to follow the directions. A half hour into my trip, I dialed a very familiar number.

"G-tech Corporation dispatch, Tony speaking."

"Hey," was all I said.

"Isis, is that you, baby?" Now he was calling me baby. I guess he was about due for some of Momma's lovin'.

"Yeah, it's me. I'm in New York. Can I come up to your job?"

"Ah, I don't think that's such a good idea. Almost everyone up here knows Monica, and—"

"And you don't want me to fucking embarrass you!" And to think I was gonna give this Negro some pussy.

"That's not it and you know it. Why don't you meet me after work? We'll get a short stay."

"Why don't we get a room at the Marriott so you can spend the night?"

"I can't do that without using a credit card. Plus, if I'm not home by a certain time, Monica will have a fit. She's got me on such a short leash I can't fart without her being there to smell it." He sighed. "And it doesn't help that you harass her constantly. You call her job almost every day. You need to stop this shit, Isis."

"I don't know why I didn't kill that bitch when I had the chance."

"Will you stop saying that? You're not killing anybody. Why do you always have to go there anyway?"

"'Cause that bitch is living my life, and you ain't got the balls to do what's right. That's why!" I hung up the phone and kept driving. He made me so mad. This was all his fault. If he'd left me alone that day in the club when we met, my sister would still be living in Momma and Daddy's basement, and I'd be married to Rashad. And now he had the nerve to tell me to stay away from his wife? Well, he had another thing coming.

After a two-hour drive, I pulled up in front of a two-story

Victorian brick house and got out of the car. I waddled up to the door, pressing my hand into my back for support, just in case anyone was looking out the windows. My back didn't really bother me, but I liked for people to know I was pregnant. In most cases, it was because they gave me sympathy when they thought I was in pain, but in this case, I had an entirely different reason for flaunting my pregnancy.

I lifted the brass knocker and knocked loudly. It took a while, but an older woman, probably about my mother's age, answered the door. "Can I help you?" At first I thought perhaps I had the wrong address, or the people I was looking for may have moved, but then I heard Monica's unmistakable voice yelling from inside the house.

"Who is that, Momma?"

Momma. Oh, this was too good to be true.

"I'm not sure. There's some woman at the door," her mother replied. "What's your name, young lady?"

"Tell her Isis is here to see her." Monica's mother froze right where she was standing. Obviously she'd heard my name before. With any luck, I'd been the topic of many discussions—or preferably, fights—in their household.

I stood there and stared the old woman down until she finally said, "Monica, she says her name is Isis."

I heard Monica slam something inside the house, then her footsteps as she stomped to the door. When she pushed past her mother, she probably thought she was being cute, giving me the once-over like I was some piece of trash. But the joke was on her when her gaze landed on my growing stomach, which I made sure was poked out as far as it could go. Because of my weight, I really looked about seven months pregnant.

When she was finally able to pick her jaw up off the floor, she said, "What do you want, Isis? I know you ain't here trying to start no trouble."

I heard the children calling in the background. Suddenly, two little girls came running up to their mother and grandmother. They were so cute. Both of them had Tony's gorgeous green eyes.

"Who's that, Nana?" They peeked from behind their grand-mother's skirt.

"Ain't nobody," Monica said, trying to rush them out of the foyer.

Did she just call me nobody? Oh, see, I was planning to be good and wait until the kids were out of the way before I said anything, but if she was gonna disrespect me like that, then it was on. "Why you rushing the kids out of here, Monica? I just came to share the goods news with y'all that your girls are going to be having a baby brother." I patted my stomach. "Tell them your husband and me are having a baby. And as for you, now that we'll both have Tony's babies, maybe you could try to be a little nicer to me. I mean, after all, we're wife-in-laws." I smirked.

She looked back at her kids. "Tonya, Tamika, go play." I could see she was on the verge of losing it, and I was relishing every minute of it.

"Who is that, Mommy?" the older one asked.

"That is a crazy woman! Now scoot!"

The girls stood their ground, looking too scared to move now that their mother had called me crazy.

"Momma, will you take them, please?" Monica gave her mother the eye, and Grandma shuffled the little ones back into the house, although I could still see the old battle-ax peeking around the corner.

"Get the fuck off my property, you crazy, certified bitch!"

"Who you callin' a crazy bitch?" I challenged.

"You, bitch. I don't care what you say. Yours and mine will never be related—I don't care how many bastards you spit out. Besides, you lie so much, I'm sure it's not even Tony's baby. Now get off my property before I call the police."

See, like I said, Monica never made this easy for me. Why couldn't she just believe me the first time I said it, the way Loraine did with her husband's other woman? Even if I was lying. But that's okay. I would give her something to think about if she didn't want to just take my word for it.

"No, we'll see whose baby it is soon enough. Besides, if you're too high and mighty to believe me, here's something to put in your little pipe and smoke: Ask Tony where he went the weekend of Fourth of July, when he told you he was going fishing in the Hamptons." I could see her tabulating the time, date, and place in her head. "That's when I conceived junior here. You couldn't give him a boy, so I guess I had to."

"You're a liar! And I'll prove it when Tony comes home. I just talked to him before your skank ass showed up on my doorstep, and he's on his way from the grocery store."

I called her bluff and then some. "What, do you think telling me Tony's on his way over here is going to get me to leave or something? Shit, you got a chair so I can wait?" I laughed hysterically. "Honey, Tony ain't stopped hitting this in all this time; what makes you think you gonna stop him? And he ain't gonna be here anytime soon, 'cause he's sitting at his job down in Yonkers, happy as shit from the blow job I gave him in the parking lot. So, unless he's got jets, he ain't gonna be here anytime soon."

"You fucking home-wrecking bitch!" Monica broke down screaming and crying. I guess she finally believed me. I thought she was going to rush at me, but she slammed the door instead.

As I left the porch, I could hear her children crying too. "Mommy, what's the matter? Who was that lady? What is she talking about we gon' have a baby brother?"

I laughed all the way to my car. All hell was going to break loose in that house when Tony got home from work later.

My cell phone began vibrating as I started up my car. I couldn't believe she'd called Tony that fast. I put on my hands-free headset, expecting to hear Tony's voice when I answered. But it was Egypt who spoke.

"Isis, where are you?" she demanded like she was my momma or something. "We've called all over looking for you. And don't try and tell me that lie you told Daddy, because Coco's not even in town."

"I'm all right."

"I hope you haven't been with that damn Tony. You know Rashad is too upset. He's been worried sick."

"No, I haven't been with Tony." In a sense, I was telling the truth. I smiled and hummed to myself. I was happy to know that Rashad was concerned. "I just had to go for a ride to clear my head. I'll be there in a minute."

Loraine

33

I said good-bye to Egypt and hung up the phone just as I pulled down my block. Thankfully, I'd managed to make it back home without being pulled over by a cop. I was drunk as hell. I knew I shouldn't have drunk half of what I did, but the alcohol was the only thing dulling the pain.

I'm sure if Jerome hadn't passed out right before I left, he would have taken my keys. I couldn't remember the last time I was this wasted; then again, I couldn't remember a time I needed to be this wasted. I don't think I'd ever hurt this much inside. If it weren't for Jerome's friendship, I'd probably be a basket case.

Over drinks, I'd told him the whole story about LaKeisha showing up at the house, telling me about the scarring on Leon's ass and admitting about the panties. He couldn't believe it. Genuine anger flashed in his eyes as he listened; then he went so far as to pull out his gun from its secret hiding spot and threaten to shoot Leon. I half expected him to laugh at me and say "I told you so," but he didn't, and I really appreciated his decency and friendship even more.

Jerome had fallen asleep a little after eleven, so I texted Egypt, looking for another sympathetic shoulder to lean on. Unfortunately, she was out of town for the Thanksgiving weekend but called while I was driving home. She turned out to be a good friend and a good listener. She did her best to comfort me and support me, but let's be honest: Nothing was really going to make me feel better—except for maybe a Mack truck hitting both Leon and his bitch.

The entire time I was at Jerome's, Leon kept calling and text-messaging me, asking where I was. I refused to respond, other than to say I'd be home soon. He had no idea what he had in store for him when I got there, though. I wasn't sure if his bitch had called to tell him that she talked to me today, but by now he had to know that I wasn't too happy with him. If he thought we were going to sit down and talk things out, he was in for a very rude awakening. My bitterness had taken my mind down a devious road. I had something very special in mind for my soon-to-be ex-husband. I hadn't even told Jerome about it for fear that he'd try to talk me out of it.

Leon's car was parked in the driveway when I pulled up. I expected to be greeted at the door, but surprisingly, he wasn't waiting there for me. I was happy about that. When I saw him, I wanted it to be on my terms.

The downstairs part of the house was dark, but I staggered into the kitchen and put on a pot of water. I took a tea bag and a cup out of the cupboard, along with some sugar. When the water came to a boil, I poured some into my cup, then placed the pot back on the stove.

Sipping my tea, I thought about the confrontation I'd had in front of my house earlier that evening. In a last-ditch effort to save the love I had for him and our marriage, I tried to give Leon the benefit of the doubt. Unfortunately, I couldn't think of any reasons why that woman would have known about the scarring on his ass or why she would chance coming to my house and getting her ass beat, other than, like she said, she was in love with him. And as far as the panties, they were most definitely hers, 'cause sister girl was more than big enough to fit in them. For the umpteenth time that night, tears rolled down my face as I had to confront facts: My marriage was over, and my husband was a damn cheater.

On that note, I took the boiling water off the stove and headed up the stairs with the pot in my hand. Leon was still staying in the guestroom. It sent my blood pressure up five points just thinking about the fact that if that bitch hadn't shown up, he would have been in my bed and we would have made love again for the first time in months. Now, just the thought of him touching me after he'd been with that hussy made my skin crawl.

I tiptoed down the hall to his room. When I opened the door, I found him sleeping peacefully with the comforter pulled up to his head. He was turned on his side, and I couldn't help it; my first thought was that he looked so cute.

"Why couldn't you love me the way I love you?" I whispered as I watched him sleep. Jerome once told me that you have to love someone in order to hate them. I think I understood exactly what he meant now, because as much as I loved Leon, I hated him. In fact, as an image of LaKeisha popped into my head, I hated his fucking guts. Without a moment of hesitation, I lifted the pot of hot water and threw it on him.

Leon sprang up, screaming. He threw off the comforter and rolled out of the bed, onto the floor. "Awww! Help me! Help me! I'm on fire!"

The loudness and intensity of his screams snapped me out of my drunken haze for a minute, enough to recognize the serious-ness of what I'd just done. If he hadn't been covered by a heavy comforter, I could have permanently injured him. As angry as I was, I really wasn't trying to kill the man. I was just trying to get his attention so I could get him out of my house. The way he was rolling around on the ground and patting himself like he was on fire, I felt sorry for him—but only for a split second.

He was in such a panic that it took him a while to even real-ize I was in the room. Even then, he called out, "Loraine, help me!" not realizing that I was the cause of his pain. Only when he heard me drop the pot to the floor did it dawn on him what I had done.

"Oh my God, woman, are you crazy?" He tried to get up but fell back to the ground.

"I'm not crazy, Leon. Drunk, yes, but crazy? I don't think so." I'm sure it was the alcohol that was giving me the courage to stand my ground. Even so, I had to stay alert and prepared for the worst, because that pain was only going to last so long, and then he would come after me.

"What'd you put on me? You trying to kill me or something?" He was rubbing his left side and still attempting to get up.

"Oh, please, Leon, the pain you feel is nothing compared to the pain you've caused me."

"What are you talking about? You're acting crazy." He was looking at me like he was trying to see through my skull and into my brain. "You've finally lost your mind, haven't you?"

"No, I'm not the crazy one—but your bitch tried to make me think I was the one losing it when she left her panties in my bed and in my house."

"Are we back to this shit again? What, did you find another pair of panties?" His pain must have subsided a bit, because he was standing up now, and his anger was evident. I wasn't ready to back down yet.

"You damn right we're back to this shit! You can thank your little girlfriend—or should I say your *big* girlfriend—for that."

I got a blank look from him. I guess his girl hadn't let him know that she paid me a visit. Good. The fact that I'd caught him off guard definitely gave me the upper hand, because he'd had no time to concoct some bullshit lies to feed me. Not that I would have believed him at this point anyway.

"How could you do this to me? I would have done anything for you!"

"Do what? What are you talking about?" he shouted. "I'm seeing a shrink two times a week—three times, if you count marriage counseling. What the hell am I doing?"

Damn, he was a good actor.

"Leon, you're pathetic. You know that?"

"And you're crazy! Did you know that?" He sat on the bed and removed his wet shirt. The skin on his side was bright red.

"What I know is that you're a liar and a fucking cheat."

"Oh, and who put this in your head? That little faggot?"

"No, your bitch, LaKeisha."

He hesitated for a second, which gave him away. "LaKeisha? LaKeisha who? Who the fuck is LaKeisha?"

"Why you denying her? You know she's in love with you? At least that's what she told me. I'm not stupid, Leon, and I'm not a fool. Now, get your shit and get the fuck out."

"I'm not going anywhere, Loraine. I've been working on my life and this marriage too hard to walk out on it." He took a step toward me, and I pulled out Jerome's gun, which I had been holding in my pocket since I dropped the pot. I'd taken it when I left Jerome's, just in case Leon decided to act up when I told him to leave. It looked like it was gonna come in handy.

"Don't make me have to kill you, Leon, because I will. Now, you're going to leave this house. The question is whether it's of your own volition or on the coroner's gurney. The choice is yours."

He kept his eyes locked on the gun and spoke carefully. "Loraine, you're making a big mistake."

"No, Leon, the mistake I made was marrying you. Now you're the one who will be making the big mistake if you don't get your shit and get out my house." I pointed the gun at his head. Nothing makes a person understand the severity of a situation better than a gun to the head.

"Do you remember what you told me about guns?" I asked.

"Don't pull one out unless you're willing to use it."

"Exactly. Now, I really didn't want to have to take it this far, but you just too hardheaded for your own good. And the way my hand is shaking, this thing could go off at any second. You might want to get your shit and go before something happens that we'll both regret."

Leon didn't say anything as he picked up a shirt and some sweats that were draped over a nearby chair. He threw a few of his belongings in a pillow case, and a few minutes later, he was down the stairs and out the door, yelling, "You're wrong for this, Loraine," as he exited. I heard squealing tires as his car left the driveway.

I was satisfied that I'd gotten him out but was still a little shaken by how far I'd gone. I needed to do something to calm my nerves, and I knew just what would work. I went to Leon's closet and started pulling out all his Armani suits, bought with my hard-earned money. Every last one of them went into the garbage bags I'd brought up from the kitchen.

I dragged the bags out to the curb, went inside, and then put the chain lock on the door. I shut off my cell phone, took two sleeping pills to calm my still-anxious nerves, and went to bed. After the day I'd had, things had to be better tomorrow.

Isis

34

From the moment I pulled up to the house, I could feel my mother's presence like a thick fog taking over a country road. She was sitting up in her Queen Anne's chair by the bay window, obviously waiting for me to come home, like she used to do when I was a teenager staying out late or when I first learned how to drive. This time, it was four o'clock in the afternoon, not one o'clock in the morning, and I was thirty-eight years old, not sixteen, so I knew I was not walking into a good situation.

I paid her no mind as I entered the house and walked over to my father. I kissed his cheek, trying not to block his view of the game as I handed him his keys.

"Where's Rashad, Daddy?" I asked. "I'm surprised he's not—"

My mother's head whipped around like it was going to fly off her shoulders. "He took his *wife* to see that new Will Smith movie."

"What?" I whined in disbelief. "They were supposed to take me to see that." *And besides, I didn't ask you. Is your name Daddy?*

"You ever think that maybe he wanted to take his wife out alone for a change, without you?"

I wanted to say something smart like, *No, not really,* or *Why would he want to do that?* but I resisted the temptation. It was never a good idea to be smart with my mother, so I reserved it for occasions when it was truly necessary.

"Yeah, I guess you're right. They could use some time alone. And to tell you the truth, I could use a break from them too. It was so nice to go and do what I wanted without a chaperone."

"Hmph. Where have you been anyway? You had us all worried to death. Your poor sister spent half the morning trying to track you down."

"For what?" I asked, unable to keep the attitude out of my tone. "I told Daddy where I was going. I went to IHOP with my friend Canard, and then I went over to the mall."

She smirked at my answer, and that's when I realized I'd messed up. Damn, I was a grown woman, and I still let my mother get the best of me every time. She was happy to let me know I'd just told on myself.

"Canard, huh? Your father said you told him you were going out with Coco."

I glanced over at my father, who was too wrapped up in the Redskins game to pay either of us any mind.

"Well, Daddy was mistaken . . . or maybe I said Coco by accident. What's the big deal anyway? I'm thirty-eight years old. I come and go as I please." She had always been that way with me, watching over me like a hawk, while Egypt could do whatever the hell she wanted. "What I wanna know is why are you questioning me like I'm a child?"

The stern look she gave me told me I'd be better off if I just backed down. My mother was not one to tolerate disrespect from anyone, especially her kids.

"As you can see, I'm home in one piece." I bent down and kissed her on the cheek, wrapping an arm around her shoulder in hopes that she would take it as a peace offering. But she didn't soften one bit. She pushed me away, not accepting my embrace.

In all my life, as many times as my mother had caught me telling lies, I'd never seen her look at me as coldly as she was now. A chill ran through my body.

"What have you been up to?"

"Nothin'," I said, concentrating hard on keeping my expression neutral. I didn't want her to know she had me rattled. "What are you talking about?"

"My office, now!" She got out of her seat, and I knew it was useless to protest. I followed her with my head hung low. If Daddy tore his eyes away from the game and realized what was going on, even he couldn't save me now. She'd ordered me to her "office."

I hadn't heard her call the kitchen her office since I was eighteen. When I was a kid, I hated when she did that, because it always meant I was in some kind of trouble. I could always bullshit Daddy and get whatever I wanted out of him, but Momma—no way. She had this sixth sense when it came to me; she could always tell when I was doing something I knew I shouldn't have been. Looking back, there were times I was convinced Momma was a mind reader; either that or she was perched up in some satellite tower and could see me acting a fool from miles and miles away. Whatever it was, she could read me like a book, and it pissed me off.

"What is it, Momma?" I said innocently when we entered the kitchen.

"I don't know what you been up to, but I hope it don't come back to bite you in the ass."

"I'm not up to anything." I rested my hands on my stomach, hoping that the subtle reminder about her grandchild growing inside of me might soften her mood a little. Not a chance. She wasn't buying it.

"Look me in the eye, Isis Rene. I know you. I carried you nine months, two weeks—"

"Three days, sixteen hours, and twenty-four minutes. I know that, Momma." She'd drilled those numbers into my head many times before, like every second was torture for her. Sometimes she acted as if she were the only woman to ever be in labor. It damn sure didn't make me feel loved whenever she pulled that line out on me.

"Who you getting smart with?" She raised her hand, and I have to admit I flinched. "I will still smack your face. I don't care if you're grown and pregnant or not. I'm still your mother."

I apologized because I knew she wasn't joking. My mother would never hesitate to smack me if she thought I needed to be put in my place. "Sorry."

"I know you are." To be honest, I couldn't tell if she was accepting my apology or if she was calling me sorry, and I think that's exactly how she wanted it. She wasn't about to let me off the hook with one little "sorry."

"It's a great thing you're doing for your sister and her husband."

Her husband. She'd been calling Rashad by his name for almost fifteen years, but now that I was pregnant with his baby, she was throwing around a whole lot of "her husband" and "his wife." I rolled my eyes, which I'm sure my mother didn't appreciate.

"Anyhow, I'm only going to say this to you once: You better not break your sister's heart when it comes to this baby. Do you understand me? You are the one who signed up for this madness, and you better see it through."

"Why are you coming at me like this? All I did was go out for one afternoon, Momma." Shoot, if I had known that disappearing for one day was going to cause this much trouble, I would have just stayed out all night and made it worthwhile.

"It's not what you did. It's what you are, Isis. You're selfish."

I felt like I'd just been punched in the stomach. I can't begin to describe how much it hurts to hear your own mother say such negative things about you. And she'd always done this to me. No wonder I had so many problems. But like always, I sat silently and took it as she continued to tell me about myself.

"You have never been able to share anything with your sister. And you expect me to believe you're going to just hand over a baby—Rashad's baby, at that? Not everyone is as gullible as your sister."

I felt exposed. They were some shitty things she said about me, but unfortunately, they weren't wrong. My mother really did know my ass like a book—though I wasn't about to let her know it. "Momma, what are you talking about?"

This time, she laughed. "What am I talking about? I'm talking about you still being in love with your sister's husband. That's what I'm talking about. I see the way you look at that man. You still want him."

I never stopped wanting him.

"Are you trying to get Rashad away from Egypt since you know she can't give him a baby? Is that what this is all about?" I didn't answer. I just stared at her blankly. I knew the way this went when my mother was lecturing me. She wasn't really looking for a conversation; she just wanted to speak her mind, so I let her ramble on and kept my thoughts to myself.

"'Cause if it is, I'm here to tell you it won't work."

How the fuck do you know? You have no idea how much he wants a child.

I offered only this much: "I'm not trying to take Rashad."

"Good, because your sister has something you don't have, and it's just as powerful as any child."

I wanted so badly to ask what, and I'm sure she knew it. That's why she hesitated so long before she finished her statement.

"You see, she's got—how does that song go? Oh, yeah. She's got papers on him. And as long as she's got papers, she got a right to half his shit. As you know, they've got a lot of shit, and he loves his shit. So instead of giving up half his shit to be with you and the baby, he's going to keep all of his shit—except for the shit he gives his lawyers—and he and your sister are going to take your mentally unstable behind to court. And not only are they going to win, since you signed surrogacy papers, but you will probably be disowned by the entire family."

Son of a bitch. Was I that obvious? Or was what I used to think as a child true? Maybe she really could read my mind. If she couldn't, she'd really given this whole situation some thought. And then to top it all off, she had to bring my mental health issues into the conversation, like that had anything to do with it. She could be so cold sometimes.

"So you see, I'm glad you don't want to take him from your sister, 'cause I would hate the thought of you not being here next year for Thanksgiving."

I swear to God, if she wasn't my mother, I would have stabbed her with a butcher knife. But I was officially on notice. Now that I knew she had her eye on me, I was gonna have to be a little more careful about staying under the radar.

Jerome

35

Lord have mercy, I am such a ho! Why? Because I had just spent the most fabulous day with Big Poppa, and now I was on my way to Washington, DC, to see Ron, my young Energizer Bunny lover. I wanted to give him an early Christmas present and a night of robust lovemaking before he left for the West Coast for a bunch of games and Christmas tournaments. We hadn't seen each other in more than a week, and even that was just a little parking-lot action, because we were both so busy. He had finals, practice, and a hectic game schedule up here in DC, and I was down South with Loraine, who was in crisis; and Big Poppa, who all of a sudden wanted more attention; and the half dozen other sponsors I was juggling. There was something about the holidays that made everyone so needy for my attention.

When I arrived at the hotel, I saw Ron already sitting in the lobby with an annoyed look on his face. I was a little late, but he'd get over it as soon as I blew his mind—along with another body part. As was always the case, we had to play like we didn't know each other in public, so I walked right past him and went to the front desk to check into our room. I took the room key from the front desk clerk and walked to the elevator, texting Ron the room number. As a precaution, he always waited five minutes before coming up.

When I got in the room, I placed his present on the dresser and removed my shirt before ordering a bottle of champagne and chocolate-dipped strawberries. That's when I realized for the first time in my life that I was actually the sponsor. I didn't have a problem with it, though, because Ron was an investment.

After I had a chance to see him play ball and ask around, I decided that he was a sure-enough keeper with NBA potential. By that time, if Big Poppa and I hadn't run away together, I'd just move to whatever town Ron was drafted to and reap the dividends of my investment. All I had to do was make him fall in love with me—and he was well on his way to that.

Speak of the devil. A knock on the door took me out of retirement planning and back to the task at hand, keeping Ronny boy happy. I checked myself out in the mirror, then opened the door. I was greeted by Ron's fist in my face, which sent me reeling backward.

"What the heck did you do that for? Is this some type of S and M role-playing game? 'Cause I ain't into that shit." I touched my lip to see if I was bleeding.

"You son of a bitch!" Ron shouted, throwing three more blows that barely landed. He looked like he was crying.

I grabbed his wrists so he couldn't punch me anymore, and we wrestled to the ground. He was so angry he looked possessed.

"Ron, what's wrong, man? What did I do?" He was even stronger than he looked, and it was taking everything I had to keep him from pounding my face.

"It was bad enough you sent them to my coach. But my mother?" He pulled his left arm free, then started swinging again, hitting me in the side of the neck and chest. "You sent those pictures to my mother, you son of a bitch."

"Your mother? What are you talking about? What pictures?" I had both arms up, blocking his blows, but he kept trying to get at me. "Ron, listen to me, man! I don't know anything about any pictures. I wouldn't do anything like that. I'm in love with you, man!"

Those words made him pause for a minute. He threw one or two more halfhearted blows, then stopped trying to fight me. To be safe, I backed up out of arm's reach, because he still had fire in his eyes.

"I love you, Ron. I wouldn't do anything like that to you."

"Don't lie to me, Jerome." He lifted his arm to strike me again. I covered my face and braced myself, but the blow never came. When I looked at him, he was seated on the bed. The way his posture sagged, he looked like a man who felt totally defeated.

I sat next to him. "Tell me what's going on."

"Somebody sent pictures of us in that parking lot last week to my mother, my coach, the university president, and some of my teammates."

Poor kid. I know he wasn't ready for that. But I needed to make sure he understood I had nothing to do with it, because he was obviously under so much stress that he could snap and get violent again at any moment.

"And you think I did that?" I asked cautiously.

"Yeah, I think you did it. You set me up, Jerome. Nobody knew we were going to that parking lot, not even me. That was your idea."

He was right; it was my idea. I was trying to be spontaneous and give him a blow job before I took him back to his dorm. Now it looked like my spontaneity had been captured on film.

"It was your dick's idea, Ron. Remember, it was you who kept talking about how horny you were. I was just trying to make you happy, man."

He looked me in the eye and stayed silent for a minute, like he was remembering that night and trying to decide if my version of events was correct. As I watched some of the tension leave his face, I felt a little safer. It looked like he was starting to believe I was innocent, though he still had another question for me, so I wasn't completely off the hook.

"You didn't tell anyone you were going to be in DC, did you?"

"Nah, man, I didn't. I wouldn't do that to you."

Now the fire in his eyes was gone. He no longer looked angry, just hurt and confused. My heart went out to the kid.

"Then who?" he asked. "Who would do this to me?"

"I don't know." One person did come to mind, but even he wasn't that crazy, was he? "I wish I knew who did it."

"Jerome, if I find out you had anything to do with this," he warned, "I'm gonna kill you. This is my future somebody's fucking with."

"I know that. I swear to God, I wouldn't do anything like that." I raised my right hand in the air.

"Man, my momma is heartbroken over this shit. I may lose my scholarship and probably any chance I got at the NBA. I damn sure won't ever be one of the boys again."

I leaned forward on the bed, trying to get comfortable. My entire upper body ached from the beating I'd just taken. I didn't even want to think about my face. It was probably bruised beyond recognition.

"Don't worry about your scholarship. If they yank that, we'll have every gay activist in the country on campus. As far as the NBA is concerned, just go out there and play ball. The rest will take care of itself."

He didn't look convinced. I tried to lighten the mood a little, because I really did care about him, and I hated to see him looking so hurt. "I don't even wanna think about how much money you can make as the first openly gay professional basketball player. Sissies from all over the world will be rooting for whatever team you play for. Man, you're gonna be like Jackie Robinson, a true pioneer."

He made a face as he stood up and took a few steps to distance himself from me. "No, I won't, because I'm not gay. And even if I was, I damn sure don't want to be a pioneer."

Even when he's out, the boy wants to stay in denial. I resisted the sigh that threatened to escape from my lips.

"Ron, there's no reason to deny who you are anymore. It's out. You said it yourself; they've got pictures."

"Fuck those pictures!" He stepped toward me, his anger boiling beneath the surface again. "You set me up, didn't you? You wanted me outed so you could use me as some type of poster child for gays."

We were back at square one. I really didn't want to get hit again. What was it going to take to convince him?

"Look, man, I'm sorry, but I didn't have anything to do with it."

"Sure you didn't, Jerome."

"Ron, I swear to you—"

"Save it, aw-ight?" He gave me the finger as he walked toward the door. Lucky for me—and my already aching body—he looked like he'd run out of steam, so the argument was over. "If anyone asks you about those pictures, they were Photoshopped and you don't know me. You understand?"

"Yeah, but what do you mean I don't know you? You just want me to pretend, right? You're not giving up on us, are you?"

He reached for the doorknob. "There is no *us,* Jerome. There never was, and if you give two shits about me, you'll keep it that way. I'm trying to get my life back."

I nodded as I watched him walk out the door and quite possibly out of my life. I didn't have the strength or energy to follow him—not that it would have done any good. I'd seen my share of men who'd been outed to the public before they were ready. It was never a pretty picture, and it usually forced them to go even further into denial.

I got up and walked into the bathroom, washing the blood from the small cut on my upper lip. I didn't look half as bad as I felt, so I put on my shirt and jacket, then headed to the parking garage.

I still wasn't quite sure what the hell was going on, but deep down, I had a feeling it had something to do with that crazy white boy Peter. The scariest part was that if it was Peter, then he had followed us to that parking lot, and who knows how long he'd been following us before then. I replayed that night in my mind, and I couldn't recall any time when I saw anything suspicious or felt like we were being followed. What the hell was this guy, some type of ninja?

I was just about to get in my car when my phone rang. I reached down to my holster and checked my caller ID. *Damn, now that's creepy.* It was Peter. What the hell did he want?

I clicked the TALK button. "What?" I yelled.

"You look a little bruised up there, sport."

I felt my stomach do a flip. I climbed in my car in a hurry, looking around the parking garage. He was nowhere in sight.

"Where the fuck are you? And what the fuck do you want from me?"

"I'm close. I'm always going to be close to you."

I'd seen enough horror flicks to know that this was my cue to get the hell out of there. A dark, deserted parking garage is not the place you want to be when a stalker calls. Feeling paranoid as shit, I pulled out of the parking space and headed straight for the exit, expecting his spooky ass to jump in front of my car at any moment.

"Why are you doing this?" I asked.

"You haven't figured out what I want yet?" He chuckled. "I want you, and I'm not going to rest until we're together."

"You're insane, Peter. Totally fucking insane. Do you know that?"

"If you say so. I'm sick of arguing my sanity with you. I know I'm sane, and even if I'm not, it's all because of you." He laughed like a hyena, and that just made this shit creepier.

When he got his psychotic ass under control, he asked, "So, how'd you like the pictures?"

I punched the steering wheel. Now I had confirmation that he was the one who took the pictures. But why did he have to hurt Ron the way he did? I was pissed. Not only had he fucked up Ron's situation, he'd also caused me to get my ass beat. I tried to keep my voice calm, because I didn't want to give him the satisfaction of knowing how much chaos he'd created. "I haven't had a chance to see them."

"Too bad. There are some really nice shots of you. My favorite one is of you sucking on his dick so good that his eyes look like they're popping out of his head. I know exactly how he felt. Reminds me of how you made me feel that night at the hotel."

"Why are you doing this?"

"I told you before, Jerome—if I can't have you, nobody will."

"But he's just a kid. He doesn't deserve this. He's having a hard enough time dealing with being gay. You wanna fuck with someone, fuck with me."

He laughed halfheartedly. "I already am, and I've just begun. Have a safe ride home. You might wanna get some gas. You're running a little low." I glanced down at my gas gauge and almost hit a parked car.

Jesus Christ, this crazy motherfucker's been in my car.

Loraine
36

It was Christmas Day, my favorite holiday of the year. Unfortunately, this Christmas I woke up bitter, miserable, and alone for the first time in ten years. I finally climbed out of bed and headed downstairs to the kitchen around two in the afternoon. I fixed myself some breakfast, then sat in the living room, finishing off a box of chocolate turtles as I contemplated whether I should open the pile of presents sitting on the love seat. Usually I was like a kid on Christmas morning, waking Leon up early so we could come down and open gifts. He would have the entire house decorated like a winter wonderland. But this year, I didn't even put up a tree. I didn't want to do anything that would remind me of Leon.

Sadly, everything reminded me of him. I was so depressed and bitter about the whole situation that the only thing I wanted to do was eat—something I seemed to be doing constantly. We'd been separated a month, and I'd already gained a good ten or fifteen pounds. My wardrobe was now a quarter of what it used to be, just because I couldn't fit into most of my clothes.

I opened a few presents, the majority of them from clients and people from my office. The gifts were all nice but nothing I would use or wear. I had no idea who'd invented gift receipts, but I felt like I owed them dinner.

My house phone rang, and I picked it up without looking at the caller ID. I'd changed my number, along with all the house locks and alarm codes the day after I kicked Leon out. It was a good thing, too, because he had been blowing up my cell phone and even came by a few times, professing his love. The last time, I had to call the cops because he wouldn't leave. Now, I don't want to give you the wrong impression, because it wasn't like he was trying to knock my door down or break into the house. No, this fool was staging a sit-in. That's right, a sit-in. He was sitting on the front lawn with one sign that read I LOVE LORAINE AND ONLY LORAINE! and another one that read I'M NOT LEAVING UNTIL YOU TAKE ME BACK.

Under any other circumstances, it might have worked, but I was done. I doubt he thought I'd call the cops, but I sure as hell did. Anyway, I knew it wasn't him on the phone, because I had given out the new number to only a few select people, and he definitely wasn't on the list.

"Hello."

"Merry Christmas!" It was Jerome and his cheerful ass. I loved him, but I could sure as hell do without his Mr. Happy attitude today. Not now, not when I wanted to be miserable.

"Merry Christmas, Jerome," I replied in a flat tone.

"Loraine, girl, you are the bomb!" God, what was he so damn cheery about?

"Why am I the bomb, Jerome?" I only asked because I knew he wanted me to.

"Because of your Christmas present, why else? They just delivered it, and, girl, I love it! I absolutely love it. And I love you for it. It must have cost you a small fortune to have them deliver it on Christmas Day."

"I love you too, Jerome." I couldn't help it; a smile crept up on my face. Now I understood why he was so happy. I'd completely forgotten about the home-theater system I'd gotten him for Christmas, since I purchased it so long ago. "That is what you wanted, isn't it?"

"Hell to the yes!" He sounded so happy. "Did you open mine yet?"

"No, not yet."

"Girl, you better open my presents." He sounded even more excited about my gifts than he did his. "I gave you two. Open the blue one first."

I shuffled through what was left of the unopened presents until I found Jerome's. One was a two-by-two-inch box that I was sure was some type of jewelry. The other was a thin rectangular box about the size of my hand. I had no idea what was inside that one.

"You open it yet?"

"No, I haven't opened it yet. Give me a minute, okay?" I took my time and unwrapped the first box. "Oh, Jerome, they're beautiful." As I suspected, it was jewelry, a pair of beautiful dangling diamond and white gold earrings. Unlike most of the presents I'd received, this was something I would wear for many years. As always, Jerome knew my taste. "Thank you so much." I was starting to feel a little Christmas cheer.

"Merry Christmas, Raine, but that's not it yet. That was just the warm-up. Your big gift is in the other box. Go 'head and take the paper off, but don't open it until I tell you."

"Big gift?" I looked down at the present. What in the world could possibly be better than the earrings he'd already given me? Okay, I was starting to get excited. I ripped the paper off the gift, exposing a blue Tiffany's box. It had to be the diamond bangle I'd been looking at online. "My goodness, Jerome, you've gone all out. You know I love stuff from Tiffany's."

"Yes, I do. Now, open it."

I opened the box, but there was no bangle or jewelry of any kind in it. It contained a small envelope, about the size of a credit card. I lifted it up to see if there was anything underneath, but there was nothing. "An envelope?"

"Yup. Confused?"

"Very," I replied. "What is it, a gift card?"

"Nope. It's not even from Tiffany's."

"Okay, so what exactly is it?"

"Loraine, I spent the better part of a month trying to find this present for you." As he was talking, I opened the envelope. "You know I usually don't play matchmaker, but I want you to be happy. In that envelope is a business card from that guy Michael Richards," he explained at the same time I was pulling out the card and reading it in confused silence.

"It's time to move on, Loraine. You're a beautiful woman inside and out, and nobody sees that more than Michael. He wrote his cell number on the back of the card. He went down to Norfolk for the holidays, but he said you can call him anytime. He's expecting your call."

"Jerome, I . . ." Wow. I didn't know what to say. Jerome had taken friendship to an entirely new level. No one had ever done anything like this for me before. Sure, I'd had people hook me up before I was married. I'd also been on my share of blind dates. But what Jerome had done and the way he presented it showed me just how much he loved me. He knew I was hurting inside; I was lonely, and he was trying to do something about it. I was touched.

"Thank you," I whispered. "I love you, Jerome."

"I love you too. Merry Christmas."

I turned the card over, and like he said, there was a number written on the back. Now it was up to me to decide what I would do with it. I can't say I hadn't thought about Michael, because that would be a bold-faced lie. He'd been the subject of many conversations between Jerome and me, before and after Leon left. I was more of a skeptic than Jerome. To me, Michael almost seemed too good to be true. I mean, after everything I had been through with Leon, what were the chances of me finding a sweet, honest man who had supposedly loved me since we were kids? There's no way he could be so perfect.

Jerome, on the other hand, didn't think so. He saw this as God's way of giving me a break after all the crap I'd put up with. He encouraged me to find Michael, saying I deserved to be happy. I thought about it for a while, even going so far as to check Facebook to see if he had a page, but I gave up before I'd even typed in his name, because it just made me feel desperate. If it was really meant to be, I wouldn't have to search him out.

And so, apparently, Jerome had completed the search for me.

"So, you gonna call him?"

"I don't know. I want to, but I don't know if I can."

"What are you talking about? You better call that man. Do you know how much trouble it was tracking him down?"

"I can only imagine, and I appreciate it, but he doesn't know me. He doesn't know the real me. What he sees is a girl who was nice to him when we were kids. I'm forty-four years old. I'm not the little girl he knew as a child. The girl he's infatuated with is long gone."

"Oh, I see what's going on now. You're scared to take a chance, aren't you? Scared you just might fall in love again."

"Scared would be an understatement. I'm absolutely terrified."

"It's okay to be scared. Just don't let life pass you by because of it. Just give him a call, okay?"

Knowing Jerome as well as I did, I was sure he wouldn't let up until I agreed to make the call.

"Okay, I'll call him. But I'm not getting my hopes up."

"Good. Let me know how it goes," he said before we ended the call.

Placing the phone on the coffee table in front of me, I studied the business card while I gathered my nerve. This was not easy for me. It had been a long time since I'd had to think about finding a man, and even back when I was single, I'd never been the most confident woman. It's funny, because people at work saw me as so strong. They weren't wrong; in my professional life, I rarely suffered with doubt. But for some reason, I'd never felt completely comfortable when it came to dating.

It wasn't that I had low self-esteem or anything. I wasn't some stereotypical big girl who hated her body. On the contrary, I was proud of my curves. I don't know, maybe it was that I was so used to succeeding at everything I did, and with dating, there's always that chance you'll be shot down. I wasn't used to failure, so I avoided anything that opened up the possibility—hence my aversion to the whole singles scene. But the sad reality was that I would soon be entering that scene once again, so I guess there was no time like the present to make that leap.

With a sigh, I picked up the phone and dialed the number on the back of the card.

"Hello."

"Hi, Michael. It's ... it's Loraine. I hope this isn't a bad time."

"Loraine, Merry Christmas!" To my relief, he sounded happy to hear from me. "When Jerome asked for my number, I didn't think you'd actually call."

"I almost didn't."

"Well, I don't know what changed your mind, but I'm glad you did."

Did he really mean that? Was he really that glad to hear from me? If Jerome were here, he would be kicking me for doubting myself, but I couldn't help it. I wasn't going to change instantly.

"My sister just said to tell you Merry Christmas and asked when you are coming down to see her."

"Tell her I said as soon as I get an invitation."

"Be careful what you ask for." He laughed. "Listen, Loraine, can I call you back? We're right in the middle of Christmas dinner."

"Oh my goodness, I'm so sorry. Sure, you can call me back."

"Before I let you go, I wanted to ask you something."

"Sure. What?"

"Jerome told me about you and your husband's split. I'm gonna be down here for a couple of days doing some stuff for the family, but would you like to do something on New Year's Eve when I get back?"

I didn't allow doubt to interfere this time. "Yeah, I'd like that."

"All right, then, it's a date. I'll give you a call a little later tonight, and we can finalize our plans."

"I'll be waiting." I hung up the phone feeling a whole lot better than I had when I woke up.

Egypt

37

The tension in the room was so thick I felt like I could suffocate. Rashad was an utter wreck, and I wasn't much better. We'd gotten up to open Christmas presents about an hour ago, and my sister was nowhere to be found. I watched as Rashad checked his wristwatch for the third time in five minutes. He kept glancing up at me with the same annoyed expression, as if this entire thing were my fault. The looks he was giving me were so evil, you would have thought he caught me in bed with another man. But it wasn't me he should be mad at; it was Isis. She was the one who went MIA, on Christmas of all days.

"What I don't understand is why the hell she would go anywhere without telling you."

No, he didn't just try to throw this at my feet! It was one thing for him to think it, but it was another for him to verbalize those thoughts. I was not about to let him make this about me, when everything I'd ever done was for the benefit of our unborn child and our marriage.

"Telling *me*?" I pointed at myself for emphasis. "Honey, contrary to popular belief, I'm not my sister's keeper. And besides, when I was keeping tabs on her in order to keep up with the health of our unborn child, you told me I was being overbearing and that I should leave her be, remember?"

"What I remember was you always being on her back, stressing her out about what she was eating and drinking. That shit you pulled at your parents' house, yelling and screaming at her Thanksgiving weekend because she went out for a few hours—you could have made her lose the baby."

Oh, brother. Whose side was he on anyway? We were supposed to be a team.

"You got this all wrong," I retaliated. "I wasn't stressing her out. I was laying down the law." He wasn't the only one who could get snippy. "She's the one who thinks I'm her maid and you're her butler. If anyone's being stressed out, it's us! Waiting on her ass hand and foot like we're slaves. And as far as Thanksgiving weekend's concerned, what I said to her was for us. Don't act like you don't know where she went when she took off with Daddy's car. She was with Tony and you know it."

He shook like a chill passed through him, but he still tried to defend her. "She said she wanted to get away from you for a few hours so she could breathe. I don't have any reason to believe she went to see him. Why would she do that?"

"You can't be serious."

"Of course I'm serious! Why would—"

Thank the Lord, the doorbell rang, because I could feel a huge argument brewing, and if he had said the wrong thing, there would have been two people missing in action.

Rashad jumped up to answer the door. When he opened it, I saw two Chesterfield County police officers standing on the porch. Rashad had called the police about twenty minutes after we realized Isis was not home. When we first checked her room and saw that her bedroom hadn't been slept in, I didn't think much of it. My thought was that she'd hopped a bus to New York and was probably at Momma and Daddy's by now. But when I called there and they hadn't heard from her, I started to get a bad feeling that she might be with Tony. I ruled that out when I realized it was Christmas Day. He had a wife and kids. No way his wife would let him out of her sight long enough to make an overnight trip to Virginia on Christmas Eve.

Seeing the officers just made the whole situation a bit scarier and a whole lot more serious in my mind. Now I was deathly afraid that something really might have happened to my sister.

"Afternoon. We received a call about a missing person?" the taller of the two cops asked as they entered the house. I could tell they were impressed with our house as they tried to inconspicuously peer around.

I walked over and stood next to Rashad, who spoke up first. "Yes, my sister-in-law's missing, and she's five-and-a-half months pregnant."

"When was the last time you saw her?" the shorter of the two asked, writing on a small pad.

"She was here when I went to work," Rashad replied, turning toward me. "But my wife was with her up until around . . ."

"Around five yesterday afternoon," I said, completing his sentence. "I went out to do some last-minute shopping."

"Does she have a car?"

"No. She doesn't have a car. And she left her cell phone upstairs in her room," Rashad explained.

"I see. Does she do this type of thing often?" the taller officer asked. "Has she ever left for long periods of time without telling anyone?"

"Never," Rashad answered quickly as he paced across the room. He was so wound up he couldn't even keep still. "She may go out for a few hours, but she always comes back home. She would never do this to us without calling. Something had to have happened to her."

The tall officer scratched his head. "Neither of you got concerned when she didn't come home last night? You did say she was pregnant, didn't you?"

"I didn't get home until late." Rashad shifted his eyes toward me. "If I had known she wasn't at home, I wouldn't have gone to sleep. I would have called you a long time ago."

Both officers' eyes were now on me. *Way to go, Rashad. Blame it all on me, why don't you?*

"Did you check on her, ma'am?"

I didn't want to lie, but I didn't want to tell the truth so Rashad could jump down my throat either.

"Ma'am?"

"Egypt, he's talking to you."

"Ah, no, I didn't. I didn't check on her because we had a little argument before I went out to the store," I admitted. A wave of guilt overtook me. "By the time my husband came home, I thought she was in her room sleeping. I never even really knew she left the house."

"See, this is what I'm talking about," Rashad jumped in, shooting daggers at me with his eyes and pointing an accusatory finger. "What are you doing arguing with her? You know how sensitive she is. Your arguing hasn't helped the situation one bit." His finger was getting very close to my face. "You didn't see her all night and didn't think to check on her?"

"Calm down, sir," said the shorter officer. "Your wife is probably right. There's really nothing she could have said that made her leave the house unless your sister-in-law wanted to leave. Did you see any sign of forced entry?"

"No," we both said in unison.

"Well, then, she's probably off with her baby's father. This type of thing happens more than you'd think."

Rashad spoke up. "I doubt that very seriously. I'm the baby's father, Officer."

"What the h—?" The taller officer caught himself before he finished. "Didn't you say this was your wife?"

"Yes," Rashad answered stupidly.

"But you got your sister-in-law pregnant?"

Rashad nodded, and both officers turned to each other, trying to hide smirks. I knew what they were thinking. They thought we were running some type of freak show, and Rashad wasn't saying a word in our defense.

I tried to explain, "Officers, my sister is our surro—"

The other officer threw his hand up to stop me. "No need for explanation. Look, that's not our business. Virginia law says we can't report a person missing until twenty-four hours after they disappear." He put his notepad back in his pocket, then handed me a business card.

"If she's not back by five, give us a call."

"That's in five hours. What the hell's the difference? That woman's carrying my baby." Rashad was visibly angry. "I thought the first forty-eight hours were the most critical in a missing person's case."

"I understand what you're saying, sir, but the law says twenty-four hours, and that's what my supervisors are going to hold me to."

I felt a coldness sink down to my toes. What if the next five hours made all the difference, and these cops were refusing to do anything before then?

I was scared for her safety, but at the same time, I was so livid I could strangle her. Lord help her if she was all right and had just neglected to call.

After the two officers left, Rashad and I sat quietly as the minutes on the clock ticked slowly by. I think he was emotionally spent. As for me, I was busy analyzing everything he had said. Sure, we were both worried, but Rashad had wasted no time turning his concern into anger—at me! And here's what stuck in my mind the most: He'd told the cops she was carrying *his* baby. Not ours, his.

Maybe my mother was right. Maybe having Isis act as a surrogate wasn't such a good idea. Was Rashad just concerned about the baby, or did he still have feelings for Isis? It hurt that I even had to ask myself that question, but his behavior today made me wonder if maybe our marriage was still on shaky ground, even with a baby on the way. Having this epiphany left me speechless for a long while.

Finally, I couldn't stand it anymore, and I spoke up to Rashad. "You're acting like she's your wife. You're so worried about what's going on with Isis that you can't see me over here dying a little inside every day. Have you even considered what's going on with me?" My eyes were starting to tear.

"Egypt, this is no time to be acting like a drama queen," he said with a sigh. "We've got to worry about Isis and our baby."

I started to say, *So, now it's* our *baby,* but I stopped myself before I stirred up more trouble. I didn't want to drive a deeper wedge between us. If I pushed too hard, I might just push him back into Isis's arms. She was already holding the trump card with that baby inside of her.

"Ain't that some shit."

I followed Rashad's gaze out the window to see what had him sounding so upset. A black SUV with New York plates was pulling up to our driveway.

"Oh, hell no! That's Tony's truck."

"Yeah, and Isis is getting out of it," he growled.

"That's *your* girl," I snapped, feeling vindicated.

"Don't start, okay?"

"I'm not trying to start. I just want you to understand that what I do is for your benefit. I'm your wife, for better or for worse, 'cause, baby, I got your back."

"You was right. I was wrong." It took a lot for him to admit that, and it meant a lot to me to hear him say it.

"Egypt, I want you to call that real estate agent in L.A., 'cause once she has the baby, I want her ass out my house. Does that make you feel better?"

"Much better," I said with a smirk.

Three and a half more months of this madness and then she was outta here.

Isis

38

Egypt and Rashad were going to kill me, and I probably deserved it. I hadn't even bothered to leave a note when I left the house after Tony showed up unexpectedly. At first I wouldn't open the door for him, because I thought he was there to whip my ass for showing up at his house Thanksgiving weekend. We hadn't spoken since then, because I was too afraid to call him. When I stood in front of his wife, telling her I was pregnant with Tony's child, it had seemed like a good idea, but as I drove away from the home, I realized that doing it in front of his kids and his mother-in-law was pretty stupid. It was one thing to disrespect a man's wife. He could handle her if he had to. But I had put him in the position of having to explain to his kids, and I was sure he was pissed.

To my surprise, though, he didn't sound angry at all as he stood outside the door, begging to come in. I was worried it was just an act so he could get inside and get his hands around my throat, but the more he confessed his love and pleaded with me to open the door, the more I remembered that Tony could never stay mad at me for very long.

When he walked through the door looking like a great big teddy bear, my heart just melted. He must have felt the same way when he saw my big belly, because he gave me a kiss that took my breath away. I was so happy to see him that I didn't think twice about getting in his truck and leaving five minutes after he walked through the door. I just grabbed my coat and my bag, and I was gone. I didn't even go upstairs to get my cell phone. I'd had an argument with my sister earlier, so calling her was the last thing on my mind anyway.

Tony showed me the best time I'd had since moving to Richmond. He took me shopping at South Park Mall in Colonial Heights, and we visited the bookstore owned by my favorite author, Carl Weber. I had so many shopping bags in Tony's trunk, I didn't know how I was going to sneak them past Egypt. Some of the stuff was for the baby, but most of it was for me. After shopping and then dinner at Red Lobster, we ended up at the Richmond Coliseum for the Frankie Beverly and Maze concert. Tony must have really planned this out, because our seats were the absolute bomb. I had no idea it was going to be an overnight stay but didn't exactly protest when he pulled into the Hilton Garden Inn on Broad Street. It was so nice to go out and not be the third wheel.

"Tony, I'm really happy." I leaned my head against his shoulder and he wrapped his arm around me as we walked from the parking area to the hotel lobby.

"So am I."

"No, I'm really happy—not to mention touched. You never spent a Christmas Eve with me before." I held his arm a little tighter.

"Yeah, I know. I'm sorry about that. But things are going to be different now. A lot different. I promise." I hadn't heard that kind of sentiment from him since the day I took those pills and he confessed his undying love to me. But that was when he thought I was halfway to the grave, and he wouldn't have to follow through on a promise he couldn't keep. I had to wonder: Obviously I wasn't dying, so what was inspiring him to make these promises now?

"Different how?"

He stopped walking and turned to face me with a somber expression. "Monica and I are getting a divorce."

I released my arm from his and said with a sigh, "You don't have to lie to me. I made my peace with you being married a long time ago."

"I'm not lying. If you want, we can go back to the truck and you can see the papers she served me with."

I searched his face for some telltale change in his expression— a flinching of his facial muscles or a lack of eye contact that would prove to me that he was lying—but there was nothing like that. He looked me dead in the eye, and his voice was steady and even. Hmmm, maybe he wasn't lying.

"So, where does that leave us?"

"Right now I'm staying with my parents, but I want you and the baby to come stay with me after I get settled. I want you to come back home to Queens. I love you, Isis. When my divorce is final, I want you to be my wife."

I was starting to believe him, until he threw in the part about marrying me. Another telltale sign of a liar is someone who throws in too much detail or makes his story sound too good to be true, and Tony was definitely doing that now. Well, I would just have to call his bluff.

"You know, on second thought, I think I would like to see those papers you supposedly have in your car."

I expected him to hesitate, to come up with some bullshit about why he couldn't show them to me now or even to admit that it was a lie. Instead, he took my hand and said, "Okay, let's go back and get them."

This had me totally confused. Was he just stalling, using this walk to the car as time to think up a good lie? Maybe we'd get there and he'd pretend he misplaced them or something. Or was it possible that he really did have papers, and he really was getting a divorce?

When he reached into his glove compartment and pulled out a thick envelope, which he handed to me, I felt my knees becoming weak. It was looking more and more like my dream was actually coming true, and Tony would soon be single. As I read the legal documents that I pulled out of the envelope, I had to lean against the truck to keep from collapsing.

"Oh my God, Tony! It's really true! You're getting a divorce." Maybe it was inappropriate, but I couldn't help but laugh with excitement. I had been waiting for a very long time for his wife to leave us alone so we could be together the way we were meant to be. Rationally, I knew this meant he would be living apart from his kids, and that would tear him up, but we could work that out. In the meantime, I would make sure he was so well taken care of that he wouldn't have time to be sad.

I threw my arms around his neck and kissed all over his face. "I really thought you were playing," I said, still breathless with delight.

"Does this look like I'm playing?" He bent down on one knee right in the middle of the parking lot and pulled out a small box from his jacket.

"Isis, will you marry me?"

"Yes! Yes, Tony, I'll marry you." I think you could put that down as the happiest moment of my life. I melted into his embrace and imagined myself there, safe and warm, for the rest of my life.

I don't even know how we ended up in our room, but somehow we did, making up for lost time. I could honestly classify the sex as the best I'd ever had. That man put something on me, and might I dare say, I put it right back on him. Whoever said pregnant sex was the best ain't never lied.

I went to sleep feeling like I was in a fantasy, a dream come true, but when I woke up, reality set in, in the form of a kick to the belly. The clock on the nightstand told me it was eight, right around the time Rashad would be in the kitchen making breakfast.

I rubbed my hand over my swollen abdomen to calm the baby, but he wasn't having it. I felt another kick.

Hungry, huh? You miss your daddy's cooking, don't you? So do I.

With thoughts of Rashad came a massive wave of guilt. He was probably worried sick, and Egypt, she was probably ready to kill me. Yeah, I always thought that what I wanted was a man of my own, but now that Tony was beside me and I was wearing the diamond he'd given me last night, I wasn't so sure I was happy about it. Suddenly, I was living proof of that old maxim, "Be careful what you wish for." What the hell had I gotten myself into?

Okay, boo-boo, Momma's gonna get you something to eat. Just give her a minute.

I tried to shift my body so I could slip out of bed, but when I moved, Tony moved with me, and his arm came to rest on my stomach.

The baby kicked again. I couldn't help but think he was trying to tell me something. Probably something like, *Get that man's hand off me. Isn't it bad enough that I'm swimming in his sperm?*

He kicked again, and you best believe I removed Tony's hand.

I'm sorry. You just don't know how hard it is, how lonely it can be. You want your mommy to be happy, don't you?

I glanced at my engagement ring sadly. It was no longer a symbol of our love; it was a reminder of the lie that had prompted Tony to ask me to marry him. I had to wonder, Would he have asked if he knew it wasn't his baby I was carrying? But then a thought occurred to me. What if, by some chance, Tony was the baby's father? I mean, there was that one time, and condoms aren't 100 percent foolproof.

Another kick told me to stop dreaming and face the facts. That baby just wanted to go home to his dad. And I'd be lying if I said a part of me didn't want to go also.

I slid out of bed without Tony even noticing. As I headed to the bathroom, I noticed the phone on the desk and decided to call Rashad so he could stop worrying.

I picked up the receiver, but before I could start to dial, Tony woke up. "Hey, you. You calling room service?"

"No, I was thinking about calling my sister and letting her know I was okay."

"That's right. You haven't called home yet, have you?"

"No, and it's gonna be a problem." That part wasn't a lie. Last thing I wanted to hear was Egypt talking shit all Christmas Day, but I had no doubt that was exactly what would happen.

He sat up. "Don't worry. I'll explain it to them."

I shook my head and put the phone down. "That would make it worse."

"Fuck it. They're just gonna have to get used to it. We're getting married and having a baby. Shit, we're family now." He got out of the bed and came to my side, wrapping his arms around me.

If I had the guts, this would have been the moment for me to tell him the truth about the baby. But he felt so good pressed up against me that I didn't want the moment to end. Plus, I knew he was already hurting over his divorce, so I couldn't bear to bring him any more pain. I needed more time. Dammit, why couldn't the baby just be his so we could get in the truck and go back to Queens right now? With a thirty-thousand-dollar payday looming, though, I wasn't leaving Virginia until I had that money in hand. So, until I could figure out this whole mess, I would just have to play my cards right and keep everyone in the dark.

"Tony, what if I told you I want to keep our engagement a secret?"

"What for? You embarrassed of me?"

"No, baby. That's not it at all. I just want to wait until the right time to spring this on them."

"Spring it on them? The right time? What are you trying to say?" The volume of his voice was escalating. I hadn't meant to make him mad, but I knew I better calm him down in a hurry before things got worse.

I led him to the bed and sat next to him. "Let's role-play for a minute, okay? I'm gonna be my father, and you're going to be you."

"Aw-ight."

"So, you're going to marry my daughter?"

"Yes, sir. I love her," he said confidently.

"Didn't you love her the first time you were engaged to her?" Tony looked a little confused and a lot less confident. "Didn't ya?" I pushed.

"Yes, I did."

"But you was married then, weren't ya?" Tony just looked at me. "C'mon, Tony. We're role-playing, remember?"

He rolled his eyes at me, but I didn't let up. I deepened my voice to try to imitate my father and asked, "Well, weren't ya married then?"

"Yes, you know I was married."

"What about now? You married now."

"I'm getting divorced."

"Well, when your divorce is final, you come see me about marrying my daughter."

Tony frowned but admitted, "I guess I see your point."

"As soon as your divorce is final, we'll have a big party, okay?"

"What if I want a party now?" He kissed me as his hand reached out to cup my breast.

"Have I ever refused to party with you?"

"No, and let's not start now."

Junior kicked me in protest, but this time, I ignored him. I wasn't going to let him, or anyone else, ruin my last bit of fun before I faced Egypt and Rashad. So, on that note, Tony took me in his arms, and we made love one more time.

Later, after we showered, we went to breakfast. I kept thinking I needed to call Rashad and Egypt, but I was enjoying myself too much, so I never picked up the phone.

Finally, around noon, Tony drove me back home. I asked him to let me off at the corner, but he insisted that he drop me off where he picked me up. Of course, you know my two jailers were waiting on the front porch for me.

I turned to Tony. "Please stay in the car."

"You know I don't like this shit."

"I know, but it's just until you get divorced. I'll call you tonight. I promise."

"All right. I'm doing this for you, so there won't be no drama. Take care of that precious cargo you carrying there for me." He patted my belly.

"I will. Promise."

I leaned over and kissed him, then stepped out of the truck. I opened the back door to get my bag, where I'd stashed my engagement ring for the time being.

"Thanks, baby." I blew him a kiss and walked up to the house to face the drama.

Egypt started the second I stepped foot on the porch. "Where the hell you been?"

To my surprise, Rashad sounded just as mad. "I can't believe you would do this," he snapped at me. To make things worse, the baby kicked me.

I know I should have told him. I'll do it when he calls tonight. Right now I got to deal with your daddy and your aunt.

Loraine
39

I hadn't been out on New Year's Eve in quite a few years. Leon and I usually brought in the New Year quietly, sitting in front of the TV watching the ball drop in Times Square. Half the time, I had to wake him up a few minutes before they started the countdown to the New Year. So I was so excited to be going out on the town on New Year's Eve. I felt as giddy as a teenager going on her first date. In a sense, that's what it was like. I hadn't dated since Leon and I met twelve years ago. But tonight was my night. I was starting a new chapter of my life without him.

To get ready for my date, I pulled out all the stops. I made an appointment at Madame McKee's Salon, which was a high-end, one-stop beauty spa in the west end of Richmond. There, I received the works: a facial, a massage, a pedicure, and a manicure, all of which had my skin glowing. I had the famous Madame McKee personally wash and blow-dry my hair. When I left the shop, my hair was bouncing in the wind like Michelle Obama's did on Inauguration Day.

After I showered, I pulled out the white beaded dress Jerome had purchased just for this occasion. I can't even pronounce the French designer's name, but I'm sure with Jerome's taste, he'd paid a pretty penny for it. The way it fit, I can tell you it was worth every dime, because I looked and felt like a million bucks. I studied myself in the full-length mirror. Not bad for a forty-something-year-old woman. Although I was thick, I was beginning to see my waist slim down and hips come back. Since Christmas, I'd gone on a three-day protein diet and dropped seven pounds in the first week, something I was very proud of.

When Michael arrived for our date, I kissed him on the cheek and invited him in. It was a little awkward for me at first, seeing as how this was the first time I'd done this since my marriage—I mean going on a date; what I had had with Terrance was just revenge sex—but any fleeting thoughts of Leon quickly vanished when I saw how handsome Michael looked with his fresh new haircut and sharp black tuxedo. Before the night was over, I would have to ask him the name of his cologne, because he smelled phenomenal.

"You look gorgeous, Loraine. I love that dress, and your hair . . ." He circled around me, checking out every inch. It didn't feel creepy or overly sexual; he just made me feel beautiful.

"Why, thank you, Michael. You don't look so bad yourself."

We didn't linger in the house long. We had eight o'clock reservations at this exclusive French restaurant, Chez Pierre, in historic Shockoe Bottom. I will tell you chivalry is not dead, because Michael held not only the car door for me when we left the house, but also every other door I went through for the rest of the night.

The restaurant was crowded—I guess the pre–New Year's Eve crowd planned to eat well before they got their party on. Of course, when the waiter escorted us to our table, Michael held out my chair. He ordered a very expensive bottle of wine—in French, no less. I ordered duck. Michael ordered the same. While we waited for our meals, we made small talk and drank nearly the whole bottle of wine. Michael seemed to sense that I wasn't ready for any kind of deep conversations about the state of my marriage, so he allowed me to steer the conversation, and I kept it light. I must say that after all the doom and gloom I'd been feeling for the past few months, it was a pleasure to chat about insignificant things, like our secret shared addiction to certain reality TV shows. Michael kept me laughing until our main courses arrived.

When our meals were set in front of us, Michael bowed his head, took my hand, and said grace. I was impressed. Leon and I had stopped blessing our food in the past few years, and I can't even tell you why. Here was another good point: The man was a Christian. I wasn't trying to get my hopes up, nor did I necessarily feel ready for a steady relationship, but I still couldn't help making a list in my head of Michael's good points. So far, I hadn't come up with anything to put in the "bad" category.

"I'm so glad you came out with me tonight," Michael said as he put down his fork. "I've been thinking about you ever since we ran into each other. This is definitely starting this new year out on the right foot for me."

"I've thought about you too," I said, then put another forkful of food in my mouth to avoid saying more. I wasn't ready to go further than admitting that he'd been on my mind.

Once dinner was finished and we'd had dessert, Michael held up his glass and proposed a toast. "To the future. May it be as bright and beautiful as the woman I'm sitting across from."

I was blushing so bad I had to lower my head. What a sweet, sweet man. "You sure know how to flatter a girl," I told him.

"I call them as I see them."

We went to the Marriott, where the governor was known to ring in the New Year. From what I could tell, Michael had just as many contacts in the city as I did, because this ball was very exclusive. Not just anyone could get into a party like this.

I love to dance, and as it turned out, so did Michael. I didn't know too many black men who knew how to tango, but Michael happened to be one of them. He was so light on his feet and was able to spin and dip me so well that I felt like I was on *Dancing with the Stars.*

"You're really a good dancer," Michael whispered in my ear.

"Thanks," I murmured back. "I was just thinking the same thing about you."

The one problem with doing the tango with him was that the dance was so sensual it was damn sure putting me in the mood. I was determined I was not going to be a one-night stand—not that I necessarily thought Michael was going there, as respectful as he'd been all night—so I tried to keep my mind off how good my body felt pressed against his.

A voice came over the loudspeaker. "Ladies and gentlemen, we are about to count down the new year!"

Michael wrapped his arm around me as we chanted along with everyone else, "Ten, nine, eight . . ." We reached "Happy

New Year!" and confetti flew up in the air, champagne corks popped, and the blare of noisemakers filled the room. Michael leaned in and gave me a gentle kiss on the lips. I reciprocated by wrapping my arms around his neck and kissing him back.

"Happy New Year, Loraine. I hope this year's all that you want it to be."

"Thank you. Happy New Year to you too. It's off to a great start."

On our way home from the Marriott, Michael asked me if I'd like to see him again. Of course I said yes without any hesitation, and we made plans to have dinner that Friday night. For the first time in months, I felt alive again, maybe even a little sexy after all his compliments. He really was an exceptional man, along with being a great kisser. I honestly felt my life would be better with him in it.

We pulled up to my house, still involved in a conversation about our favorite books. We stayed in the car to continue the conversation, and the next thing I knew, it was almost four o'clock in the morning. I can't even remember half of what we talked about, as the subject shifted from books to friends to other topics, but no matter the subject, I felt like I was hanging on every word he said. He was one of the most intelligent men I'd ever met. Brainy men have always done something to me, especially the good-looking ones.

When I started yawning and decided it was time to call it a night, Michael was out of the car, running around to my side before I could even get my door open. He walked me to my front door, and as I put the key in the lock, he turned me toward him and kissed me. Unlike the fairly tame "Happy New Year" kiss we'd shared, this time he surprised me by sliding his tongue in my mouth. Talk about turning up the heat.

I'd had enough wine and champagne to loosen my inhibitions, and I was considering asking him to spend the night. By the time he started kissing my neck, I was trying to remember if I had kept any of those condoms they gave out as favors at the bachelorette party I went to last month. I could only pray that sleeping with him on the first date wasn't going to run him away, because at this point, I was pretty much committed—that is, until some headlights blinded us as a car pulled into the driveway like a bat out of hell.

"Loraine, what the hell are you doing?" I couldn't see him because of the glare of the headlights, but I recognized Leon's voice. Then again, who else would be pulling into my driveway at four o'clock in the morning, harassing me?

"Leon, get out of here before I call the cops." By the time my eyes adjusted to the light, he was stumbling toward us.

"Who is this clown?" Michael stepped in front of me.

"I'm her husband! That's who I am. Who the fuck are you?"

"Leon, you're drunk, and you're going to wake up the entire neighborhood. Someone's going to call the cops."

"If they don't, I will," Michael added.

"Fuck those siddity motherfuckers. Now, who the fuck is this, and why is he kissing all on you?" Leon stepped closer to Michael, but Michael stood his ground. I watched the muscles tensing in his shoulders, and I knew things could get explosive in a moment. I pulled my cell phone out of my purse.

"Look, man, the lady doesn't want you here." They stared each other down like two gladiators about to do battle.

"You fucking my wife?" Leon was starting to cry.

"I don't think that's any of your business."

"You fucking him, Loraine?" He looked past Michael and directed his accusatory stare at me.

I held up my cell phone. "Leon, I just called the police. You have about five minutes before they get here. Unless you want to get arrested for DWI, I suggest you get out of here."

Luckily, he was drunk enough that he didn't question my lie. "I'll take that as a yes." Without further incident, he turned and went back to his car. "I never cheated on you with that woman, Loraine. Not even once."

Isis

40

Egypt was so pissed off at me for hanging out with Tony on Christmas Eve that she had been trying to make my life a living hell ever since. It seemed like all we did was argue—about *my* body, no less—from the minute I got up to the moment I went to bed. She had a comment about every bit of food I put in my mouth, how many hours of sleep I was getting, or if I was getting enough exercise. She even had the nerve to comment on my maternity shirts being too tight, as if they might strangle the baby or something. If I said up, she said down; if said I blue, she'd say brown.

What I didn't understand was why she was so upset with Tony being back in the picture, because all of a sudden, she and Rashad were all lovey-dovey. The more she fought with me, the closer they got to each other. They'd been going at it like two rabbits in heat. I even caught them doing it on the damn washing machine one day, which upset my stomach worse than any morning sickness.

In the good old days, it would have taken me no time to make Rashad forget why he was mad at me, but now things were different. I couldn't convince him to forgive me, because I couldn't even get him to talk to me. His revenge for my night out with Tony was the exact opposite of Egypt's approach. He wasn't speaking to me at all, which, I'm sure he knew, was much more painful than Egypt's constant arguing. He had always been this way. When Rashad and I were dating, he never argued after the initial fight. He'd state his position, then give me the silent treatment, sometimes for days or weeks. He would barely acknowledge my presence, which drove me crazy. One thing I inherited from my mother was a need to be seen.

As bad as things were now, I still held out hope for us. With the baby's due date only a few months away, he would have to come around, or he'd miss out on a lot of joyful moments.

He almost broke the other day when Egypt and I were arguing about the sex of the baby. He was very passionate about wanting a boy. That's why I was sure that once we had the sonogram today, his silence would end.

When we arrived at the doctor's office, Rashad and Egypt were still treating me like a pariah, sitting as far away from me as they could in the waiting room. I sat alone and rubbed my belly, wondering when they would wake up and realize that without me, this baby wouldn't exist. They had better start showing me some respect real soon, or I might just pull another disappearing act for a few days to scare their asses.

The nurse called me in to the exam room, and Rashad and Egypt both jumped up from their seats. Rashad had never gone into the exam room with me, thanks to Egypt's paranoid, jealous ass, but this time he insisted. Nothing was going to stop him from seeing this sonogram and learning the sex of his child. Still, Egypt made one last attempt to control the situation.

"Baby, you don't have to go in the examination room with us."

"Yes, I do. I want to know what we're having just as much as you do." Usually, he backed down pretty easily from Egypt to keep the peace, but today there was a determination in his voice I hadn't heard before. I saw it as an opportunity to get back on his good side.

"I think he should be there," I chimed in.

"Nobody asked you, Isis. This is between me and my husband." I wanted to race across the waiting room and choke the shit outta her ass, but with the nurse standing right there watching us, it wasn't gonna happen. I bit my tongue and headed toward the exam room. I wasn't surprised when Rashad followed right behind me. This was one argument my sister was definitely not going to win.

When we crowded into the small room, Rashad had no

choice but to stand close to me. As soon as his body was near mine, I felt the baby move.

Oh, you're happy, aren't you, junior? You want your mommy and daddy together. I know what you mean; Auntie Egypt needs to take a hike.

When the technician came in with the machine, he put the gel on my stomach and moved the ultrasound wand over my abdomen.

"Is this your first sonogram?" he asked.

"No, they gave her one last month, but the baby was turned with its back toward the front," Egypt answered for me.

I wanted to say, *Well, I'll be damned. I thought he was talking to me,* but Rashad spoke before I could.

"So, will you be able to tell us the baby's sex today?" he asked.

"Sure. As long as the little bambino cooperates. Sometimes they move around so much we can't get a good look at the important parts."

He moved the wand around some more, clicking keys on the computer every once in a while to capture certain images. "This is a big baby for six months," he commented.

"Takes after his daddy, I guess," Rashad said proudly.

"Oh! Here we go," the technician announced. "Talk about being big!"

He pointed to the screen, and I saw the proof of what I'd known all along. I could clearly see a penis. It even looked like he had a little erection.

"I told you I was having a boy," I said smugly.

Egypt jumped her big behind in front of the screen so nobody else could see anything. "M-my God, it *is* a boy!" She stuttered like she couldn't believe it. "Baby, it's a boy!"

Rashad pushed his way up to the computer. "Stop trying to bogart the screen, baby. Let me see."

She stepped aside, and Rashad let out a laugh as Egypt pointed to the baby's penis. He stared at the screen for a minute before he said anything. Then he turned to Egypt and said, "It's a boy. First boy in my family since I was born. I can't believe it."

As I lay there and watched them hug each other, I couldn't

help but feel sorry for myself. Here I was the one making this all possible, and I might as well be invisible. Then Rashad turned to me, and everything was good again.

"Isis, I don't know what to say."

Those were the first words he'd spoken to me in weeks. He broke into this big smile that made all this discomfort worth it. Like I said before, men could never stay mad at me for very long. I breathed a sigh of relief.

"I told you it was a boy," I said again, though there were a million other things I wished I could say to him.

Rashad looked at me now with tears in his eyes. "Thank you. Thank you so much."

He held my gaze for a moment, but then Egypt started pushing up on him, putting her arms around him. "Baby, I'm so happy. We're having a son. This is wonderful."

He kissed her, but I knew that kiss was meant for me. She had to steal the moment, but it was all right. I knew that secret look Rashad had given me. Egypt's days were numbered now that I had given him a son.

When they left the room, I whispered to my baby, "Yep, looks like me and your daddy are back on the same page. I'm going to make sure I do whatever I have to do to make it right for us again."

Jerome

41

I was at my desk daydreaming about the great sex I'd had with Big Poppa the night before when I felt someone entering the room. People didn't just walk in my office without knocking, except for Loraine, whose office was behind mine as part of our suite, and she was out to lunch with Michael. With everything going on with that crazy stalker Peter, I casually took hold of my letter opener before I looked up. If by chance it was him, I was going to show him exactly who the crazy one was, 'cause I was getting sick of his shit. Everywhere I went, that motherfucker seemed to show up, and if he wasn't there, he'd call me up to let me know he knew I was there. Shit, I felt like a fool to be asking myself this now, but did his crazy ass have a job? I don't see how he could have, because it seemed like he was making a career out of following me. Maybe from now on I should learn a little more about a person before we got naked.

A simple glance around the room told me it wasn't Peter hovering over me, but my coworkers, Egypt and Hannah, who was from reception. When we made eye contact, they were both giggling at me like two teenagers who had a secret and couldn't wait to share. I expected this sort of thing out of Hannah—she was a young girl who was always in the middle of office gossip—but Egypt needed to quit. She was about to become a mother.

"Jerome"—Hannah laughed playfully—"when I die, I want to come back as you."

"Me too." Egypt chuckled along, raising her hand as if she were testifying. "'Cause, honey, you are the man."

I kind of laughed along with them, although I didn't have a clue what was so funny. "Excuse me, but could you two clue me in on what the hell is going on?"

Egypt walked over and placed a hand on my shoulder. "Jerome, honey, I owe you a big-time apology."

I raised an eyebrow. "Why's that?"

"Because when you used to tell us about Big Poppa and how fine he was, I thought you were lying. But, honey, you were right. He is some kind of fine. Mmm, mmm, mmm." She stomped her foot.

I was totally confused. "And you know this because . . . ?"

This didn't even sound right, because Big Poppa would never show up at the job asking for me, especially not using his nickname. It would blow his cover, and he was all about staying on the DL. Besides, he was too well known; if he strolled into our offices, Egypt and Hannah would have recognized him right away.

Hannah chimed in. "You know, Jerome, I have to admit, I would have never expected Big Poppa to be a white guy."

I had to suppress a scream. That was definitely not Big Poppa they were talking about.

Before I could ask for more details, Egypt said, "Who cares if he's white, black, green, or yellow? The man is drop-your-drawers fine."

"I care if he's white," I snapped as I stood up. I was through with both their nosy asses and was feeling a little more than threatened, since I suspected the white guy they were talking about was Peter. "Especially since Big Poppa is black."

"Uh-oh," Hannah murmured.

"Uh-oh is right. Where the hell did you meet this guy?"

They exchanged guilty glances; then Hannah said quietly, "In reception. He's waiting for you."

I picked up my letter opener and headed out the door with both of them in tow.

Peter was standing in the reception area like he didn't have a care in the world. He was holding what must have been three dozen roses and a big-ass box of candy.

"Happy Valentine's Day." He tried to hand me the flowers and candy, but I threw my hands up in refusal.

"What the hell are you doing in my office?"

"Big Poppa's come to give you your Valentine presents and take you to lunch."

I shot him a disgusted glare. "I'm not going anywhere with your lunatic ass. And you're not Big Poppa."

"Jerome, I'm so sorry," Hannah said. She and Egypt stood a safe distance away from me and Peter. I guess they now realized that we had a psycho in our office. "When I saw the flowers and the candy, I asked if he was Big Poppa."

"It's not her fault, Jerome. It was just a slip. But what I want to know is, just who is this Big Poppa?"

"That's none of your business." As crazy as Peter was, Big Poppa's identity was the last thing I wanted him to know. He would make both our lives hell.

"Everything about you is my business, Jerome. How many times do I have to tell you that?"

"How many times do I have to tell you that you're one sick individual?"

"As many times as you want, I guess. But I'm not crazy. I'm in love. Haven't you figured it out yet?"

"None of that matters if I don't love you."

"So, you used me? I was just a piece of flesh for your enjoyment. Do you enjoy using people? Ruining their lives?"

Egypt and Hannah stood there, totally engrossed in the drama. Neither one of them made a move to call security.

"Look, man, it was a fling for both of us. Something to do. Besides, you're the one who's married. You left your wife's bed to sneak out and get a blow job."

"Oh, shit!" Egypt let slip. I cut my eyes at her. God, I hated office gossip, and this was a story that was going to be told for years to come.

"Peter, I'm sorry if you've been hurt, but you gotta move on."

"So, who do you love? That young boy up in DC, or is it this Big Poppa nobody seems to know about?"

I could see it in his eyes. It was driving him crazy that he hadn't known about Big Poppa.

"Who I love is none of your business."

He laughed. "Like I told you before, Jerome, you are my business. And now, so is Big Poppa."

I hate to admit it, but his words struck true fear in my heart. I couldn't let him know it, though, so I barked, "Hannah, call security."

"No." He shook his head. "You don't have to do that." He placed the flowers and candy on the reception desk. "Happy Valentine's Day, Jerome. I wish I could have spent it in your arms . . . but I guarantee nobody else will, because if I can't have you, nobody will."

I watched him walk to the elevator and leave.

"That man ever comes back here . . ."

"I know," Hannah said, "call security."

"No, call the police. That man is crazy. Next time he shows up around here, I'm betting he's going to have a gun."

After talking to Loraine, I decided that this whole situation with Peter was getting way out of hand. At her suggestion, I went down to the police station to file a stalking complaint. The station was filled with people milling around. Some police officers ran out on calls, some officers sat around shooting the breeze, and others were working on computers. I went straight to the desk sergeant, who was a husky, out-of-shape white guy.

"How can I help you?" he asked. He peered over his glasses, giving me the impression that he really didn't want to be there.

"I'd like to find out what the stalking laws are here in Virginia."

The sergeant paused, rolling his eyes. "So, which one are you, the stalker or the stalkee?" He chuckled, but I remained stone-faced.

"I'm the stalkee."

"You know, women are crazy these days." The sergeant opened up a three-ring binder, lowered his head, and started to write. "Okay, what's her name?"

"It's not a her. It's a him."

He lifted his head. "It's a him? Your stalker's a guy?"

I nodded. "Yes, sir."

"Well, that's a new one." I can't even describe the look he gave me. He might as well have just called me a fag to my face. "What's the relationship between you and this *guy*?"

"None. We have no relationship."

The sergeant looked up from what he was writing again. "So, he's stalking you, but you have no relationship at all? How do you know each other? Are you fucking his wife or his ex-girlfriend or something?"

"We were intimate for a short period of time. He thinks he's in love with me."

"Ok-*ay*," the sergeant said, not even bothering to hide his disgust. "So, how exactly is he stalking you?"

"The guy follows me wherever I go. He takes pictures of me and my friends. He came to my job today with flowers and candy."

"Flowers and candy. Some might say he's courting you."

"He's not courting me. The guy's friggin' crazy."

"Has he violated your person or property? Has he harmed you at all?"

I paused. The truth was that Peter was never standing close by when he was trailing me, so I couldn't say he was violating my physical space. To my knowledge, he'd never broken into my house or trespassed on my property, and although I suspected he'd been in my car, I had no proof.

"No." I shook my head.

"Is he calling you and/or threatening you?"

"Well, sort of. He told me that if he can't have me, nobody will."

"That's a rather vague statement. Is that all you got?" He looked like I was wasting his time.

I knew I could make him take me seriously if I told him about Ron and the pictures, but I wouldn't violate Ron's privacy like that. I tried one last time to convince the officer that this was not a joke.

"Look, this guy is crazy, and somebody's gonna get hurt if you don't do something."

"I understand how you feel, but unless he commits a crime,

my hands are tied. What's this guy's name? Maybe he has a warrant."

"Peter McMann."

The sergeant sat up straight in his chair. Finally, the smug, amused look on his face was gone. Something had definitely grabbed his attention. "Did you say Peter McMann? *The* Peter McMann?"

"I guess. Is there another one?"

"Oh my God. Did you say you were sleeping with him?"

I nodded.

"You trying to tell me Peter McMann is gay? Jesus Christ, I know his entire family. My kid plays ball with his son."

"Look, I'm not here to pull anyone out the closet. I just want the man to leave me alone. I take it you know this guy?"

"Everyone knows Peter McMann."

I was gonna shit my pants if this guy told me Peter was some kind of career criminal. "Peter McMann is the top investigative reporter for the *Richmond Times Dispatch*. That guy has blown the lid off a hundred stories."

"Well, if he looks like George Clooney, then that's our man. Has he been known to stalk people?"

"Only for a story. What exactly do you do for work?"

"I'm the executive assistant to Loraine Farrow at BLAZE. Why?"

"Because Peter McMann doesn't stalk people; he investigates them. He's cracked more cases than most of the detectives in this building. Who do you think cracked the James River murders last year?"

"Peter?"

"That's right. He's also the one who led to the takedown of the Browns' drug cartel down Southside."

I'd heard about the Browns thing. It was all over the news. Well, this explained how Peter had been able to take down Ron the way he had and why he seemed to always know where I was. Of all the men in this world to turn out, I had to pick a psycho investigative news reporter.

"What I wanna know is why a man like Peter McMann has an interest in you."

"We were just lovers. Obviously, he read more into the situation than was there."

He looked doubtful.

"Look, I can see where you're trying to go with this. I'm not a crook, a drug dealer, or anything else illegal. If you want to know why Peter is so interested in me, it's because I give a hell of a blow job." The sergeant flinched. Idiot had probably seen more blood and death than I could imagine, but the thought of two men having sex was more than he could handle.

"Now, can you help me or not?"

"Mister, the only help I can give you right now is a little advice. Whatever you're doing, if I were you, I would stop, because Peter McMann is not somebody you want to play with."

Tell me something I don't already know.

Isis

42

It was two in the morning, and the house was quiet. I was alone with my thoughts. I held on to the railing as I slowly climbed the stairs from a late-night pantry raid. Lately, I'd been addicted to salt-and-vinegar potato chips and mango salsa.

I was more than thankful that the lovebirds had finally calmed their hormones and gone to sleep. They'd been going at it ever since they came home from their little Valentine's Day dinner cruise.

I almost let Tony scoop me up and take me out for Valentine's Day. I hadn't seen him since Christmas, and he was begging me to let him come down so he could spend time with me. A night on the town away from Egypt's controlling ass and some good dick would be just what the doctor ordered right about now too. Unfortunately, that was sure to piss off my baby daddy, Rashad, so I told Tony no and stayed home alone on Valentine's Day. If only Rashad could have been as thoughtful toward me and kept it quiet in his bedroom tonight.

I waddled down the hall past my room and into the nursery. The truth was, I hated this room, if only because of what it stood for. To me it was a constant reminder that Egypt planned on taking my baby when he was born and shipping my ass to California. I almost puked as I watched her damn near break her back, painting and putting up wallpaper to put this ugly-ass room together.

I wanted to say, *What the fuck is the point? He's never going to spend a night in here,* but obviously I knew it wouldn't be smart to reveal that plan. Better to let her continue in her fantasy world, where she thought that my baby was going to be hers.

The closer it got to my due date, the more she played the role of expectant mother. Last week, some white chick named Hannah from her job even threw her a baby shower. They had the nerve to have me there front and center, rubbing on my belly like I was some kind of Buddha. Meanwhile, they presented Egypt with all the baby shower gifts. It took all my strength to get through that charade.

The one thing I did like recently was that I'd started Lamaze class, and Rashad was my official coach. I say official, because, of course, Egypt had to tag along. But I didn't care. I just ignored her as much as I could, focusing on my breathing and allowing Rashad to hold my hand and encourage me the way the teacher instructed. Egypt was so into the whole experience that when the pregnant women in the room practiced the breathing techniques, she was panting right along with us. She looked like such a fool.

I laughed at that image as I sat down in the glider rocker next to the bassinet and opened the bag of chips. Egypt hadn't put up any curtains yet, so the room was partially illuminated by the streetlights. Unfortunately, even in the half-lighted room, I could still see the ugly lavender she'd picked out for the walls. Why the hell she would pick such a girly color when we'd already found out the baby was a boy made no sense to me. As far as I was concerned, it was just another sign that she wasn't fit to be a mother.

It didn't really matter anyway, because she was never going to be a mother to this child. I had a plan, and as long as the arrival of my mother in a few weeks didn't ruin things, I would be keeping this baby and the money. I wasn't sure if she was coming to help Egypt after the birth, as she claimed, or to keep a close eye on me, but with her intuitive behind, she was the only person who could really stop me.

I patted my stomach gently.

"Did you know they plan on shipping me out right after you're born, junior?"

The baby started squirming.

"Calm down, little one. I'm not going anywhere, not without you, at least, and perhaps your daddy. "

After one last kick, he settled down.

"That's right, junior. You're gonna be with your real mommy, not an auntie who wants to pretend she's your mommy. They think I'm moving to L.A. and you're staying here, but I have news for them. . . . Oh, I'm moving all right, but they don't have any idea where. Although once he finds out, I really believe your daddy will come follow us." I smiled at the thought.

"'Cause, baby, ain't no way in hell am I giving you up to Egypt. Nope. I'm not giving up my baby to that bitch who stole your daddy from me in the first place. That's what's wrong with this whole picture."

Suddenly, the nursery door opened. Light from the hallway flooded the room.

"Isis?" It was Rashad, and he was carrying a baseball bat. "I thought I heard someone in here. What are you doing up?"

I answered him once my heart rate calmed down. "I was talking to your son." I placed a hand on my belly. "He keeps kicking me."

Rashad walked into the room and sat down on a short stepladder Egypt had used to hang wallpaper. He looked rather GQ-ish, sitting there with no shirt and his plaid pajama bottoms, holding the baseball bat.

"Hey, Rashad, can I ask you something?"

"Yeah, I guess."

I pointed at where the bat was positioned between his legs. "Is that a baseball bat, or are you just happy to see me?" I said with a laugh.

"Huh?" It took him a second to catch on to the joke, but then he laughed too. "You stupid, Isis. You know that? Real stupid."

"Yeah, I know, but—" The baby kicked me hard, and I held on to my stomach. "Oh, there he goes again."

"You okay?"

"Yeah, I'm fine, but you need to talk to your son."

"I wish I could."

"Why can't you? You're his daddy, aren't you? Put your hands on my stomach." I guess all he needed was an invitation, because he didn't hesitate to lean over and touch my belly with both hands. "Now talk to him."

Rashad looked up at me. I was giving him a gift, and his smile let me know he appreciated it.

"Go ahead, talk to your son."

He leaned his face close to my stomach and spoke softly. "Hey there, little man. This is your daddy talking to you. I just want you to know that I love you, and I can't wait until you come out into the world."

Rashad pulled his hand away quickly. "Oh my God, I could feel your stomach moving. I didn't do anything wrong, did I?"

"No, silly. He's moving because he likes what you said. He was just trying to let you know that he heard you."

"Really? Can I talk to him some more?"

"Of course you can."

He placed his hands on my stomach again. "Like I was saying, I can't wait until you come into the world. Me and you, we're going to be tight, man. Just like me and your grandpa before he passed away. I'm never gonna let you down, man. I promise." You should have seen the pride in Rashad's eyes as the baby moved around under his hands. It truly was a beautiful sight.

"I can't believe I was just talking to him. Man, that was crazy cool. Thank you, Pooh."

I took a deep breath, then sat back in the chair, his hands still on my belly. "Pooh. Wow, you're taking me back." He had called me by the pet name he gave me when we were a couple.

"Yeah, we do have a lot of history, don't we?" His voice softened, and his eyes looked kind of distant for a second. Like me, I'm sure he was thinking of what used to be, in another place and another time.

"We'll have even more history in a month or two."

"I can't believe I'm going to be a father." He started to rub my belly, but it felt more like a massage.

"I can't believe I'm going to have a baby."

After a few moments of silence, during which he kept massaging me, I said, "Can I ask you a question?"

"Uh-huh, ask away."

"Are you going to be satisfied with just one child?"

"Of course I'd like to have more than one child, but right now I'm satisfied with the one that you're carrying." He removed his hands from my belly.

"Don't stop. It relaxes the baby," I said, though it was really for my own benefit.

He smiled and put his hands back on me. "Have I told you how much I appreciate what you're doing for me and Egypt?"

"Uh-huh, you sure have, but I'll tell you a secret."

"What?"

"I'm not having this baby for Egypt. I'm doing it for you. Only you."

He stopped rubbing again. I almost wished I hadn't said what I did, because I could see that my confession bothered him. "Really? Why? She's your sister."

"Because I could see how much you wanted a baby. It was tearing you up inside. You're not a drinker, but you were drunk every night. If I hadn't agreed to have this baby for you, who knows where you might be right now? Heck, you might not even be married."

"Yep," he admitted, "that was definitely a low point in my life."

Then he tried to minimize his own pain by saying, "Don't get me wrong. Egypt and I would have been okay even if we didn't have a child, but this is so much better."

I wasn't interested in hearing about Egypt, and especially about the strength of their relationship. I kept the focus where I wanted it. "I couldn't bear to see you that way. You haven't realized by now that I'd do anything for you? I never stopped loving you."

"Whoa." He moved back to put a little distance between us. "This conversation is getting a little uncomfortable for me."

"Why? Because you feel the same way?"

"No, because I'm married to your sister. Doesn't that mean anything to you?"

"Well, I'm having your baby. Does that mean anything to you?"

He sighed. "Of course it does. But that doesn't change the fact that I'm married to your sister."

I was getting so sick of everyone considering Egypt's feelings, like I didn't matter.

"What if I told you I was willing to have another baby by you?"

I guess I'd caught his attention with that one. He stood there speechless, just long enough for me to complete my thought. "Instead of moving to L.A., what if I move to Petersburg or Williamsburg? Nobody has to know but me and you. Egypt can have this baby, but the next one can be mine. Matter of fact, we can have two: another boy and a girl. It'd be nice to have a daughter, wouldn't it? Plus, all your kids will have the same blood."

He stared at me for a while. At first I thought maybe he was considering my plan, which was a pretty good one, if you ask me. But finally he just shook his head and turned to leave the room without saying anything.

"Think about it, Rashad," I said to his back before he exited. "How many men have a chance to have the best of both worlds? You can have two sisters, and you know you want some of this. You do remember how good it is, don't you?"

He left without giving me a response, but I told myself that was a good thing. I knew I had gone out on a limb by propositioning him so directly, especially when he was still talking about my sister like theirs was a match made in heaven. So, the fact that he didn't go off on me was a good sign. If I made it to the breakfast table tomorrow without Egypt killing me, I'd know he was at least thinking about it. And then I could feel confident about putting the rest of my plan into action.

The baby started squirming again.

"Relax, junior. I know you don't want to live with Auntie Egypt, but your daddy's going to be there, and it's only a temporary solution. Your momma still loves you. She just has to get your daddy back in bed. Once Auntie finds out we're sleeping together, she's going to divorce your daddy, and you're both going to come live with me and your baby sister or brother. And that, my little darling, is a promise."

Loraine

43

I woke up lying on my back with a smile on my face, physically and mentally satisfied for the first time in five years. It was still dark outside, and I didn't want to wake Michael, so I lay there next to him, reminiscing about the wonderful evening we'd shared. The night started with a fantastic Valentine's dinner cruise on the James River that one of the girls in the office had set up. I'd been on these dinner cruises before, with their dry chicken and hard rolls, but all I could say this time was that the chef outdid himself. The food wasn't just good; it was excellent. I don't think I'd ever had salmon that delicious, and Michael's steak was like butter. The comedian had us all in stitches, and let's not forget the DJ, who was off the chain and had me dancing up a storm.

I was sure there would be a lot of talk at work come Monday morning about how the boss went wild. Most of my staff was probably still in shock, because I never showed that side of myself around the office. I was out on the dance floor, doing the Electric Slide and the Macarena—and I know I took everyone by surprise when I started dirty dancing with Michael. When I was with Leon and we went out, I was usually rather reserved. Michael brought out a confidence and freedom in me that had been missing for quite some time.

Speaking of something I hadn't had in quite some time, I'd finally made love to Michael, after a month and a half of holding out. All I can say is he put it on me last night. I hadn't had sex like that in a long, long time, and the orgasms came one after another in waves that reached from the top of my head to the bottom of my feet. He'd done things to me I hadn't thought possible with a woman my size. I don't know where he got his formal training, but he sure knew his way around a woman's body.

The only real question was, could he do it again? Well, I was about to find out. I kissed his exposed shoulder, then made my way up to his ear, blowing in it lightly.

"Mmm, hey, beautiful." Michael turned over and kissed me.

"Hey yourself, handsome." I kissed him back, reaching down between his legs to take hold of his penis and massage it gently. I loved the way it felt as it grew in my hand.

"You trying to tell me something?"

I shook my head and grinned. "Not you, but him." I tightened my grip on his now fully erect penis.

He kissed my neck as he laughed. "I see. Well, I guess that's a good thing, since he seems to be controlling everything when I'm around you."

"You know what they say—all men think with their dicks." I purred when he nibbled on my earlobe.

"Is that right? Is that what they say?" He gently rolled me on my back.

"Uh-huh, that's what they say." His lips had moved their way back to my neck. My body felt like it was on fire. "So, baby, right . . . right now . . . I need you to be a genius."

"Well, in that case, let me introduce you to my dick." He mounted me. "Loraine Farrow, I'd like you to meet my friend Albert. Albert Einstein." He slid himself inside me. It felt like a perfect fit, like we were made for each other.

"Michael, I think Albert and I are going to be friends for a long time."

"I sure hope so." He kissed me, and we made sweet love until we were both spent, falling asleep in each other's arms.

A few hours later, I woke up feeling contented, not to mention worn out. I got out of bed and slipped on my satin nightgown, careful not to disturb Michael's sleep. I wanted to make him breakfast in bed as a reward for a job well done.

As I put on my slippers, I looked out the window and caught a glimpse of something very disturbing across the street. It was

Leon's car. He had the driver's side window down, and I could see the frown on his face plain as day. He wasn't a happy camper, most likely because he'd seen Michael's car in the driveway. What the hell was he doing here anyway? And how long had he been sitting outside?

Jesus Christ, can I have one decent day without the weight of the world falling on my shoulders?

I turned back to the bed, where Michael was sleeping. I wondered if I should wake him and tell him about Leon but decided to let him sleep. Leon was my problem.

I picked up my cell phone and walked down the hall to my home office. I sat on the love seat near the front window, where I could see out but couldn't be seen. I dialed Leon's number. I wanted to deal with the situation personally, but I didn't want to deal with it face–to–face.

I didn't even give him a chance to say hello. As soon as I heard the call connect, I said, "What the hell are you doing across the street from my house?" I didn't realize I was so angry until I started to talk.

"Just sitting here. Was that you or that guy I saw peeking out the window?" He didn't sound angry like the last time when he ran up on me and Michael. This time, he sounded like a lost soul.

"Leon, how long have you been out there?"

"I don't know. A couple hours maybe."

"What do you want?" I was trying not to blow up at him again.

"I wanted to ask you a favor." I didn't say anything. I just listened. "I wanted to know if you'd come to therapy with me tomorrow. Please, Loraine."

"I'm sorry, Leon. I can't do that."

"Why? I'm not asking you to be with me. I'm just asking you to go to therapy with me. I'm doing good, Loraine. You can ask the doctor."

"I'm sorry, but you're not my problem anymore. You need to go home."

"This is my home, Loraine. At least it used to be."

Have you ever felt sorry for someone you knew you shouldn't

feel sorry for? Well, that's how I felt talking to Leon. He sounded so pitiful, and as much as I didn't want to care, I couldn't help it.

"Well, then go to LaKeisha's house. She loves you. Why don't you give her a chance?"

"Loraine, I don't even know who that woman is."

I couldn't believe he was still denying it. Well, that was enough to make me stop feeling sorry for him. "You know what, Leon? My man is calling me back to bed, and I'm sick of your lies. If I were you, I'd be gone before he comes downstairs." I hung up the phone.

Isis

44

It was Easter eve, and everyone in the house was asleep when I sneaked into Rashad's home office to use the computer. The only reason I was doing it so late at night was because my mother was in town, and she'd been hovering over me like a swarm of bees at a picnic. I needed to use the computer, because I'd been approved for an apartment in Petersburg, and the landlord was e-mailing me the lease.

Rashad still hadn't said a word to me about my proposal to start a second family. The good news was that neither had Egypt, so I assumed it was still our little secret and that I should go ahead with my plans. Although we hadn't spoken about it, I was sure he would take me up on the offer, because he hadn't tried to distance himself from me like he'd done in the past. On the contrary, he'd actually been friendlier, or maybe more forward was the proper way to put it. As a matter of fact, Egypt couldn't make it to one of our Lamaze classes, and during that session, Rashad was touching and feeling on me in ways I know Egypt wouldn't have appreciated. I never said a word, because I was sure he was just testing the waters—the same way I was testing the waters when I left an apartment listing on his office chair last night. It was only a matter of time before I'd be in Petersburg and he'd be making daily visits.

Feeling content after I printed out two copies of the lease, I walked back to my room. I'd just made it there when all of a sudden, I felt a gush of warm water run down my legs.

My first thought was, *Oh my God. I peed on myself.*

I ran to the bathroom. When I sat on the toilet, I was shocked to see blood in my panties. "Oh, shit. I think my water broke," I said aloud.

A wave of fear took over me for a few seconds. This was really happening. Suddenly, I felt a tightness that rippled from my back to my navel. I braced myself for some serious pain, but it never came.

"Aw, this is a cinch. That little cramp ain't nothing. I'm going to get through this labor easily."

As soon as the little wave of pain passed, I opened the bathroom door and shouted out, "Rashad, come here! I think my water broke! Rashad!"

I could hear Egypt and Rashad scuffling around in their bedroom, and then they both ran to the bathroom in their robes, followed by my mother and father. I sat there with my panties pulled down, still sitting on the toilet, pointing to the blood.

"Let's get ready to go," Egypt said.

"Hold on." My mother took control of the situation. "How far apart are your contractions?"

"I don't know. I only had one, I think."

"Well, we better time them. You got a long way to go before this baby comes, Isis. This is just the beginning. How about if you take a shower, because it's going to be a long night."

I didn't like the sound of that. The whole time I was pregnant, I was so focused on what would happen after the baby was born that I never gave any serious thought to the actual delivery. Now the moment had come, and I was not looking forward to the hard work that my mother was predicting.

By three in the morning, the contractions were coming eight minutes apart, and Dr. Collins told us to get to the hospital. Although this was my first baby, they wanted to be on the safe side because of my weight.

It was still dark outside when we left for the hospital. At Egypt's insistence, we had already done a dry run, so we knew exactly to the minute how long it would take to drive there. Rashad helped me to the car, and Egypt had to lug the heavy-ass suitcase that she'd packed for me. I loved every minute of the attention I was getting, until we got to the car and Egypt jumped in the front seat next to Rashad. If I wasn't so uncomfortable from the contractions, I would have put up a fight. Instead, I just lay against my father in the back seat.

I started having harder contractions on the drive. I was moaning so loudly it drowned out the sound of the radio.

"Breathe, Isis," Egypt ordered from the front seat. "Concentrate on breathing."

I felt like reaching around the headrest and choking her ass to death. How the hell was I supposed to concentrate on breathing when the only thing I could think of was the godforsaken pain I was in?

"I'm trying." I panted between the sharp pains.

When we arrived at the hospital, they rolled me to the labor and delivery room right away.

Egypt turned to Rashad. "I've got this, baby. You can go sit in the waiting room with the other fathers."

"You're kidding, right?" Rashad asked firmly. "Fathers don't sit in waiting rooms anymore. You think I took those Lamaze classes for my health? I'm going to see my baby be born."

"Rashad," she whined. I wanted to punch her in the face right about now. How could she deny Rashad the experience of seeing his own child being born? But I didn't have to put my two cents in, because Rashad handled it on his own.

"I'm not going to argue with you, Egypt. I'm going to be in that delivery room. You coming or staying here with your parents?"

Although I was in pain, I felt like cheering him on. Egypt was always trying to control everybody around her, just like my mother. It was about time he put her in her place. I was relieved, too, because as the pain got worse, I was starting to get scared, and I was glad he would be there with me through the whole thing.

Egypt said, "Okay, baby, I'm coming," to Rashad, but she looked crushed.

They both got suited up in cloth scrubs and masks. Everything happened in a blur after that. They put a monitor on me, and my contractions started coming faster and faster. I think I heard them say I had dilated to five centimeters when I first got there, but now I was to seven.

I remember Rashad putting crushed ice cubes on my dry, parched lips, and I loved it. Oh, how I wished he was my husband at my side, but this was just as good. We could get married later on. Right now, I was about to have our first baby.

A nurse took care of me at first, but when I made it to about nine centimeters, they called Dr. Collins, who showed up within a matter of minutes. As the labor progressed, the pains became almost constant and more intense. It felt like one long, continuous contraction. The pain was worse than anything I could have ever imagined. I tried to take my mind off it by imagining my life with Rashad once Egypt was out of the picture, but it hurt so much I couldn't even concentrate. It got so bad that I wanted to kick Rashad's ass for getting me pregnant in the first place.

This labor went on for what seemed like forever, although later I found out it was only about four hours. I screamed, I hollered, I cursed out everyone in the room.

"Oh, hell naw," I said when Dr. Collins tried to examine me for the hundredth time. "My coochie is on fire. Get away from me."

"They've got to examine you to see how far along you are," Rashad said, wiping my sweaty forehead with a towel.

"Can't y'all give me something for the pain?" I asked Dr. Collins. "This shit hurts."

"Isis, you're too far dilated to give you anything," Dr. Collins said. "It's time for you to start pushing."

"You know we agreed no drugs, so the baby can come out alert," Egypt interjected with her know-it-all self.

"Fuck that shit! I'm the one having this baby, not you!" I kicked at Egypt's ass, then looked at the doctor. "Give me some damn drugs! I can't take this." I was crying now. "Fuck! This is killing me! Get this baby outta me!"

The only thing that calmed me down was Rashad. "Come on, Isis. You've been brave so far. We don't have much further to go. All you have to do is breathe. I'll help you."

"Okay, it's time," Dr. Collins said.

Rashad stood near my head and placed his strong hands on my shoulders. "Breathe, Isis. Pant, pant, push," he coached, just like we'd been taught in the Lamaze class.

Egypt was shouting the same thing, but I ignored her. Rashad was the only coach I needed. Just his presence was soothing. He stayed calm as he coached me to keep pushing through each contraction.

All of a sudden, I felt a burning pain, like I was splitting in two.

Through a haze, I heard Dr. Collins say, "The head is out. We just need one more push for the shoulders, Isis."

Rashad left my side and went down to the end of the bed. I didn't care that he could see all up in my coochie, with everything hanging out. It wasn't like it was something he hadn't seen before. Then again, he'd never seen it stretched this wide.

"Oh my God, I can see the head! Push, Isis, push, and he's going to come right out!" Rashad shouted.

I was in so much pain I thought I was going to pass out, but with Rashad's encouragement, I gave it one more push. I let loose one long, piercing scream, and then, just like that, I felt something slip out of me, and all the pain was done.

Suddenly, I heard a cry. A sweet, wonderful baby cry.

"Oh my God, look at him!" Rashad was so excited. "You did it, Isis! You did it!"

I felt a rush of love for Rashad at that moment that was so intense, I started to cry. I know I had told him that I was having the baby for him, but until now, I hadn't realized just what that meant. We had been through an ordeal together, but it was worth every second of pain, because the outcome was a beautiful baby boy who was part of each of us. The joy on Rashad's face was something I would never forget.

Rashad bent down to kiss me, but then my beautiful fantasy was shattered. Instead of embracing me and telling me he loved me, he only gave me a quick peck on the cheek before he stood to face Egypt. He wrapped his arms around her, and the two of them started crying.

"We did it, baby," he whispered to her, and I wanted to die. Mercifully, Dr. Collins interrupted their moment.

"We've got to cut the cord."

"I want to cut it," Rashad said.

Dr. Collins handed him the scissors.

"Let me see him," I said, sitting up and reaching my arms out for my baby. "Let me see him."

The doctor placed the baby in my arms, and again my eyes filled with tears. This time, it wasn't love for Rashad; it was for this beautiful child I was holding.

Egypt must have noticed that I was getting emotional, because she moved next to me and hovered over the baby like she was getting ready to snatch him up. If I could have made her disappear into thin air, I would have done it in a second.

"I've got to weigh him," the nurse said. I don't know if she noticed the tension between me and Egypt, but she sure stepped up at just the right time. I handed the baby to her, and she took him to the scale.

"Eight pounds and ten ounces. He's a big one."

While she finished washing the baby, checking his Apgar score, and wrapping him in a blanket, I felt like an outcast. Rashad and Egypt stood there gazing at each other and then at the baby as if I weren't even there. As if I had nothing to do with the baby's birth. My hormones were so scrambled up, all I could do was lie on the table, shivering and crying quietly. This was not at all how I'd imagined things would be.

The nurse finished what she was doing and then turned to carry the baby back to me. That's when Egypt staked her claim.

"Nurse, that's not a good idea," Egypt said.

The nurse stopped in her tracks. I'm sure this wasn't a situation she encountered every day. "Excuse me?"

"She's our surrogate."

The nurse glanced at me as if she felt my pain.

"I just want to see how he looks. I want to make sure he has all ten fingers and toes," I pleaded with outstretched arms.

Egypt's reply was cold as ice. "Don't worry. I'll check for you. Dr. Collins, can you please tell her to give me my baby?"

The nurse turned to the doctor, and he nodded.

Egypt walked over and took the baby from the nurse's arms. I don't think I ever truly hated my sister until that exact moment as I watched her kissing and cuddling my child. Rashad walked over to her and placed his arm around her, and I almost couldn't see through my tears.

He turned back and looked at me. "Thank you, Isis."

I couldn't even answer. I turned my head away and felt the tears dripping down my face.

The doctor directed the nurse to bring Rashad and Egypt to another room with the baby. I, on the other hand, would stay on the cold-ass table so the doctor could deliver the placenta and stitch me up. As Egypt left the room with my child, all I could ask myself was, *What in the world have I done?*

Loraine

45

"I am so jealous."

"You should be," Jerome said with a smirk. "By this time to-morrow, I'll be pissy drunk from Bahama Mamas and as black as the ace of spades from sitting under the Caribbean sun all day. What's not to be jealous of?"

"Have I told you how much I hate you lately? Because I do!" I was being sarcastic about hating him, but I really was jealous.

We were sitting at our usual Friday night happy hour table at T.G.I. Friday's. Jerome was waiting for a car service to come pick him up, because he and Big Poppa were sneaking away to a private villa in Jamaica for Easter week. I knew I shouldn't be too jealous, though, because I was also going away, with my new boo, Michael. We weren't headed to a tropical island; we were headed for a weekend in Roanoke, in a romantic cabin up in the mountains. I couldn't wait until tomorrow morning.

"That's my ride," Jerome said, gulping down the last of his cognac. "Well, Raine, I guess I gotta go. Tell my man Mike I'll see him when I get back. And you have a good time in the moun-tains."

I couldn't help but pout a little when Jerome stood up and kissed me on the cheek to say good-bye. I loved my friend so much.

"I will. Have a good time." I was sad to see him leave, but I really did hope he had a great trip.

After he was gone, I sat alone and nursed my Long Island iced tea for a little longer. I wasn't ready to go home and be alone.

But as I looked around the bar at all the people talking with friends or trying to hook up with strangers, I realized I was already alone, even in this crowded place. I thought of Michael. Maybe I could call him and ask him to have a late dinner with me.

That idea disappeared quickly, too, because I knew it wouldn't be fair to Michael. He had a lot of work to do tonight if we were going to leave for Roanoke in the morning, so it probably wouldn't be a good idea if I was around to distract him.

Things were moving fast between me and Michael, much faster than I would have expected. He was telling me he loved me on a consistent basis, and I was starting to do the same. He'd even started talking about when we got married, like it was a certainty, and he was constantly asking me when my divorce would be final. I already had my lawyers working on the papers. It was time to push Leon to the side and get on with my life.

At least that's what I thought, until a man approached me with some information that would change my perspective on quite a few things.

"Excuse me, miss." I turned around and was startled to see a rather handsome white man with salt-and-pepper hair sitting in Jerome's seat.

"Sorry," he said with a friendly smile. "I didn't mean to sneak up on you."

"It's okay," I said, and I meant it. I didn't feel threatened by this guy. He was wearing a suit, probably some professional just out for a few drinks after work. He wasn't really my type, but I figured it couldn't hurt to be nice and have a polite conversation for a few minutes.

"Loraine, right?"

Now that made me pause. If he knew my name, then we must have met somewhere before. I hoped he wasn't a client, because I was going to look like a complete idiot if I couldn't remember his name. Upon giving him a second look, he did seem vaguely familiar, but I had no idea why, so I couldn't even play it off like I knew him.

"Yes. I'm sorry. I'm drawing a blank right now. Have we met?"

"Well, no, but we have a mutual friend."

I'd had enough alcohol at this point that I didn't even bother to censor my reaction. Client or not, his choice of words just set me off. "Mister, last time someone told me we had a friend in common, she ended up telling me it was my husband and she was sleeping with him." I drained the last of my drink. "Please don't tell me you're sleeping with my husband."

He chuckled. "No, I can assure you I'm not sleeping with your husband."

"Thank God for small favors." I laughed along with him. "So," I asked, my curiosity getting the better of me, "if it's not my husband, then who is this mutual friend?"

Without answering, he reached down to his briefcase and pulled out a manila envelope, which he placed on the table in front of me.

I looked down at it, but all I saw was a blank envelope. I had no idea what was inside. I gave him a questioning look, wondering if maybe I should have been a little more cautious when he first sat down.

"I'm sure you're gonna wanna see this."

"What is it?"

"Take a look for yourself."

I put my hand on top of the envelope but then hesitated for a second. I was dying to know what was inside, but I was also a little scared. Then I realized I'd already been faced with the worst surprise of all—a visit from my husband's mistress. This guy told me that he didn't know my husband, so this couldn't be that bad, could it?

I would soon find out how wrong I was.

I opened the envelope and pulled out the contents. The picture on top made my stomach lurch like I was about to throw up all the alcohol I'd consumed.

"Is this some kind of a fucking joke?" I asked him as I waved the photo of LaKeisha in his face.

"No, but you know who she is, don't you?" He was totally calm in spite of my growing agitation. I guess he hadn't figured out yet that I was gonna fuck him up if he didn't come up with some explanations in a hurry.

"Yeah, I know her. She's the bitch who's fucking my husband." I sat back in my chair and glared at him. "And who the fuck, exactly, are you?" A warning bell was beginning to ring in the back of my mind, like I was seconds away from figuring out how I knew this guy, but I still couldn't quite put two and two together.

"I'm the guy who's going to get you and your husband back together."

Now he really had my attention, because nothing short of finding out that Leon was Jesus Christ reincarnated could get us back together. I still had no clue what was going on, but there was no turning back at this point. No matter how loud that alarm was ringing in my head, I couldn't walk away before I heard what he had to say.

"Take a look at the next picture."

I leaned forward and flipped to the next photo, which almost made me fall out of my chair. It was a picture of Jerome handing money to LaKeisha. With shaking hands, I quickly flipped through the rest of the pictures. There were a few more of Jerome handing her money, and the rest were of the two of them talking over what looked like lunch at the Tobacco Company, one of his favorite spots.

"That's Jerome," were the only words I could manage.

"Any reason why he'd be giving the woman who is supposedly sleeping with your husband a wad of cash?"

"No . . . I mean, I don't know." Nothing made any sense.

"I do. He was paying her off."

"What? Why would he be paying her off?" And then it dawned on me that I still had no idea who the hell this guy was. "And how would you know anyway?"

"Oh, let's just say that I've taken a special interest in Jerome."

His vague answer set off those alarm bells again, but I was too busy trying to wrap my head around the images I'd just seen to worry about how I knew this guy.

"Okay, so let's just say you didn't Photoshop these pictures. I still don't understand why Jerome would be talking to that bitch."

"I don't know. Maybe to break you and your husband up?"

It took no time for me to reject that theory. "Jerome's my best friend. He wouldn't do that."

"You sure?" he asked, still as calm as could be.

I stared at him, challenging him to prove it.

"Take a look at the dates on the photos. I took these pictures of her and Jerome the day before Thanksgiving. That Saturday, she showed up in front of your place." He handed me some more pictures. Each was of me and LaKeisha.

At this point, I was speechless.

"Put the pieces of the puzzle together, Loraine. That man gave that woman money, and then she came to your house. Do you really think that was a coincidence?"

The truth swept over me like a tidal wave, and suddenly I felt like I couldn't breathe. Jerome and I had been through hell and high water together, and it tore me apart to realize that he could somehow be involved with everything I'd been going through. I still wasn't sure what the implications were, but I knew that my whole world felt like it had just shattered.

"Look." He stood up to leave, having already inflicted all the damage he could. "There are a lot of things Jerome hasn't told you. All I'm going to say is that your husband's an innocent man. He doesn't know that woman." He looked down at the pile on the table. "You can have those pictures. I have plenty of copies."

I was too stunned to reply.

"And, by the way, just in case you still don't believe me, here's the woman's name and address. Maybe you need to pay her a visit. I'm sure for some cash she'll sell out old Jerome in a New York minute."

He slipped me a piece of paper with the name Tina Lauderdale printed on it. The address was in a seedy part of town off Jefferson Davis Highway.

"And when you talk to Jerome—because I know you will—tell him Peter said hello."

Snap! The last puzzle piece fell into place. Now I knew who this guy was. I watched as the man Jerome had described as his stalker left the bar. Considering the source of the information, I was still left with plenty of questions. Based on everything I'd been told about this guy, it was possible he was just making this up to hurt Jerome. But armed with these incriminating photos and Tina Lauderdale's address, I intended to keep searching until I got the answers I was looking for—no matter whose ass I had to kick in the process.

Isis

46

I was lying in my hospital bed, suffering with horrible cramps, when my mother walked in smiling and singing. She was carrying her digital camera, which I had no doubt she'd used to snap a million pictures of the baby—probably in Egypt's arms, I thought sadly. Unlike my own foul mood, my mother looked like the happiest woman in the world.

I hadn't seen her since we'd arrived at the hospital. My father, God bless his soul, had been sitting with me all afternoon. Daddy didn't say much; he just sat there and watched the game on the TV, but it was a comfort to know he was there. I loved him so much.

"Bobby, you better come on in here if you want to see the baby again. We're getting ready to go back to Egypt and Rashad's."

My father nodded to my mother, then turned to me. "Isis, honey, we'll be back in the morning. You going to be all right?"

"I'll be okay." He leaned in to kiss me, and I wrapped my arms around him, holding tight. "I love you, Daddy."

"Love you too, princess. You did good today." He glanced over at my mother, then said, "Don't let anybody ever tell you any different."

He walked past my mother, but she didn't follow him. "You coming?" he asked from the doorway.

"You go ahead. I'll be right there. I wanna say good-bye to Isis."

After Daddy was gone, my mother sat in the chair next to me. She handed me an envelope. "Your sister wanted you to have this. I think it's the rest of your money."

"Thanks." I placed the envelope on the table next to my bed. I was now officially thirty thousand dollars richer, but it didn't feel nearly as good as I'd expected it would.

"How you holding up?" she asked. "Are you bleeding much?" Her eyes were wandering around the room, so I doubted she was really interested in my answer. That was fine with me, because I was too tired for a long conversation anyway.

"No, it's already slowing down, and the nurse gave me some Tylenol for the cramps. I'll be all right."

"I know you will. This whole thing is hard on everyone."

On everyone? The only person this was hard on was me. I was the one who just went through nine months of pregnancy only to have my sister rip my baby out of my arms right after his birth. If it wasn't for the fact that Rashad and I were going to have our own secret life and family, I'd probably be a basket case. I changed the subject to stop myself from screaming at her.

"I see you got your camera. You take any pictures of the baby?"

"Yes, I took quite a few."

"Can I see?" I reached for the camera, but she pulled it back.

"No, baby girl, you can't see the pictures. You need to leave this alone."

"Leave what alone? All I want to do is see pictures of my baby. It's not like I'm running up in here with a lawyer trying to have the surrogacy annulled."

Her eyebrows shot up, and her mouth flew open. "And you won't, will you?" I didn't answer, and she repeated herself even more sternly. "Will you, Isis?"

"No, ma'am," I finally said to appease her.

"Good. I'll tell you what. I'll let you see all the pictures when we get on the plane day after tomorrow."

"Plane? Day after tomorrow? Where are we going?"

"Your father and I are going to take you to Los Angeles to get you settled."

Where the fuck did this come from?

"I'm not supposed to go to L.A. for a few weeks. I don't even have a place."

"You do now. Rashad just wired the apartment complex a check."

I didn't say anything. I knew that if I opened my mouth, I would curse her out, so I just shut up.

She changed the subject when she saw I wasn't going to share what I was feeling. "I love you, Isis. This is a brave thing you're doing. It's like the real mother in the Bible who was willing to give her baby up so that he could live."

Oh, Lord. She wasn't really going to start preaching to me now, was she?

"I want you to read your Bible."

Yep, she was going to preach. I lay back and stared at the ceiling as she began her lecture.

"It's found at 1 Kings, chapter three, verses sixteen through twenty-eight. It's the story where the two mothers came before King Solomon claiming the same boy child. The real mother wanted the child to live and not be split in half, whereas the mother whose child had died wanted the live baby split in half."

"What has that got to do with me?"

"As the biological mom, you want what's best for Little Rashad. You've got to be willing to sacrifice your feelings for your baby's best interest. You don't want your baby to be split in half between you and Egypt, do you?"

"Mom, what are you talking about?"

"He's not going to do it, Isis."

"Who's not going to do what? What are you talking about?"

She gave me a look that said, *You know exactly what I'm talking about.* But I didn't.

"Rashad."

"What about him?"

"He told me everything."

For a second, I felt panic, but then I realized she was probably just on a fishing expedition. I refused to believe he'd said anything to my mother, especially since he hadn't even told Egypt.

"What exactly did he tell you?" I wasn't about to admit a damn thing until I was sure what she knew.

"Let's just say he told me enough that I canceled the lease on your apartment in Petersburg."

Oh, damn. She did know everything. "You can't do that. I'm a grown woman."

"I already have. And the landlord was very interested to know about your mental history."

"You fucking bitch," I spit out before I could stop myself.

I felt a stinging pain I hadn't felt in twenty years, the heavy-handed smack of my mother. She was standing over me, her eyes daring me to fight back, the same way she did when I was a teenager. "Don't get slapped again," she warned. "You may be grown, but I'm still your mother."

Tears dropped from my eyes. At that moment, I think I hated her even more than my sister.

"Now, that man is not going to have another baby with you, so I want you to get that out your head. He's in love with your sister, and the two of them are going to raise this baby whether you like it or not."

I was too numb to explain what I felt anyway. Not only was I hurt physically by my mother's slap, but also emotionally I was devastated. I'd been betrayed again by the one man I never thought would betray me after I'd given him the gift of a son. How the hell was Rashad going to live with himself? Well, I knew one thing: After all the pain I'd gone through to deliver, there was no way I was giving up my baby. I didn't care what kind of papers they had. They could all kiss my ass.

Loraine

47

"You wanna tell me what I did?" Michael asked as he pulled in front of my house.

He was trying to hide his irritation, but after riding with him in silence for two hours, his true feelings were finally beginning to show. Hell, I couldn't blame him if he was pissed off after the way I acted this weekend.

We'd just returned early from what was supposed to be a romantic weekend in the Roanoke Mountains, the key words there being *supposed to be*. Although the hot tub was hot and the champagne was chilled, I was as cold as ice, and no matter what Michael did to try to warm me up, it just seemed to make matters worse. I went on the trip thinking it would take my mind off the pictures Peter had shown me. My plan was to try to forget about the photos, at least until Jerome came back from vacation and I could get some answers, but it consumed my thoughts to the point that I ignored virtually every romantic gesture Michael made.

He'd finally given up this morning when he asked me flat out, "Do you want me to take you home?"

I nodded my head. Fifteen minutes later, he'd packed our bags and we were on our way home. Neither of us said a word during the entire two-hour trip.

"Who said you did anything wrong?" I asked him as I unbuckled my seat belt.

Michael slammed his fist against the dashboard. "Dammit, Loraine! Why are you playing games? It's pretty damn obvious I did something. We just left a fifteen-hundred-dollar-a-night chalet in the mountains because you were ready to go home. Somehow, I doubt it was the four-hundred-dollar-a-bottle Cristal or the chocolate-covered Godiva strawberries that brought you to that decision."

I'd never seen him this upset, and I did owe him some type of explanation. I placed my hand on his leg and turned to face him.

"You didn't do anything wrong. I just have a lot on my mind. I really didn't mean to take it out on you, but you're the one who's here."

"Well, tell me what's going on."

"I will, I promise, as soon as I figure everything out myself."

"Tell me what you know. Maybe I can help." He was so sweet. Here I was giving him only the vaguest of explanations, and instead of kicking my ass out of his car, he seemed genuinely interested in helping me. Still, I wasn't ready to tell him the whole story.

"I wish you could help, but this is something I have to deal with on my own before I can move on with you. It's very complicated." I tried to give a reassuring look. "Do you understand?"

"Oh, I understand completely." He leaned back in his chair, no longer looking so patient and understanding. "And it's not very complicated at all. In other words, it's got something to do with your husband, right?"

"Yes, it's got everything to do with Leon, but it's something I have to work out on my own."

He nodded. "Okay, you do what you gotta do, but don't let this guy mess us up. I love you, and I'm not going anywhere." His words made me feel good. The only problem was that I couldn't make the same promise to him. If it turned out to be true that Jerome had staged the whole thing with LaKeisha, then I didn't know what I was going to do. Would I apologize to Leon and try to make my marriage work again? Things with Michael had been going so well, and in a lot of ways, he was better for me than Leon, but I couldn't say for sure that I would choose him over the man I had vowed to God I would love for better or for worse. This whole thing was getting more complicated by the second.

I leaned over and kissed Michael's cheek, then got out of his car. I waved good-bye as he pulled off. There was a knot in the pit of my stomach, and I wondered if this was the last time I would ever see him.

When Michael's car disappeared down the block, I closed the front door and went straight upstairs to my bedroom. I found the manila envelope Peter had given me and the pictures of Jerome and LaKeisha—or Tina Lauderdale, if that's what her real name was—spread out all over my bed, just as I had left them. I sat on the bed and flipped through each picture as I contemplated the whole bizarre situation. I still didn't know what the truth was.

Even with the photographic evidence in front of me, I was finding it hard to believe that Jerome could have done this to me. I wished I could call him—hell, I'd have settled for an e-mail—but he'd promised Big Poppa no communication during their romantic trip. Wasn't that convenient? This guy Peter just happened to give me this evidence right after Jerome left on a weeklong trip where I wouldn't be able to contact him. The more I thought about it, the more it seemed that Peter was setting Jerome up—and I wouldn't be surprised if Leon had something to do with it too. He'd never liked Jerome, probably because Jerome was the only one who ever stood up to him. Just the thought of those two evil bastards getting together to set me and my friend up made my blood boil.

I fell asleep with those pictures in my arms, and my dreams were filled with images of my best friend doing me wrong. When I woke up, I still had no idea what to believe. Either Jerome had set me up, or Peter, and possibly Leon, had Photoshopped the pictures to come between me and Jerome. I decided to drive over to Tina Lauderdale's house to see if I could learn the truth there.

"You have arrived at your destination," my GPS chimed as I pulled in front of apartment 234A of the Hillside Court Housing Projects. I knew I was in the right place, because the car in front of me was the same car that LaKeisha, aka Tina, had been driving the day she showed up at my house.

I was nervous about confronting this woman. These projects

were definitely not my neck of the woods, and I had no way of knowing who else might be in the apartment with her. What if she really was Leon's mistress and she jumped me when I knocked on her door? I sat in my car and let my imagination get the best of me for quite a while before I finally gathered the nerve to go talk to her. It was the only way I was going to get the answers I needed. "Just get it over with," I told myself as I got out of the car.

"Who is it?" someone called out after I rang the bell. I was pretty sure it was the same voice I'd heard from the woman who introduced herself as LaKeisha. I took a chance and called her by the name Peter had given me.

"Tina, open the door." I rang the bell again.

"What? Who is it?" she asked angrily. The door opened up, and there was LaKeisha. My heart started racing now that she was standing in front of me. I willed myself to stay calm; I refused to show any weakness in front of this woman. Whether she had set me up or she was sleeping with my husband, this bitch was my enemy as far as I was concerned.

"Remember me, Tina? Or are you still going by LaKeisha?" I couldn't help but smile wickedly when I realized that she was the one with fear written all over her face.

"Oh, shit!" She tried to slam the door in my face, but I put my foot out to stop it. I had purposely worn jeans and sneakers just in case things got out of hand.

"Get your foot out my fucking door." She tried to push the door closed. Obviously she knew nothing about leverage.

"You keep cursing at me like that and I'm not paying you a dime for the information I need."

This got her attention.

"You gonna pay me?"

"Yeah, if you give me the information I'm looking for."

"How much?"

"Five hundred. Now, can I come in?"

Tina—or LaKeisha or whatever she was called—stuck her head out the door and took a look around, as if she was afraid I'd brought the police with me. Satisfied when she didn't see any, she beckoned me into the house.

She offered me a seat in her sparsely furnished living room.

I remained standing and got straight to the point. "Did you set me up?"

She stared at me silently for a moment. "The money first," she said, gazing down at my purse.

I don't know why I was surprised. Considering the dump she was living in, this woman clearly wasn't bringing home a steady paycheck. Taking money up front for services rendered was probably second nature to her. You should have seen her eyes light up when I handed her the money. She stuffed it in her bra— as if I wouldn't go down there and get it if I thought she was lying. Truth is, I didn't want to give her shit other than my foot in her ass, which, I thought, I might end up doing just for GP when I was finished questioning her.

A cat came up and rubbed itself against my leg, and a queasy feeling started to ease into my stomach. "How long have you had the cat?"

"Him? 'Bout three years. His momma's around here some-where. I had her for about seven." The queasiness got worse.

"Do you even know my husband? Because my husband's al-lergic to cats. He couldn't spend five minutes in this house."

She lit a cigarette and took a long drag before answering. "The truth is, I never met the man."

The queasiness now felt like a punch in the stomach. "What the hell do you mean, 'never met the man'? Why did you tell me you were sleeping with him? Why would you do this to me?"

"Same reason I'm talking to you now. For the money." She shrugged casually, like wrecking someone's life was all part of a day's work. I wanted to reach across the room and slap her ass.

"You ruined my marriage for money?" I stood up, fists clenched. "Do you even know what kind of a person that makes you? Do you care about anybody but yourself?"

"Shoot, for two thousand dollars, I would have ruined my momma's marriage—if she had ever been married." She got a lit-tle attitude herself, but she didn't stand up. Lucky for her, be-cause the way I was feeling, I might have knocked her out. "Anyway, don't be judging me. Look at this place. I've seen your house and your car. Your ass is rich. Just go get you another man." She took another long drag of her cigarette. "You wanna trade lives with me? 'Cause we can do that shit anytime you want. "

I needed to leave there soon before I killed that woman. "I got just one more question."

She shrugged again. "Might as well get your money's worth."

I pulled out the pictures of her and Jerome. "Do you know the man in this picture?"

She looked down at the photo and then up at me, but she hesitated to say anything.

"Don't look at me; look at the goddamn picture. I just want the truth so I can get the fuck out of here." I took a step toward her. "Unless you want me to take back that money you shoved in your bra."

She sighed like a petulant child, putting out her cigarette in an overflowing ashtray. "Yeah, that's Jerome. We grew up together back in Danville."

"Oh God, no," I let slip. I was so sick to my stomach that I suddenly felt like I might throw up. I stiffened my back and held my head up high, trying not to let this woman know just how devastated I was.

"Why'd he give you the money?"

"He wanted me to help him split you and your husband up. He said he'd tried everything, but you were too stupid to leave. Said he needed something to push you over the edge so you'd leave your husband. That's when he asked me how good an actress I was and if I wanted to make some money."

What hurt the most was that her explanation made sense. It was no secret that Jerome wanted me to leave Leon. I just had no idea he would go to such lengths to make it happen. I had a flashback to the boiling water I'd thrown on Leon and to the fact that I'd actually had the nerve to pull a gun on him. Jerome had succeeded in pushing me over the edge.

"Do you know why he would do this?"

She was starting to look bored. I guess she figured she'd given me my five hundred dollars' worth of information. "To be honest, he acted like he was jealous. I got the impression y'all were sleeping with each other."

"Jerome is gay."

She raised her eyebrows. Obviously, this was news to her. "He doesn't look gay. And he wasn't gay in high school, I don't think."

"Well, he's gay now. And when he gets back from vacation, he's in a lot of trouble."

"Well, don't tell him I told you shit. The last thing I need is more drama in my life."

I turned to leave and then remembered something. "Before I go, one more thing."

She sighed. "What?"

I looked down at her hand. "Give me back my gotdamn rings."

"Uh-uh, you gave me these."

"Have it your way. But don't be surprised when the police show up at your door to retrieve my stolen property."

I knew it would only take that one small threat. She rolled her eyes at me and pulled the rings off her finger. I took them from her and stuck them in my pocket. I'd have to be sure to disinfect them when I got home.

I walked out of that house fuming. What the hell was Jerome thinking? He knew how hurt I was when I found the panties in my house. I'd been living through hell ever since I first suspected Leon was cheating. If this all turned out to be some elaborate plan concocted by Jerome, I didn't think he could ever offer me a good enough explanation. Why would my supposed best friend want to make me miserable?

I remembered that Peter told me there were things about Jerome I didn't know. Then I thought about what Tina had just told me. She thought Jerome and I were sleeping together. Was it possible that was his motive? Could my gay best friend really be in love with me?

Damn! I'd come to Tina for answers, but I still had questions. The biggest one of all was now that I knew that Leon had probably been telling the truth all along, what the hell was I going to do about him? And how was I ever going to face Michael with this? There was, however, one thing I had to do immediately.

I pulled out my cell phone, then punched in the numbers to my lawyer.

"Johnson and Swartz," a woman said.

"Hi, this is Loraine Farrow. Can I speak with Brad Johnson, please?"

"Sure, Ms. Farrow. Hold on one minute."

Some elevator music started playing until a familiar voice clicked in. "Hey, Loraine, what's up?"

"Did they serve my husband yet?"

"No, not yet. The process server's going by his office this afternoon."

"Well, stop him. I'm not sure if I want a divorce."

"You sure?"

"For now. Yes."

"Okay, I'm on it."

"Thanks, Brad." I hung up.

Isis

48

Rashad had really played me well, but I still couldn't help but think he was nothing but a damn coward. If he really didn't want me to move to Petersburg so we could start our own family, why didn't he just tell me himself? Instead, he had to stab me in the back by going to the one person he knew could do the most damage. Now that my mother had called my landlord, I didn't even have a place to go. Looks like my plan to start another family with Rashad had blown up in my face.

What Rashad and the rest of my family didn't count on, though, was that I had another plan. If he didn't want to help me have another baby, then I would just have to make sure I kept this one. In the end, he'd be sorry he'd taken Egypt's side. In fact, he might be sorry he ever chose Egypt over me in the first place.

I picked up the phone next to my bed and called the lawyer I'd been corresponding with. Rashad and Egypt might have a good lawyer, but I had a whole team of lawyers at my disposal. Just to cover my ass, I'd sent a copy of the surrogacy papers to my lawyer last week so he could look them over. Now I needed some advice about how I could get out of that contract and take my baby back. Unfortunately, the news he had for me wasn't good.

After some preliminary legal talk I barely understood, he said, "So, Isis, unfortunately this agreement is pretty airtight."

"So, basically what you're saying is I don't have a fucking leg to stand on?" I wanted to throw the phone across the room.

"I don't know if I'd put it that colorfully, but essentially, yes, that's what I'm saying. Legally, that baby is theirs, although your sister has to go through an adoption process. The fact that he's the child's biological father makes their case even more open and shut."

"I thought as a surrogate I had forty-eight hours to change my mind."

"You've been watching a little bit too much TV. You see, technically this is not a surrogacy case. Virginia law only allows a woman to be a surrogate if she's married with at least one child of her own. This is a custody and parental rights case. By signing the consent form relinquishing rights to the child, you've basically given up your parental rights. Now, we can fight this, but it's not going to be cheap at all."

"Wait a minute. Isn't Prepaid Legal gonna pay for that?"

He got quiet for a second. "No, but we can recommend an attorney at a lower-than-average rate. Our services—"

I cut his ass right off. "Hold the fuck up. When I signed up for this thing, they told me that anytime I needed a lawyer, I could get one. That I'd have a team of lawyers at my disposal."

"That's true. And you do, for some basic services. But in certain cases, there is a charge."

"And this just happens to be one of those cases?"

"Unfortunately, yes."

"You know what? This is bullshit right here. I been paying you motherfuckers for over two years, and when I finally need you, y'all want more money. Thanks for nothing, shithead." I hung up on his ass. And to think the crook who sold me this useless policy just sent me a postcard from the Dominican Republic, talking about how he appreciated my business. Oh, he was gonna get a piece of my mind when he came back from his little vacation paid for on my dime.

I felt defeated, like the whole world was sitting on my shoulders and I had no one to help me carry the weight. And people had the nerve to ask me why I wanted to kill myself. 'Cause this world ain't shit, that's why.

"Excuse me." A nurse came into my room, wheeling a blood pressure machine. "My name is Jessica, and I'm going to be your nurse for the night. I just have to check your vitals." She pulled my medical chart out of the holder on the front of my bed and glanced at it. "Isis. What a beautiful name. Very exotic."

"Best thing my mother ever did for me was give me that name."

Jessica laughed. As she checked my vital signs, she made small talk about the weather and about her kids. She seemed a bit distracted, like her mind was somewhere else. It turned out that one of her kids was sick, and she was feeling guilty about being at work, instead of home taking care of him. It was actually good for me to listen to her ramble on about them, because it helped me take my mind off the mess that my own life had become. Instead of treating me like an incubator for Egypt's baby, which is basically how I'd been treated by my whole family for nine months, she treated me like a human being. She treated me like I was the same as any other new mother on the ward—and that's when it dawned on me: She had no idea I had given birth as a surrogate.

"Would you like me to bring you your baby?"

Her offer was like a sudden ray of sunshine on a stormy day. My mother wouldn't even show me a photo of the baby, and here was this nurse offering to bring him to me. I didn't hesitate to say, "Yes, I would."

When she returned about ten minutes later, she was pushing a small bassinet. "Let me see your arm. I have to match up your wristband."

I was nervous. My wristband had my name and some numbers on it, but I had no idea what was on the baby's band. For all I knew, it had the word *surrogate* in big red letters, and she would take the baby away before I had a chance to even see him.

She lifted him out of the bassinet, and I got my first look at my son since his birth. He was gorgeous, wrapped snugly in a blanket and sleeping peacefully. I felt my eyes fill up with tears, but I tried to remain calm so the nurse wouldn't suspect anything. She checked the band on his ankle, then the one on my wrist. "Yep, the numbers match. This one's yours," she said with a smile as she handed him to me.

My heart melted as soon as he was in my arms. No question about it, he belonged there.

He started squirming. The nurse said, "Maybe he's hungry. Are you breastfeeding?"

I nodded my head, though technically I wasn't. How could I breastfeed a baby they hadn't even let me see? They had brought me a machine earlier so I could pump my breasts. The doctors explained that it's good for the baby's immune system to get breast milk, even if it's just for the first few days. Egypt had me pumping my breasts so she could feed the milk to the baby in a bottle. It was just one more demeaning thing I had to go through, hooked up to a milking machine like a cow, all so my sister and Rashad could have their happy little family.

I pulled up my gown. No one had taught me how to breastfeed, but it just felt right. I can't explain it; having him in my arms, I felt a natural instinct to nurture my child. My breasts started tingling, like they'd done earlier when I pumped. Another nurse had explained that this was a sign my body was releasing the milk. She said it was purely a hormonal process, but I knew that it was happening now because my body recognized this baby that I'd carried for nine months. He was mine, no matter what it said on some damn piece of paper I'd signed.

He turned his head sideways, and Jessica said, "Oh, he's rooting. That means he smells your milk and he's trying to find it."

I lifted my breast toward his tiny mouth, and he latched on right away. I winced a little from the pain, and Jessica showed me how to help him latch on correctly. Once I got the hang of it, it didn't hurt at all. In fact, it was the most beautiful feeling in the world, knowing that I was the only person who could provide this milk, this perfect food that God had created just for Little Rashad. I had never felt such a warm bond, such unconditional love for another human being. I knew at that moment that I would throw myself in front of a truck to save this boy if I had to.

"He's a good feeder," Jessica commented. "Is this your first baby?"

"Yes."

"Well, you're nursing him like an old pro. So many new mothers have a hard time expressing the milk."

"Thanks," I answered as I put the baby on my shoulder to burp him. "It just feels like this was meant to be, you know what

I mean? Like God had always planned for me and him to be together in this life. Was it like that with your babies?"

"Mmm-hmm. There's nothing in this world that compares to that mother/child bond," she said with a smile as she leaned down to admire my gorgeous son.

"Oh my goodness!"

I looked up at her. "What? Is something wrong?"

"No, no, it's just the first time I've seen him open his eyes. He has the most unusual green eyes I've ever seen."

"What did you say?" I took him off my shoulder and looked down into my baby's eyes. They were a beautiful shade of green. To Jessica, they were unusual, but to me, they were very familiar.

"Yep, he sure does have green eyes. Just like his daddy—my fiancé, Tony." A smile a mile wide took over my face as I looked up at Jessica. As soon as she left the room, I had to make a very important phone call to New York.

Jerome

49

I'd just returned from the most spectacular trip to Jamaica. Big Poppa and I stayed at a private villa in the hills of Montego Bay, where we had a private chef and a driver who took us sightseeing all over the island. We had such a good time that by the end of the week, I was seriously considering buying a place there and renting it out until I was ready for retirement.

Then again, the whole trip wouldn't have been half as good if I hadn't been there with Big Poppa. I missed him already, and it had been only six hours since his flight left. We'd taken separate flights to and from Jamaica, for discretionary reasons. Big Poppa was paranoid enough as it was, but with that crazy-ass Peter lurking around every corner, neither one of us wanted to take a chance.

I hadn't been home more than a few minutes when my phone started ringing. I was hoping it was Loraine so I could tell her about my trip. No matter how well her weekend with Michael went, she was still going to be jealous when I told her the glorious details of my week. I glanced over at the caller ID and was happy to see her number.

I didn't even give her a chance to say hello before I started bragging. "What's up, girl? I'm back and I'm black, literally! You should see how dark I got."

"You need to come over here right now. We need to talk."

Talk about killing my mood. The tone of her voice was so cold, she might as well have thrown a bucket of ice water on me. I guess she wasn't interested in hearing the details of my vacation.

"All right, what's up?"

"We'll talk about it when you get here," she snapped.

Damn, what had her panties all in a bunch? It had to be something dealing with work, because Loraine never talked to me this way unless I messed up on the job. The only thing I didn't understand was why she couldn't wait until we were at the office to talk about it. With the mood she was in, though, I wasn't about to question it.

"I'll be right over."

"Good." She hung up.

No, she didn't just hang up on me without so much as a good-bye! Damn, I really must have fucked up something at work. Part of me was afraid to go over there, and the other part was afraid not to. There were a lot of things Loraine would put up with, but fucking up at work wasn't one of them. The girl was like a pit bull in a skirt when it came to the business. This was really killing my postvacation high.

Five minutes later, I was in my car headed to Loraine's house. I'd just gotten on Parham Road when I spotted Peter in my rearview mirror. I pounded the steering wheel in disgust. With Loraine in a tizzy, the last thing I needed was to have this fool following me to her house. Hopefully he didn't know the area like I did, and I'd be able to ditch him, but I wasn't so sure that would work. I'd been taking cabs and car services to go out and meet my sponsors lately, because I had a strong suspicion that he'd put some type of GPS tracking unit on my car. If that was true, I had no hope of losing him now.

To test my theory, I made a quick U-turn, then ran a red light, taking back streets toward Loraine's house. Surprisingly, he was no longer behind me. After a few more turns, I was pretty convinced that I'd lost him, and I finally relaxed. Well, I relaxed as well as I could, considering I was driving to see my best friend, who was pissed off for some unknown reason.

I was startled by the sound of my cell phone. It was Peter. I checked my rearview mirror again, and he was still nowhere in sight.

"What is it gonna take for you to leave me alone?" I screamed into my phone.

"I tink you gots some 'splaining to do!" he said in a weird Ricky Ricardo imitation, then started laughing with that crazy hyena laugh of his. This guy was nuts. He was really fucking nuts.

"What the fuck are you talking about?"

"You'll find out. You're headed to Loraine's, aren't you?" How the fuck did he know that? Dammit, did he have my phones tapped too?

"That's okay. You don't have to answer me, Jerome. I already know that's where you're going. Maybe I'll meet you there. Me and Loraine have become such good friends since you've been gone."

"If you've done anything to her, I'll kill you. Do you hear me? I'll kill you with my bare hands."

"Jerome, Jerome, don't you know making a threat against someone like that is against the law? You could get locked up for that. But since emotions are high and I'm sure you didn't mean it, I'm gonna let you slide." He laughed. "Oh, and you better hurry. Loraine's waiting. Like I said before, I tink you got some 'splaining to do!"

He disconnected the call, and I held the receiver in my hand, staring at it like it might somehow help me decipher Peter's strange words. What did he mean, I had some explaining to do? And what did that have to do with Loraine?

The possibilities were frightening. I had a few secrets I'd never revealed to Loraine. I had no way of knowing what, if anything, Peter had told her, but there was plenty that he could have said, and none of it would be good for our friendship. I was tempted to turn my car around and go home.

My phone rang again, and this time it was Loraine's number on the caller ID. Whatever was on her mind, she wasn't going to let it drop until we talked about it. I had no choice but to go see her. I let the phone ring. Might as well face her in person.

I pulled into her driveway, then took the longest walk of my life to her front door. I rang the bell, and before I even had my hand away from the buzzer, she snatched the door open, stepped outside, and slapped me so hard I stumbled backward.

"What was that all about?" I held my stinging cheek. Goddamn could she hit hard. Now I knew why Leon hit her ass back. She was throwing blows like a man.

"You son of a bitch! I hate you. I hate your fucking ass."

"What are you talking about, Loraine? What did I do?" I hoped it wasn't what I thought it was.

"You know what I'm talking about."

She threw some pictures in my face, and they fluttered to the ground. It was déjà vu. Just like that night with Ron, I was getting my ass beat over some pictures Peter took.

I bent down to pick up the photos to see what she was yelling about, but there was no need, as Loraine blurted out, "I talked to Tina and she told me everything."

"Shhhh-it." I didn't know what else to say. What could I say, with a picture of me handing Tina money staring me in the face? That son of a bitch Peter had done it again.

"I thought you were my friend. How could you do this, Jerome?"

"I'm sorry."

"Sorry! Is that all you can say? Aren't you going to deny it? Tell me it's not true. Beg me to call this woman up so you can confront her and prove your innocence? Why don't you just fucking lie?" Loraine had tears in her eyes—first time I'd ever seen her cry—but the sadness in her eyes did not belie her anger.

"Loraine—" Before I could say another word, she was screaming again.

"You fucking asshole! It was all you, wasn't it? The panties, the thong, that woman coming to my door—it was all you trying to ruin my marriage." Her eyes flashed with an icy fire through her tears.

"I wasn't trying to ruin your marriage, Loraine. I was trying to save you."

She was silent for a long while, with her arms crossed over her chest, giving me the coldest glare. I stood waiting for her to talk, praying she would understand that I had her best interests at heart when I did those things. I didn't want to lose my best friend.

Finally, she spoke up. "I don't know if Leon will ever forgive me—all because of your lies. I had the nerve to be confiding in you. Gay man, straight man, it doesn't matter. As long as you have a dick, you're all conniving liars."

"But, Loraine—"

She interrupted me. "Just tell me why. Why did you do this to me, and you're supposed to be my best friend in the world? Why would you do that?"

"I did it because I love you, girl. You know I'd never do anything to hurt you. "

"Well, you did hurt me. In fact, you broke my heart. What kind of monster are you?"

"Look, I did it to help you. He's not good for you."

"Who the fuck are you to say my husband is not good for me? Have I ever tried to tell you how to conduct your life with all your tawdry affairs?"

"No, but—"

"I could be sitting in jail right now behind what you did. I almost shot Leon, and I damn near scalded him to death. And now I've filed for divorce from a man who didn't even do the shit I accused him of." She shook her head and gave me a disgusted look. "You really set me up good."

"I'm sorry. I didn't mean to cause trouble."

"Trouble. Hah! This ain't trouble. This is goddamn hell you caused in here now. I dropped out of my sorority race because of this crap. And what about Michael? What am I supposed to tell Michael?"

"Don't worry about Michael. I'll talk to him. I'll explain everything. He's a good guy. He'll understand."

"He'll understand!" she repeated. "I don't want him to understand. I want him to be able to be with me. Goddammit, Jerome, I'm in love with Micheal!"

"Loraine, I'm sorry. I'm really sorry, and I'll do whatever it takes to make things between us better," I pleaded. "Just understand, I had your best interests at heart." I tried to take Loraine's hands into my own, but she knocked my hands away.

"You know what, Jerome? I'm done! You haven't just ruined my life or even Leon's—you've ruined Michael's too. I don't know what you were thinking, but I'm done!"

I didn't like the way that sounded. Nobody other than Leon

had ever survived Loraine's "I'm done," and even he had been kicked out eventually. I felt like a criminal awaiting his sentence from the jury. "So, where do we go from here?"

She went into her pocket and pulled out a check. "Severance, one year's salary. I don't want you back in my office. I'll have Hannah send over your personal belongings."

"Raine, no, please. We don't have to do this. I can fix this. Just give me a chance." I gave her an imploring gaze, but this new Loraine was not my friend. She had already cut me off in her mind, and now she was doing it physically.

"Are you kidding? I can't stand the sight of you right now."

"But I love you."

"You know Leon meant the world to me. If you really loved me and cared about my best interests, you would have never done something this low-down and underhanded. I thought I knew you, but now I don't think I ever really did. I knew you would stab your own grandmother to get somebody's husband, but to try to break up your best friend's marriage?" Loraine heaved a deep sigh. "Well, it is just too incomprehensible. As long as I live, I'll never understand it. Now get the hell out of my house!"

Egypt
50

I walked out of the shower to find Rashad fully dressed, gazing out the bedroom window that overlooked the backyard. I'm sure he was trying to remain patient, but the baby's car seat on the floor next to him gave away his eagerness to get down to the hospital and retrieve our son. Rashad had been a ball of nervous energy ever since we'd come home from the hospital last night. He was so wound up he'd barely slept most of the night. I know this because he'd woken me up three times to have sex. I obliged the first two times, hoping it would help him to sleep, but I had to draw the line the third time, because I was just too beat from my own lack of sleep. I'd slept only two hours the night Isis went into labor, and after Little Rashad was born, we were at the hospital almost eighteen hours.

"Good morning, handsome," I said.

"Morning, baby," he replied, but he never turned from the window.

"How long you been up?"

"I don't know. A couple hours. I was out back, mapping out the playground I'm gonna have built for the baby."

I walked up behind him and wrapped my arms around his waist, pressing my naked flesh against him. "I'm gonna put a swing set right over there, a sandbox there, and build him a clubhouse over there." He pointed out each of the spots, making me smile.

"Why don't you make me some coffee while I get dressed, so we can bring him home before we do all that? What do you think?"

"Sounds like a plan." He turned toward me and we kissed. Life was as perfect as it could be, just knowing I had this great man who loved me, and we had this sweet little boy sitting at the hospital waiting for us.

"I'll meet you downstairs, Mom."

"Okay, Dad."

Rashad walked out of the room, and I hurried to get dressed. Before I went downstairs, I went to the nursery and checked it one more time. Everything was in place. I had Little Rashad's diaper bag all packed, and I'd picked out a blue knit outfit for him to come home in. I had two receiving blankets and a fluffy soft yellow bunting blanket.

My parents and Rashad were waiting for me in the foyer. Rashad was holding my favorite travel mug in one hand and the car seat in the other.

"Guess everyone is ready to go, huh?"

"Early bird gets the worm," my father said.

"I don't know how early we're going to be. It's already eight-thirty," Rashad said.

"I'm sorry," I said sarcastically. "I wanted to get up earlier, but I didn't get much sleep. Someone kept waking me up in the middle of the night." I took my coffee from Rashad.

"I think I had that same problem," my mother said, rolling her eyes at my father as we headed toward the door. "Besides, we're still on schedule. You said you wanted to have the baby home by eleven. We've got plenty of time."

The plan was to take two cars. We were doing this because not only did we have to pick up the baby, but Isis was being discharged as well. So, while Rashad and I retrieved the baby, my mother and father were going to get Isis and check into a hotel for two days. If it were up to me, I'd have her behind on a plane to L.A. tonight, but they wanted to give her a few days to rest after the delivery. Just to make sure she had no excuses to come back to my house, I'd already packed all her stuff, and UPS was coming to pick up the boxes tomorrow.

When we arrived at the hospital, Rashad and I went straight to the nurses' station on the nursery floor.

"Good morning. My name is Egypt Robinson, and this is my

husband, Rashad. We're here to pick up our baby." I smiled and lifted the car seat to show her.

"Well, congratulations. I can check that car seat off my list." She looked down at her computer screen. "Baby's name?"

"Rashad Robinson Junior."

She typed the name into the computer and clicked her mouse a few times. "Has Daddy signed the birth certificate?"

"No, not yet," Rashad replied.

"Okay, maybe that's why I don't see anything under Robinson. What's the mother's last name?"

"Connors. The birth mother's name is Isis Connors." Rashad handed me the folder with all of our paperwork, which I passed to the nurse. "Here's the consent form relinquishing the mother's rights to the child and our custody agreement."

The nurse took the paperwork without even looking up from her computer screen. "Isis Connors. Here she is." I watched her expression change as she read something on the screen. "Can you wait here a minute? I'll be right with you."

She got up, looking alarmed, and rushed through the door behind her, returning shortly with two nurses and a woman in a lab coat who was probably a doctor. None of them said a word, but they all huddled around the computer screen while the doctor looked over the file.

Finally, the nurse who we originally spoke to pointed at the screen and said, "Look. It's right here." The doctor looked at the screen, then grimaced like she suddenly had a very bad headache.

I said in a panic, "What's the matter? Is our baby all right? Why didn't someone call us if something's wrong with him?"

"Mrs. Robinson, the baby is fine." The doctor paused. She looked very uncomfortable, like she wished she didn't have to deliver the news. "He's just not here."

"Excuse me?"

"He's not here."

"We heard what the fuck you said!" Rashad shouted. "What I wanna know is where the fuck is my son?"

"Sir, there is no need to use that kind of language."

"Rashad, calm down for a second, honey. He's probably on

another floor or in a different part of the hospital." Even as I said the words, I felt myself trembling because deep down, I knew it could be true that he was gone.

"No, he was discharged to his mother and father about an hour ago."

"What the fuck you mean, he was discharged to his father? I'm his goddamn father! And this is his mother! Look at the damn paperwork."

"I'm sorry, but none of this paperwork was attached to his chart."

Rashad turned to look at me, and I could see it on his face. If the baby was gone, he was going to blame it all on me. And I have to admit I did feel guilty. I can't believe that after controlling everything so carefully for nine months, I'd let my guard down. I was so ecstatic about spending time in the nursery with the baby that I practically forgot about my sister. Plus, she'd been fairly quiet; no complaints or anything after my mother gave her the check for the final installment of her thirty grand. For some reason, I'd let myself believe that now that she had delivered the baby and he was in my arms, we were home free.

The doctor continued covering her ass. "And even if it was in the chart, these papers were only rescinding the mother's parental rights. The biological father still had the right to take his child."

"I'm the damn biological father!"

"Not according to the mother."

"What?" That's when Rashad went totally off on the doctor and the hospital staff. He was cursing and screaming so loud that patients and their families were coming out of their rooms to see what all the commotion was about.

"Sir, if you don't calm down, I'm going to have to call security," the doctor said.

"I don't give a shit if you call President Obama! I'm gonna sue every one of your incompetent asses if you don't find my son."

I couldn't take it anymore. I broke down crying. Rashad put his arms around me, but I was inconsolable.

My mother and father came rushing toward us.

"Isis is gone," my mother yelled.

"So is Little Rashad." I could barely get the words out of my mouth.

My mother closed her eyes and shook her head. "I should have known something was wrong with her when she called me a bitch."

"She called you a bitch?" My mother was no joke. She was bigger than both Isis and me, and didn't put up with anyone being disrespectful. Even Isis's rude ass knew better than to call her anything but Momma.

"She sure did, and I slapped the taste outta her mouth. She's probably got postpartum depression."

My father cut his eyes at my mother. They were definitely going to have words later about her slapping Isis. They had a very weird bond, those two.

"So what exactly happened? Did she just walk on outta here with the baby?" my father asked.

"No, they discharged her, along with my son!" Rashad shouted.

"This is crazy," my mother muttered, turning to the nurses and doctor. "Which one of you brain scientists discharged my daughter?"

It took a few seconds, but one of the nurses finally raised her hand. "I did, but I didn't do anything wrong. All her paperwork was in order. So was the man's who signed the birth certificate. It was her baby, and like the doctor said, there wasn't anything in her charts that said she wasn't to leave with the baby." The nurse sounded scared.

"I think she's with Tony," I told my mother.

"It figures. Whenever she gets herself into any kind of trouble, he's usually lurking in the shadows somewhere. I just don't understand what she sees in him."

"Yes, Anthony Owen is down here as the father," one of the nurses added.

"I hate that son of a bitch," Rashad snapped.

"Get in line," my mother added.

When I regained my composure, I said, "What are we waiting for? Let's call the police. Maybe they can put out an Amber alert or something."

"No police!" My father's deep voice echoed down the hall. "We're going to handle this as a family. The nurse by her room said she'd only been gone about an hour. Has anyone tried to call her cell phone?"

Rashad and I both said no in unison.

"Well, let's see if she picks up." My father pulled out his cell phone and walked about ten feet from us. All I heard him say was, "Princess, where are you?" Then he walked farther down the corridor so I couldn't hear him.

The doctor asked us to move away from the nurses' station, so my mother and I sat in the waiting room while Daddy spoke to Isis. Rashad stood in the doorway the whole time, watching my father as he paced back and forth on the phone.

Twenty minutes later, my father walked past Rashad, who was on his phone talking to our lawyer. Daddy sat down in the waiting room. Momma and I were sitting on the edges of our seats, waiting for him to speak. Rashad was listening but was still on the phone.

"Okay." He sighed. "Well, she and the baby are safe, and they are definitely with Tony."

"Did she tell you where they are?" I asked.

"No, but she mentioned going to Vegas to get married."

"Oh, Jesus." My mother threw her hands in the air, then sat back in her chair with a disgusted look on her face. "Isn't he already married? Why do I feel like we've been down this road?"

"Momma, please." I put my hand up for her to calm down so I could listen to my father. "What about my son? Are they going to bring Little Rashad back, Daddy?"

My father turned to me and shook his head. "No, sweetie. They don't have any plans on doing that until after they're legally married and have seen a lawyer."

I started to cry again. "Then I'm calling the police."

"That's your prerogative, sweetie, but I wish you wouldn't do that."

I stared at my father like he was on drugs. What had gotten into him? "Daddy, that's our child she's got running around who knows where. He needs to be with his parents."

"Your sister seems to think the baby's not Rashad's, which would technically make them the parents."

"Not possible, Daddy! I was on her like white on rice during the entire month she got pregnant. She couldn't pee without me knowing what shade of yellow it was."

"That's what she said, but she also wanted me to remind you of a certain girls' night out around that time. Something about you asking her to do you a favor and babysit your friend Hannah's baby because her sitter had the flu."

I remembered that night. Isis was at Hannah's house the whole time, watching her kid. It wasn't like she had time to sneak off with Tony. "What does that have to do with anything?"

"To make a long story short, it seems Tony came over for a visit. Isis says there was a very good possibility Little Rashad was conceived that night."

"That's bull! We were right up the block at my other friend's house." I said it with confidence, but now that I thought about it, Isis was pestering us about what time we were going to be home and telling us to stay out as long as we wanted to. Plus she was singing the whole ride home. I'd never admit it to Rashad, but it was possible they got together that night. That still didn't mean Little Rashad was Tony's baby.

"Your sister has never lied to me." He glanced over at my mother, who sucked her teeth; then he looked back at me. "Now, maybe like your mother says, I don't ask the right questions. Nevertheless, she's never lied to me, and I believe what she says."

"Daddy! You believe her over me?"

"No, but she made a very convincing point, one that I brought up to your mother last night and she dismissed."

"What's that?"

"That boy's eyes look like they were plucked right out of Tony's head."

"That don't mean a damn thing. Rashad's grandmother had green eyes."

"I'm sorry, sweetheart. I'm just calling it as I see it. If you guys don't believe her, she said she'd give you a blood test."

Rashad had just hung up his cell phone. "I don't want no goddamn DNA test. I want my son. Call that bitch back and tell her to bring me my son."

My father stood up and got in Rashad's face quick. "That's my daughter you're talking about, and I ain't raised no bitch! Now, sit your ass down. I got a few things to say to you."

Rashad did as he was told. I didn't have a good feeling about this at all.

"For three years I held my tongue when it came to you."

"Bobby, don't—"

He cut his eyes at my mother. "Stay out of this, Karen. You know this conversation's been a long time coming."

He turned his attention back to Rashad. "First of all, don't act like you're all innocent in all this. You either, Egypt."

I sat back in my chair. How the heck did I get in this? Rashad was the one who called her a bitch.

"You been screwing my daughters for fifteen years now. You was going with Isis, gave her a cheap-ass ring to keep her from finding a decent man for five years, then moved down to Atlanta without her."

"Hold on," Rashad protested. "I asked her to come with me."

"Yeah, but she stayed put because you wouldn't marry her. I wouldn't have moved down there with you either. Why should she give up her life if you didn't want to commit?"

Rashad kind of huffed and rolled his eyes. Where the hell was my father going with this? I thought all this was water under the bridge a long time ago.

"Then you come back to New York and have some epiphany that she's the one thing missing in your life. And you're probably right, only Tony's standing in your way. So you two duke it out for her affection like a bunch of goddamn imbeciles. Messed up part for you is that you get your ass beat."

Rashad was squirming around in his chair. I know he didn't like what Daddy was saying. I didn't like it either, but I wasn't about to protest and put myself in the line of fire. At least not yet.

"Now, this is the part that I'm in the dark about: What the

hell made you think that sleeping with her sister was the right thing to do? You get dumped by one daughter, then decide to screw the other. You're lucky my wife stopped me, because I was gonna beat your ass myself."

Rashad glanced at me. I knew he wanted to say something, but I was so glad he was holding his tongue. One wrong word could make this whole thing even worse.

"Oh, and don't get me wrong; I'm not saying Egypt was in the right on this either." He looked at me, and I knew it was my turn to get blasted. "Screwing your sister's ex-fiancé is about as trifling as a woman can get."

While I sat there stunned, he turned back to Rashad.

"I ain't got no choice when it comes to Egypt. She's my child, and I got to love her. But what made you think I'd be cool with you sitting at my dinner table with one daughter after I know you were screwing her sister for ten years? Did you think I'd be cool with that? 'Cause, for the record, I've never been cool with it. I just love my children."

His words were like an arrow through the heart. I never even knew Daddy had an opinion about my relationship with Rashad. And I definitely didn't know he disapproved. It appears he just didn't want to rock the boat.

I made a weak attempt to stop him. "Daddy, we've been through all this. Isis has told me plenty of times that she's over Rashad. Why don't we figure out how to get the baby back?"

He cut his eyes at me. "Can't you see I'm having a man-to-man conversation with your husband?"

Yeah, but you're the only one talking.

I glanced at my mother for help, but she shook her head in warning, which told me this was something that had been weighing heavily on my father's mind for quite some time.

"You see, it's not that I dislike you, Rashad. You've been a decent son-in-law, and you take care of Egypt real good. Truth is, I was almost past all this until I found out you had the audacity to ask Isis to have your child."

"I didn't ask her. Egypt did. I didn't know anything about it until I got home that night."

That's it, baby. Throw me under the bus.

My father let out a derisive laugh. "Is that when they took you dragging and screaming down to the fertility clinic so you could give sperm to inseminate her?" He shook his head. "Do you have any idea why Isis agreed to have your baby?"

Rashad hesitated long enough that it made me feel uncomfortable. Something was running through his mind, and I had no idea what it was. When he answered my father, he sure didn't sound confident. "The money?"

"Don't insult me, okay. I know my daughter, and she did it because she loves you. In her mind, having your baby was like having a piece of you that her sister could never have."

None of us said anything, probably because if we were being honest with ourselves, we were all in agreement on that point.

Rashad tried to get a word in. "But none of that matters now. What matters is she signed those papers, and then she took my son."

Daddy looked like he wanted to punch him.

"What if he's not your son? What if by the slightest chance he's Tony's? What you gonna do then?"

"You don't want us to fight for our son, Daddy?"

"I never said I didn't want you to fight. What I want you to do is what's right. Your sister said she'd give you guys a blood test. I'll make sure she does. If Rashad's the father, you guys split custody. If Tony's the father, you leave your sister be."

"What about the money she took from us?" I asked.

The look he gave me told me he thought I was being petty. "You'll get your money back."

I turned to Rashad. "What do you think, baby?"

Of course, he didn't look happy, but I think he knew that this was the only choice we had at this point. There was almost no chance Isis would talk to either one of us. It would take us who knows how much money to fight this in court, and even then, we might need private investigators just to find Isis. Daddy was the only hope of staying in touch with her and working this whole thing out, which meant we had to play it by his rules.

"I want your father there when they take his blood," Rashad said.

"I can do that."

"And we use a facility that my lawyer agrees to." He looked my father straight in the eye. "For the record, I never intended to fall in love with Egypt. Truth is, I tried to avoid it, but you never know who you're going to fall in love with. So, I respect what you said; I just want you to respect that she's my wife."

My father nodded his understanding, and I felt the tension in the room lift ever so slightly.

"Oh, and as far as my son goes, if I find out he has one drop of my blood, I'm fighting for full custody. I don't care what you or anyone else says."

Loraine

51

I cried so hard last night I could barely sleep, and when I did finally doze off, I had horrible nightmares. I kept asking myself over and over again why Jerome would do something like that to me. Sure, he gave me that cockamamie story about how Leon was no good for me and that he was doing it for my own good. Who the hell was he supposed to be anyway, my father? What hurt the most was that up until the moment I heard him admit it, I still had faith in him. I honestly believed he was going to have some type of explanation, or at the very least an immediate denial. A part of me still couldn't believe he hadn't attempted to lie. I'm sure some would say at least he kept it real and didn't deny it, but to me, the lies he'd told had already done all the damage, and this one might have saved me a little heartache.

When I woke up, I realized I needed to get away. The absolute last place I wanted to be was at work. I was an emotional wreck, and there was no way I could walk past Jerome's empty desk all day without breaking down at some point. I had a lot of things to work out in my head, including who was going to take over Jerome's position as my right-hand man. Even more importantly, what was I going to do with the two men in my life? I loved each one very much in his own special way.

I got dressed and called into my office to tell Hannah I'd be taking a week or two off for some personal business. I'm sure she thought I was going somewhere exotic with Michael. I told her to pack up Jerome's belongings, because he was no longer working with us. She asked what happened, but I just told her Jerome no longer worked for our agency . . . period. No way was I telling her my personal business. I liked Hannah, but she was the biggest gossip in the office, and my life was disastrous enough already without the added trouble of everyone in the office whispering about it behind my back.

To start off my little soul-searching adventure, I decided to ride down to Virginia Beach and get a room by the water so I could sort out my feelings. When I was younger, I used to take long walks along the beach whenever I broke up with a boyfriend or had a problem. Usually, by the time I'd gotten home, I'd have everything kind of worked out in my head. I knew it wasn't going to be quite that easy this time, but by the end of the week, I hoped to have a little clarity in my life.

I drove down I-64 with the top down on my convertible and the wind blowing in my hair. For the moment, I felt like I had peace.

The open road was a nice distraction, but that's all it was. It didn't solve any of my problems. I was still in love with two men, and one of them, Michael, had been blowing up my phone all morning. I wasn't sure if he'd spoken to Jerome or if he'd called the office and Hannah had mentioned that I was taking some time off, but he obviously knew something was wrong, because he was calling every five minutes. I didn't want to answer the phone; I didn't know what to say.

After I checked into the Hyatt Hotel, I went to my room, shut off my phone, and went to sleep. I was mentally and physically exhausted from the drive, lack of sleep, and the entire ordeal.

The next morning, I went for a long walk down the beach to look for answers. I was glad that the beach was empty. I wanted to be alone. I took off my sandals and let the sand ooze between my toes. I breathed in the smell of the ocean. Just the feel of the morning sun warming my back was comforting. Every so often, I would scoop the sand and pick up flat stones, then skip them over the water. To amuse myself, I ran away as the tide came in, then trudged back into the wet sand after the waves receded, like a child.

I stayed at the edge of the water, which was how my life felt. I was at the edge, both mentally and spiritually. Should I take the plunge, or should I step back? Lord, what should I do?

My cell phone chimed, letting me know I had a text message. I already knew who it was; the only person who sent me text messages was Michael. I missed him so much. Not just in a physical way, but as a companion. The two of us had so much fun together.

I read the text Michael sent: PLEASE CALL ME. I'M WORRIED ABOUT U. I DON'T KNOW WHAT'S GOING ON BUT WE CAN WORK THROUGH ANYTHING. I LOVE U.

I texted back: I'M OK. JUST NEED SOME TIME TO THINK. I LOVE YOU TOO.

I don't think Jerome had any idea just how much he'd screwed up my life. Because of his lies, I was stuck in the middle of a love triangle I didn't create. I still couldn't believe I'd gone to a lawyer to divorce Leon. Signed papers too. Thank God I was able to stop them before they could serve Leon with the papers. So I was still married, but who knew if my marriage was even salvageable after everything that had happened during the past few months.

And then there was Michael. The most wonderful, yet tragic thing that had happened since kicking Leon out was that I'd let my guard down. I'd fallen in love with Michael. I'd fallen hard too. I thought I was ready to spend the rest of my life with him.

But now I just didn't know. I asked myself over and over again, was it fair to walk away from Leon, now that I found out he'd been telling the truth all along? We didn't have the greatest marriage, but it was okay, and we were working on it, trying to make it better. Truth is, if I hadn't found those panties and Tina hadn't shown up at my door, I never would have given Michael the time of day romantically. Why, when he was so fine and had everything going for him? Because I was loyal like that to my husband. I only let Michael in because I thought Leon had betrayed me.

After about two hours of walking, I was tired, but I felt a cloud had lifted off my shoulders. My answers had come to me at the ocean. By the time I returned to my hotel room, I knew what I had to do. I took out my cell phone and dialed Michael's number.

He answered after two rings. "Hey, where are you? I've been worried sick about you."

"I'm okay. Like I said in my text, I'm just trying to work through a few things."

"Yeah, but I haven't seen you in a week."

"I know, and I think it's going to be a little longer."

I heard him sigh on his end of the phone, but he said nothing. I stayed quiet too. There was nothing I could say that would make this any easier.

"Can I ask you a question?" he finally said.

"Mmm-hmm."

"Are you somewhere with Leon?"

"No, I haven't seen Leon in weeks."

"Thank God. I was starting to think you two were back together."

I didn't comment. I just went on to another subject. "Michael, do you believe in soul mates?"

"Yeah, I think you're my soul mate. I can't stop thinking about you. I feel like I've waited for you my entire life."

He made me smile, but I was still sad because of the terrible situation I'd put this sweet, wonderful man in.

"Was it worth the wait?" I asked.

"Hell yeah. You're great. I love you."

How could I give this man up?

"I know you love me, but what if I told you that you had to wait a little longer to be with me?"

There was silence for a while, and then he asked, "Loraine, are you going to tell me what's going on?"

Now was the moment I had been dreading. I had to tell Michael the whole truth. "Remember I told you I kicked my husband out because he was cheating?"

"Yeah, he was messing around on you for like five years, wasn't he?"

"Well, not exactly. I recently found out my husband wasn't cheating."

Michael got quiet.

"Michael, you still there?"

"Yeah, I'm still here. I'm a little confused, but I'm here."

"I know. I'm sorry. I never wanted things to be like this." I went on to explain to him everything I'd learned, from the moment Peter approached me at the bar to the confrontation with Jerome that confirmed the truth.

"So, if he wasn't cheating, where does that leave us? What does it mean?"

"Michael, this is really hard for me. I'm trying to do the right thing here." I was so nervous that I was pacing back and forth as I talked to him.

"You're breaking up with me, aren't you?"

"I want to be fair."

"Fair to who, him?" he shouted for the first time.

"He didn't do anything wrong, Michael. Don't you understand?"

"Well, neither did I, Loraine."

"I know that. But he's my husband. I took an oath in front of God to love him for better or for worse. I have to give him a chance."

"But I'm in love with you." The pleading in his voice broke my heart. I wished I could reach out and hold him, make everything all right.

"I'm in love with you too. I just can't be with you right now."

"Loraine, I've loved you since I was a young boy, and I've never gotten over you. No woman has been able to touch you. Now, here I finally think I've got a shot at happiness, and you tell me this?"

"Just trust me, Michael. What's meant to be will be. Just let me work this thing out. I want you to know that no one has ever made me as happy as you have these past few months."

"If you're going to break up with me, at least do it face-to-face."

"I can't do that."

"Why not?"

"Because if I see you, I won't be able to let you go, and this is hard enough as it is."

"Don't do this. Please don't do this."

"You take care of yourself. Always remember I love you." I hung up without saying good-bye, because I couldn't stand to say those two little words. They were so permanent. I hurt so badly; I felt like my heart would burst.

I lay down on the bed and stared into space for the longest time. Eventually, I turned on the TV to drown out my own thoughts, and I finally fell asleep.

After my nap, I ordered room service, then took another walk on the beach. I felt the need to gather myself before I made my next phone call.

Leon answered on the first ring. "Hello? Loraine, are you all right?" He sounded surprised, probably because I hadn't been accepting his calls for the past few weeks.

"Yeah, everything's fine. I was just sitting here kind of thinking about us."

"I do that a lot myself."

"Where'd we go wrong, Leon?"

"I don't know. I guess a lot of it has to do with me and my insecurity. I've learned a lot about myself from going to therapy. I will say this much—and if you want to hang up on me, you go right ahead—but I do not know that woman."

"I believe you."

"You do?" Of course he was shocked. Those were the first kind words I'd spoken to him since Jerome started this whole nightmare.

"It took me a while, but I finally figured it out."

"So does this mean I can come home?" He didn't even ask me how I knew he was innocent. In the end, that didn't really matter anyway, did it? All that mattered was that there might still be hope for our marriage.

"No, but you can come down to Virginia Beach and take me out to dinner so we can talk about it. I've learned what it's like to be treated like a woman should be, Leon. I've also cut a lot of things out of my life, so I'm not going to accept anything less than what I am now accustomed to. So we need to talk."

"I'm on my way."

"I'll see you when you get here."

I hung up the phone. I wasn't sure whether I was ever going to tell Leon about Jerome setting him up. If he asked why Jerome wasn't around, I'd tell him we just had a falling out.

Right now, though, Jerome was the least of my concerns.

From the looks of it, his stalker was giving him a taste of his own medicine anyway. As for me, I knew I had a long road ahead of me if I was ever going to get Michael off my mind, because right now, the reality was that I was hopelessly torn between two lovers.

Epilogue

Six months later

Leon pulled in front of Egypt's door, then glanced over at me with a smile. I smiled back, leaning over to kiss him good-bye. We'd been doing a lot of kissing lately. My husband had actually become very passionate and romantic these past few months. The sex hadn't gotten any better—he was still faster than a speeding bullet—but he'd been working on that with the therapist. Maybe one day soon we'd have sex again that lasted more than a few minutes.

A lot of the problem wasn't his fault at all. You see, it turned out that Leon had some serious issues, a lot more serious than I would have ever expected. He'd been abused as a child by his uncle. His abuse was so traumatic that the doctor felt he'd repressed most of his memories. Once he dropped me off, he was headed to talk with the doctor about finding a way to help him remember parts of his childhood. The doctor felt that by confronting his past, he'd somehow be set free from his personal demons.

I reached for the door handle, and Leon gently took hold of my left arm. "What time should I pick you up?"

He was so thoughtful as of late. "That's okay. You don't have to pick me up. I'll have Egypt drop me off or I'll catch a cab. Just make sure you call me and tell me what the doctor says, okay?"

"All right, but if you need a ride, I'm just a phone call away. I love you, Big Sexy."

"Love you too."

I winked at my husband, then stepped out of the car and walked to Egypt's door. She opened it before I could ring the bell.

"Hey, girl," she shouted, then hugged me tight. When she released me, she waved at Leon, who waved back as he pulled off.

I'd called Egypt early that morning to see if she was going to be around so we could do a little catching up. I had a very special favor to ask her, and instead of doing it over the phone, I really wanted to do it face to face. Lucky for me, she told me Rashad was out of town on business and she would love a little company.

"Look at you, looking all fly with a new do," she said, giving me the once over. "It looks good, Loraine. I like you in short hair."

"You don't look too bad yourself. Motherhood agrees with you." We hadn't seen each other in weeks, so I gave her an observing glance. She had lost a little weight, and looked good in a pair of jeans and a snugly fitted top, which I noticed had a little milk spit-up on the shoulder.

"Motherhood is hard work," she said with a sigh. "It's non-stop, twenty-four/seven, but I swear, Loraine, I absolutely love it. I wouldn't give it up for the world." Her smile was so bright and she looked so happy.

"I guess that means you're not coming back to work anytime soon?"

There was a silence. "Is that why you wanted to talk to me? 'Cause if you need to hire someone to replace me, Loraine, I think you should do it. I love my job, but I love my baby even more. I can't say when, or even if I'm gonna go back to work."

"Don't worry. I understand. And no, that's not why I wanted to see you." I glanced around the room. "Speaking of which, where is that little godbaby of mine anyway?"

"Up in the nursery taking a nap. We'll go up there in a few minutes. Right now I'm a little curious about what you wanted to speak to me about."

She offered me a seat. "Well, I don't know if you knew this, but Leon and I were married at the courthouse by a justice of the peace."

"I would have never guessed that. I just envisioned you as a woman who had this huge church wedding."

"Don't I wish. At that time in my life, I was trying to save every nickel I could. I'd only been in business for about four or five years. Back then it was just me and Jerome trying to make ends meet."

"You've come a long way."

"Yeah, I have. Funny thing is I always wanted that big wedding I missed out on, and now I can afford that wedding. That's why I came over here."

"Are you saying what I think you're saying?"

"Only if what you think I'm saying is that I want you to be my maid of honor when Leon and I renew our vows in a couple of months."

"Really?" She raised her eyebrows like she was surprised by my request.

"Yes, really. I can't think of anyone I'd want to be by my side other than you."

"Not even Jerome?"

"Especially not Jerome." Just the mention of his name got my blood boiling these days. "I'm sorry, but I don't have anything to say to him."

"Loraine, he's your best friend. You should at least call and check on him."

"That's ex-best friend," I said sternly. "I'm serious, Egypt. I don't have anything to say to the man. I can do bad all by myself."

"Well, girl, I saw him the other day when he came by with a present for the baby." Her face contorted. "Loraine, he looks a wreck. That stalker guy is still after him, and I think he's getting the best of him."

"See, that's what I'm talking about. He's always going around messing up people's lives, and that stuff just came back on him."

"Aw, Loraine, y'all two were so tight. How you gonna just end your friendship like that?"

"Just like this." I slapped my hands up and down. "Girl, I'm finished. Done."

"I'm sorry to hear that."

"Nah, don't be sorry. Just be my maid of honor. I want you to help me plan my wedding."

"Okay." She nodded. "I'll do it, but we haven't finished talking about Jerome."

Luckily, the baby began hollering. I didn't have the time or the energy to explain to Egypt what had come between me and Jerome.

Egypt sighed and stood up. "Let me get the baby."

While she was upstairs, my cell phone rang. I answered it, speaking quietly. "I'll be right there. Give me about twenty more minutes. I'll text you when I'm on my way outside."

I hung up just as Egypt was walking into the room with the baby in her arms. "Here's Aunt Loraine."

"Hey, precious, come to Auntie," I said, reaching out for the pretty little girl.

"You know she'll be nine months next week," Egypt said.

The baby started crying. "Yeah, she's being feisty," Egypt said. "Can you hold her while I get her bottle?"

"Sure."

I took the twenty-pound baby, who was dressed in a beautiful red velvet dress with white lace socks, looking pretty enough to be in a baby ad. The sweet scent of Johnson's baby lotion made me smile as I hugged her close to my chest. She stopped crying as soon as I patted her back.

It had been a long, hard road for Egypt and Rashad to finally have a child, and I could see how they doted over her now that she was here. After Egypt's sister, Isis, had the baby boy and it turned out to be Tony's baby, Egypt and Rashad were devastated. I introduced them to a woman I knew in the Dominican Republic who handled overseas adoptions. They were able to get baby Jessica, who was three months at the time, within two weeks, and the adoption was finalized within five months.

When Egypt returned with the bottle, I handed her the baby, then glanced down at my phone to send a text.

"Egypt, I'm sorry, but I really have to go," I said. "It's the Morris account. Judith Morris just caught her husband, Hal, with his pants down. I've gotta go save his ass."

"Oh, no. I was so looking forward to us having lunch and spending the afternoon together."

"Yeah, but you know this type of thing happens all the time in public relations. I'll come back and we'll spend the day together with my new godbaby, okay?"

Egypt relented and gave me a bear hug like she didn't want to let me go. I had to pull myself away from her.

"Besides, as my maid of honor, we'll see each other all the time," I assured her.

"Okay," Egypt said reluctantly. I'd never seen her act so needy and lonely. I hate to say it, but it made me glad I didn't have any kids tying me down.

"Look, I'll let myself out so you can feed the baby." I kissed her and the baby on the cheek, picked up my Coach bag, and left.

When I got outside, I climbed in a car waiting in front of a house down the block.

I turned and gave Michael a kiss.

"How much time we got?" he asked.

"Until about ten or eleven tonight. After that, he'll be looking for me."

Yes, I loved Leon and I'd given Michael up, but not for long, because I loved Michael too. Now, like the song, I was truly torn between two lovers.

Dear Readers,

Wow, I hope you enjoyed reading *Big Girls Do Cry* as much as I enjoyed writing it. It was quite a ride, wasn't it? Of all the books I've written in the past ten years, I think this one and *So You Call Yourself a Man* were my favorites. It was just a fun story to write, and I really got into the characters as the story progressed.

As many of you know, I love writing about the big girls, but I have to admit that about three quarters of the way through, Jerome, along with crazy-behind Peter, had become my favorite characters. It was about that time that I came to the realization that I couldn't bring their story to an end in just one book. Although I feel for now that Isis and Egypt have had their final run, I also feel there are a few loose ends I could tie up with Loraine, Leon, and Michael.

With that being said, fasten your seatbelts and join me this fall for my second release of the year, *Torn Between Two Lovers*.

Carl Weber
A man who loves a woman with some meat on her bones

BIG GIRLS DO CRY

CARL WEBER

ABOUT THIS GUIDE

The following questions are designed to facilitate discussion in and among reading groups.

1. Did you read *Something on the Side*? If you did, do you feel *Big Girls Do Cry* is a sequel or a companion book?

2. Which sister was your favorite? What did you think of their relationship with each other? Was there love there?

3. Would you be able to be a surrogate?

4. Did you think Rashad still had feelings for Isis?

5. Do you think the sisters' mother was on point with her concerns about Isis? Did Egypt make a bad choice by asking Isis to carry Rashad's baby?

6. If you were a father, would you let Rashad sit at your dinner table? Why do you think he waited so long to speak up about the whole situation?

7. In every scene, Loraine took the first swing. Does this make her in any way responsible for Leon's reaction? Would you classify this as an abusive relationship?

8. Would you automatically assume your partner was cheating if you found someone's undergarments in your bed? If so, would you remain with them?

9. Did you like Jerome, and do you think he should have been a member of the BGBC? Did his desire to turn out married men change your opinion of him?

10. Were you surprised at Jerome's actions to break up Loraine and Leon? Do you think he was wrong?

11. Did you feel any compassion for Leon? If you were in his position, would you have taken Loraine back?

12. Who would you have picked, Leon or Michael?

13. What was your opinion of Jerome's stalker, Peter?

14. On a scale of 1 to 10, what do you think of this book?

15. Which character or characters would you like to see again?

Catch up with Loraine, Jerome, and the other members of the
Big Girls Book Club in

Torn Between Two Lovers

Coming in September 2010 from Dafina Books

Leon

I eased back on the soft, buttercream leather armchair when Roberta walked into the room. For us, it had been the same place, same time for almost a year. I'd been waiting for her, not long, only about five minutes, but long enough to wonder if her damn phone had cut into my time with her again. If so, it wouldn't be the first time. Her phone was constantly ringing whenever we were together. Most of the time she ignored it, but there were a few occasions when she glanced at the caller ID and excused herself. Sure, I knew the calls were work-related and she wouldn't take them if they weren't important, but damn, this was supposed to be my time. If she were anyone else, I would have kicked her to the curb a long time ago, but her pros so outweighed her cons. Roberta had a way of making me feel so good about myself. I don't think I could ever find someone who did for me what she'd done. I always left her with an incredible yearning to see her again. When we first met, I was such a broken man, but with her help, I was starting to put the pieces of my life back together.

She sat down next to me, adjusting her body until she was comfortable. I immediately noticed she was wearing a new scent. It was a little lighter than usual, but sexy all the same. She always smelled so good.

"New perfume?" I asked.

"Why, yes, it is." She gave me a smile that could have lit up the room.

I'm sure she was surprised that I noticed. She probably thought that like most men, I didn't pay attention to the little things. But what she didn't understand was that when we were together, just like her, I paid attention to everything. Oh, I tried to play it cool; what type of man would I be if I didn't? But I left no stone unturned when it came to the time we spent together. It was that important to me.

We'd started this little Monday and Thursday afternoon ritual about six months ago. Back then, you couldn't have paid me a million dollars to think I'd still be seeing her after all this time. She was without question the only woman I'd ever let in my head—other than my wife, Loraine. In fact, I'm sure Loraine would be shocked at how much more Roberta knew about me than she did. All that withstanding, I still wasn't quite ready to let the world know I was seeing Roberta. I liked keeping things on the Q.T., or on the D.L., as they call it nowadays. I didn't care what anyone said; I was convinced that if anyone found out about us, my life as I knew it would be ruined.

Funny thing is, it all started rather innocently around the time my wife and I were having relationship problems. I'd ended up getting kicked out of my own home and losing all of Loraine's and my mutual friends. Roberta was there for me when no one else was. I was under so much stress at that time, I don't know if I could have made it without her. It seemed that fate just brought us together.

"So here we are again. I've been giving a lot of thought to our last conversation, Leon. Did you happen to do what I asked you to do?" She was no longer smiling. Her face was serious; she wanted an answer. An answer I wasn't sure I was prepared to give.

I gazed down at her stilettos. There was no doubt in my mind that they were expensive. As was customary with her, they looked brand new. There wasn't a scuff mark on them. You can tell a lot about a woman by looking at her shoes, and hers almost screamed how classy she was. But, I wondered, how could such a classy woman talk to me about such lewd things, even if it was for my own good?

"Are you ignoring me?"

"No," I replied, but I'm sure she knew I was.

"So, answer my question. Did you—"

"Did I jack off first? Yes, I jacked off first, all right?" I finished her sentence in my own words. I just didn't want to hear her say it again.

My eyes traveled from her shoes, up a little farther. Her legs were crossed neatly at the knees, showing off her well-built calves. She had an amazing hourglass figure, while her face and hair defied her almost fifty years of age.

"Leon, are you embarrassed?"

Was I embarrassed? Of course I was embarrassed. Here was this beautiful woman sitting across from me, wanting to know if I'd masturbated. What was even more embarrassing was the reason she'd asked the question in the first place. You see, I had a little problem in the bedroom. And no, it wasn't that I couldn't get it up. I got it up just fine. My problem was that . . . well, my . . . my stamina wasn't quite what it should be and . . . I ejaculated a little faster than I should.

"Leon, there is no reason for you to be embarrassed. We've been through this before. Plenty of men go through premature ejaculation. Masturbating before sex should help with your stamina. You just get too excited. There's nothing wrong with being excited. We just have to find a way to harness that excitement."

After all these months, she still didn't get it. She still had no idea what made me tick.

"Roberta, I don't think I know how to harness my excitement."

I looked up at her, our eyes meeting for the first time. I was hoping she would understand like she always seemed to. This had been the topic of conversation between us for quite some time, but this time she tried to hide a frown. It didn't work. Her disappointment was written all over her face.

"Why are you looking at me like that?" She was making me feel self-conscious.

"I'm just trying to figure out how serious you are about this. Do you want to stop prematurely ejaculating? Do you want to enjoy a normal sex life?"

What the hell was that supposed to mean? Was she taking a pot shot at my manhood? If she was trying to humiliate me, she was doing a good job. My embarrassment was now defensive anger.

I stood up. "Of course I wanna have a got-damn normal sex life. Why the fuck do you think I've been paying your sorry ass a hundred dollars an hour for the past six months?" I pointed my finger in her face. "I should be asking your ass when I'm going to have a normal sex life. You're the damn therapist—oh, excuse me, psychiatrist! So what's up, Doc? When am I going to be cured? When am I going to be able to fuck like I used to?"

Roberta straightened up in her chair, her bottom lip quivering just a bit. There was no doubt in my mind she did not appreciate my sudden use of profanity or my accusatory tone, but this wasn't the first time I'd gotten loud. Truth is, I just wanted her to snap back at me, give me a reason to walk out that door and feel sorry for myself, but she never did. No matter how ignorant I got, she always kept it professional.

Surprisingly, her expression softened. "You know what, Leon? You're right. I'm sorry. I know you're trying. And to be totally honest, I can't say when you're going to be cured. But I'm committed to finding a solution to your problems. I just need your help."

Well, if you haven't figured it out, Roberta is my shrink.

"What can I do?" I asked.

"Why don't you have a seat so we can talk about that?" I did what I was told and sat back down.

"So, I take it you and Loraine made love this weekend and things didn't quite work out as you planned?"

"I did exactly what you said." I sighed. "I took her out to a nice romantic dinner at Luigi's. When we got home, I went in the bathroom, locked the door, and took care of business."

"Okay, that's good. What'd you do next?"

"I broke out the massage oil and gave Loraine a massage from head to toe. You would have been proud of me, Doc. I took things nice and slow, just like we talked about." My eyes panned her office, which was trimmed in cherrywood molding that matched her Queen Anne desk.

"I'm already proud of you, Leon." She patted my knee like I was a schoolboy who needed approval. I have to admit I did appreciate her words. "What happened after that? How were things afterwards? Did you get intimate?" She was trying to get back in my head. She knew we'd gotten intimate.

I hesitated before I answered. I really didn't want to tell her the truth. I twiddled my fingers and started feeling my palms get sweaty. I swallowed deeply before answering, "Yeah, we did."

"So how was it?"

I lowered my head and closed my eyes. Once again, I could see Loraine's look of disgust when I collapsed on top of her within a minute of beginning our lovemaking session. I'd even tried dropping some Viagra beforehand, but that didn't work. I just knew that last night was going to be the time I held out until Loraine reached her climax, but once again, I came too quickly. Loraine didn't say anything, but I could tell she was getting sick of my Speedy Gonzalez performances. I felt about as low as a man could get.

"Horrible. Worse than ever."

"What do you mean?"

"I tried to hold back, Doc, but it seems like the more I try to hold back, the more excited I get. Once I got inside her, that was all she wrote. I exploded like a short fuse on a firecracker—quick, fast, in a hurry."

"I see . . . Maybe we're going about this wrong. Maybe we should be looking at the cause of your excitement, not the effect." Roberta gave me a compassionate look, which encouraged me to open up. "What do you find attractive about Loraine?"

I let out a low whistle. "Wow, I mean where do I start? She's just so . . . so sexy to me. Roberta, I've told you this before. I just love a big woman, and when Loraine takes off her clothes, she just makes me feel like exploding." I glanced down at my pants. "I'm all excited just thinking about her being naked."

"Yes, I can see that." Roberta raised her eyes. "Have you ever been attracted to smaller-framed woman?"

"Not really. I've been with a few, but they did absolutely nothing for me."

"Hmmm, interesting. So when did your attraction for big women begin?"

I shrugged my shoulders. "I don't know. I don't know. I've always loved big women."

"I see. Any large women in your family?"

"My aunt, who raised me after my mother's death, was a big, beautiful woman."

"Oh, you've never mentioned your aunt before. Tell me more."

I heaved a deep sigh before I started. I was treading in some dangerous waters that I preferred to keep locked away inside my heart. "Well, my mother passed away when I was seven, and her brother, my Uncle William, and his wife, Catherine, raised me until I got grown."

"How about your father?"

"I never knew my father."

"Sorry to hear that. So did you and your auntie have a good relationship?"

"Yeah, Aunt Cathy was the best. She was like a mother to me."

"Interesting. Tell me more."

"I can't. She died when I was fourteen."

"So tell me what you remember."

"Every time I think about a woman adoring me, I always think about my aunt. Funny thing is, I can't even remember anything about her other than she was nice to me." I sighed. "So is that why I like big women? Because of my aunt?"

Dr. Marshall began to scribble on her notepad. "That makes sense. A lot of our adult lives are based on our childhoods. We are often attracted to people who remind us of our parent figures. It's not unusual for a lot of men to look for mother figures."

I nodded. "Maybe so. But I don't see what this has to do with not satisfying my wife. I'm really worried I'm going to lose Loraine if I don't step up my game and handle my business in the bedroom. It's been a long time since I've satisfied her. After all, she's only human."

"Does Loraine remind you of your aunt?"

I paused. "Yes. No. I don't know. Maybe." I started feeling confused.

"What do you think about your aunt that has to do with your issues?"

"Why should she have anything to do with what's going on

with Loraine and me?" I noticed my heart start racing. I didn't know what was wrong with me.

"Let me rephrase this. What do you remember about your aunt when you were a teenager that was so kind that makes you think of Loraine?"

I shook my head. "I can't remember."

"Leon, do you realize that every time we try to go back into your teenage years, you have a blackout?"